TO END ALL
WAR

TO END ALL
WAR

A Historical Novel

Nicholas Lambros

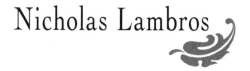

TO END ALL WAR

iUniverse books may be ordered through booksellers or by contacting:

iUniverse
1663 Liberty Drive
Bloomington, IN 47403
www.iuniverse.com
1-800-Authors (1-800-288-4677)

ISBN: 978-1-4917-4383-6 (sc)
ISBN: 978-1-4917-4385-0 (hc)
ISBN: 978-1-4917-4384-3 (e)

Library of Congress Control Number: 2014914253

Print information available on the last page.

iUniverse rev. date: 04/10/2018

Dedicated to the men and women of the armed services
of the United States without whose personal sacrifice and
dedication to duty America and many other nations would not
be enjoying the freedoms that are so often taken for granted.

An introduction by
John Charles Roemer III

TO END ALL WAR IS the result of years of research and thought about World War I and about how to shape it into a work of fiction both true to the facts of the times and passionately devoted to its heroic main characters. The tactics and technologies of the war, particularly those pertaining to air combat, are rendered compellingly enough to guide a history class, while the artfully developed characters will have every reader rooting for them.

This is not one of those modern everybody-is-vile-and-corrupt exercises. It's much more in the romantic vein of good people struggling to make sense of horrific circumstances. The reader doesn't see them as distant lab specimens; instead we want them to prevail because they're decent and moral and engaging.

There's an old-fashioned sense of right and wrong in *To End All War*, but not in some simplistic comic book sense. These are people you might know (and would certainly like to know) who feel compelled to do the right thing in wartime for their country but who are keenly aware of the horrors of war for everyone, including enemy combatants.

In addition to the historical accuracy and the nicely developed characters, *To End All War* is simply a wonderfully exciting read, full of rich detail, gripping plot lines, suspense, and rousing action. You'll learn a lot about the Great War, while at the same time enjoying a beautifully written Great Adventure.

John C. Roemer III
BA History, Princeton University
MAT, Harvard University
History Teacher, 35 years
Executive Director, ACLU of Maryland
Peace Education Chairman, Middle Atlantic Region
American Friends Service Committee
Vice-Chairman, Baltimore Congress of Racial Equality

Preface

ONE-HUNDRED YEARS LATER, THE SHOCK waves of the guns fired between 1914 and 1918 still can be felt. The Great War caused forty to fifty million casualties—military and civilian, killed, wounded, or missing. Over nine million combatants died. Historians say six to ten million civilians lost their lives. American combat casualties are roughly set at three-hundred-twenty-thousand. In 1918, the war ended at 11am, on the 11th day, of the 11th month. Over one-hundred-sixteen-thousand Americans died—one in three—a ratio of dead to wounded that exceeds any norm in modern war.

On April 6, 1917, after a number of *overt acts* on the sea and the discovery of the *Zimmerman note*, neutral America finally joined the Allies against the Central Powers. A small number of untrained and poorly equipped Americans began to arrive in France in late June, 1917. They were greeted by their commander, General John

"Blackjack" Pershing. Except for their uniforms and rifles, our "doughboys" were essentially equipped and supplied by the French. French and British military leaders repeatedly pressed Pershing to replace their heavy losses. Under orders from President Wilson to keep his army intact, Pershing lent mere handfuls to the Allies. Before fighting as an army, the vast majority of doughboys trained for over a year under French and British instructors. In May, 1918, the 28th Infantry Regiment of the US 1st Division recaptured Cantigny in thirty-five minutes. Days later, a small unit of US marines halted a German advance at Château Thierry. In June, US marines won Belleau Wood.

After much quarreling, Marshal Foch, the commander of all Allied forces, grudgingly agreed to allow General Pershing to lead his First Army in battle, under the American flag, on condition that Pershing redeploy his 600,000 men on crowded, muddy, French roads, and immediately engage an entrenched enemy in fog and rain on September 26, 1918. Pershing agreed. It meant Pershing had twelve days to secure the Saint-Mihiel salient, which he largely accomplished on September 12, 1918, the first day of battle. The Meuse-Argonne offensive was a different story!

That single battle was the most costly ever fought by an American army. In roughly eight weeks, twice as many American soldiers died as did in the eight years of combat in the jungles and rice paddies of Vietnam. A memorial wall to the American dead of WWI would run the length of the reflecting pool in Washington, DC. Hence, the vast majority of American deaths occurred within the last two to three months of the war—a rate of carnage that wasn't unique in the Great War. The battles named Verdun and the Somme produced nearly twice as many Allied and German casualties in two months as were caused by our entire Civil War, the war America still remembers as the deadliest in its history.

The consequences of the Great War are so numbing and so far-reaching, we must ask why the war is so little appreciated in our history classrooms. Americans I've spoken to, young or adult, have little knowledge of the war. Other wars Americans fought–the Revolutionary War, the Civil War, World War II, Korea, Vietnam, and today, Iraq and Afghanistan–command our attention.

The Russian Revolution began before the war ended, bringing Stalin into power. His purges killed an estimated two million Russians before the start of WWII–many of them military officers. We forget that the squalid trenches of the Great War bred and spread the pandemic called the Spanish flu, resulting in the deaths of some sixty million men, women, and children worldwide before running its course. Taken together, the number of lives lost as a direct result of the Great War closely matches the entire population of the United States in 1914.

The First World War was the bloodiest war history had ever seen. When it ended, the world had lost a generation of young men. Yet today, many see World War One as little more than an event that forced historians to attach the number Two to the next world war. America's late participation is downplayed, but the war would have ended differently without it. Unfortunately, *the war to end all war* did not fulfill its promise. Rather, it set many precedents.

Modern warfare was born in WWI. For the first time combatants had motorized vehicles, telephones, and motion pictures. Advances were made in all sorts of munitions and the means to deliver them–the first true machine guns, semi-automatic rifles and pistols, high-explosive artillery shells, huge mortars, flamethrowers, deadly gases, tanks, fighter and bomber airplanes, zeppelins, the ship called the Dreadnought, and diesel-fueled submarines. Had the war never occurred, its weapons alone were reshaping world politics. Employed against Napoleonic tactics, both sides were forced to dig trenches along the entire front—a front that moved only grudgingly up to the end of the war. The most ominous first of the First World War is the civilian slaughter. Not since Oliver Cromwell's scourge of Irish Catholics had non-combatants suffered such wholesale death.

Histories written just after 1918 stress the war's immediate impact. Historians seldom attempted to speculate on its lasting consequences. The fact is, the Great War set the course for the remainder of the Twentieth Century. Largely overshadowed by its successor, the war's impact is often overlooked. One need not look very hard or very long to realize its impact. European and Russian monarchies fell. Communism was born. The Ottoman Empire dissolved leaving the fate of the Middle East to the victors. Arthur Balfour, the British foreign secretary, promised a Jewish homeland. Among other things, the Treaty of Versailles made Germany destitute. The sheer cost of the war spawned world depression and fostered a socio-political environment that gave rise to Fascist Italy, Fascist Germany, Imperialist Japan, and ushered in a wider Second World War. Communist China was born in WWII. British, French, Dutch, and German colonialism withered. Gandhi's India and Pakistan became belligerents. Communism swelled to Southeast Asia, causing Korea to split in two. Followers of Islam who lost much of Palestine to Israel gave rise to militant and fundamentalist Moslems, leading to today's global war on terrorism.

Key figures who survived WWI played important roles in WWII— Franklin Roosevelt, Winston Churchill, Dwight Eisenhower,

George C. Marshall, Douglas MacArthur, George S. Patton, Harry S. Truman, Adolf Hitler, and Hermann Goering to name a few. Marshal Foch dictated the German Peace Commission's route through France to his private coach in the forest of Compiègne. The dialog between Foch and the German delegates led by Matthais Erzberger gave us Armistice Day. Twenty-two years later, Foch's coach was rolled to the same spot as Germany returned the favor to France on June 22, 1940. Hitler ordered the site destroyed after the French signed the German terms of armistice.

I was born nearly four months after WWII began. I enjoyed searching for foreign music on my parent's Philco console radio. One of my earliest memories is hearing Adolf Hitler's guttural voice as I played with the modulating transmissions on its short wave radio bands. A child of four years, I didn't know who Hitler was, what he was saying, or why he sounded so angry. I was surprised when he paused and a large audience shouted, "Sieg Heil, Sieg Heil," endorsing his anger. Four-year-olds knew little about the war. But even then, those shouts had an ominous sound.

Later, as a young boy, I watched old films made during the Great War. My impression of them inspired a lack of appreciation for that war. The unsynchronized film speed showed a bewhiskered Kaiser wearing a ridiculous plumed helmet riding his horse in front of a goose-stepping army marching impossibly fast down a German street. The German soldiers resembled characters from a Mack Sennett comedy. The airplanes both sides flew looked like toys I played with on a rainy day.

Decades later, I found a letter [reproduced within the novel] inside an old book in an antique store. Monroe's letter was genuine. His imagined voice sprang from its pages. Written in 1918, the letter made that era worth researching. Research stirred old questions I had about WWII. Germany was a civilized western nation! How could the world tolerate the start of a Second World War? Wasn't the first enough? How had Hitler convinced Germans to overlook his crimes against the Jews? Answers came in research. Monroe's letter became a story worth telling.

Originally written to inspire student interest in the Great War, the novel's characters turned it into a book suitable for adult consumption. A snapshot of the Great War is found in its pages, which span the period from the winter of 1916 to early 1919. Factual details were often hard to pin down. Historians might mark the start of a battle as the onset of a barrage [which could last for weeks] or the start of the ground campaign. The number of men involved and the casualties they sustained differed in historical accounts. As a result, statistics were averaged to serve as a context for the human cost of the war.

If the war is the antagonist, the fictional characters are protagonists. Research allowed nonfiction characters to be presented accurately in time and place. John, a fictional character, sails to France on the Saint Louis and meets Eddie Rickenbacker who actually sailed on the Saint Louis at the time. The British officer, French official, and Sister Cecilia on the bus to Senlis, as well as Arnaud Giraud, the hotel owner in Belfort, are all fictional. Their tales of German atrocities are not. Those were taken from accounts produced by the Michelin tire company directly after the war (*Michelin Illustrated Guides to the Battlefields*, in booklets printed from 1919 to 1920). The Michelin guides offered tourists useful maps to the battlefields after the war.

The novel owes its existence to that fascinating letter written by a man who simply signed it, *Monroe*. It's impossible to give credit to its writer. In reading the letter, it's obvious that Monroe served the Morris family as their chauffeur. The letter serves as his memorial.

The main characters retain the Morris family name, but Monroe merely mentioned it. Who they were and where they lived is not known. Research unearthed several candidates for the distinction, but it doesn't matter. Miss Morris and her brother, the "high Medical inspector," were totally fictionalized, as was Monroe. Thanks to that family is limited to employing Monroe for the trip to the Brooklyn Navy Yard. Had he not driven their car, he'd never have written his letter, and the novel would never come before a reader's eyes. A special acknowledgment must go to Rahaleh Nassri of the French embassy in Washington for finding the elusive address of the American embassy in Paris in early 1917. Lastly, to two great teachers and historians, Dave Clements and John C. Roemer III, and to all the others who suffered reading drafts, commented, suggested, and helped to improve the novel, I offer my limitless thanks.

Nicholas Lambros
June, 2014

John Edward Morris 1915-1916

JOHN ENTERED THE STUDY WHERE his father could usually be found making notes on the patients he'd seen earlier that day. Dr. Samuel Morris was sitting at his desk, pen in hand.

"Father, do you have a minute? I need to discuss something with you."

"Just a moment, John. Let me finish this entry. There! What's on your mind, son?"

A crucial moment for John, the opening he'd practiced seemed puny to him now. "I think it's best to come right to the point. I've decided to go to France as soon as possible." Watching his father's reaction, he knew Sam had spoken against war many times and was particularly opposed to the current war in Europe.

Sam instantly looked up. John knew that look. It always came when he proposed to do something his father was against. Nevertheless, John was twenty-six, no longer a child.

"I see. You've apparently given this some thought. I don't

suppose you have an idle tour in mind. John, you know how I feel about this war. What brought you to this decision, and what makes you think you would make any difference?"

"Father, let me explain. I want to join the French. It's the right thing to do. I certainly can't make a difference as a spectator. We were appalled when the *Lusitania* went down and those innocent women and children died. Wilson simply protested to the kaiser!"

"John, he was elected because the country wants no part of European wars. So far ..."

"Please, let me finish. I know you're against the war. Both you and I believe problems should be solved without war. Yet the war is a fact. I can't stand by and watch neutral countries like Belgium get overrun. I can't sit still as they kill women and children. The country is witnessing murder on a daily basis, and doing nothing about it!"

"I know how you feel about that, John, but it's not our fight. Wilson declared neutrality."

"Then why does he send support to the Allies? That's not neutrality. That's business as usual. It's hypocritical to say you're neutral and ship war materials overseas."

"I agree, John. You know very well that I've never believed war is an answer for anything. But why risk your life before America enters the war? Why not wait? You could enlist here in Maryland. With your education, they'd probably give you a commission right out of training. That makes more sense than to go rushing straight into war. It would make more sense if you joined the English! How would you communicate with the French? Your sister may be fluent, but you've never studied the language!"

That much was true, but John reasoned he would overcome the problem in time.

"Father, this is the most defining war in France since the French Revolution. The Central Powers are bent on destroying them. They need volunteers. The war cuts straight to the heart of what you've always said about civilized behavior. That's what makes the war something I can't ignore. It's not just to save France. It's to save those values you've preached to us since childhood. They're my values now, and they're worth fighting for. The Atlantic isn't going to separate us from Europe forever. Sooner or later, we'll have to fight. You may not believe it now, but I believe we have a personal stake in its outcome."

The surgeon in Sam tried his strongest argument. "Suppose you're seriously wounded? The medical care over there isn't much advanced beyond our Civil War! Men are dying over there, John. Many aren't killed outright, but they die from infected wounds."

"I know that. We'll all die someday. Compared to all that's happened, the danger a man faces is almost absurd. They torpedo women and children! How can I stay here? For me to duck a few bullets just doesn't compare. Belgium fought as best they could, and they were neutral! You've always said it's how we live that counts, not when or how we die. You've said it many times. Most never face the challenges our world throws at our feet. Father, I didn't choose this war, this war chose me. I just hope I can go with your blessing."

John knew Sam Morris was dead against the idea. Yet his arguments carried weight. He knew that Sam loved his children. Sam knew John was serious, and Sam never disappointed him when it counted. To let John go without his blessing was unthinkable.

"You know I don't want you to go, but you have my blessing and my prayers. However, I don't think your mother will be as easy to convince as I."

"That's why I spoke to you first. She never quarrels with you once you've made up your mind." The comment brought a wry smile from his father.

Only then did he reveal his thinking and the steps he'd already taken to fulfill his mission. He wanted to join a group of fliers led by the French but composed wholly of Americans. John had written the commander of the escadrille. He withheld the fact that his departure date would not allow him to await a reply, a fact that may well have weakened his argument and given his father reason to withhold his consent.

John chose to become a pilot for several reasons. He ruled out joining the French army. The first reason he gave his father was good enough by itself: he didn't speak French. He envied his sister's fluency. At Bryn Mawr, Catherine had majored in French. He knew he'd have to learn some French no matter which service he joined. When he arrived in France, the language barrier was guaranteed. Nevertheless, he must go to learn to fly and be accepted into the escadrille. John wasn't completely certain how all that would happen, but he was determined that it would.

His second reason suited his father. If he joined the French infantry, he must take an oath to France and risk losing his American citizenship. Should he survive the war, he wanted no political albatross hanging about his neck. Beyond that, he couldn't imagine himself charging recklessly, rifle in hand, from a French trench into a German machine gun. Tens of thousands of Frenchmen had been futilely sacrificed doing so for little or no gain. Attacks made from British trenches had proved no better than those from French trenches.

He'd ruled out the navy, as well. John didn't relish the idea of becoming a seal pup swimming on hostile seas while killer whales cruised below, waiting to pull a meal under the waves. Beyond all that, he was simply too independent to waive total control over his destiny. If he was to die, he wanted his death to be his fault, not the blame of some French army commander or the unlucky course steered by a ship's captain. The choice that remained was to fly. A pilot had total charge of his airplane, and orders were impossible to hear at ten thousand feet. Commands given to them on the ground would be impossible to enforce in the air. His choice to fly suited John's independent frame of mind.

American fliers he'd read about, who made a difference, belonged to the Escadrille Américaine, a unit formed through the efforts of Norman Prince and William Thaw. As fliers, they belonged to the French Foreign Legion. The oath they took was to obey their commander. They did not swear allegiance to the French flag. Moreover, the French needed fliers, and he was willing to learn and to defend France. To be turned away from the start was unlikely. John's only concern was how long it would take to learn and how he would do in combat. He left his father's study feeling better than when he'd arrived.

John knew that skill in the air was his only chance to survive. Learning to fly topped his list of things to do. His country had concentrated power in its navy. Finding anyone at home who'd flown in combat was impossible. Military airfields were uncommon, and schools for combat pilots didn't exist. He needed to learn from experts. Combat training could only be found in England and France. If he wasn't trained in England where language wasn't a problem, he'd go straight to France.

While waiting for his ship to sail, he spent time reading about airplanes. In fact, his only source of learning was what he read. He read anything he could lay his hands on—from the Wright Brothers' experiments with wing warping to flight controls and instruments. Mechanical problems were common. In 1911, the first flight across the country took nearly twenty days, and fewer than three had actually been spent in the air. The remainder was spent repairing the aircraft.

Many had once laughed at the idea that man would ever invent a machine that could fly. That mentality didn't exist in Europe. Necessity had made that thinking obsolete. His reading helped convince him that he'd made the right choice. Combat pilots were the vanguard of aviation. He believed the invention of the warplane meant that naval power alone was not enough to protect America and that neither the Atlantic nor Pacific would forever keep war from reaching its shores. He sincerely believed that the shortsightedness in an America flanked by two oceans blinded the military to the plausible future of airpower.

He thought it strange that in the land of its birth, powered flight amounted to delivering mail or pilots taking people up for the fun of it. The government's interest in warplanes was practically nil. The Signal Corps had fifty-five obsolete planes, and fewer than forty qualified pilots flew the handful still airworthy. This was not true in England or France. The French appreciated the value of warplanes, and advances in aircraft had come at an accelerated pace. They found uses for airplanes far beyond photographing enemy lines and spotting targets for artillery. He avidly read any news report on the air battles over France.

When he read about the protest of Count Johann-Heinrich von Bernstorff, the German ambassador, over the existence of an American escadrille, he'd gotten angry. Everyone knew America was neutral. The squadron was entirely volunteer and supported entirely by the French. Bernstorff demanded that American fliers on leave in America be interned by their own country. He'd couched the demand in neutrality law. His complaint mentioned nothing of Germany's invasion of Belgium, in disregard of its neutral neighbor. To John, Bernstorff was the epitome of the cynical, two-faced diplomat who played games with words—a politician who used diplomacy when it served his government while ignoring international norms. He distrusted diplomats and politicians in general, and he didn't exclude Woodrow Wilson or certain members of Congress.

He'd told his father that diplomats had failed miserably at preventing the war. Political figures on each side had totally underestimated the war's duration, its cost in lives and property, and the cost to his generation and those to follow. He believed governments should apply themselves to ending the perennial problems that plagued mankind—the first being war itself, hunger, disease, housing, and education. The list of priorities was obvious to John. He'd have avoided political studies entirely were it not for his pursuit of a career in journalism. His political studies amounted to learning about the rivalry between nations, petty quarrels between political parties, the use and misuse of power, how to bend the truth in support of national ambition, or to justify war based on a pack of lies. As far as John was concerned, politicians lived in a world separate from reality. John saw no good coming from war. Wars might be won or lost, but they had no winners, only losers.

His brother, Michael, and his younger sister, Catherine, also loved history. Catherine had studied French history. Michael's interest was American history. World history was John's passion. He devoured it. As a boy, he'd dreamed of playing some small part in the history of his day. His university studies dwelled on the Renaissance and beyond. He recalled reciting Lafayette's full name to point out an objection to a statement by his history professor trying to justify the slaughter of French nobility at the end of the French Revolution.

"Wasn't it a French noble by the name of Marie Joseph Paul Yves Roch Gilbert du Métier who helped America fight King George, sir?"

"What was that, Mr. Morris?" the professor asked.

John had crossed his fingers hoping for such a response. He especially loathed vague generalities when applied to justify anything, particularly anything related to whole groups.

"The Marquis de Lafayette, sir. One of those French nobles you described as self-serving, pompous potentates—a rather alliterative description, wouldn't you agree?"

Surprised by the rebuff, the professor's reply was forced. "I meant no disparagement of Lafayette. I was speaking about the nobles executed in the Revolution."

John took the response as a confession. Most of his student colleagues agreed that far too many nobles had met their fate in the guillotine.

In a political discussion John had with a classmate, they considered how family relations between European, English, and Russian royalty might figure in the start of the war. They decided to blame national rivalry. European alliances complicated the debate. Many such treaties had been ignored in the past. States joined in defense became warring states and then warring nations. An anomaly did arise. They found irony in how time could make enemies of allies and allies of former enemies. Each of them could cite such instances. John loved these vocal excursions into history. To John, it was important to discuss national issues. Discussion was the foundation in preventing similar mistakes that led to war.

John often questioned his own ideas. He was aware that his decision to go to France was suspect. Killing a man he'd never met had to be justified, especially a man who could easily have taken up arms for reasons that matched his own.

An army chaplain who'd come to the university to speak to the graduates had touched on the question. Of the soldier's old dilemma, he said, "We can choose to be instruments of God or man. God said we are our brothers' keeper. In war, men must become the instruments of God." To John's mind, the reasoning was too vague. Killing was not something he wanted to believe his God sanctioned. "Thou shalt not kill" left the question of killing in wartime unanswered.

As a flier, killing seemed less personal to him. Shooting an airplane down was easier to digest than killing a man charging you from a trench. The distance between opposing airplanes was a comfortable span compared to those who fought with rifles and bayonets. At any rate, he knew the time to discover how he'd react would come at ten thousand feet, fifty yards behind an enemy plane. He'd know what it really meant only then.

This much he knew. If a German pilot approached with the intention of sending him to a flaming death, he wanted no doubt or reservation to cause him to hesitate. His survival in the air meant shooting or being shot. That was war, whether at sea, on land, or in the air. The war had clearly demonstrated that nothing and no one was sacrosanct, not civilians, male, female, elderly, or diapered.

John's passage to Europe was arranged sooner than expected. Within hours of his father's blessing, his request for a booking on the *Saint Louis* was confirmed. His passport had arrived days before. Originally, John hoped to enter France directly, but the *Saint Louis* was the only ship sailing to Europe that still had tickets available. Several days remained before it sailed from New York to Liverpool. He'd requested an entrance permit weeks before. He needed it to enter France. Famous for its inefficiency, Washington had failed to send it. Entrance into England would not be permitted with only a passport. His father immediately arranged to have a permit sent by wire directly to the embassy in London and asked that copies be forwarded to the customs authorities in Liverpool. The rest was up to John.

The winter of 1916 brought the cold and the *Saint Louis*. As John left the house in Guilford to board the train to New York, he paused by the portrait of Teddy Roosevelt hanging in the lobby— the one man in the house who totally shared his desire to go to war. At the station, he said his good-byes to Catherine, Michael, and his father. Elizabeth, his mother, hadn't come. Instead, she'd handed him a letter. She deeply opposed his going. For his sake, she wanted to avoid an emotional scene at the station. Sam Morris canceled a surgery to see John off. He gave him a postcard with a picture of the battle flag flying over Fort McHenry. He took John's hand and said, "It's for luck. Stay alive, and come back home, son." The words spoke the sentiment of them all and raised the only question none of them could answer with certainty.

John on the Saint Louis—1916

TO APPEASE WILSON, KAISER WILHELM halted unrestricted U-boat warfare, removing the menace to ships sailing on the seas. Yet after several days on the *Saint Louis*, the rolling of the Atlantic seemed anything but peaceful as the ship cut a path to Liverpool. The waves that slapped at the bow made a seemingly endless barrage. John almost wished a U-boat might break the surface to have a look and end the tedium. Urgency to reach England came with a cost.

Since leaving New York, he hadn't recognized or spoken to anyone, except casually, and another morning had passed to the constant drumming of the waves. The doorway of his tiny stateroom took up fully a third of one wall. John decided to lunch in the cafeteria and to look for an interesting face. His room offered nothing but time to think of what might go wrong in England. He needed to talk, to think, to settle his mind.

The cafeteria was luxurious is size compared to his room.

Seating was plentiful, and meals were reasonable. By pure chance, he immediately saw a man with an angular jaw and prematurely receding hairline seated at a table twenty feet from the entrance. A confident air radiated from the familiar face. If he was the man John thought he was, the day might prove interesting. John walked toward the table to introduce himself.

"Good afternoon, sir. I noticed you were eating alone. I thought I might join you."

The man glanced at John and said, "Why not, Mr. …?"

"John Morris. Call me John, Mr. …?"

"Rickenbacker, Eddie Rickenbacker. I prefer Rick to Eddie, John."

It *was* him! John had read about the exploits of the famous race car driver. He admired the man, and he believed he shared Rickenbacker's zest for adventure.

"Glad to meet you Mr. Rickenbacker. I've read a lot about—"

"John, take a seat, and please call me Rick. Can I order something for you? Would you like a menu?"

"No, thanks. What you've got looks fine." John stopped a passing waiter and gave him his order. Before continuing the conversation, John made a quick personal appraisal of his famous tablemate. Assessing Rickenbacker as an honest man, John wanted to know if the stories he'd read were really true. After offering a hand, he risked saying, "So you're the crazy Rickenbacker I've read about—the one who picks up racing trophies like he was playing marbles."

Without expression, Edward Vernon Rickenbacker looked squarely into John's eyes. John didn't know whether he was rising to knock him down or take his hand. After an awkward pause, a smile rounded Rick's face. His grin allowed John to count every tooth in Rickenbacker's upper jaw. He took John's extended hand in the tightest, most painful handshake he'd ever felt.

"Well, I guess a guy's got to be a little crazy to do what I do. My pleasure, John. Where are you from?" Both men took their seats.

"Baltimore. The pleasure is mine, Rick ... I think," he said, prying his fingers apart and using his good hand to massage blood back into the other. "What brings you to Liverpool?"

"Wolverton. We're building a new racing team. Going to work on some cars. You've got to stay on top in this business, or the competition will eat you alive. How about you?"

"Well, compared to what you do, it seems a little tame. Don't laugh, okay?"

Rick smiled. "Okay. That's a deal," he said, going back to his meal.

"I'm going to get flying lessons with the English or maybe the French. It depends. I'll find out when I get there. I wrote to the commander of the American squadron in France to ask if I could join after I learn to fly. I couldn't wait for an answer. The ship was about to sail."

"I'm not surprised. Wasn't long ago that German subs were sinking anything that floats. Mail from Europe to the States had to risk it. So, you don't know anything for sure?"

"No. Not yet."

"Well, I wouldn't worry if I were you, John. They need as many fliers as they can get."

"I figured they needed pilots too. I'll probably go to the embassy in London first. They can help. I don't think I'll have any trouble once I get to France."

"You might, John. I wouldn't bet on it being tamer than racing. From what I've heard, there's plenty of shooting going on in those clouds. It's funny you mentioned it. I've been thinking about trying it myself. You never know ... maybe I'll see you there one day. Don't shoot all the Heinies down. Save a few of 'em for me, okay?"

If Rickenbacker was really considering learning to fly, he hadn't made up his mind. However, he was right. The fighting over the northern provinces was anything but tame. If Rick decided to fly, there was a small chance they'd see each other. John didn't think it would happen. Rickenbacker was famous for racing. Why should he risk his life by joining a squadron and become just another target in the air? It didn't seem likely.

Meatloaf with gravy and potatoes arrived, and the conversation turned to other subjects. For the first time on board, John was enjoying himself. As it turned out, they were more alike than either had guessed. John's interest in Rick's stateside racing drove the conversation, and Rick was more than willing to talk about his hair-raising close calls.

"There was this race in Sioux City, Iowa. Fred Duesenberg and I sank every penny we had in the Mason car. It was either win that race or go bankrupt. My mom's advice, bless her superstitious heart, was to tie a bat's heart to one of my fingers and then everything would work out. I'm not lying, John. A hunk of dirt flew up from the car ahead and knocked my mechanic senseless. I had to pump oil myself to keep the pressure up. We won that damned race with him out cold and a bat's heart tied to my finger. God's truth! That bat was worth $12,500 in prize money! Saved me from becoming a full-time mechanic. Let me buy you a drink, John. You aren't in a hurry, are you?"

"Okay. I'll have whatever you're having."

The stories continued to flow, and John listened, admiring a man who was willing to risk death for what he loved—racing against the fastest cars on the circuit. One of his tales was less spectacular and more informative.

"I met Glenn Martin in California. He showed me the bomber he built for the navy and offered to take me up. I said okay before thinking it over. I didn't tell Glenn I don't like high places. By the time he stopped climbing, I looked over the side and was surprised

I didn't get dizzy. It's the first time I've ever been that high and didn't get sick."

"It's a good sign, Rick. I haven't even thought about how I'd react physically. I don't think heights bother me. I've never been up high enough to know. I guess I'll find out."

John felt it odd that a man who'd seen others crash and die right in front of his eyes could be afraid of heights. If true, he had second thoughts about ever seeing Eddie Rickenbacker in an airplane. What chance would he have in a fight if he was busy throwing up his guts?

"Rick, you ought to write a book. I can't remember hearing stories I enjoyed so much. If we ever get together again, dinner and drinks are on me. Okay?"

Their drinks emptied, they stood and shook hands without as much pain.

"My pleasure, John. I wish you the best of luck. You'll probably need it where you're going. If we do see each other, you buy dinner, but I'll buy drinks."

"It's a deal. Good luck with your new racing team. I hope we see each other again. If we don't, I'll look you up after the war. I'll buy you a dinner either way."

"Okay. Keep your head down. I'm going to order a meal that'll flatten your wallet!"

"I'll bring my checkbook."

"So long, John."

Waves still pounded the bow. Not a ship or periscope was in sight. It didn't matter. Rickenbacker made his whole voyage worthwhile. John's spirits were higher than they'd been since he'd decided to go. Rick's aura of confidence reassured John.. The change in his attitude was diametric. He hadn't realized how apprehensive he'd become during the seemingly interminable voyage.

The *Saint Louis* finally docked in Liverpool. John took his bags to British customs. The line of passengers wasn't overly long. He was glad he hadn't waited for a large liner. Slowly, the line moved through customs. He looked for Rickenbacker and thought he caught a glimpse of him being escorted to an office. Sorry he hadn't had a chance to speak to Rick, John supposed a man like Rickenbacker had friends waiting to meet him. Being famous had its advantages. He wondered whether Rickenbacker would remember him.

When John's turn came, he was asked to explain the purpose of his trip, name his destination, and state how long he intended to stay on the isle. His responses revealed he'd come to England in order to go to France.

"I'm going to the American embassy in London. I hope to join a squadron in France. I'm not sure how long I'll be in England. It depends on how things go."

"A rather roundabout way of getting to France, don't you agree, sir? May I see your passport and papers, please?"

"My papers should be here."

The customs officer found John's papers and scrutinized the photograph on his passport. He took his time. John began to worry. The agent seemed helpful. At the same time, he was being extremely cautious and professional.

"Did you bring any restricted materials into the country?"

"I don't think so. I'm not sure what's restricted."

"You should have read these papers, sir! It lists things you are forbidden to bring into England."

"I apologize. I didn't get copies of my papers. I just boarded the ship."

"Very well, sir. The baggage inspector will need to check your luggage. He's the man in the line on the extreme left. When finished, he'll apply a sticker and tell you to return to this station. I'll keep your passport until you return. Do you have any questions, sir?"

"No. Thank you." John was disappointed. It meant more time

to go through another line. Understandably, Britain was in the midst of a war and must be very careful about who and what entered England. The officer pressed a button signaling the inspector in the other line that another passenger was being sent to him.

The luggage inspector waved his hand to attract John's attention. The agents were very thorough. Ten minutes later, John finally got to the inspector.

"Luggage on the table, please. Is there a key?"

"No, sir, they aren't locked."

"Very good. Are you carrying any restricted materials?"

"I don't think so. I hadn't read the entrance papers."

The inspector looked at John as if he might be a smuggler. The back of John's neck grew warm. What if he was carrying something on the list? What would happen then? Would they arrest him, deport him, or simply confiscate the item? He mumbled softly to himself, blaming himself for his predicament.

"Did you say something, sir?" the inspector inquired.

"No. I was just wishing I'd had my papers earlier." John tried not to look guilty. It wasn't easy. He *felt* guilty.

"Right, sir. We'll soon see. That's why I'm here. I'll be a minute. You'll be on your way if you've done right. Have you ever been to England before, sir?"

"No, sir. This is the first time. I shouldn't be here very long." John thought this last comment might help ease the inspector's concern.

"Too bad. There's quite a bit to see, sir, even in time of war."

That wasn't the reaction John hoped his comment would evoke.

"I didn't mean to say … I mean, I'm glad to be here. It's just that my business may not take long. Actually, I hope to see as much of England as I can."

"To be sure, sir." The inspector sifted through everything in John's luggage. He even inspected the bags, feeling along their sides and bottoms, turning them upside down, looking for a suspicious seam. Nothing slipped his gaze.

"Right, sir. Now if you'll just turn your pockets out, sir, we can finish."

With some embarrassment over having to reveal his father's postcard and his mother's letter, John complied. Satisfied, the inspector placed a sticker on his bags and told him to return to the customs officer. The officer stamped John's passport and allowed him to pass.

None of the other passengers had taken as long to get through customs. He regretted being singled out for the full treatment. Rickenbacker hadn't had any trouble. He'd been escorted into the country. International fame had its reward.

John could not have been more wrong. His delay was caused by his limited association with Rickenbacker on the *Saint Louis*, not by his baggage. British agents detained Rickenbacker after observing his Atlantic crossing. They believed Rickenbacker to be a possible spy, and the British were taking no chances. He'd changed the German *h* in his last name to an American *k*. He was told to return to the ship. Christmas came and went before one of his influential friends in London convinced Britain's agents that Rickenbacker was not a German spy.

Now that he was here, John wanted to get to London as soon as possible. The city lay nearly two hundred miles from Liverpool. At the bus terminal, the ticket agent told John he'd reach London by the next day and recommended that John go to Manchester to board a train.

"If it's on schedule, you might reach London tonight, sir."

John took the advice.

The agent was right. The train was late. John met a British airman stationed in southern England on leave from the Royal Flying Corps. His name was Richard Sloane.

"I've always wanted to see 10 Downing Street," the airman said. "Never been before."

Sloane's face was badly scarred. John didn't ask how and didn't tell Sloane why he'd come to England. Having told his story to Rickenbacker and two customs agents, he didn't feel like recounting it again.

Curiosity arose at Sloane's insignia. It was enough to start a conversation. Richard rattled off short, cryptic explanations of the insignia. John wasn't familiar with RFC jargon. Military rules prevented Sloane from discussing sensitive information.

"I can tell I'm now a mechanic. Confidentially, old man, the FE2 pusher is no match for the Albatros. Our designers will have to do better. At the rate new models are turned out, it shouldn't take long."

Several of John's questions brought "That's hush-hush, old man. Sorry. They enforce restrictions on what we say. Loose tongues risk our boys in the trenches. Ears all about, you know. Hard to say where a Hun might be lurking. Some fellows think Old Willie has a copy of our plans before they arrive at the trenches."

"Old Willie?"

"The kaiser. Jolly old Wilhelm. Bloody bastard, if you ask me."

"I see. Have you been in France?"

"Yes. I'm very much pleased with my posting in the isles, thank you. In spite of the glory you hear about, I'm not keen on the life expectancy of an RFC pilot these days. Once landed in a flaming FE2, if you'll pardon the pun." That explained his scars.

"Were you a combat pilot in France?"

"Right. For a relatively short period, I'm afraid."

"What's it like up there?"

"Damned risky, old man! The Huns get rather annoyed when we fly across their lines."

Getting Richard to talk in detail about his combat flying wasn't easy. John searched for a way without forcing him to remember things he might be trying to forget.

"I'm hoping to get to a training center, myself."

"To be a mechanic?"

"No. A fighter pilot."

"Never flown before?"

"No. I came to learn."

"I see. From what I've read, you haven't got much of a flying corps. I suppose the pond has a lot to do with that."

"The Atlantic?"

Sloane nodded.

"That's why I'm here. Just arrived in Liverpool today."

"Plymouth is closer. I suppose they're still a bit anxious about the blasted U-boats."

"I didn't see one on the way."

"Fortunate for you, old man. They do their worst on the surface. The bastards sink anything that floats our way."

The conversation grew lighter after that. They refrained from speaking about the war. They decided to go to the dining car for a late dinner. The choice lay between sandwiches and some sort of meat pudding. John ordered a ham sandwich. Richard got the meat pudding. Both ordered a draft of Irish beer that came in a mug so large that John couldn't finish it.

"Do they still issue alcohol to British servicemen?"

"Rum for sailors. I believe the infantry gets it, as well. I've never visited their mess."

"I guess not, you being an airman." His attempt to steer the subject to air combat failed. He didn't press Sloane into talking about something so sensitive to Sloane.

They returned to the compartment. To John's surprise, Richard raised the topic to combat.

"I was nearly two weeks with a squadron in Amiens. Saw enough to last a lifetime."

Relieved he hadn't had to press Sloane, John encouraged him to continue. "It must have been a demanding post."

"Not at the physical level. It's what you see from two miles up. A God-awful sight when you're not looking for Fritz flying about. Until you see it, it's impossible to describe. Shell craters by the thousands, splintered trees, towns in rubble. Trenches gash the earth for miles. Those are the quiet sights. When the artillery is having at it, it's too terrible to describe. You've got to see it. If you last more than a week or two, you'll outlive the average British pilot. That's the life expectancy in the RFC these days. It's no vacation up there! A well-placed bullet and you've bought the farm."

John was too stunned to reply.

The train slowed, veered onto to a siding, and stopped. John slumped back in his seat and looked through the window. It was too dark to distinguish anything. He tried to imagine what Sloane said. Was it really that bad? Was a French pilot's life as short as an Englishman's? What was it like to be shot? How did it feel to shoot at another flier? Sloane's description raised old questions. A less confident man might have turned for home. John didn't.

A newspaper bought in Manchester did nothing to encourage him. Wilson was trying to get all sides together to discuss terms and settle the war peacefully. Germany's initial response was to call for a conference table in Germany. Such a ploy would obviously fail. Britain and France would never agree to that. It would take more than words or political maneuvers to end the war. Words had done no more good in the summer of 1914 than they did in the winter of 1915. Words weren't enough to end it. It could take years. It would certainly take more lives.

John in London

JOHN ARRIVED IN THE CITY of Charles Dickens at King's Cross Station on the morning of December 22, 1916, the day after his debarkation from Liverpool. Somewhere in central England, his passenger train lost priority to allow a military train to pass. The conductor told him it was an infantry transport. John guessed it was taking replacements to the front after the fighting on the Somme.

He had good reason to believe that was the case. The Manchester newspaper listed preliminary casualty reports, including the total casualties from the Somme. The estimates on both sides were staggering. The corner of the newspaper these dispassionate numbers occupied struck him as ironic compared to the large byline on the death of the emperor of the Austro-Hungarian Empire.

Franz Joseph had arguably been the man who started the war. He started it by allowing his ministers to issue an ultimatum to Serbia and not accepting its reasonable reply. The death of old monarch was ludicrous compared to those mind-numbing statistics.

An article said the fighting on the Somme gained the Allied eight miles. The numbers revealed that it had cost the British 420,000 men. French losses numbered nearly 200,000. Mathematics put the carnage in more graphic terms. Combined allied losses totaled 77,500 per mile. German losses were suspected to be even higher than those at Verdun.

John's eyes continued to move glumly over the figures in the upper-left corner of the page. Official numbers were undetermined. The newspaper claimed "authoritative sources" had losses to the French surpassing 450,000 dead or wounded in recapturing the forts of Douaumont and Vaux in their counterattack at Verdun. German losses were also estimated. Those were equal to French losses. It was a scale of carnage John knew of no equal in history.

You didn't have to be Bertrand Russell. According to the figures, in the space of a few months, two million men had died or been wounded in France. The carnage was so great that only numbers could describe it. The cost was unimaginable compared to wars John had studied. The worst war in American history looked like a family quarrel compared to it.

Gettysburg wasn't far from Baltimore. His father had taken John and Michael to see it when they were boys. His memory of the day was clear. John's interest in history began that day as he read the plaques commemorating the events of the first three days in July of 1863. He'd stood at the High-Water Mark, where the Confederate charge was stopped after their hellish rush into the teeth of Union cannons, rifles, and bayonets. Major General George E. Pickett lost half of his fourteen thousand men in less than an hour. Union cannons shredded them, scattering blood and bodies over the wheat fields along with their hope for Southern independence.

To compare the Civil War with the statistics in the Manchester newspaper, John had to count all of its casualties. It had been a question on a high school history test. He remembered it as the easiest question, because the number impressed him at the time. The Civil War, the deadliest in American history, had killed or wounded an estimated one million men. Over half were numbered among the dead. Of those, many had died of disease, not battle. Yet here, in a handful of weeks, the destruction on the Somme and Verdun had doubled the losses of the Civil War. The magnitude of the numbers turned something in the pit of his stomach.

He never imagined his view of the war in Europe could change so much in less than two days. Men had learned how to kill each other at a rate unknown in human history. The news both saddened and humbled John. Before anything else, he now knew what he must do on his arrival in London. It was something he hadn't done in a long time.

Outside King's Cross station, the clock on the tower showed 7:01 a.m. John was in a crowd representing every British service. Military hats of all kinds were everywhere. Many women also wore hats bearing strange insignia.

It occurred to John that he had much to learn. He needed to learn to read military insignia, how to fly, and learn enough French to get by. All of that could wait. First, he wanted to learn the direction of the nearest church. His new perspective on the war had shaken him. He wished he could speak to his own father. The nearest was God.

A young soldier wearing a hat bearing insignia John believed was an officer's was nearby.

John asked, "Excuse me, could you direct me to the nearest church?"

"Protestant or Catholic?"

"Either one. It doesn't matter, sir."

The officer's eyebrows rose. "I see. You must be new to London. Several are nearby. Our finest should do. It's not far. That's Gray's Inn Road over there. Take it to High Holborn and cross to Chancery Lane. Go left on Fleet Street and just keep walking. You can't miss it. Sorry, old man, I've got to run."

The officer turned briskly and trotted toward the station. John's thanks went unheard. The officer disappeared into the crowd moving toward the platforms.

John followed his suggestion and passed Lincoln's Inn. He suspected it wasn't named for the sixteenth president. At the end of the lane, he saw Fleet Street. The street wound around. It seemed too narrow for a main thoroughfare. On his right, a large stone building with cone-topped turrets bracketed by two towers at either end drew his attention. Three men wearing white wigs and full black robes walked toward its entrance.

As he passed a tiny lane, a sign announced that it led to Dr. Samuel Johnson's house. He became curious about his surroundings. He began looking into shop windows and down the maze of tiny courts and alleys. A stranger could easily get lost in London. It certainly wasn't laid out in neat rectangles like Baltimore. He supposed the Thames River had an influence on its design. One had the feeling that an attempt was made to compress a large city into a few thousand acres. He'd already passed a small church but was sure it wasn't the one the officer said he couldn't miss. He kept walking. Not long after, he understood what the officer meant. The unmistakable mass of a huge cathedral emerged at a bend in the road a few blocks from where he stood. It seemed built in the middle of the street. Stopping another British soldier, he asked the name of the sooty cathedral.

"A Yank, what? It's Saint Paul's. I expect you've never been to London. Walk on in, old fellow. No formality. Everyone's welcome."

Again, a British soldier walked off before John said thank

you. He developed the impression that British soldiers were all red cheeked, short on words, and in a hurry to be somewhere.

John climbed the steps to the landing outside the entrance. He arched his neck to look at the towers on either side of the twin-tiered portal. Pairs of columns supported an elaborate pediment. A Roman numerals on the clock tower read 7:12 a.m. He climbed the remaining steps and entered the nave. Inside, the cathedral was starkly magnificent and unlike anything he'd seen in Baltimore.

Huge stone arches bordered the nave, leading his eyes to a large altar at the other end. Vaults supported the ceiling. A great space opened up under the dome. John noticed chapels on either side of the entrance. He chose the one dedicated to Saint Michael and Saint George. There he knelt to honor the men who'd died by the Somme and around Verdun and whose only epitaph was a column of numbers in the upper-right corner of a Manchester newspaper.

Down the vaulted nave, he came under the dome and looked straight up. It was like standing under a huge ornate bell with sunlight pouring in one side. The light dispelled the starkness of its great space. John decided not to climb to the top but walked behind the high altar. He was surprised to find another chapel dedicated to Jesus. A Catholic, John made the sign of the cross. He left Christopher Wren's cathedral utterly impressed. Not a praying man, John was relieved to join the people walking about Fleet Street.

For all their willingness to war with their brothers, John believed people needed each other. Today, their world was being tested, and they needed each other more than ever. Far from his family, the thought reassured him, and John needed reassurance. Lighter in spirit as he walked down Fleet Street, his mind returned to the reason for his trip. According to the clock in the tower, an hour had elapsed since his arrival in London. He hailed a taxi and asked its burly driver to take him to the American embassy.

"That'd be Grosvenor Square, governor. Not far. 'aven't 'ad a Yank in the cab for weeks. You're the first this month." John had never heard a Cockney accent. He enjoyed it so much that he relaxed and hoped the driver would keep talking. He needn't have worried.

The driver took Fleet Street west and became a traveling tour guide for his Yankee passenger. The corners of his moustache moved freely as he spoke, adding a curious congeniality to his descriptions of London's more famous landmarks.

"Over there's the Royal Courts, Yank. Proper fellas, those blokes, aye, gov?"

John recognized the building he'd seen on his way to Saint Paul's, busily ingesting wigged figures in long black robes.

"Them's the judges, barristers, and such like. Trafalgar Square's named for the battle what Lord Nelson won. That's old Horatio 'isself up there. Looks small from 'ere, but 'e's eighteen feet top to bottom. The national gallery's beyond. Mind now, a bloke walking 'ere under all them pigeons best be wearing 'is 'at, if you know what I mean, gov. Ruddy blighters'll poop on anything."

John wasn't sure it was the accent or how he described things that appealed to him more. Hardly pausing to breathe, the driver pointed out each English icon, sometimes two or three in the stretch of a city block. The cab barely moved at rolling speed.

"Say, gov, would you like a short tour? There's things you really oughta see whilst you're in London. My guess is you 'aven't been in town before now."

"I just got in. Not a long tour, please. I need to be at the embassy."

"Tell you what, gov, I'll pay the fair 'til we gets to 'yde Park. It won't cost you a king's copper. Fair enough?"

"That's generous of you, but I'll pay the fare, Mr. ....?"

"Albert. Albert's the name, gov."

"Okay, Albert. You've got the wheel."

With that, the tour began in earnest. Albert kept as slow a pace as possible, paying little attention to the protests of taxi horns and yelling of other drivers. He'd wave them around and carry on a rolling commentary about the sights as they passed. His pride in London shone through an endless portrayal of the city he so obviously loved. Before the ride finished, John was familiar with the Admiralty, the King's Horse Guards, Big Ben, Parliament, Westminster Abbey, the Victoria Memorial, and Buckingham Palace.

"Albert, you missed your calling. You should head a London tour service."

"I'd rather be the guide than lead the guides, Yank." Albert thought John might enjoy his last speech. Yanks had fought England in part over the right to free speech.

"That's 'yde Park. Anyone what's got a mouth can talk about anything on God's good earth. Mind now, gov, I mean anything! Why the other day, I was walking by this very corner. Blimey, I heard this old bloke, standing right on that spot 'e was, proclaiming Parliament ought to outlaw corsets and other such trap the ladies use to 'old their breasts, if you know what I mean. Said they oughta be free as a pair o' love birds, 'e did. The way God made 'em, 'e says! Loose as cow's tits."

John broke into laughter from deep inside. The taxi filled with laughter and spilled into the street. People standing outside looked at him as though he'd gone insane. War made them forget such laughter still existed.

"It's the honest truth, gov! You can take—"

John finished the phrase. "Take your word for it?" No sarcasm was intended. Unsure, Albert sensed a Yank might see humor in repeating the expression.

Albert joined tentatively at first but soon surpassed John with a deep, hearty laugh that spilled to the edge of Hyde Park. John stopped. Albert stopped too, their sides hurting. He turned onto Grosvenor Square and parked near the building marked number six. The square had been the home of America's Ministers to the Court of Saint James since John Adams was appointed its first in 1785 and had stayed in the house at number nine. John was truly amazed that Albert knew where John Adams had stayed.

Before leaving the taxi, John asked Albert what he owed.

"Not a farthing, gov. I wouldn't take a bloomin' penny for this trip. I can't remember when I last laughed so 'ard. Worth every penny. Take care, gov. I 'ope you enjoyed our tour."

"I insist, Albert." He was worth whatever he asked. John learned more about London in thirty minutes than he would have learned on his own in a week.

Albert just waved him off, saying, "Keep your money, Yank. It's my pleasure. Good luck with whatever the Lord sends your way." Albert drove off, heading back to the railroad terminals in the city he loved so thoroughly and knew so well.

At the entrance to the embassy, John showed his passport to the guard. The guard nodded and directed him to a receptionist seated behind a desk just beyond the entrance hall. John thanked him and went inside.

"Good morning. I'm John Morris from Baltimore. I just arrived from Liverpool hoping to see Ambassador Page." John had noticed a nameplate resting on her desk. "I need his help with a personal matter, Miss Andrews."

"Welcome to England, Mr. Morris. Unfortunately, the ambassador is temporarily out of town. However, I might be able to assist you. May I ask the purpose of your visit?"

"I need help in joining the American Escadrille in France. I'm not a certified pilot and hoped he could advise me." John hesitated. "It's somewhat complicated. I was really hoping to see the ambassador." John considered his problem too personal for discussion in a public hall. It was more suited to a man's ears. Miss Andrews eyed him for a moment, realizing the issue surpassed her authority.

"I understand, Mr. Morris. The ambassador would be able to assist you better than I. I'm not sure he can help you join an escadrille. As you know, America is neutral. As the ambassador to Great Britain, he normally goes through our ambassador to France when contacting French authorities. However, he might be willing to contact the ambassador for you. Would that be of any help?"

"It would, Miss Andrews. You said he's out of town?"

"Yes. I expect Ambassador Page to return by noon tomorrow. May I see your passport, Mr. Morris? I'll set up an appointment for you." She opened the passport, wrote his name and address on a card, and scribbled a note to the ambassador.

"Thank you. The sooner the details are settled, the sooner I can begin. I've been traveling quite a lot lately, and I'm anxious to get started."

"I understand. Would tomorrow at 2:00 p.m. be convenient?"

"Yes! Thank you, Miss Andrews."

"You're quite welcome, Mr. Morris. I hope the ambassador will be able to help. If there's anything I can do, please let me know."

"Actually there is a small favor." John asked whether he might leave his larger bag at the embassy until he met the ambassador. She granted the request. John knew her main job was to filter the ambassador's visitors. Her willingness to help was gratifying.

John left, having forgotten to ask her about a place to stay. He was sorry he hadn't asked Albert to wait. If anyone knew the answer to that question, Albert certainly would.

John Meets the Ambassador

JOHN WALKED TOWARD HYDE PARK, spending time thinking about the train ride to London, Albert's grand tour, and his future. The tour was the least troubling. He'd really enjoyed Albert's tour. What would Albert do if he had an entire day?

Tomorrow, when he returned to the embassy … Damn! His passport! He felt his pockets twice to be sure. It wasn't there. He'd left it at the embassy with Miss Andrews. John ran back to the building. The same guard was on duty, so he wasn't stopped as he breezed by the doorway and hurried to her desk.

"Miss Andrews? I must have left my passport here."

"I'm terribly sorry, Mr. Morris. I forgot to return it. I didn't know where you were staying, or I'd have brought it to you. I'm really very sorry."

"It's my fault, Miss Andrews. I should have remembered."

She handed him the passport, somewhat hesitant to return it. It occurred to him that she'd taken more than a passing interest in him. Not wanting to pursue the issue, he thanked her and left the building. Outside the embassy, a taxi with the same markings as Albert's stopped near the curb right next to a No Stopping sign. For a moment, he thought it might be Albert. It wasn't. The driver looked nothing like Albert. Disappointed, John walked toward the taxi. After all, any taxi driver could suggest a good hotel. Before he could ask, the driver spoke.

"Pardon, sir. Are you the gent what Albert brought 'ere this morning?"

Surprised, John wondered how the cabbie knew Albert had brought him here. His accent might easily be taken for Albert's echo.

"Yes, the driver with a big moustache."

"That's Albert, sir. Got a fine pair of 'andles. Said I should treat you like bloody King George 'isself. 'e asked me to ride over in case you might be needin' a lift. Said to ask whether you'd got a place to stay."

"No. How many times have you driven by the embassy?"

"Four or five, sir. Can't park 'ere, you see. You'll be needin' a place then, right, sir?"

"Yes. Can you suggest a hotel?"

"I shan't be keeping my promise if I did that, sir! 'op in, sir. I know just the place." John got into the cab, still curious. "Right, sir. We're off to Albert's place, sir."

"Where did you say?"

"Albert Dunne's flat, sir. 'e said if you need a place to stay, I'd should bring you to 'is flat. 'is very words, sir. Said, ''arry, if 'e needs a flat, bring 'im to my place, and don't take no for an answer.' Thought I'd best get you in the cab before you could turn the offer down, sir. Bit of a dodge, I suppose. It worked well enough."

John smiled. He wondered whether all London taxi drivers were as generous.

"You said your name is Harry?"

"Rightly 'arold, sir. My friends call me 'arry. Yours, sir?"

"John Morris. Call me John, Harry."

"Not likely, sir. If you don't mind, sir, I'll stay formal like. Wouldn't do to get into a bad 'abit whilst drivin' gentleman about London. I'd get careless with my gentlemen fares."

"Okay, Harry. You know best." He admired Harry's professionalism.

"Right, sir. Best to be proper. It gives the taxi a bit more shine, if you know what I mean."

Albert's modest flat was near Cheapside and within the sound of the bells of Saint Mary-le-Bow. He was a Cockney in the true sense of the word.

"Thanks, Harry. It was nice of you to wait for me."

Harry would not accept a tip. "Not necessary, sir. Albert's place is up a flight, sir."

Albert answered the door, glad to see John. He introduced his wife as Bertie, explaining her given name was Bertha. Albert said they had two sons. The younger was named George, after King George. The oldest was Edward, after the former king. Bertie giggled. She didn't seem to need much cause. It was the sort of giggle that helped brighten the dim flat. What light there was came from a single window and four oil lamps.

Albert felt the need to explain. "Saves electric, John. Bertie and I don't mind the dark. London 'as its share as well from the soot off the coal burnin' about town."

That was the only time Albert had anything negative to say about London.

Bertie showed John a couch she'd made up as a bed. From what he saw, they barely lived within their means. Even so, Bertie fashioned a fine dinner from what was on hand in her tiny kitchen. She bubbled over at the thought of a real Yank eating dinner in her very own flat. John was grateful for their generosity. Albert told

John how he'd met Bertie and when they were married. He spoke proudly of his family. John told Albert about his sister and brother, carefully avoiding mention of his family's relative wealth.

After dinner, Albert suggested he and John visit a nearby pub.

"I'd enjoy that, Albert. Thanks for dinner, Mrs. Dunne. I was starved."

"My pleasure, I'm sure, Mr. Morris."

John insisted she call him by his given name.

The two men excused themselves and walked down Milk Street. Albert mentioned it was the street where Sir Thomas More lived. "Milton was born on Bread Street farther down."

The tour guide in Albert was impossible to suppress. John supposed it sprang from his occupation as a taxi driver. It must have pleased those passengers who were new to the city and asked him about things they saw on the way.

They crossed Cheapside and walked by the church of Saint Mary-le-Bow. John couldn't make out the design of the weather vane that topped its tall, slim spire.

"Looks like a rooster, don't it, John?"

Ahead, a small square appeared, and Albert was impatient to show John the statue of a man wearing baggy pants.

"You've likely 'eard about this old bloke, John."

John read the dedication to Captain John Smith, the noted explorer.

"You're right, Albert. I have heard about this old bloke."

"Don't poke fun, John. I know I don't speak the King's English, but folks understand me well enough about town."

"I wasn't poking fun, Albert. I was borrowing your accent. Besides, I said 'have heard,' not "ave 'eard.' I enjoy your accent, and I enjoy you knowledge of London."

Albert smiled. "Right. Then no offense taken, John. Blimey! I'm thirsty as a dog with no tongue. Let's get on with it, shall we?"

They entered Williamson's Tavern. Albert said it was built on the site of a seventeenth-century house once used as a residence by the old lord mayors. He simply couldn't resist! In or out of his taxi, Albert was more London tour guide than taxi driver.

They ordered tankards and became familiar with each other. More beer was ordered when the conversation turned to the reason John had come to England.

"You know, John ... I 'ope you don't mind me calling you John. I feel as I've know you a bit better than most. I s'pose I talk too much about London at times."

"This is a nice pub, Albert. But if you call me anything else but John, I'm leaving. I'm not your fare now. I'm your guest. I've enjoyed your stories about London as much as you enjoy giving them. I want you to consider me your friend."

"That being the case, John, then this is a mighty fine pub, and I'm proud to be your friend. As I see it, friends know each other. You might as well know I've been a bit on edge waiting to 'ear yours. I don't get many Yanks as fares, and I'm curious. What brings you to my town, John?"

"I've told just about everyone I've met so far, Albert. There's no reason to keep it from a friend."

John explained why he'd gone to the embassy. Albert listened with admiration for a man who'd volunteer to leave the peace of his home and family to risk death in Europe's war.

"America's not at war, John. What made you come? There are others like you, as well. It's beyond my ken why anyone would come and risk gettin' 'is arse shot off."

John smiled and tried to explain.

"I'm willing to take the risk. The risk is not what's important. Englishmen have better reasons for fighting. That's true. Our ties with England are strong."

"Our ties are one thing. I'd like to know your reason for coming."

"Albert, America will have to get involved eventually. We may be an ocean apart, but the war affects us too. We haven't been bombed, but this past summer, someone blew up the Black Tom munitions depot in Jersey City. It flattened the whole area. Twenty-six people were killed. One was a friend of mine. The U-boats sink our ships. You know about the *Lusitania*. It was a passenger ship! What happened to those people could happen again. We live in the same world, Albert. Wilson hasn't asked for war because he thinks America isn't ready. Americans see the war thousands of miles away. London was raided a few months ago. America can't imagine something like that happening to our cities. I don't see it that way. The world gets smaller every day, Albert. War will come our way someday. No ocean will stop that."

"You're probably right, John. We've never seen the like before. These new contraptions … zeppelins, aerial bombs, and such. It makes you wonder what they'll do next. It's bad enough in France, what with their artillery and machine guns. I've 'eard some sad stories from our lads. They say the boys are getting blown to splinters by the thousands. Known a few of them, I 'ave. Fine lads. No end of it in sight. Nothing is gained for long. It makes no sense. No sense at all."

Albert didn't add his usual trailer to his comments, and John took its absence as significant. Albert surely knew some of those boys. A sadness had come over his voice, slowing his speech and lowering his tone, a side of Albert that John had not seen.

Reminded of the statistics he'd read earlier, John wanted to change the topic. The war would still be there tomorrow, but he may never see his friend Albert again.

"Let's leave it there for now, Albert. We should be enjoying ourselves. I really enjoyed your tour today. Now that I know where you live, I might look you up if I have the chance to come back."

"And welcome, John. Fact is, if you didn't, it'd be a slap in the face, take my word for it."

The familiar words made John feel better. Albert was himself again.

Their tankards empty, they ordered again. The conversation drifted to lighter topics.

"Do you think it'll be a cold winter, Albert?"

"'ard to say, John. We're due for one. When are you due at the embassy?"

"Tomorrow afternoon. At two."

"We could take in the Tower of London tomorrow morning. I've got a bit of time coming. With an early start, we can 'ave a look and come 'ere for a beer."

"Are you sure you should take the day off, Albert?"

"I've more than one day coming, John. Things are better now that Bertie's driving the tram part time. That reminds me. She won't be coming. She's got to make the mornin' run."

"I can't think of a better way to spend a morning, Albert."

They walked back to the flat singing a bawdy British barrack song Albert had learned while driving a soldier in his taxi. Bertie was still awake.

"You still up and about, love? You got the tram bright and early."

"Shhh. Keep your voice down. Edward's out, but the young one's asleep. As for the other, it's no different than the week before, you old fart. You'll have to get breakfast on your own."

"Never worry about that, my old beauty. I was bachelorin' long before I met you, and I can still crack an egg." Nevertheless, Albert spoke more quietly. He gave Bertie a good night kiss.

"Mrs. Dunne, I want to thank you for putting me up tonight. You and Albert have been very kind. I hope I'm not too much trouble."

"Oh my, think nothing of it, I'm sure. It's not every day Albert brings a real Yank home. All we 'ears about you Yanks is from the *Times*. You ain't nothin' like they say. I expected you all wore cowboy 'ats, you know. I'm glad Albert didn't take you to Soho! The girls would 'ave eaten you alive!" A hand covered her mouth as she giggled.

"Now, now, Bertie, none of that! Why, you'll 'ave John thinking all sorts of things 'e shouldn't—and 'im going off to war. Best 'is mind is clear of that trap."

"Well, my, my, aren't we the careful one now? Pay no mind to him, John. 'e's been a ladies' man 'is whole life, ain't you, Albert?"

John could have sworn he saw Albert blush.

"Get to bed, love. The sun will rise before you know. You'll miss your bus."

What a pair! It was incredible. This little woman had Albert in the palm of her hand, and he loved it. It raised John's awareness of the true nature of people. Below the surface, what really mattered were the things that made them happy.

The next morning Albert took John to the Tower of London. There were really four towers. John admitted he had little knowledge of its history.

"Albert, all I know is it's a place where a lot of people were relieved of their heads."

Albert laughed. "There's no denying that, John, and some fairly lofty 'eads at that."

Albert related facts that weren't found in guidebooks. John didn't know about the remains of a crumbled Roman wall on the grounds, the wives of Henry the Eighth, or that the ravens walking around the yards had their flight feathers clipped so they wouldn't fly away.

"'enry took six wives, as though one isn't enough! Not a boy child from any of 'em. Elizabeth came through that gate. It weren't certain she'd be leavin' by it. Roger Casement was the last to die 'ere—an Ulster Protestant. Caught 'im off the coast dealing with a U-boat captain to get rifles for Irish rebels. They showed 'im no mercy. Strung 'im up over there near five months ago. Nasty business that, John. I don't think much good will come of it."

John had forgotten the man but remembered the clamor the hanging had caused in Washington. Albert said their cause would gain more sympathy if more Irishmen fought Germans instead of Englishmen.

Time passed quickly. John had to return to the embassy. It was too late to go back to the tavern. Albert was sorry the time had gone. They took his taxi to the embassy.

"You're welcome to the flat anytime, John. If you can't come, write and let us know what you're about. It's the devil's own playground over there. Look out for yourself, lad."

At the embassy, Miss Andrews greeted him. She wore the same smile as before but practiced more eye contact than she had the day before.

"The ambassador is waiting to meet you, Mr. Morris. I've told him the purpose of your visit. If there's anything I can do for you, anything at all, please don't hesitate to call on me."

This time, John recognized her signals, though he was a bit surprised to find them coming from a woman working at the American embassy in time of war. She'd be a prime target for a wily German spy who had a way with the ladies.

She escorted him to an office with three rows of brass letters mounted on the door–Walter Hines Page, United States Ambassador, Court of Saint James. She knocked, opened the thick wooden door, and announced him to Ambassador Page. The ambassador was a distinguished old gentleman in his early sixties who might easily be mistaken for a balding college president. An ample mustache didn't completely hide a sincere smile.

"Sit down, young man. Miss Andrews said you'd be here at two, and two it is. I admire punctuality in a young man. I see you're from Baltimore." Page rose from a red leather chair and advanced to shake John's hand. His brow had the furrows bred of concern. His tone was friendly and warm. "I'm familiar with Baltimore. Good food. A very busy port city."

"Thank you for taking the time to see me, Mr. Ambassador. You must be very busy."

"Don't think that way, young man. We're here to help our citizens. Now what exactly do you want me to do for you?" Ambassador Page resumed his seat behind a massive mahogany desk held down by stacks of papers. Wilson's photo hung on the wall behind.

"Sir, I only recently arrived in town. As you know, our country has not yet entered the war. It's my intention to join the French as a flier with the American escadrille. I wrote to its commander, but my ship left New York before I received a reply."

"I see. You are right about us not being at war. Colonel House thought we'd be in it after the *Lusitania* went down. The president didn't see it that way. He hopes they can settle it before we need to get involved. I have my doubts."

The ambassador swiveled his chair to look toward Hyde Park, a hand cradling his chin. The ambassador pondered the problem. His authority as an ambassador did not include military questions, and Miss Andrews had told him that John had no flying experience.

"John, many American boys rushed to join the French army when the war began. Most happened to be in Paris at the time. It's caused no little grief for their families back home. I assume yours know what you intend? How do they feel about it?"

"Yes, sir, they do. My father, Dr. Morris, and my mother didn't like the idea. My father said he'd rather I became an officer or a doctor like my brother, Michael. I just couldn't stand by and watch what was happening. I feel obligated to serve."

"Your father had good advice, John." Swiveling the chair to face John, the ambassador held up a hand to interrupt a response. "You said your father is a doctor?"

"Yes, sir. Dr. Samuel Morris of Johns Hopkins."

"Sam Morris? A fine man! I was a fellow at Hopkins. I met your father when I went to Hopkins for a fund-raiser some years back. I can understand why his sons are willing to act on principle. He impressed me as such a man. John, a lot of young men went to war thinking it would end soon. They looked at war and saw nothing but glory. I can tell you with certainty that there's nothing approaching glory in this war." The ambassador gazed directly at John. "Most of Europe felt that way at first. Now they're bent on self-destruction." Page stood and began to pace behind his desk, alternately staring out the window then at John. "I understand why you want to do this. However, as ambassador, I'm duty bound to say I cannot openly assist you in achieving your goal. We are a neutral nation, and the rules of conduct apply here. The things that I do, I can do under those rules. My hands are tied when it comes to others. You may have heard we had to change the name of the American squadron when the German ambassador complained it violated our neutrality."

"Yes, sir. I read about it in the newspaper." John wasn't sure he'd come to the right place. If the ambassador couldn't help, he was only wasting the ambassador's valuable time. "I appreciate your position, sir, and apologize if I'm putting you in bad—"

Page interrupted, "That's the government's policy, John. It's kept us out of war so far and probably saved many young men's lives."

The ambassador's words rang true. John said nothing in response, but he grew more discouraged. Once again, the ambassador turned to look toward Hyde Park. For a moment, he said nothing. He turned and looked John squarely in the eyes with a stare that would have burned a hole into steel. John prepared for a lecture on the ill-advised impulsiveness of youth.

"John, I believe I've explained our government's position on the matter. It's policy. I don't happen to agree with it. I wanted to be sure about your sincerity. Promise me something. What I'm about to say now is strictly between you and me, understood?"

The words surprised John. "Certainly, sir." Whatever came next, John hoped it was something that would not force him to go back to America with nothing but a sad tale to tell.

"I repeat, this is confidential and must not leave this office. I took the liberty to call William Sharp, our ambassador in Paris. I told him what you intend to do. I can't promise he'll be willing to help. If he chooses to, he has the connections to help you. I've asked him to send one of his staff to meet you in Le Havre. He'll take you directly to the embassy to see Sharp.

"You'll need a visa to get through customs. I can help you with that, but you never know how French customs will act. The French government changes so often that it's impossible to predict what their border people will do. Once you've landed at Le Havre, Sharp's contact will help you get through customs. That's the best I can do, John. Do you have any questions?"

John was stunned by his words. "Yes, sir. I need flight training. I've been reading everything I can get my hands on about it. Should I find a combat flying school here in England or in France?"

"The British won't train you unless you join the RFC. The French train a lot of our boys. Once you're trained, they'll assign you to an escadrille at their discretion. It's best to learn from the French. You'll learn to fly airplanes you will actually fly into combat. Any other questions?" "I'll need to get to France, sir. Do you have any advice?"

"You board a shuttle tonight at 11:00 sharp."

"Tonight, sir?"

"Tonight. Can you do that?"

"Yes, sir! That's sooner than I'd hoped."

"Good. I thought you'd agree. I managed to pull a few ambassadorial strings for you. Transportation is arranged to Portsmouth. That's where your shuttle is docked. Are you packed?"

"Yes, sir. Both bags are downstairs."

The ambassador opened a desk drawer and fetched two tickets. One was for a bus and one for the shuttle. He handed John a letter written in his own hand, expressing his personal approval for John's entry into France. A letter bore the wax seal of the embassy. Page handed both to a very surprised John. Page had planned his departure before he'd even met John! He'd anticipated everything, apparently meeting John to test his commitment.

"Hand the sealed letter to Ambassador Sharp. No one but Sharp! I can't stress its importance more than to say it's vital you deliver it to him personally. Understood?" The words "Letter of Introduction" were handwritten on the envelope. Page's explicit instructions for its delivery gave it a deeper significance. John either held something to help him enter the escadrille or was acting as a courier for the ambassador.

In an effort to discover which was true, John asked, "It's confidential, sir?"

The ambassador looked squarely at John and said very deliberately, "Let's just call it a letter of introduction, John. Hand it to the ambassador. The French won't open it when they see the seal. They have no reason to. There's nothing unusual about it. Now, do you need money?"

"No, sir. I have enough." John was certain of two things. First, the letter looked like a letter of introduction, and second, it was nothing of the kind. He didn't press the issue. The ambassador would not have confirmed or denied either case.

"John, if I were your age, I'd be using those tickets. I'll call Sharp later to confirm its delivery. Good luck, and give my regards to your father. John, no father in his right mind wants to see his son go to war. Still, I have to believe he's very proud."

John shook the ambassador's hand. "Thank you, sir. I appreciate everything you've done for me."

Page smiled and said, "Stay safe, and good hunting."

John walked from the office in a sort of daze. He found it difficult to imagine that he'd be sailing to France tonight. Passing the reception desk, he'd forgotten about Miss Andrews. She smiled as he went by. On impulse, he went over, leaned across her desk, and kissed her lightly on her forehead. "Thank you, Miss Andrews."

Wide-eyed and open mouthed, she was speechless, but she felt much better about her feminine charm.

Leaving the embassy, his mind fairly raced with anticipation. In less than nine hours, he'd be on a cross-channel shuttle. By morning, he'd be in France. Two troubling points couldn't easily be shaken. Would he be allowed into France? Would he ever make the trip in the other direction?

After talking to Richard Sloane, it wasn't unreasonable to assume that he'd be lucky to survive the war. Realistically, the odds of a pilot surviving were slim. It occurred to him that worrying about the odds might easily distract a flier who needed to be alert. John didn't want statistical burdens added to his technical burdens. Learning to fly was the only issue. The more he learned, the better his chances. The rest was out of his control. Whether he survived the war or not, it made no sense to worry about it. In war, death and survival were two sides of the same coin. Either could turn up once the coin was flipped. He'd do what he came to do. That much was settled. The future would decide what followed.

John Arrives in France

JOHN BOARDED THE CROSS-CHANNEL SHUTTLE an hour ahead of its scheduled departure. Before sailing, its captain received several reports of submarine sightings. Things grew worse when rumors arose that spies were signaling U-boats cruising near the coast. Five minutes after sailing, the captain changed their destination. He'd sail southwest, avoiding Le Havre and the Norman coast. The captain didn't want to risk his ship or its passengers for the sake of a few hours. He told the passengers that no one aboard was allowed to leave the boat or communicate with anyone on shore. Their new route was to be kept secret. He would notify the French of his decision en route, using prearranged radio codes. The French, in turn, would notify English authorities.

The crossing was made without incident. On the morning of December 24, 1916, John landed in Saint-Nazaire at the mouth of the Loire River on the west coast of France. He could only hope one of the embassies had learned of the change and had made other arrangements for his arrival. Unfortunately, this had not happened. Ambassador Sharp sent his agent to Le Havre as Ambassador Page had planned.

The agent was disappointed when the shuttle didn't arrive on schedule. He assumed it was forced to return to port, sunk by a mine, or torpedoed. Several days passed before the landing was confirmed by the embassy in Paris through regular dispatches.

In Saint-Nazaire, the customs agent immediately became suspicious of John. Americans and Englishmen normally used the cross-channel ports, not Saint-Nazaire. John was asked for his passport and entry papers and to state his reason for entering France. He told the agent he was going to the American embassy in Paris. While this made sense, it suggested that John might be lying. Why come to Saint-Nazaire? Port facilities in Saint-Nazaire were primarily designed for cargo ships. Foreigners traveling from England used the northern ports to enter France. Le Havre was much closer to Paris. He asked John the nature of his business at the embassy.

"I'm not here for business. Not the way you mean. I have an appointment to see the ambassador," John explained.

That raised more doubt in the customs agent. Ambassadors were busy people. If not here on business, why had he come to France? He was certainly not a tourist! The interview was not going smoothly. The agent grew impatient, partly because John spoke no French and partly because he knew only enough English to pass the examination for customs agents.

John was worried. He hadn't expected trouble on entering a country he wished to defend. The sealed letter hadn't made an impression on the agent. The war—and the unexpected arrival of an English shuttle—raised suspicion. All customs agents were advised to thoroughly interrogate foreigners attempting to enter French ports, especially ports not normally used by travelers.

John felt his next answer might make the difference between entering France, being indefinitely detained, or being forced to leave immediately as an undesirable. The last two weren't choices he was prepared to accept. The truth was his only chance.

Opening his English-to-French dictionary, John paged through the volume in a desperate search to find a phrase that might help. The problem was that phases like "I need a doctor" and "How much does the bread cost?" were no help to him. At best, language dictionaries made conversation awkward. He had no choice but to speak English and broken French.

"I come to join the *Escadrille des Voluntaires Américaine*."

As these were the only French words that might help, he said them slowly. His interrogator actually understood!

"*L'Escadrille des Voluntaires?*" The agent's expression changed from serious to puzzled. He raised an eyebrow. John, in turn, grew concerned. What was wrong now?

"*Quoi?*" John asked. The French word his sister always used for "what" seemed to mollify the agent. This was fortunate, since John had reached his limit in French vocabulary. It would be awkward if he was forced to use it again.

"*Mais monsieur, l'Escadrille des Voluntaires. C'est…* ah, how you say, it is no more. *Que voulez-vous dire?* You mean perhaps *l'Escadrille Lafayette,* no?"

Relief came immediately. It was stupid of John to forget the change in name. The pilots didn't like the name chosen for them when German Ambassador Bernsdorff complained. They'd changed it to the Lafayette Escadrille.

"*Oui,* sir. Eh … what you said. The Lafayette Escadrille."

The agent smiled, "*Mais monsieur,* you should say from the beginning. This makes a big difference."

John felt better but was annoyed by his poor command of the French language.

His mistake nearly cost him entry into France. Inwardly, he swore at Germany's ambassador over the existence of an American escadrille. After all, they'd volunteered! America had nothing to do with it. Things progressed when the agent called for the baggage inspector to look at John's belongings. The inspector spoke English well. He reexamined John's passport picture almost microscopically. He began to scrutinize John's face after opening a large picture catalog that looked as if it had been used for months.

John noticed handwritten names next to photographs pasted into the crudely assembled volume. Most of the men in the photos were older than John. From time to time, the agent glanced at a photo and then at John. Several times he made a low humming sound and looked at John again. Luckily, John didn't resemble the younger men in the catalog of spies.

The inspector explained, *"Procédure, monsieur."* He opened John's bag and repeated nearly every question the first agent had asked. John responded to each.

"To go to Paris, you must take a bus."

Again, relief came to John.

"This is best. The train comes tomorrow. The soldiers, they have priority. *C'est la guerre.* Passenger trains are not coming so much as before the war, *n'cest pas?*"

John had no intention of debating the form of his transportation to Paris with a more cooperative customs agent. If the inspector said he should go to Paris by bus, he'd go by bus. The agent's brother probably owned a bus. John wasn't about to risk offending a man who could prevent him from entering the country.

"Oui! The bus. *Merci."* His thank you was genuine, if not its pronunciation.

The baggage inspector finished destroying his carefully folded clothing, having checked everything, including all of his shirt pockets. It took John several minutes to repack well enough to close the lid. The problem of entering the country seemed solved. The inspector told him to return to the customs agent. Now what?

"*Bon, monsieur!*"

The customs agent stamped his passport and wished him well in the escadrille. Before letting him go, he told John to notify Parisian police of his arrival when he reached the city. They must be made aware he was in Paris and traveling alone. France was at war. A record of his presence must be made.

John nodded, not wanting to say anything that might renew the process. He left the terminal resolved to learn more French. He was glad he'd snacked on the boat before arriving. Ordering a meal in town would certainly require his dictionary.

Until he found a bank willing to exchange dollars for francs, the bus station would have to wait. Needing directions, he looked around hoping to see a friendly face. He sifted through the dictionary looking for a phrase. He must have appeared lost, because an elderly bearded gentleman approached, touched his arm and said in perfect English, "Is someone meeting you, *monsieur?*" John was astounded. This was the third person to speak to him in France, and this one spoke flawless English! The man wore pince-nez glasses that reminded John of TR's portrait in Guilford. He held a silver-topped walking cane that made him seem out of place.

"No, sir. I'm looking for a bank. I need to change money into francs. Can you tell me where I might find one, Mr. ...?"

"I have guessed correctly! My name is André du Montrey. I instruct English in the local school. It is not often I have an opportunity to speak with a native. But I must inform you the banks are closed. *La Fête de Noël.* Your expression is Christmas, I believe. Will you stay in Saint-Nazaire tonight, *monsieur?*"

"I hadn't planned on it. I need to get to Paris. I'm due at the American embassy. I should wire them about my arrival. Is there a telegraph office nearby, Mr. du Montrey?"

"Ah … an American. I thought you might be British. But again, I must remind you of the holiday. The telegraph station is also closed, Mr. …?"

"Forgive me. My name is John Morris from Baltimore, Maryland." John offered his hand.

"Maryland! This is one of the first states, yes?"

"Yes. Baltimore's not far from Washington."

"I have heard of Washington. But there are two, yes?"

John hadn't considered how the omission of DC might be confusing.

"Yes. The state called Washington is on the West Coast. Maryland is on the East Coast. It gave land for the national capital, the city we call the District of Columbia."

"Ah. I have much to learn. Forgive me. I know little American history. I studied the language of our ally, King George. Perhaps you can help me learn about America. Instructors may occasionally need instruction." André laughed good-naturedly.

John was amused, but it was getting late. He hadn't any francs, couldn't take a bus or send a telegram, and needed a place to stay.

"I'd be happy to oblige, Mr. du Montrey. But I must find a place to stay."

"Please. You must stay with me tonight. My pension is small, but there is room for an American." The old man smiled. John didn't refuse the offer. He'd stay overnight and get a fresh start in the morning.

"That's very kind of you. I'd be happy to accept, if you're sure it's no trouble."

"*Bon!* My daughter will make us a meal. You can go to Paris in the morning."

André led the way, walking quite briskly in the cold, moist air. Carrying his baggage, John had trouble keeping pace. Through town, John asked the same question several times. He'd point to signs over the shops and ask, "What does it mean?" He knew only one without asking, a restaurant. André explained each—a butcher shop, shoe store, a tailor's shop. John's vocabulary steadily grew.

He guessed several of them by looking in the windows. Many weren't too different from those in Baltimore. Here, the proprietors specialized in one product or service. He attributed this to local culture. The stores in Baltimore were more diversified to attract a wider range of patrons.

Paris might be more like Baltimore. Tomorrow, he'd be looking at the Seine.

Noticing that John was having trouble keeping up, the old man stopped beyond the center of town. The old man said his pension wasn't far. They sat on a bench overlooking the Loire. They were walking next to one of the most storied rivers in France. Watching the Loire flow to the Atlantic, André began to talk about the châteaus along the river. The largest, he said, was Chambord, a sixteenth-century castle built by François the First as a hunting lodge in the Forest of Boulogne.

"It has 440 rooms built on a small tributary of the Loire called Cosson."

"He called 440-room castle a lodge? I thought our hotels in Baltimore were big!"

John had never seen a château before. He recalled engravings in the pages of history books. The illustrations were small. He resolved to visit a château while he was in France. "My favorite is Chenonceau, a white Renaissance château on the Cher. Its gallery lies across the river. When the water is still, the gallery is reflected like a mirror."

John tried to imagine it. The old man's eyes seemed to see the palace. *"C'est un château pour des dieux."*

"I beg your pardon, Mr. du Montrey?"

"Ah. Forgive me, John. You don't know French. I merely said

it was a mansion built for the gods. Perhaps we should not speak of mansions. The Loire is beautiful by itself. They build *châteaux* to be near it. I have lived here many years. I love the peace it brings. Shall we go on? You must be tired and hungry."

As a bachelor, John's father traveled to France and toured the country for weeks after graduating medical school. Once he married and had children, if no patients were to be seen that evening, he'd gather them together and invent stories to put them to sleep. Many were centered around his trip.

"Dad loved to tell us stories. He once traveled on the Seine by barge. He fished on the Doubs near the town of Besançon. He visited the fortress on the hill. He said the river nearly circled the fort. My favorite story was of Besançon under siege. He invented a hero, a young boy he called John."

"A story maker, your father. Perhaps those stories brought you here."

"Perhaps they did." The idea hadn't occurred to him until André mentioned it.

France had many rivers, and John was aware of their acclaim. Histories of France were barren without their mention. The Loire was known for its castles. The Seine was famous for flowing through Paris. The Rhône and Soâne Valleys were loved for their wines. Today, the Loire, Rhône, and Soâne were no longer the best known. Other rivers in France were much better known. The Lys, the Somme, the Oise, the Aisne, the Meuse, and the Marne were also French rivers. They'd gained eternal fame as the names of bloody battles—fame they hadn't sought but they had certainly earned.

André led John down the Avenue de Lesseps, taking pleasure in saying it was named for Ferdinand de Lesseps, builder of the Suez Canal. But remembering his American guest, he added that he had not completed the canal across Panama.

"Your former president who speaks softly and carries a club finished it."

John smiled. He didn't correct the expression tied to TR's foreign policy. What he said was meant to express the difference between digging canal and digging a trench. "At least the Suez wasn't dug to defend your country."

The old man smiled at the comment. Lowering his eyes, he said, "*C'est vrai.* Very true indeed!"

John asked the old man, "How much farther, sir?"

"We are near the bakery, John."

Assuming the bakery was a landmark, John gave it no significance. As they neared the bakery, the unmistakable odor of freshly baked bread grew strong. John's mouth watered. He offered to buy a loaf, forgetting he had no francs.

The issue was solved when Mr. du Montrey thanked him and said, "Don't worry, John. I know the owner."

André entered first. John followed, putting his bags down as soon as he was inside. Noise from a kitchen in the rear indicated the baker was busy at the ovens. John was surprised when the old man called to the baker.

"*Michelle? Vient-tu. Un visiteur.* Come meet him."

The reply came in English! Her voice was impatient, young, and very feminine.

"I'm almost finished, Papa. The bread is cooling. I must clean up. I have no time for strangers."

André knew his daughter well enough to know that she didn't like to meet the young men he sometimes brought home. He also knew what she liked. He called again, knowing the words would bring her from the kitchen.

"He is an American. Should I send him away?" He winked at John. Michelle wanted to visit America and had never met an American. She'd either leave her ovens or he didn't know his daughter.

"American? Yes. One moment, Papa. I must wash my hands." Her tone became more excited.

André knew his daughter very well.

"She will come, John. My daughter runs the bakery. She bakes in the evening for the morning and cannot easily come from the ovens."

"I understand, Mr. du Montrey. Running a business is demanding. Did you say your daughter's name is Michelle?"

"Yes. My only child. I tell her to speak English. I taught her in our rooms above the bakery. She is not my best student. She prefers to watch the boats come to port. Anything but English lessons! She rides her bicycle to town to watch or goes shopping when the store is closed."

Michelle appeared in the doorway, untying an apron dusted with flour. She placed it on a peg behind the door. She smoothed her hair by running her hands along her temples to the nape of her neck. She looked at John and smiled. Something inside him turned to jelly. Michelle was the loveliest girl he'd ever seen. He guessed her age at twenty-four. She was like the girls he and his friends had fantasized dating someday without believing they actually existed. Caught flat-footed, composing a greeting in French to impress her was totally beyond him.

Michelle spoke first. *"Bonjour, monsieur, je—"*

André interrupted. "English please, Michelle. Mr. Morris does not speak our language."

Again, she smoothed her hair.

"Yes, Papa." Her eyes returned to John. "Good evening, Mr. Morris. My father brings you from the town?" Her voice had a lilt.

"Actually, from the port. I just arrived. Your father graciously invited me to stay tonight. I hope it isn't any trouble for you."

"Papa, what does it mean, 'graciously'?"

"Gracieusement, mon petite avec la tête du pépin!"

"Papa!" she cried in mock protest. She certainly did not have pebbles for a brain! She hadn't recognized the word!

"Excuse me, Mr. Morris. Father is very, ah … critique for my English. He says I must know the words because I am his daughter. You are welcome to stay. But I was not expecting a guest. I must go to town to buy our dinner."

"Please call me John. May I call you Michelle?"

Her English was good enough, and it had a charming accent. John was more attracted by her eyes. They were shy, blushing eyes, yet full of life. They were the color of the midday sky.

"Please do. Papa, I must go. The butcher works late, but he may close sooner tonight."

"Michelle, please don't go to any trouble. Your father was very kind to offer his home. I shouldn't be imposing on you."

André interposed, "Please, John. You accepted my invitation. You are our guest. This is no trouble. Michelle often goes to town." With no francs in hand, John couldn't offer to buy food for their meal.

"*Oui!*" Michelle confirmed. "You must stay. It is no trouble. If you wish, you may come with me."

John would have accepted the invitation immediately, but he looked at André to gauge his reaction to her suggestion. After all, he was a stranger. André misunderstood John's glance.

"Michelle, Mr. Morris has made a long journey. He must go to Paris tomorrow. He should rest before dinner."

"I'm okay, Mr. du Montrey. I don't mind. If it's all right with you, I'll go."

Had he recalled his youth, André might have anticipated John's response. "Ah. Of course. Use my bicycle, John. It is next to hers." André turned to speak to his daughter. "*Attendez-vous a l'heure, Michelle.* And wear your coat. It's cold outside."

"*Oui*, Papa. Come, John. We must go before he is closed."

"Thank you, sir." John waited to ask Michelle what André said to her. Perhaps his ignorance of French would work in his favor for a change. It gave him an excuse to speak to her.

He was surprised to feel a return of shyness he hadn't felt since his teens. As a boy, he didn't give girls much thought. He got along with girls, but they were girls, not things that captured a boy's attention. He'd had a crush on one pretty girl, but that was as far as shyness would let him go. When a girl flirted, he'd find an excuse to do things boys did. His father had advised him more than once that girls came second to studies.

Now twenty-six and about to go to war, the shyness he'd felt as a young boy returned. He'd only just met Michelle. Why the sudden shyness? She was pretty, but other girls he'd known were pretty. A magnetism attracted him to her. In fact, magnetism described what he felt exactly.

John mounted André's bicycle. "Are you ready, Michelle?"

"Yes. May I call you 'Jean'? This is how we say it in French."

"Sure. When in France, do as the French do." *What a dumb thing to say*, he thought. *Is that the best you can do?*

"*Bon!* You are a good sport, Jean. But, I am too."

Michelle smiled. John didn't understand. Then she sped off. It was a clear challenge for him to catch her. He accepted the challenge. Her boldness surprised him. The girls he'd known never dreamed of being so bold the first time he'd met them. John admired boldness. It was refreshing—especially in a girl. His mother would disapprove.

With her head start, Michelle reached the river first. She waited until he came, not sure whether he was slower or if had simply allowed her to go first.

"You must not ride a bicycle in America, no?"

With that, she renewed the contest. This time, he kept up with her, but it wasn't as easy as he'd thought it would be. As André had said, Michelle had done this often.

Saint-Nazaire to Le Mans—1916

DREAMS PLAY A LARGE PART in life. John hoped to meet a girl like Michelle. She had spirit, and the effort she put forth to race proved it. Michelle also had a dream. She dreamed of meeting a handsome, young American who'd take her away from Saint-Nazaire. The race gave their dreams new life.

She was surprised when she saw John. He was young and handsome, too young to be rich. She'd earned her living for years. It didn't matter. The fact that John was leaving Saint-Nazaire in hours did matter. Dreams ended in the morning when you awoke.

As they reached town, he finally asked her what her father had wanted her to attend.

"Attend? I don't understand, Jean."

"Your father said, 'Atten-day-voo.' What does he want you to attend?"

"Ah, *attendez-vous*. We must be quick. He says I waste too much time in town."

John was reminded of his ignorance in French.

The evening air was damp and cold. They maintained a brisk pace to stay warm, retracing the route John and André had taken. Michelle stopped at the butcher shop that John had asked André to identify earlier. It was the only shop still open.

The owner was a brusque middle-aged man, whom Michelle called Maurice. They spoke entirely in French. John listened, trying to discern what was said. When she asked, he told her he had no lamb. Before she could ask, he told her he had no bacon and no beef, the goose was reserved for the mayor, and he was keeping the pork chops for himself.

"Mon Dieu!" he complained. He was reduced to selling sausage and poultry! If things got worse, he'd have to start selling fish! That would make him very unpopular with Monsieur Moulet, the fish merchant. *"La guerre … toujours la guerre!"*

For a moment, Michelle thought his complaining was finished. It wasn't. This was a terrible fate for a butcher to be reduced to selling scraps of meat, and worse, fish!

This emotional state wasn't uncommon for Maurice. Michelle was often exposed to his anguish, even before the war. For Maurice, it was normal. Normally, Michelle ignored him. Tonight, she attempted to soothe Maurice by saying rationing hadn't made it easy to be a baker. She understood his problem. She said that once the Germans were driven from France, things would be normal. She asked Maurice about the chicken hanging from a hook in the store window.

Maurice wasn't quite ready to become the proprietor of his butcher shop. His reply to her remark was loaded with sarcasm. *"Naturellement!"* he snapped, *"C'est cela, et ils ont vécu heureux le reste de leurs jours."* The phrase common to the ending of fairy tales was spoken with sarcasm, a strongly paternal tone, and was accompanied with wild gestures. Maurice was in no mood for sympathy, even if it came from the pretty daughter of Monsieur du Montrey.

Michelle raised a hand in the gesture a traffic cop would use to stop traffic. *"Assez, monsieur! Il est tard!"* Her words followed in rapid succession. Roughly translated, she told him, "If you are intent on feeling sorry for yourself, that's your affair. Sarcasm is misplaced with me, *monsieur*! You know very well I run a bakery! I need not remind you that the government allows so much flour each month. What I bake is sold before it goes into the oven! I earn less because coal is expensive! You have no reason to speak to me as if I were a child. I have come here for years, but you are not the only butcher in Saint-Nazaire!"

She'd shown him no mercy. Her rebuke took instant effect. His apology was epochal. To prove it was sincere, he told her he'd sell her the chicken for what it cost him. He didn't mention that he was adding two francs for his injured pride, his forced apology, and the humility she'd forced from him.

Michelle felt better, and Maurice made a small profit from an angry customer. The next closest butcher was two miles away, and his prices were higher. On balance, nothing unusual had taken place. He'd complained, and she'd gotten a bargain. French commerce survived.

"C'est la vie," he said as they were leaving.

"Non, monsieur. C'est la guerre!" she corrected. Unwilling to rebuff, Maurice let out a long sigh. Outside, Michelle looked toward the sky and said, "The idiot!"

Fascinated, John had watched the whole affair. He'd never witnessed the likes of it in Baltimore. Yet he knew Michelle had won the quarrel. He asked her to explain.

"It was nothing, Jean. He thinks he is the only one suffering from the war. I had to remind the old bull he is a butcher, not one of the hogs he sells."

John laughed. Her mention of the animal Maurice sold in slices struck him as more than coincidental. He gained a renewed respect for Michelle he'd never felt for another woman.

The following morning, Christmas morning, he thanked André for his kindness. John asked his advice on getting a train to Paris.

André assured him that until he got to Le Mans, he should take the bus. Trains were often late, and the soldiers and military equipment had priority over civilians.

"I taught many who work the trains," André said. "They go to Calais, Boulogne, and Le Havre. They bring the guns and ammunition from the port. Coaches are rarely added for passengers. The war comes first. Take the bus to Le Mans. From there, you may get a train."

André personally exchanged francs for John's dollars to pay his fares to Paris. John thanked him and shook his hand.

Michelle waited for John by the entrance to the shop. That night, he'd asked her to teach him how to say hello and good-bye. She'd said the time of day was important. He could always say *bonjour*, but to be correct, he should say *bon matin* in the morning and *bonsoir* in the evening. *Adieu* meant "good-bye," and *au revoir* meant "until we meet again." John promised he'd write to her and try to return. She wiped the corner of an eye with her apron. John took her hands and gently rubbed his thumbs over their backs. She didn't speak, but her sorrow was plain.

"*Au revoir*, Michelle." He'd never forget the sight of her running back to the kitchen. That one Christmas morning would remain the most cheerless in his memory.

Paris was over two hundred miles from Saint-Nazaire. In town, John went to the bus station. The buses had a limited schedule, running only when enough fuel was available. On Christmas Day, they ran to accommodate travelers. Taking André's advice, he bought a ticket to Le Mans.

John hadn't slept well that night. The thought of Paris had his mind racing. In Le Mans, he had to be awakened. The driver spoke French, but John recognized the words "Le Mans, *monsieur*" and realized he'd slept most of the way. He thanked the driver and walked to the train station. The station was more chaotic than King's Cross. Its atmosphere was oppressive, filled with French soldiers showing utter fatigue.

Many wore heavy pale-blue overcoats with their lower corners buttoned at the hips. Dirt tried to hide bright red trousers. Strips of gray cloth, called puttees, wound around their lower legs. Those without head wounds wore the helmet called an Adrian. Some carried field packs slung over their backs, with rubberized blankets strapped securely on top. Nearly all carried rifles.

Unwounded soldiers helped those who needed support. Bandages abounded, circling heads and covering necks, arms, or chests. Gas victims were led, their eyes covered by an oily gauze. Dozens were carried on stretchers to waiting ambulances, a long row of red-crossed vehicles that bent around the station and out of sight.

John was struck by the expressions on their faces and the way nearly every one of them moved. They were more than weary to the bone. They were worn to the soul. Habit kept them upright. The swagger and bravado he'd expected to see in famous French army was nowhere to be seen. When they spoke, their voices were low, subdued. Many were pained. Occasional moans were interrupted by orders barked by a sergeant directing them to the ambulances.

In America, the French army was known as the greatest in Europe. These men didn't exude greatness. They moved like men who'd been peeled back a layer at a time, torn by a war that clouded their legendary fame. They weren't defeated men. They were men who'd seen too much war. The sight of them opened his eyes to how war changed young and once vibrant men. A few were leaving Le Mans. Most were arriving. It was likely they were returning from the battle to recapture the fortresses near Verdun. John knew about the French attack that began a month before Thanksgiving. Looking at these men, he wondered if they'd won or lost. Sailing to England, he'd been removed from news of ground war.

King's Cross station wasn't like this at all. He'd seen fewer wounded there. The awful statistics in the Manchester newspaper had impressed him. But here, in Le Mans, he saw hundreds of those statistics moving before his eyes. Many were going home for Christmas. Many were going to hospitals, never to see or walk in the snow again. They'd given their eyes, legs, an arm, a foot, and also their lives to defend France.

Many would recover. When restored to a semblance of men, they'd return to fight on some mutilated field in northern France, perhaps the same fields from which they'd come. Their leaders had told them glory was found on the battlefields. John saw no sign of glory here. Here, there were only soldiers who'd been granted time to heal.

In a discussion with a college friend, John recalled they agreed that war, whether political or religious, amounted to the same thing—taking land to subjugate people. Germany claimed to fight for political reasons. But war meant taking French soil and capturing land. France hadn't forgotten the humiliation of Alsace and Lorraine. Bismarck had retaken Alsace and Lorraine in 1871, the same territory that had changed hands between them six times in six centuries. John bet his friend a steak dinner that France would win it back for a seventh time.

Returning to the present, a curious thought crossed John's mind. If France won, would the contest end, or would Germany try to regain what was lost in a future war? History validated the idea. If the Great War wasn't the last war of its kind, they'd have to give the next a number. Inconceivable! Only madmen would dream of doing this again! Outside, snow swirled in wild eddies. John grew cold not from the snow but from the thought that any man would dare start another such war.

John Goes to Paris

LE MANS WAS THE HUB for trains from ports as far as Bordeaux, Brest, and Cherbourg. John discovered that leaving Le Mans by train was all but impossible. Trains going north were military transports. He should have stayed at the bus station. He was only halfway to Paris, and the telegraph office was crowded with soldiers waiting in long lines. He decided not to send a telegram to the embassy on the assumption they'd already received news about the shuttle. He used his remaining francs to buy a bus ticket to Paris.

This time, he stayed awake. In Chartres, two nuns boarded and began singing Christmas carols in their native language. The passengers sang along. Tunes he knew, John joined in English. The singing helped him to forget Le Mans and made the trip shorter. Listening to the lyrics, he picked up a few words. By the time he reached Paris, his French vocabulary had doubled. In Paris, a tall structure came into view. The Eiffel Tower was undeniably Gustave Eiffel's best-known work.

Eiffel had built the framework for the Statue of Liberty at the entrance to New York Harbor. At nearly a thousand feet, the Eiffel Tower surpassed the pyramids as the world's tallest structure and was the most visible feature in the Parisian skyline. At first, Parisians said it was ugly and would collapse from its own weight. Its existence was still debated. A million rivets and strategic importance as an observation tower for the war had saved it from the scrap heap.

To John, the tower stood as a symbol of the imagination of French thinkers and writers. He listed them mentally—Descartes, Pascal, Voltaire, Dumas, Rousseau, Hugo, Sand, Zola, de Maupassant, Gide, Apollinaire, and lately Proust. It surprised him that only the names of philosophers and writers had come to mind and not the warrior Napoleon. It occurred to him to ask a nun about the American embassy.

The bus stopped near a circle that served as the hub of twelve avenues. At its center stood the Arc de Triomphe, a massive arch he'd thought much smaller. The nun indicated that he could walk to the embassy from here. Using gestures, she pointed in its direction.

"*L'ambassade, monsieur. Là-bas, là-bas!*" Her repetition was of no help, but her gesture was.

Off the bus, John saw two or three avenues that led in the direction she'd pointed.

"*Là-bas, là-bas!*" she said through the window, pointing directly over his head.

Military trucks rumbled slowly down snow-filled streets in every direction. A horse-drawn artillery train crowded the length of one avenue for as far as he could see through the snow. Parisians trudged in every direction, seemingly oblivious to the traffic. John walked down the snowy avenue. His feet quickly grew cold. Down Avenue Kléber, leafless trees separated street lamps spanning its length.

Buildings on either side would have been proud additions to parts of Baltimore. They awarded the city with dignity. Their gables and chimneys inspired an almost royal panorama. Ordinarily, he'd have peered into the shop windows, but the evening was ripe, and nothing he saw remotely resembled an embassy. He quickened his pace to stay warm, passing people on the sidewalk. To his dismay, Kléber led to another smaller circle acting as a hub for more avenues. Not knowing which to take, he asked a nearby policeman for directions.

"*L'ambassade des États-Unis? Oui, monsieur.*" The policeman physically turned John to face the Avenue d'Eylau.

"*Voilà à droit, monsieur. Allez tout droit. L'ambassade. Là bas.*" The policeman pointed a finger. John didn't understand his phrases, but since he'd pointed the way, it made no difference.

The building across the street was visible through the snowflakes. John saw the American flag flying high at front of the building. He spoke to the marine wearing a .45-caliber semiautomatic on his hip standing guard at the entrance.

"My name is John Morris. The embassy in London sent me. I was supposed to see the ambassador early yesterday. He sent an agent to Le Havre to meet me, but our ferry changed course."

The guard didn't bother to absorb the information. " Sir, you only have to show me your passport."

"Certainly." John fumbled for his passport.

The guard looked it over and handed it back. "Sir, the receptionist is in the main lobby on your right." The marine resumed his post, oblivious to the snowfall.

Two guards were posted inside on either side of the lobby. Each wore the same sidearm.

The receptionist, a young woman, asked for his passport. She verified his identity and immediately picked up a telephone and dialed two numbers.

"He's here, sir. Mr. Morris just walked in …yes, sir, right away."

She signaled the nearest guard. "Corporal, escort Mr. Morris to the ambassador. Ambassador Sharp will see you now, Mr. Morris. He expected you yesterday." Her point was well made.

"This way, sir."

Saving explanation for the ambassador, John followed the guard. The guard knocked, and an impatient voice from inside cried, "Come in! Come in!"

The guard opened the door announcing, "Mr. Morris, sir."

John walked to the center of the office. Ambassador Sharp stood in front of his desk. He was not in a good mood. John waited for Sharp to speak.

"Where in the hell have you been? We turned Le Havre inside out! Looked in every damned channel port for hours. I've been on the phone all afternoon. No one's even heard about you! I must have called everyone but the French president, whoever he is this week! Well, don't just stand there. Where were you?" This wasn't the greeting John hoped for. He cleared his throat for time to gather his wits.

"I'm sorry, Mr. Ambassador. He rerouted the shuttle. The captain said submarines were reported in the channel, and no one was to leave the boat or make calls. I couldn't notify Ambassador Page. The telegraph office in Saint-Nazaire was closed for Christmas."

"Saint-Nazaire? I thought they'd sunk you, son. Of all places! Hell, that's on the west coast! The nincompoop! It's four times as far! The idiot exposed his boat to a greater threat than if he'd crossed where he was supposed to! I'll call Page to let him know you're here. He wanted me to confirm your arrival."

John said nothing and remained standing. He'd gotten past his initial welcome and was curious to hear what the ambassador said to Page.

The ambassador picked up his phone. "Miss Brooks, get Ambassador Page for me."

Sharp hung the phone without waiting for a response. An awkward silence followed. John took the opportunity to retrieve the letter of introduction.

"Sir, Ambassador Page asked me to give this to you personally."

"I was going to ask you about that." Sharp took the letter and walked behind his desk. "Sit down, John. You're making me nervous. I should be by the fire at home sipping a drink. I'll get to you as soon as I look this over." As instructed, John sat and remained silent.

Sharp opened the letter. His eyes flew past the text. His telephone rang as soon as he put it on the desk.

"Put him on, Miss Brooks. That you, Walter? ... Yes, he's here. Just walked into the office ... No. Saint-Nazaire ... That's right ... Damned if I know, Walter. Captain said U-boats were in the channel. Look, Walter, does the admiralty or that idiot decide where to land? ... That's what I thought. Hell, Walter, I wouldn't use him anymore. You can't depend on him if he changes his route every time somebody thinks he sees a periscope. I thought Wilson had worked this out with the Prussian jackass ... I agree, Walter. He's not stupid enough to give away a U-boat's position just to punch a hole in a damn channel shuttle ... I've got it ... No. It's in code ... You bet, Walter. I'll ring you tomorrow. Don't worry. I'll take care of him ... Okay, Walter. Regards to your family." Sharp hung the phone. "He thinks pretty highly of you, son."

Their conversation left no doubt in John's mind. The letter was more than it appeared to be. The fuss Sharp made over John being late had more to do with that letter than concern for John. He hoped the ambassador's comment to Page meant he would help.

"Okay. Let's get down to business. I know why you came. Joining the escadrille shouldn't be a problem, though Lord knows why you want to take a risk before your country. I took the liberty of calling their commander, Captain Thénault. He said he'd gotten your letter and mailed you a reply. Did you get it?"

"No, sir. My ship sailed before it came."

"In a hurry to get here, I suppose. He said you'd be welcome on condition that your training goes well. They're a fine bunch of fliers. Have an outstanding record. According to Thénault, they do their jobs and don't complain. You'll fit in if you can fly. I guess I was a little rough on you at first, son. I should have given you a chance to explain."

"I understand, sir. Thank you for calling Captain Thénault."

"Stop by Miss Brooks's desk before you go. She'll give you the address of the house where you're to stay tonight. I'll let the commander know. He may want to contact you, so stay in the house. No sightseeing! Good luck. From what I've heard, you're going to need it!"

The receptionist wrote down the address 80 Rue Boissè. She told him a Boston woman, Mrs. Alice Weeks, sponsored the home to honor her son, who'd been killed in action. American volunteers received the best treatment from Mrs. Weeks. She handed him an envelope containing enough francs to last several days. John thanked her and promised to return it. Miss Brooks said that wouldn't be necessary.

Outside, John gave the address to the taxi driver. Mrs. Weeks was cordial. He was fed and given a bed for the evening. The men told him the best cup of coffee in Paris would be waiting downstairs in the morning.

The next morning, in the lounge, John was happy to see a legionnaire, a man from Knoxville, Tennessee. The sergeant said his unit was among the first to be sent to Verdun to help contain the German advance. He said he was on leave and didn't rise to take John's hand.

John hardly had time to finish his coffee before he was contacted by telephone. An officer named Alfred de Laage was calling from Groupe de Combat Treize. De Laage told him to go to the French Ministry of War to meet Captain Réne Jacquot and enlist in the Légion Étrangère. The captain would give him a pass to Pau. From there, he was to go to the Gare des Invalides. All that remained was his training. He asked whether John had any questions. John said no, grateful that their conversation was held in English.

John returned for his coffee and to thank Mrs. Weeks. Under rationing, he assumed it might be the last good cup of coffee he'd get until he returned. In the lounge, the same legionnaire was still sitting. Again, John extended his hand. With some effort, the man rose without stepping forward. John noticed the sergeant was missing a foot. John leaned over the coffee table to take the sergeant's hand.

"Leaving so soon, sir? A shame. Paris is beautiful in winter."

"I'd like to stay, but I'm traveling to Pau. Take care, Sergeant."

"It's a bit late for that, sir. My football days are over. Guess I'll become a lawyer like my dad." The soldier slowly sat back on the couch.

"Well, good luck. By the way, courtroom law is something like football. It takes a lot of strategy. One side wins, and one side loses."

The comment brought a smile to the sergeant's face. "I hadn't thought of it that way."

John left to find Mrs. Weeks. "If I ever get back to Paris, I'll return."

She assured him he'd be welcome.

He'd forgotten to ask the sergeant his name and hadn't given his own. It bothered him to remember the oversight of the courtesy. At first, when the man hadn't stood, John thought he didn't want to exchange names. With de Laage's orders on his mind, he'd simply forgotten. From now on, he'd give his name first and not make assumptions about men who didn't rise to offer a hand.

In joining the legion, he was disappointed to learn that Pau was near the edge of the Pyrenees in southern France. Pau was as far as he could get from the war and remain in France.

The letter he'd carried contained plans based on the response to Wilson's latest peace proposal. Ten days later, news arrived at Pau that Ambassador Sharp had learned that the French rejected a German counterproposal to hold peace talks in the Reichstag. The matter was dropped after the French insisted on reparations as a precondition to peace talks. The war would continue.

America's army had less than half the men the French had lost in their counterattack at Verdun. In June, Congress increased the strength of the National Guard to 450,000 or as many as the British lost in the battle on the Somme. America's navy ranked third in the world, and most of its warships were obsolete. Airworthy fighters could be counted on one hand. America was unprepared for war. Its unarmed merchant vessels comprised America's war effort. The merchant marine sailed on Atlantic waters, the domain of German U-boats. On the last day of January 1917, the kaiser ordered unrestricted submarine warfare to resume the following day.

He ignored Wilson's threats. America's military was impotent. Wilson traded with his enemies. Italy posed a greater threat to Germany than America. Isolationism would keep the United States out of the war long enough for his U-boats to win victory.

The German army began to secretly withdraw to hardened positions prepared above the current line. The withdrawal eliminated a German salient and created German divisions to hold the high ground. They'd wait for the Allies to wither on the vines of broken supply routes, which the U-boats would surely cut.

The British lion would starve, forced to eat its pride. The lion tamed and America a wingless eagle, France could not win alone. France would sue for peace. Germany would win the war. The more merchant ships were sunk, the quicker Germany would win, and nothing America did could happen soon enough to change the outcome.

JJ Goes to War—1917

ON APRIL 6, 1917, THE United States finally declared war. James Jefferson, nicknamed JJ, decided to quit Howard University during the summer break. Mr. John had already gone off to France. Mr. Michael had told JJ's father, Monroe, that he was going to become a medical officer in the navy when he graduated Hopkins. Dr. Sam was a good man. He was a second father to James, always asking Monroe how James was doing. Monroe, the family's chauffer, was also a good man. A clean-shaven man in his fifties, he didn't like the fact that JJ had asked him to keep a secret. No one but Monroe and James knew about the scholarship Dr. Sam had set up for James. He'd made the scholarship a trust. It would still be there when James returned. James thought it wasn't right for him to stay at Howard while Dr. Sam's boys went off to war.

"I've worked it out in my mind, Papa. You know why I have to go," JJ told Monroe.

"I know. I understand. I feel proud. I wish you'd finish school. School's important too."

"It's the right thing to do, Papa."

"I know. If your mama was alive, she'd be sad. But she'd be proud."

His decision made, James wanted to go to Newburgh. Monroe often talked about it. He'd brag about the scenery on the Hudson River. JJ wanted to see for himself before he joined. He left for Newburg early that summer.

When James arrived, a local paper said the Fifteenth Infantry Regiment of the New York National Guard was in Peekskill. With the exception of its commander and some officers, it was an all-black unit. The regiment was already formed. Originally, he'd planned to join the unit being formed in Camp Meade, Maryland. Since the Fifteenth was already formed, he decided to join before going home. Colonel William Hayward, its commander, was more than willing to have him.

"I can give you six days. Take the train home to get what you need. If you still want to join us, I'll swear you in when you come back."

"I don't need to go home, sir. Everything I need is in Newburgh. I just need to let my father know I'm joining the regiment."

"Okay. I take you into Peekskill this afternoon and pay for the telegram, James. The Fifteenth will be glad to have you." Other than Dr. Sam, that was the only time a white man offered his help.

The colonel asked JJ once more, "Are you sure you want to join the regiment?"

"I'm eighteen, sir. I'm as sure as any man can be."

The first statement wasn't true. James was only seventeen, but he looked older. The colonel believed him. His birthday was a few months away. By the time they found out, it'd be too late. The telegram sent, Colonel Hayward swore him in that evening with an orderly acting as witness. James ate supper with the regiment. He had trouble getting to sleep, thinking about his new life. He'd acted impulsively. But, he was Private James Jefferson—the newest member of the Fifteenth Regiment. He was in a tent and lying on a bunk, excited, proud, and a little scared. It all seemed a bit unreal. Thinking about it, he believed he'd done the right thing for the right reasons. The next day, the Fifteenth took a train to New York to join other units marching up Riverside Drive. James wrote a letter to tell Monroe why he joined the regiment. The letter became a good luck charm to Monroe. He'd carry it for over a year. Monroe liked to read the part about the parade.

> New York gave us a fine welcome. We were judged
> best in the parade! The whole regiment was proud.
> I worried about my blanket roll, but it stayed on. It
> was a great day, Papa.

The Fifteenth Heavy Foot, the name they gave themselves, was mustered into the US Army in July by President Wilson. The regiment received orders to go to Camp Whitman in Dutchess County. The new camp was better than the one in Peekskill, but they had to declare war on the cooties that invaded their tents. Training continued until new orders arrived.

The next order broke the regiment up for many weeks. Units were sent in every direction to guard whatever headquarters deemed was in need of guarding. James went to Ellis Island with a small group of men. The group guarded German prisoners detained for the duration. In October, the regiment was called together with orders to go to Spartanburg, South Carolina. The move was made public.

Spartanburg's Mayor Floyd wrote to military authorities warning them against posting black men in his town. He said

Spartanburg would not welcome a black regiment. Their arrival would not change the way the town treated blacks, and no special Jim Crow shops would be set up for the regiment. Local Negroes had shops that supplied their needs. Newspapers published his letter.

When the army insisted on coming to town, the mayor called on Major General O'Ryan to warn his high-minded Northern Negroes to behave. If they understood the customs, they'd get along. If not, the customs would be observed just the same. On October 8, the Fifteenth Regiment boarded a train to Spartanburg. James wrote another letter to Monroe.

> Dear Papa,
>
> We are on a train to Spartanburg. Did you read what their mayor said? The men are still talking about the article in the *New York Times*. He doesn't want us, whether army men or not. I don't know those people. I've never been south. Maybe if the war got to Spartanburg, the mayor wouldn't mind as much if we came to save his white skin. You never did talk about the whites and us. I often wonder how you feel. I'm not worried. The Morrises treated us kindly. Colonel Hayward will make it right, so don't worry. He's a lot like Dr. Sam. I guess we will see when we get there.
>
> Did you know Jim Europe is on this train? He's a lieutenant! They assigned his band to the Fifteenth. Do you want me to ask him anything for you?

I got your letter this morning. I'm glad to hear things are better with Miss Catherine. She just needs more time. Did Miss Elizabeth go to Arizona?

I'll write again later.

JJ

That evening, the regiment got off the train in Spartanburg. Pine trees grew on one side of the camp. The other was a cotton field. The camp's engineering was done. Only finishing touches remained. They planted flowers to make it look more like the area where white troops were quartered. After they'd settled in, officers called them together to hear Colonel Hayward. Hayward climbed on top of a bathhouse so they could see him.

"All you men are aware of what took place in Houston, Texas, to the Twenty-Fourth Infantry. You either read or heard about Mayor Floyd's statements in the *New York Times*. The possibility exists for trouble from some people living around Spartanburg. The mayor made us aware that we are Northerners and not welcome."

The men got restless and began to murmur among themselves.

"At ease, men."

The men quieted down.

"If that attitude reflects the feeling of people in Spartanburg, it's due to ignorance. No one should have that attitude. Those that do don't understand who we are and why we've come. Most of you are highly educated. All of you have a sense of responsibility. The treatment you get back home is earned because you are responsible, and your communities know you. Most of you have never been in the South.

"Being here in Spartanburg gives you an opportunity to gain respect. Your country will notice how well you conduct yourselves. You will be tried. As decent men, I expect you to conduct yourselves with honor and restraint. Don't lower yourselves to the level of those who may cause trouble. Do not confront troublemakers. What happened in Houston last August must not happen here. People died making this situation worse.

"I want you to avoid places where you are not welcome. Your behavior reflects on you and the Fifteenth Regiment. Therefore, I'm asking you to take an oath to refrain from violence no matter who provokes you or what provokes you to do violence. Attention! Dismissed."

The entire regiment took the oath, whether officers or not, whether white or black. The oath intended to demonstrate the honor of the Fifteenth and prevent the possibility of another Houston. To show the goodwill of the Fifteenth, Colonel Hayward instructed Lieutenant Europe and the band to hold open concerts at the camp. The concerts helped relieve racial tension. Those who came from town to listen were sorry when the playing ended.

A minor incident occurred when Captain N. B. Marshall was told to leave a trolley he'd paid to ride. Realizing the potential for trouble, the captain got off. By doing so, he set an example for the regiment. They came to train to fight in France, not in Spartanburg. No one in the camp thought less of him. Marshall left the bus to uphold his oath and the honor of the regiment. All were reminded of what they were up against.

The Seventh Regiment, a white regiment, hadn't taken an oath, a fact that became apparent when two of their soldiers saw a black from the Fifteenth being thrown from a sidewalk to the gutter. Not content with the original abuse, the townsmen involved began to beat him even after the soldier told them he'd sworn not to fight. The two whites intervened. They beat the bullies into the street.

The incident made the men in the Fifteenth proud. It also made the Fifteenth equals in the eyes of the Seventh.

James had a sour experience when he stopped at a small grocery store to ask directions. He didn't enter the store and wasn't going to enter. An elderly white lady told him, "You can't go in there. You'd better turn around, or I'll tell the owner!"

The woman's threat caught him off guard. He didn't respond. The last thing he wanted was trouble. He'd never experienced prejudice from people he'd been taught to respect. Similar such incidents occurred. Many of the people in town expressed regret that several citizens had acted in that manner and apologized for the behavior.

The potential for trouble helped Hayward convince his superiors that the unit should be in France. Each incident had to be reported to military authorities. Headquarters expressed admiration for the way the men conducted themselves. General Phillips expressed the sentiment directly to Colonel Hayward.

"The men need to concentrate on training. The Fifteenth deserves to be where prejudice can't distract them. I'm going to recommend that Washington send the regiment to France. They can finish training over there."

Training in Spartanburg ended a few weeks later. For the regiment, the move was good news. They wanted to sail to France from the time they enlisted. For Hayward, the welcome news could end a long road filled with obstacles to form, train, and ship his black regiment to France.

In June, a group of soldiers from the First Division, along with some marines, had already landed at a port called Saint-Nazaire. General Phillips gave Hayward a letter and arranged a meeting with the secretary of war in Washington. The letter expressed the general's belief that the discipline the Fifteenth demonstrated was outstanding. The letter recommended the secretary approve the unit's immediate embarkation to France for training as combat infantrymen. Secretary Newton D. Baker agreed. The orders were issued. On October 24, the regiment entrained for New York and immediate embarkation to France.

On the train, James decided not to write to Monroe about the lady who'd confronted him on the sidewalk. The incident seemed unimportant now that the Fifteenth was leaving town. Thinking back, he felt sorry for the woman. James thought prejudice was the only form of slavery still practiced. Her prejudice couldn't allow her to see him as a man. She'd somehow appended the words "except for blacks" to the words "love thy neighbor." Prejudice was a wall she'd built to defend her from her fear. It made the woman a slave, not very different from the slavery his grandmother once knew. That was why James felt sorry for the woman.

As the train passed through South Carolina, he couldn't help seeing how pretty the state was in fall colors. Autumn was everywhere, scenery that called a man home. Looking at the mass of color, he wondered if color was a cause for prejudice. No. The problem began before he was born and had survived generations. Mayor Floyd's prejudice could be explained, coming from a man who was born in the first state to secede from the Union. Yet prejudice had limits, even in South Carolina. Black soldiers were welcomed in the state capital, Columbia.

Studying constitutional law appealed to James more than ever. Spartanburg had convinced him. He hoped he'd live long enough to see the last of the prejudice the Civil War had failed to erase. First, he and the rest of the regiment must see the end of a larger, deadlier, and more current war.

The Regiment Sails

On Friday, October 26, 1917, the train carrying the Fifteenth Regiment rolled under the Hudson River through the new tunnel. It passed the rail yards in Manhattan and followed the tracks beyond the East River to Long Island. At Montauk Point, the regiment would board the *Pocahontas* as part of a large convoy formed to sail to France. Captain Little, the commander of James's company, told them, "We can't board her yet, men. The ship is in for repairs. We'll wait for the next convoy." Only convoys risked the voyage. Unescorted ships were sunk—and not always by submarines. Germans had boats the British called Q-ships, warships disguised as merchant vessels.

The convoy sailed without them. In the days that followed, James made a friend in Josiah Williams, a friendship that helped pass the time waiting for the next convoy.

On November 12, they boarded the *Pocahontas*. In the wind and cold, James went on deck with Josiah to watch the convoy sail. Many in the regiment joined them on deck.

"All these ships are going to France, Josiah!"

"It's a sight, ain't it, Jim? I nevah seen nothin' like it!"

Hours later, something was obviously wrong. The ship's speed was cut in half. They couldn't keep up with the convoy. Captain Little explained, "Men, one of the engines failed. We have to go back to New York."

After waiting three weeks, they were back in port. The whole company watched the second convoy sail east. Their spirits sailed away with the ships disappearing over the horizon.

The Fifteenth bivouacked at Camp Merritt while the *Pocahontas* underwent repairs. Train fare was reasonable and made travel possible. Some went on leave as far as Pittsburgh. A few went AWOL and were brought back by MPs.

James and Josiah never left camp. They said they were staying to be sure they sailed when the ship was ready. In truth, their legs were their only means of transportation. They had no money to spend in New York, since they regularly sent nearly all of their pay home.

Three more weeks were needed to complete repairs. The ship was scheduled to sail on December 2. For the second time, the Fifteenth boarded the *Pocahontas* in Hoboken. It left port to join the other ships assembling in the convoy. Unbelievably, a fire broke out in a coal bunker below deck. The flame was extinguished, but the bunker still smoldered. Once again, the ship returned to port to unload the coal and clean the bunkers. It was too much! Twice they'd started to sail, and twice they'd had to return. The men became sullen because they could do nothing about it.

"I sometimes wonder if we were meant to get to France, Josiah!" JJ pined.

Their shipping orders remained. What they needed was a boat that wasn't jinxed.

Captain Little told them, "Be patient, men. We've trained too long to let this get us down. The regiment is going to France if we have to row this pile of scrap across!"

The men cheered but were aware of the situation. They had no choice but to wait.

Eleven days later, another convoy was formed, and the ship was once again ready to sail. The next chance to go came on Sunday, December 16, at 8:45 p.m. Once again, they boarded, and *Pocahontas* raised anchor.

The problems with the ship would have been comical if their desire to get to France hadn't been as strong. The present concern was the weather. A blinding snow swirled around the gathering convoy. In the cold darkness and wind, visibility was so poor that the ships crawled from the harbor. Soundings were taken to be sure they stayed in the channel. Calls from the mate indicated the bottom was coming up fast. Thirteen fathoms became ten and then eight.

"Five fathoms!"

At thirty feet, the bottom was getting too close. Along with the other ships, the captain ordered the anchor down. A few men on deck went below, stamping snow from their feet and mumbling about another delay. As bleak as the weather was, they felt bleaker. Others on deck made snowballs from some of the very flakes that forced the ship to drop anchor. Snow wasn't the worst a blizzard could bring. Some of the men became angry at thought they may have to return to port.

"We ain't never going to get to no damn France!" Josiah pathetically told James.

Ships anchored near the channel ran the risk of being rammed. True to form, the bad luck of the *Pocahontas* persisted. The anchor chain of a nearby tanker dragged, becoming entangled with theirs. Momentum and the wind did the rest. The ship collided with the *Pocahontas* in the snowy gloom. Officers of the *Pocahontas* and the commander of the regiment surveyed the damage. The impact had buckled several plates above the waterline. The captain said the damage had to be repaired. He said they'd have to return to port.

The adjutant of the Fifteenth commanded several officers to go to their companies wearing sidearms. The order was meant to prevent trouble should the men fear the ship might sink. He needn't have bothered. They were mad but not afraid. By 7:00 a.m., the anchor chains were untangled. The British tanker was freed. The damage was serious enough to need repair. Colonel Hayward convinced the captain that men with the talent needed to repair his ship were already aboard the *Pocahontas*.

Several men in the Fifteenth were expert welders. Others were engineers and mechanics. They only needed the equipment and enough material and time to make repairs. The flag officer warned them that the convoy wouldn't wait for them past the hour it was scheduled to sail. Repair crews were hastily formed. Welding equipment was found. The task was organized, and the men began in earnest. As the work neared an end, news came that the captain had raised a second condition. He refused to weigh anchor unless everything repaired was also repainted.

The men worked like demons in the cold, wind, and snow. The last man hoisted from the side dropped his paintbrush into the ocean from the numbness in his fingers at the hour scheduled for sailing. The new plates were secure, and the paint was still wet when the *Pocahontas* rejoined the convoy. The Fifteenth was finally on its way! Sighs of relief could be heard on the bridge. No one dared to cheer. Fingers were crossed and prayers made asking God to end the ship's jinx.

"Maybe we won't need to row this damned barge, after all," Little said.

The system of convoys had reduced sinkings, but in nearing England, the men's nerves grew edgy. U-boat captains had orders to sink on sight, without warning, any ship in the war zone, whether destined for or departing from England. The men were relieved when a flotilla of Allied destroyers joined the convoy in the war zone. James and Josiah went on deck with others to watch their protectors sail alongside the convoy.

"They're faster than we are, Josiah."

"You got that right, Jim. They runnin' round us like our anchor was down!"

Wireless messages warned the convoy that at least six German submarines were operating in these waters. To double the chance of landing the convoy, the flag officer split the ships into two sections the day after Christmas. Half sailed to Brest, the others to Saint-Nazaire. James and Josiah were with the half headed for Brest. The ships sailing to Brest weren't delayed. The ships headed directly to Saint-Nazaire were attacked. The soldiers who'd beaten the bullies in Spartanburg were in the section that went to Saint-Nazaire. When the alarm sounded, they went on deck to watch the destroyers in action. Three broke away from the convoy and sailed at high speed to starboard, tracking the wake of a torpedo that missed their troopship by yards.

"They see something out there!" a soldier exclaimed.

"Damn! I wish this worthless boat was that fast," the man beside him responded.

The first hostile sounds they heard were the reports of the forward guns on the destroyers followed by the impact of their shells causing narrow walls of water to be heaved high in the air. The spray refracted rainbows of light in the lowering sun. The guns went silent. One destroyer sailed on, chasing the submarine, dropping depth charges that produced brief hills of boiling seawater. The other two returned to the convoy.

"I wouldn't want be a sub in this ocean! That black boy in Spartanburg got a better reception than that U-boat."

The return of two destroyers signaled that their presence was still needed. The men grew quiet. A submerged submarine was more threatening than one sighted on the surface. Underwater enemies turned the ocean into a minefield that could blow up in their faces without warning. Sinking this close to France would be cruel after waiting so long to sail. Fortunately, the U-boats didn't return. An hour later, the coast of France was in view.

The last day of 1917, the regiment landed in France at the port of Brest, the side door to the battlefields. In a brief ceremony, the band played "Auld Lang Syne." Then they boarded boxcars headed for Saint-Nazaire. Each was marked *Hommes 40, Chevaux 8.* The standard military train transport in France, each car was able to carry forty men or eight horses. Their floors were covered with straw. Though hosed clean, the cars retained a familiar odor.

Boarding drafty a car, Josiah asked, "How they gonna get eight horses in here with us?"

"Josiah, it's forty men *or* eight horses, not men *and* horses," James explained.

"Okay. But my nose says horses was in here before us."

The old straw of the floor of the car told James it hadn't carried horses. The car ahead of theirs had. They discovered that when the train left the station. To relieve themselves, a pail was provided. The 220-mile trip to Saint-Nazaire took seventeen hours. They arrived in Saint-Nazaire at half past three in the morning, tired, cold, and hungry. The train's average speed was roughly the average speed of a schoolgirl on roller skates or a boy using a stick to roll a barrel hoop on a street in Harlem.

The camp was a two-mile march from the station on a cold and windy night. Hot coffee was waiting for them when they arrived. Open-pit fires burned along the long line of men waiting for coffee. Josiah joined James in line. Hot coffee, food, and the thought of sleeping without concern for submarines dominated their minds. Restless with the slow speed of the line, Josiah finally broke the silence.

"Did you see any submarines when you was on deck?"

"No. Did you?"

"No. But it coulda been a bunch out there for all I know."

"Let's be glad we didn't see any, Josiah. I wonder if the other ships did."

"You jokin'? They went straight there! Didn't come close to no channel!"

"I guess you're right, Josiah."

"Anyways, I'll ask them boys when I see 'em."

Weeks later, the Fifteenth was still working under the direction of engineers. Saint-Nazaire was becoming the port of entry for troops and supplies from America. Swampland had to be filled for the many warehouses needed. Miles of track had to be laid to move millions of tons of supplies. The men in the regiment wanted training in combat tactics. They wanted to go to war.

"Jim, I feel more like a gandy dancer den a soldier. I thought we was s'posed to be trainin' for war, not buildin' a damn railroad! Hell, I can walk to war faster than this track is takin' me. Damn war gonna be over before we get there."

"I know, Josiah. I don't think the officers like it much. No use complaining. We got to do whatever they tell us to do." Neither Colonel Hayward nor the Fifteenth Regiment had come to France to build railroads. They'd come to fight. Officers and men needed to train. The only weapons they had were their Springfield rifles. They wanted to fire them, not push wheelbarrows.

General Pershing himself had told them to get the port ready to service the transports carrying men and materials. His army was poorly equipped and needed depots for the Service of Supply. Food, fuel, ambulances, tents, trucks, and medical supplies were needed along with any weapons the States could send. America's neutrality had crippled them. The French were supplying Americans with practically everything.

Congress hadn't foreseen the need to form an army large enough to do more than chase the bandit Pancho Villa back to Mexico. The National Guard was untrained and ill equipped. As a result, General Leonard Wood promoted sporting clubs whose members could buy Springfield rifles. Advertised as hunting clubs, they were formed so the men joining the army wouldn't be reduced to carrying broomsticks to practice. Fewer than two hundred thousand Americans were on active duty when Wilson declared war. Very few were issued rifles, and most had never fired one, because ammunition was scarce.

If General Wood could invent sporting clubs, so could Colonel Hayward. Hayward laid claim to many of the rifles set aside for the clubs. As men joined the Fifteenth Regiment, they became members of Hayward's sporting club and applied for their Springfields. Over time, fifteen hundred requests went to the state quartermaster for hunting rifles to supply Hayward's club members.

James got a letter from Monroe asking him to tell Mr. Europe that he was a bandleader. He told his son to say he wouldn't mind if they met when the war was over and talked about the new jazz being played. Monroe's requests had to wait. JJ saw Lieutenant James Europe only briefly as the band was leaving camp to begin a two-month goodwill tour. The band was to play a charitable concert at the opera house in Nantes to honor Abraham Lincoln's birthday. James could only write that he'd seen Lieutenant Europe. The regiment remained in Saint-Nazaire, filling in marshes, laying rails, and building depots.

On the brighter side, James discovered that French people didn't care about the color of his skin. They only cared that he was in France. Here, he was another American soldier, one of many coming to help them defend their country. The regiment was told that they represented the American Expeditionary Force and should conduct themselves accordingly. It wasn't necessary to make them swear to restrain themselves for the sake of their race. It was a pleasure to go into Saint-Nazaire without having to take an oath to behave or to become punching bags for bigots without fighting back. In France, the race they belonged to was the human race.

Saint-Nazaire was a postcard town. James and Josiah had permission to go to town on weekends. They enjoyed walking along the river and watching the ships entering and leaving the harbor. The town was packed with American soldiers. Walking through town one Sunday, a pair of white soldiers came walking the other way. Josiah grew curious.

"When'd you boys get in?"

"Last night," the sergeant replied.

"You stayin' or goin' into the lines?"

"The captain said we'd be here a couple days. We got orders to train with French instructors behind the line. What about you guys?"

"Humph. We been movin' dirt since we came, trying to make dry land outta swamp. I never pushed so many wheelbarrows in my life."

"Well, from what I've heard, that's what they do at the front. Dig trenches. We didn't come here to dig. We want to fight."

"You bet! We been ready to go for weeks. Don't look like we're goin' to fight anytime soon."

The other soldier, a corporal, was sympathetic but hungry.

"Right now, the only thing I want to dig into is some hot biscuits and soup. March is too cold for here. Is there someplace around here we can buy fresh biscuits?"

"Sure is! Up the road," Josiah said. "A lady runs a bakery up there, name of Miss Shell."

"Thanks. We'll try it out. Good luck, fellas. I hope you aren't here long. Rumors say the Germans got something big coming up this spring." The soldiers turned around and walked up the street toward Michelle du Montrey's bakery shop.

"I keep telling you, Josiah, her name is Michelle, not Miss Shell. It's one name. It's a French girl's name."

"That's what she said. Miss Shell!" Josiah replied. "Bet you a whole loaf of bread!"

"You've got a bet! Bring some money next time."

"Listen, Jim. Ain't no white woman gonna let you call her name without sayin' Miss first!"

The next time never came. In March, the regiment left Saint-Nazaire to train behind the lines near Givry-en-Argonne. Their spirits soared. They exchanged their Springfield rifles for French Lebels and became the Trois Cent Soixante Neuième RIUS, the 369th Infantry Regiment. Hayward and Little retained direct command as their unit became part of the French Sixteenth Division under General Le Gallais. The French supplied them with everything. The instructors were also French, men seasoned by more than three years of war.

The first night in camp, Josiah saw flashes of light in the distance and heard rumbling sounds coming from that direction. He poked James in the ribs and pointed to the commotion.

"You see that, Jim? That's a mighty big storm up there. I'm glad we got these tents! Hell, I ain't dried out from filling in that damn swamp yet."

"I see it, Josiah. I don't think that's lightning, my friend. It looks like artillery to me. Lightning is white. Those are orange flashes. The rumbling is from the shells exploding."

"I'll be damned, Jim. I guess we finally made it to the war."

"We're finally here, Josiah. I hope we get to come back once it's over."

"Where? Back here?"

"No, my friend. I mean back home."

Catherine Anne Morris—1918

"Miss Cath'rine! Mr. Michael wants to know how much longer you gonna be. His bag is tied behind the Stutz, an' he's ready to go!" The deep, impatient voice was their chauffeur's, Monroe, a clean-shaven man in his fifties, returning once more to call to her from the bottom of the stairs. Monroe always pronounced her name in two syllables instead of three.

"I need more time, Monroe. Tell Michael for me, will you?" Catherine wasn't ready, neither at the moment nor for the moment. In truth, she dreaded its coming.

"All right, miss. But he been waitin' longer than he want already. He ain't gonna like it."

Monroe's last remark strongly hinted time was up. When they started made little difference to her, and it was enough reason to continue to delay. This was the last day she'd have direct contact with what remained of the family in Guilford and the last moments she had any control of the time that remained.

Saturday, the first day of June in 1918, shone radiantly. It was the sort of day that Catherine normally loved. Today was different. Michael was leaving for New York, and John had been gone for over two years. Only twenty-two, her Victorian parents were gone. Elizabeth, her mother, was in Arizona, and her father was dead. Events had seen to that. Today marked a journey into loneliness and an indefinite future.

Elizabeth Morris had refused her doctor's advice, wanting to stay home to care for her invalid husband. After the death of Dr. Sam Morris, she no longer had good reason to refuse.

Other families had gone through similar trials. Wilson had declared war, causing many changes to families throughout Baltimore. Yet other families weren't Catherine's. Michael's departure would be the last in a series of events over which she had not the least control.

The precipitous plunge into an uncertain future was about to hit bottom. As far as she was concerned, Michael could wait. She continued to ready herself for the trip to New York, where he'd begin to serve as a doctor—another young man seduced by the endless European war. Except for Monroe, the house would be empty. The constant dread of waiting for bad news to arrive from overseas didn't seem fair. What else could she do?

The oval mirror behind the vanity framed movements she'd used since childhood to brush and pin her tawny-brown hair. The mirror reflected a face that needed redder cheeks and a nose that shone too brightly. It also reflected a sadness in her deep blue eyes. The girl who once returned her gaze was gone. Not even the familiar movement of the brush changed that.

Pinning her hair helped her forget the automobile trip to the navy yard. They could have started hours ago. Michael had been waiting in the motorcar for twenty minutes. He had to report to the hospital in the Brooklyn Navy Yard by the third. The trip would take two days, and he'd set aside an extra day in case something occurred en route.

Last week, she insisted on coming. He'd flatly refused, which prompted, "Michael, it's time I had some part in my brothers' lives!"

Unimpressed, he again refused. He couldn't deny her winning argument.

"The war's changed everything. John is in France. Now you're leaving. There's nothing left for me here. You know how it was when father died. I'm coming whether you agree or not!" Seeing him waver, she added, "Please, Michael, I want to see you off. It's such a little thing to ask. I worry about John. He seldom writes. My imagination runs riot thinking about him."

When she cried, Michael agreed. He always gave in to her when she cried.

"All right, Cath. But remember, the navy yard is temporary. I may only be there a few days. I worry about you traveling alone."

He didn't want her to travel unescorted on a train. That forced travel by motorcar. Catherine had won very few debates with family. Thinking of her victory, she smiled at the mirror, an impulse as much from relief as pride.

As early as she could remember, her father either called her Catherine or Lady. He never said Cathy or Kate. When she was small, he called her "my little lady." As she grew, he shortened that to "my lady." In a good mood, he'd even shorten that to "milady." Hearing it had always made her feel special. She missed her father. When she boarded the train to Bryn Mawr, he'd spoken to her in the fatherly fashion he reserved for occasions when giving advice.

"You're a young lady now, Catherine. All you need is some polish." Now that he was gone, the memory of the advice brought a tear. Since his death, a series of contrasting moods plagued her, changing as often as the weather. Her present mood was uncertainty. These shifts in mood added to her concern for her future. Despite her degree, she had no idea what was to become of her once Michael was gone.

At Bryn Mawr, French became a second language. Professor Thorn had suggested she become an instructor. Goucher College was only a few miles from Guilford. Elizabeth strongly objected. Her mother held to Victorian principles. She didn't think women should seek careers. Her father hadn't entered the debate, thereby conceding to Elizabeth. Catherine postponed plans until the moment came when her mother might be persuaded.

The war, departures, and then death intervened. With brothers abroad, there'd be no one home to advise on careers. Her girlfriends were content to write letters to their army beaux. Not one was fatherless. They'd never understand her need to work for a profession. Her only problem was that Elizabeth would want to know what she was doing.

Her bachelor's in French language and literature was her finest accomplishment, and her father hadn't lived long enough to see her graduate. His first stroke had come unexpectedly. Catherine hadn't slept well for days, thinking how close she'd come to losing him. When Samuel Morris died, it was the most tragic day of her life. The stroke killed him as he napped. The shadow it cast about her never lifted. His last words to her were "I can't talk now, Catherine. I need rest."

Wiping her tears brought the mirror back into focus. Catherine resumed pinning her hair in the manner of women who traveled in open cars. Nearly finished, it made her head look like an inverted pear. Braids were better, but took longer, and Michael's patience had a limit.

From Bretton Place, Monroe would drive the 1916 HCS Series III touring car south through Baltimore and then northeast to New York. The vehicle had personality. Monroe, their chauffeur for nearly twenty years, called it the Stutz.

She'd never been to New York. It was farther than she'd ever gone. Seven years earlier, she'd refused her father's offer to take her there. The fire at the Triangle Shirtwaist Company prompted him to go. Many had chosen to escape the fire by jumping to their deaths. The girls who'd survived were burned. A specialist in dermatoplastics at Johns Hopkins, Sam Morris knew they needed help. Their need didn't engage Catherine. Most of the girls were her age, and Catherine wasn't ready to confront mortality, especially hers. Sam was familiar with death.

On May 7, 1915, the day of the doctor's first stroke, the *Lusitania* was torpedoed. Afterward, she couldn't help linking the two events. They'd come without warning, and both had terrible and irreversible outcomes. Her father was unable to practice. His mind remained clear, but his spirit had died as surely as the passengers on the liner. His work at the hospital went unfinished. Dedicated to healing, Sam Morris spoke to her about the war with a loathing that ran as deep as hers.

She linked his fatal stroke to the war in Europe. That came the day after America declared war. With one son in France and the other decided to go, the declaration was too much for Sam. Since then, all four events were fused. Thinking of one reminded her of the others. Luckily, there'd been no letter from the War Department saying that John was dead.

Though ill, Elizabeth was alive. She'd left for dryer climes six months ago, finally able to take her doctor's advice. Her lung condition had improved, and Arizona might yet be her cure.

Catherine returned to the mirror. Dutifully, she grabbed one last bunch of hair to pin to her fretful head. Finished, her eye caught the picture John had sent to her from Pau. Surely, he must be the handsomest flier in France. She wrote letters that usually went unanswered. Before he sailed, she overheard him tell Michael, "Pilots are the first to cross enemy lines. They send them up to spot enemy positions. They take photos. It sounds crazy, but the idea of flying over German lines is exciting."

That comment horrified Catherine. Yet that was John. He was first to try anything. Years before, it made sense. He was the oldest. His eagerness troubled her now. He could easily be killed. What would happen should Michael be hurt? At twenty-five, Michael was two years younger than John. John could die any day. Now, Michael! If the worst happened …

"Dear God, Catherine, that is not something you should think about! For heaven's sake, finish this! Michael is itching to go!" It wasn't like Catherine to talk to herself aloud. It was the way her mother relieved tension.

Michael had volunteered to serve fresh from Johns Hopkins School of Medicine. The navy promised to appoint him to the medical service. He hadn't followed his father's wish to become a general practitioner. He'd become Lieutenant Michael Morris. His mother's concern muted any pride over his choice. Assigned temporary duty at the yard, he could be reassigned to a ship, a hospital in England, or even France. He'd told Catherine, "There's a chance I'll be assigned to a base hospital. Anything's possible, Cath. They'll send me where I'm needed."

Catherine was closer to Michael than to John in spirit and in age. John was always the brave one. She was proud of John, but Michael had the higher calling. Fighter pilots took lives; surgeons saved them. She loved her brothers, but in her eyes, their different choices made a distinction between them. She blamed the war for forcing her to judge her brothers. To Catherine, war was madness raised to the scale of disbelief.

Emptied of thoughts for the first time since she'd sat down, Catherine was finished. Her excitement grew in spite of her concern. New York would mark a turning point in her life, and nothing would change that. Putting on her sunbonnet, she drew a scarf across the top and tied the ends under her chin. The scarf would keep her hair from blowing in the Stutz. At her door, she again heard Monroe's deep voice calling.

"Miss Cath'rine? Mr. Michael wants to know if you're comin' or not. He says we either go now or you ain't!" Monroe's accent always got strong when he was troubled. He'd be driving the whole way and had wanted to start early. New York was two hundred miles from Baltimore, two days by motorcar. Their only stopover was in Philadelphia.

"I'm coming, Monroe."

Monroe called her "Miss Cath'rine" when the family was home. If guests were near, he called her Miss Morris. Catherine attributed Monroe's manners to his mother's upbringing, though she'd never met Hattie.

He once told her that Hattie Jefferson was the daughter of former slaves. Knowing that Monroe's ancestors were slaves bothered her. Slavery was possibly more abhorrent than war. Though less destructive, it was more organized, a terrible injustice to human beings. Monroe was the standard by which she judged black people. As he was kind and loyal, all black people must be kind and loyal. His son, James, was always kind. Shy, just speaking to him often embarrassed him. She hadn't seen James for months. His life was a total mystery to her.

Monroe had little schooling, but the family felt fortunate to employ him. Over the years, he'd never ceased to amaze Catherine with his skill. He had an instinct for fixing things. This was the first weekend Monroe was needed for months. Catherine wasn't sure what he or James did with their weekends. If anyone in the family knew, it had been her father. Sam had taken a special interest in Monroe and especially James.

"I'm coming down now, Monroe," she repeated. She forgot to mention the valise she'd packed but decided against calling Monroe when the front door closed. She'd carry it herself, like some women she knew. Unlike some friends, Catherine didn't need pampering. She was interested in the suffragette movement. The speeches of Emmeline Goulden Pankhurst had been the talk of Bryn Mawr. What a woman! She feared no man. Catherine nearly joined the movement, but her mother wouldn't dream of letting her carry a placard in public while strange men hooted from the sidewalk. Her brothers didn't encourage her. They said women would win the vote after the war. They suggested she be a nurse.

"They need nurses," they had told her.

Catherine chose family. Her mother needed attention, and John likely got more mail than anyone in his squadron. She hoped it stayed in one place long enough for him to receive it. She sometimes wondered if it got there at all. Before he sailed to England, John spoke to Michael about the war. Catherine caught the last part of the conversation.

"Wilson will have to get in it. Kaiser Bill doesn't like America's neutrality. Woodrow told him he's welcome to buy all the arms he can transport but knows damned well Britain won't let that happen!"

Michael laughed. "Not past the Royal Navy's blockade."

That's when Catherine broke into their conversation. "Mr. Wilson said the war should remain a European affair. I hope you're wrong about our entry, John! Nothing is sacred to the kaiser, and he wouldn't treat you any better than the rest! You should stay out of it! I don't understand why you want to take part!" Quiet followed.

Catherine pulled the strap of her handbag over a shoulder. She grabbed the valise and left the room without looking back. It wouldn't be the same when she returned. Down the hall, she passed her father's empty bedroom. Mother's was on the opposite side of the hall. His practice at Hopkins had forced odd hours during the night. She wondered what advice he'd have given her.

At the bottom of the stairs, she couldn't help noticing her father's favorite picture. A stern-faced Theodore Roosevelt hung there in spite of her mother's opposition. Her father admired TR, a man he repeatedly said "wouldn't stand for what the kaiser is doing." Roosevelt wore pince-nez glasses secured by a golden cord leading to a place hidden under his vest. His eyes were fixed front. Catherine once tried to avoid his narrow stare but couldn't escape it. No matter where she moved, Roosevelt's eyes followed, looking right through her. She never liked that portrait.

Catherine heard the front door open and knew that Monroe was checking on her. He saw her carrying a valise.

"I'll take that, Miss Cath'rine." Monroe was thoughtful of her, helping whenever he could. Since her father's death, he'd been more attentive to her.

"Thank you, Monroe. Is Michael all right?"

"Yes, miss. Been waitin' the whole time. He wanted to get started a hour ago."

Monroe's kindness reminded her of a more provincial time she missed terribly. Outside, she turned to look at the house.

"It is a grand house, isn't it?" she asked of no one in particular.

Monroe was less concerned about her tardiness than the tires on the Stutz. The four on the axles were worn but had the best tread. The spare clearly showed wear. He'd checked each a second time and remained skeptical about the pressure in the rear tires.

The front tires were inflated to fifty-five pounds, the rear to sixty-five, following the manufacturer's recommendations. The difference was supposed to account for added weight of luggage and passengers in the backseat. Monroe didn't like the idea of high pressure in the rear tires even though Michael agreed with it. To his mind, it didn't account for the condition of the roads. Many were in disrepair, and some were unpaved. Gravel and cinders covered many secondary roads. A few were badly rutted dirt.

Monroe had parked the Stutz on the street in front of the house. He took pride in letting the neighbors see the shiny car he polished and drove. Catherine got in the rear next to Michael. Monroe strapped her bag to the luggage rack with Michael's. The warm sun and clear skies made riding in the open ideal, but as usual, Monroe asked, "You want the side curtains up, Miss Cath'rine?" He always asked, even on short trips to the park. The top was in place. Side curtains would keep wind off of her.

"No. The air is warm. Thank you for asking, Monroe. Michael, I'm sorry I made you wait," she said, trying her best to be sincere. He didn't answer. She could see he was restless and anxious to get started.

Catherine watched Monroe move the curious levers under the steering column that had something to do with starting the car. Fascinated by his intuition in their placement, the throttle, spark, and choke adjusted, he went to the front of the car to crank the engine. It almost never responded on the first pull but merely gasped and hissed.

"Is the tank full, Monroe?" Michael was aware of Monroe's impeccable care of the Stutz. He simply used the opportunity to express his impatience to anyone.

"Yes, sir, Mr. Michael, to the top. Gas in the carb'rator been evaporatin' waitin' out here in this heat." He stopped short of criticism, conscious of Catherine's presence.

The Stutz backfired on the second try, startling her. The engine sputtered to life at a less-than-rhythmic idle. Monroe raced to the driver's door, reaching over to adjust the choke. The Stutz immediately stopped rocking. Monroe replaced the crank and got behind the wheel.

Catherine understood none of it but watched all the same. Monroe's efficiency with mechanical things fascinated her. He was the only man she knew with a talent for it. She was glad he was their chauffeur. Since her father's loss, she'd come to depend upon Monroe.

With a clatter of gears, the Stutz began to roll lazily through Guilford to Charles Street. They were on the way. At the intersection with Charles Street, Monroe launched the trip with some advice for the city between two rivers.

"Look out, New York! Here we comes!"

Michael's Journey Begins

MONROE WANTED TO GO NORTH to Cold Spring Lane but wasn't sure it reached Philadelphia Road. Michael didn't know, either. They decided to turn south on Charles Street to the center of Baltimore. They immediately passed the newest part of Johns Hopkins University campus, the section called Homewood.

Michael glanced at Gilman Hall. He told Catherine it had only been used for two years. The hospital and medical school, where his father had once taught, were farther south, not far above Fells Point near the Inner Harbor. Michael had recently graduated with the class of 1918.

Catherine didn't register his comments. She was emotionally worn out from her earlier reflections.

"I'm glad you're here, Cath," he said. "It's nice to have some company."

"Thank you, Michael! I'm glad you agreed to let me come."

"You didn't leave me much choice, you know."

"Traffic's startin' to get heavy, Mr. Michael," Monroe said, worried they'd get caught in a traffic jam. The city streets reflected war activity with every sort of khaki-colored military vehicle. Baltimore's port was busy loading war material into merchant vessels. President Wilson had ordered cannons to be fitted on the vessels to defend against U-boats.

"I see it, Monroe. It should be better once we leave the city."

Monroe's primary duty was to chauffeur the family. He also ran errands and did odd jobs for Dr. Sam. After the doctor's death, Monroe had taken personal responsibility for Catherine's well-being. She was aware of his increased attention. He knew he'd never replace Dr. Sam, but the need to look after her became much stronger in him. He believed Dr. Sam would approve.

"There's the park, Miss Cath'rine. We had good times there this summer."

Baltimore was often humid in summer. Catherine sometimes asked Monroe to drive her to Druid Hill Park. She enjoyed the shade of its trees, and its open spaces permitted a breeze. She liked to feed the birds. Pigeons dominated seagulls, but the gulls were braver. She admired the way they hovered, waiting for her to offer up a piece of bread. They'd pluck it straight from her fingers. Pigeons ambled about in chaotic herds, erupting in a flurry of wings whenever someone approached. Pigeons preferred the land. Seagulls loved the air. John was like a seagull. Catherine was more like a pigeon wondering how to become a seagull.

"It's a lovely park, isn't it, Michael?"

"Yes, it is." Michael sensed her mind was preoccupied, but she didn't pry. When he bothered to notice, the change in her moods seemed to occur without reason.

Monroe turned onto Saint Paul Street. The car slowed with the traffic. Near Penn Station, they stopped entirely. Clouds of steam boiled up from the station. The exhaust of motorcars mingled with acrid, black coal smoke drifting up from a huge steam engine idling on the tracks below as passengers entered the train. Catherine wiped involuntary tears caused by the smoke.

Michael watched a group of soldiers near the entrance. Each had large khaki bags resting on the sidewalk. Nearly all had family or girlfriends on hand to see them off to training camps in the south. Those who'd completed training were going to New York to board troopships.

A policeman directing traffic in the intersection stopped a trolley at Mount Royal Street. Soon, he waved an arm, and the wheels of the trolley made rhythmic clacking noises as they crossed the trolley tracks in the intersection. Monroe immediately thought of jazz rhythms.

"It's a lotta traffic 'round here, Mr. Michael. Preston Street might be better."

"It's the station traffic, Monroe. We're nearly past it now. Orleans Street isn't much farther."

"Yes sah, Mast...ah, Mr. Michael, sah. It's lookin' just dandy down there!" Monroe's generous touch of sarcasm came as he looked at the mass of traffic down Saint Paul Street.

Years before, Michael had told Monroe to change the title "Master" to "Mister," saying it was more appropriate for a man entering medical school. Monroe had called him Master Michael since he was a toddler. It took him months to get accustomed to the new title. When Michael's indifference to his opinions upset him, the old title sometimes slipped out.

As Monroe looked for a way through traffic, Catherine asked, "Michael, when will we arrive at the hotel?"

Michael looked at his watch, paused to think, and said, "Well, it's nearly twelve twenty now. We should get there in time for supper. We're expected around four. Are you worried?"

"No. I was just wondering."

Catherine hadn't spoken to divert attention from their disagreement. The dispute over which road was best was between them. Disagreement among men sometimes fostered an argument. Women she knew seldom argued their differences. Women held different points of view without argument. Men were different. She remembered the words her father had with John two years before, when John said he was going to France. She couldn't remember a time when her father had raised such a strong objection to John.

"Don't do this, John! If you must join, join here! Get your commission first! If America enters the war, you'll probably be a captain by that time and in charge of a whole company."

John argued his position, saying that rank was not the point. "If you were French, you'd tell me to join. Whole towns are being destroyed. Women and children are being murdered!"

Father insisted, "That's war, John. Murder is a different matter."

John rebutted, "What about Belgium? That matters! What about the U-boats? I know you respect Roosevelt's judgment about what they've done."

John's argument was strong. The more he debated, the fewer arguments Sam Morris could find to rebut. Nevertheless, he asked John to wait one last time. The debate ended when their father yielded. The energy behind John's conviction had startled Catherine. It ended the debate, and their father no longer tried to stop John. Michael hadn't had to face his father. He was gone.

At Orleans Street, Monroe turned east toward Philadelphia Road. It took longer than Michael expected. He couldn't remember seeing so many trucks. Many were marked with the red cross of the Ambulance Corps. All were headed toward the docks, destined for France. Michael didn't point them out to Catherine. Her somber expression clearly showed she'd seen them. Any comment from him would only make things worse.

With relief, Monroe finally turned onto Philadelphia Road.

Beyond Baltimore, the route north roughly followed the tracks of the Pennsylvania Railroad all the way to New York.

No one in the Stutz had spoken since Catherine asked Michael about their arrival in Philadelphia. Now that they were headed north, the only sound was the accelerating Stutz, reminding them that Michael was truly on his way. The silence worried Monroe.

"How you doin' back there, Miss Cath'rine? You okay? It's awful quiet back there!" Monroe didn't normally ask her how she felt when she was moody, but he was genuinely worried about her. He was aware of the position she'd shortly be in and knew she wasn't prepared.

"I'm fine, Monroe."

Monroe wanted them to start talking. "You sure?"

It wasn't like Monroe to omit her title and name in direct conversation. That familiarity was more common to her childhood. Nevertheless, it pleased her not to hear it.

"Really, Monroe, I'm fine. I'm taking in the sights. I don't remember being here before."

Michael wasn't sure she was being completely honest and noticed a lack of sincerity in her tone. The sight of the ambulances had ruffled her. "Cath" was Michael's pet name for Catherine. He knew she liked it and always used it when the time seemed right.

"Cath, this is new to me too. I usually stopped at the Pratt Library. Sometimes the market in Fells Point. I've never traveled this road. It's good we're finally headed north." He paused and said, "We'd drown if we kept going east."

His grin and silly reference to the harbor gave away his intent. Though her father hadn't always recognized her moods, Michael did. Being silly was his way of teasing her out of a bad mood. He'd say something ordinary to set up his punch line then something silly. He always caught her off guard. Her reaction was predictable. She sighed. It was an old tactic.

"Really, Michael! You do that when I least expect it."

Nevertheless, the means had the desired end. Her mood softened, and Michael's silly ploy proved successful.

Minutes later, a train sped by going north. Through its windows, Michael saw passengers wearing flat-brimmed, Montana-peaked hats like those worn by the soldiers saying good-bye at Pennsylvania Station. They could easily be the same men he'd seen standing near at Penn Station.

A disturbing idea entered his mind. Michael looked forward to service in the medical branch. He was taught to view patients as people needing medical attention. At that instant, he wondered if he would have to pull a blanket over the face of one of those men in some ether-filled operating room. It was not beyond the realm of possibility. At Hopkins, he'd seen photographs of Civil War wounded, showing the incredible mess that shells and bullets made of human flesh. The thought of saving lives had inspired him. It was the reason he chose service in the medical corps instead of private practice.

After driving almost an hour, they were approaching Aberdeen. For a paved highway, Philadelphia Road was in awful shape. The pavement was broken along much of its length. The Stutz was a fine motorcar, but motorcars didn't like potholes. Monroe spent half the time trying to avoid them. The other half he worried about a blowout. He'd have preferred cinders, even dirt, to this. Sharp-edged potholes didn't form in cinders or dirt. He avoided as many as he could but couldn't miss some for their size. In his own defense, he commented on the condition of the road.

"That was a big one! This damn ... I mean, this old road got lots of holes. I seen swiss cheese look better den dis! Looks like a darn battlefield in France." Monroe's accent always became more apparent when he was troubled. Swearing in front of them was not normal for Monroe, but he was usually more informal on weekends. He'd foregone his to make the trip. That was enough reason to be informal. They rarely heard him swear in Guilford. Usually, he'd swear to himself, especially when he hurt himself using some uncooperative tool. He swore after hitting his thumb with a hammer trying to mount that "damn portrait" of Mr. Roosevelt for Dr. Sam. The wall was solid mahogany, and he bent four nails trying to penetrate the hardwood. The accident made Monroe mad at Roosevelt. TR's face didn't seem to appreciate his pain.

The speedometer wavered around thirty-eight miles per hour. Monroe gradually slowed the Stutz. Thirty-two was fast enough. Going slower wouldn't make much difference in their arrival time. The trip through Baltimore had already done that. Aberdeen was in sight when the Stutz hit the mother of all potholes. Monroe saw it, but an oncoming truck prevented him from avoiding it. The sound of the blowout made Catherine shriek. It was all Monroe could do to keep the vehicle on the road. Brakes screeching, the car swerved right and came to a stop on the shoulder, three feet from a large oak tree. He'd avoided a deep drainage ditch by inches. Monroe sank back in the seat softly uttering the words, "Sweet Jesus." His heart was pounding. His temples throbbed.

Michael's reaction was instinctive. His right hand grabbed the back of the front seat. His left grabbed the top of the door on Catherine's side, putting his arm in front of her. When the car stopped short of the tree, he put his arm around Catherine's shoulders. Her face was pale. Her eyes closed, her hands shook, pressing the sides of her scarf against her face. Tears of fright ran down her cheeks in twin streams. Her body shook involuntarily. Michael had never seen her in such a pitiable state.

"Are you okay, Cath?" Drawing no response, he asked again. "Catherine, are you okay?"

Her sobs subsided. Catherine had never come that close to

being injured. She'd also never faced the remotest possibility of death.

"Good Lord, Michael! We might have been killed!"

Clinically, Michael knew her reaction came in response to a huge surge of adrenaline. He rubbed her shoulders and waited for calm to return. "It's all right, Cath. It's over."

"I'll be all right, Michael. I need a little time."

Monroe set the brake and turned to face them. "You folks okay back there? You take all the time you need, Miss Cath'rine. We ain't goin' nowhere with that tire!" His lowered voice nearly choked. He felt badly that Catherine was shaken. He wanted to help, but she didn't respond to his comments. The tremor in her voice had made him aware of her condition.

Catherine had never seen such anxiety on Monroe's face. Shaken as she was, she felt sad for him. Concern for Monroe finally calmed her down.

"We're okay, Monroe. I'll look after Catherine. Cath, I see a bench just up the road. The walk will do you good. It's only a little way."

Her eyes dried, she said, "Thank you, Michael. I'm fine. Can't we just sit here for a moment?"

"Sure." Then Michael spoke to Monroe. "I'll never know how you managed to avoid that tree, Monroe. Check for damage. It may be just the tire, but you never know."

Monroe was more worried about Catherine. On Michael's suggestion, he resumed his place as chauffeur. It was his profession. His duty was to take them to Philadelphia, and no damned pothole was going to stop him from performing his duty.

"Yes, sir, Mr. Michael. I'll look. You leave it to me!"

Catherine spoke to Monroe as he stepped from the car. "Thank you, Monroe."

A tremendous feeling of relief came over him. Everything was right again. A smile lit his face as Monroe leaned through the open door.

"I'm sorry, Miss Cath'rine. Tried to miss that pothole. I'm glad you're feelin' better, miss. You had ol' Monroe terrible worried!" He was truly grateful she'd spoken. He blamed himself for the accident, somehow associating its cause with being too informal. That feeling instantly disappeared. Catherine smiled at him. She was assured in knowing he felt better.

Monroe walked around the Stutz looking for damage. He hadn't heard or felt anything break, but he knew he should check the axle to ensure that the steering arm and shock absorber weren't loose or broken. Serious damage could end the trip below Aberdeen.

"You folks go sit awhile. I'm gonna jack the car up, so it'll take some time. Don't y'all worry none. I'll make it right as rain."

"Let's go, Cath. Let's walk."

By the time they sat, Catherine was calm. Michael was becoming more concerned about the condition of the Stutz. He glanced toward the car to see what was happening. Monroe was kneeling beside the car. He'd taken his cap off to put his head under the right front fender. Michael couldn't see his face. Minutes seemed to pass as Monroe examined the undercarriage. As of yet, he'd said nothing about the car. Michael's concern grew. If the car was damaged, time was not his ally even though he'd allowed an extra day for the trip.

"Everything looks fine, Mr. Michael. We'll be on our way soon as I get this tire changed."

Michael breathed a sigh of relief.

Monroe had a friend in Philadelphia called Tinner. He moved north to start a tire repair and towing business. He'd stay with Tinner overnight and ask him about getting a new tire. With any luck, Tinner would have one on hand. As it turned out, Tinner gave Monroe a new Dunlop. He mounted the tire the following morning.

The Brooklyn Navy Yard

LONG TRIPS IN THE STUTZ were tiresome. Catherine was grateful for the ferry's leisurely pace across the Hudson River. In Manhattan, Monroe turned south on Broadway. New York was busier than Baltimore. They caught glimpses of the towers that supported a bridge. Named for the borough it connected to Manhattan, Colonel Roebling's Brooklyn Bridge was called the Eighth Wonder of the World. Suspended 135 feet above the East River, it would save considerable time compared to a ferry crossing.

The bridge stirred a clinical feeling in Michael. He recalled a lecture at the medical school at Johns Hopkins. Many who'd dug the footings for the towers suffered from a disease the men called the bends. Caisson disease caused workers to stoop over in pain from nitrogen bubbles in their blood. Washington Roebling still suffered its effects. Michael decided not to tell Catherine of its connection to the bridge.

Catherine watched boats sailing on the river. At this height, they seemed like toys. The long wake of a steamer captured her eye, spreading like an unfolding fan. She wondered if it was going to France, carrying someone's brother to war. Upriver, Michael noticed a second bridge and another beyond that.

"Do you know the names of those bridges, Monroe?"

A practical man, Monroe wondered why three bridges crossed the East River while the Hudson hadn't even one. A bridge over the Hudson would have meant a warm meal by this time.

"I think that's the Manhattan Bridge, Mr. Michael. I only been here once. I wish they had one over that first river, Mr. Michael. Makes more sense than puttin' three on this side."

"They'll build one over the Hudson someday."

"If you asks me, they coulda done it sooner. We gotta go back that way."

By the time Monroe finished, they were across the East River. Sands Street took them to the entrance of the Brooklyn Navy Yard. A group of officers were talking nearby. As the Stutz approached the gate, a guard wearing a brimmed steel helmet and a scowl dropped his pencil and stepped from the gatehouse, his hand raised in the universal gesture to stop. A wide band with the letters MP girdled an arm. His other hand rested on the handle of an ominous revolver jutting from a well-oiled leather holster strapped to his right hip by a khaki-colored webbed belt. Walking toward the Stutz, he addressed Michael directly in a tone of authority.

"Your name and the purpose of your visit, sir," the guard stated gruffly.

Michael guessed the guard didn't like being interrupted. His impatience was made clear in the manner he exercised authority.

"Lieutenant Michael Ryan Morris reporting for duty, Sergeant." Michael saw no reason to provide more information than asked, especially to a guard showing no respect for his rank.

"Orders, sir. I must verify your orders."

Michael reached inside a coat pocket and handed a paper to the guard.

"Wait here, sir!" The guard's words sounded more like a command than a request. He strode toward the gatehouse to retrieve a clipboard. After looking over Michael's orders, he reviewed the page on his clipboard and then turned to look at Michael. Then he repeated the process.

Irritated by the guard's inability to confirm his orders, Michael opened the side door of the Stutz and said, "The name is Morris, Lieutenant Michael Morris."

The guard looked up, glaring disapproval. Given the opportunity to issue another command, he said, "Please remain in the vehicle, sir!" Once again, he looked at the page on his clipboard. Finding nothing, the guard walked slowly toward the Stutz. He peered at Michael with the same scowl he'd worn when they first arrived.

Questioning Michael, he asked, "Who are you supposed to report to, sir?"

Now, Michael became irritated. The name of the officer was in his orders. Michael had forgotten the man's name in the heat of the encounter.

"It should all be there, Sergeant. May I have my orders?" Reluctantly, the guard handed Michael his orders. Michael looked for the name of the man to whom he was to report.

At the same time, one of the officers who'd been standing nearby walked toward the Stutz. The guard stood at attention as the officer approached and saluted. The officer ignored the guard and continued to walk toward the Stutz.

"Excuse me, Lieutenant. I'm Captain John Turnbull. Perhaps I can help. Did I hear you say you are Lieutenant Michael Morris?"

Michael began to get out of the Stutz in order to salute but was waved at ease with a simple gesture of the captain's hand.

"Don't bother on my account, Lieutenant. Commander Fields said he expected an officer to report shortly. If that's correct, you've just completed a rather lengthy trip."

"Yes, sir, we have. It's kind of you to offer your help, Captain. I am Lieutenant Morris. Allow me to introduce my sister, Catherine, and our driver, Monroe. We left Baltimore yesterday, sir."

"I see." Nodding toward Monroe, the captain's glance fell on Catherine. "A pleasure, Miss ... or is it Mrs.?"

"Miss, if you please!" Catherine was not accustomed to answering questions from a man inquiring about her marital status. Victorian upbringing instilled a certain reserve. But in this case, her spontaneous reaction was immediately regretted. The captain's familiarity was totally innocent. Besides, he'd just offered Michael his help.

"Excuse me, Miss Morris. My manners have become somewhat rusty in the navy. I didn't mean to offend."

His apology embarrassed her more than her remarks. She'd overreacted and must set the situation right.

"It's I who must apologize, Captain. I spoke too quickly. The trip was indeed tiring."

Turnbull smiled. "I understand. There's no need for you to apologize." Turning toward Michael, he asked, "Lieutenant, would your father be Dr. Samuel Morris of Johns Hopkins?"

"Yes, sir. I'm afraid he passed away over a year ago."

The captain's smile faded. A glance at Catherine caught her tilting her head downward.

"I'm very sorry to hear that, Lieutenant. I didn't know your father for very long, but his reputation is well known. We'll save that story for a later time. Let's get you through the gate. I'm sure you'd all like to find a place to rest."

"Yes, sir. I'd like to hear that story when you have time."

"That's a promise." The captain asked for Michael's orders. He asked the guard why he hadn't passed Lieutenant Morris through the gate. The guard explained that the lieutenant's name wasn't on the roster of arrivals. Turnbull reviewed the roster. The page was dated with the current date and did not contain Michael's name. Turnbull flipped the page, looked at it, and turned the roster toward the sergeant pointing at the first entry.

"What's that, Sergeant?"

Confused by the captain's question, the guard said, "It's tomorrow's date, sir!"

"Indeed it is. You read his orders? Did you look for tomorrow's roster, Sergeant?"

"No, sir. Our procedure is to check the roster for today, sir. Tomorrow's roster is for tomorrow, sir." Positive he'd acted within navy yard policy, the guard was bewildered at his interrogation. He became more erect to demonstrate his devotion to duty.

Turnbull's annoyance became pronounced. "As of now, Sergeant, your new procedure takes effect immediately. You will look at tomorrow's roster as well, and I mean now, Sergeant!" Turnbull shoved the roster into the sergeant's midsection.

"Yes, sir, Captain, sir!" Stricken by the captain's displeasure, the sergeant saluted and flipped the page on the roster. Standing at attention, his eyes flew over tomorrow's roster. "Sir, Lieutenant Michael Morris appears on the page, sir."

"Had you read his orders more carefully, Sergeant, you'd have realized the lieutenant was to report here tomorrow. Some officers may be more punctual than others! In the future, you will pass these men through no matter which page their names are on! Is that clear?"

"Yes, sir!" The sergeant's scowl was gone when he approached the car. "Sir, you may pass. Sorry for the inconvenience, sir." He didn't look at Michael's eyes as he spoke. He jogged to the gate and raised the wooden barrier that barred entrance to the compound.

The captain returned his attention to Michael. "I'd go with you, Lieutenant, but I have some business to attend to. You'll find the hospital on the other side of the compound. Look for signs with red crosses. Call on me once you've settled in. I'd like to talk to you about your father. Miss Morris, it's my pleasure to meet you."

"Thank you, Captain." She was impressed by the captain's intervention and was made keenly aware of naval authority after being a witness to it.

Michael thanked the captain on behalf of the three of them.

Monroe eased through the gate, smiling at the guard as he passed. Speaking softly, he noted, "Man! I wouldn't want to be in that fella's shoes next time that captain is around!"

The remark brought snickers from his passengers. Watching the sergeant being dressed down, however well earned, wasn't pleasant. Michael's next comment brought a burst of laughter.

"I guess I should have told him I wasn't due 'til tomorrow!"

Monroe stopped at the entrance to the hospital.

Michael left to find Commander William Fields. "I'll be back. Wait for me."

"Miss Cath'rine, this sure been a trip!" Monroe sighed, glad it was nearly over.

"You did very well, Monroe. I hope Michael finds the commander. I'm anxious to get to the house Michael rented. You must be too. Michael said there's a room for you near the kitchen. It sounded very nice. Any house is better than the navy yard."

Since the house was off-site, she knew Monroe could be around during the day. The thought comforted her. She wouldn't be alone while Michael was working in the navy yard. Minutes later, Michael came running from the hospital. For a moment, Catherine feared he'd been told to report to a ship immediately.

"It looks like we'll be here awhile. Commander Fields said my transport isn't assigned yet. When I told him you were waiting outside, he suggested we go to the house and freshen up. He wants to take us to dinner in Manhattan. He rattled off the names of at least a dozen restaurants! He seems nice, Cath. I think you'll like him. How about it? Shall we take him up on his offer?"

Though tired from the drive, Catherine didn't want to disappoint Michael, and the commander might give them a sense for when Michael had to ship out.

"All right, Michael, if that's what you want."

She preferred to stay at the house, but the commander's invitation was important to Michael, and she wanted to spend as much time with him as possible.

"Good. I'll let him know. He's waiting for an answer so he can reserve a table."

Men! she thought. *Always trying to impress people!*

Michael forgot to ask Catherine what she wanted to eat. When he told the commander, Fields said, "Don't worry. I guarantee she won't be disappointed."

Michael's curiosity was piqued. The commander picked up the telephone and dialed Delmonico's.

"Hello, George? This is Commander Fields. Listen, I'd like to reserve a table for three, but don't hold it after eight, okay? ... I appreciate it George ... Yes, thank you, George."

The commander dialed again. "Hello, Robert? ... Commander Fields ... I'm fine. Look, Robert, can you hold a table for three until eight tonight? ... No, I'm not sure yet, but I'd be grateful if you did ... Yes. They're friends of mine ... Okay, I'll wait."

As the commander listened to Robert's reply, he covered the mouthpiece with a hand and turned to Michael. "Is six thirty or seven okay?"

"Yes, sir."

"Good. You needn't wait, Lieutenant. I've got to make a few more calls. Take your sister to the house to give her a chance to clean up. I'm looking forward to meeting her. Do you need directions?"

Michael pulled a paper from a jacket pocket on which he'd scribbled a small map. "It's 103 Abingdon Road in Kew Gardens, right, sir?"

The commander simply nodded. "For God's sake, Lieutenant, drop the 'sir.' I don't want your sister to think I'm a stickler for formalities!"

"Yes, sir ... I mean, Commander."

"Good. We'll meet here around seven!" Shooing Michael away with his free hand, his attention returned to the voice on the receiver. "Thanks, Robert. I owe you one."

Michael smiled, admiring the commander's way of reserving tables to let Catherine make the choice. He heard the commander speak again as he walked to the door.

"Yes, then give it to someone else. Don't worry, Robert. I'll take care of it."

Back in the Stutz, Michael announced, "It's all set. We'll go to the house and meet here by seven and decide where to go. Do you have an idea what you want, Cath?"

"I don't know, Michael. I haven't given it any thought."

"Okay. There's plenty of time to decide." Michael gave Monroe directions. "Monroe, turn left at the gate and left onto Flushing."

"Yes, sir, Mr. Michael."

As they approached the gate, the guard looked up. His scowl had returned, but when he recognized the Stutz, it immediately disappeared. He jogged to open the gate. Words were not exchanged as he saluted. Michael simply returned his salute.

On Flushing, Michael said, "Turn right, Monroe. Go three blocks and then turn left on Myrtle. Follow Myrtle to Kew Gardens. It's only a few miles. I'll let you know when we get there."

"Yes, sah, Mister Michael." Monroe's voice showed he was

tired of driving. To cheer him up, Michael said, "It won't be long, Monroe. We're almost there. You've done a great job. I'm really indebted to you for working on a weekend. I won't forget it."

"Michael, do we have to go to New York tonight?"

"I think so, Cath. He's making a lot of calls. He must know every maître d' in town."

Not wholly impressed, Catherine thought it was a lot of fuss to go to for a meal. Nevertheless, her interest stirred at the prospect of meeting a man who'd go to all that trouble for total strangers. The evening showed a spark of promise, she decided on the dress she'd wear before arriving at Kew Gardens.

Catherine's Choice—1918

AT DELMONICO'S, CATHERINE, MICHAEL, AND Commander Fields were enjoying the evening. The restaurant impressed her even as they arrived at its columned entrance. Commander Fields told them it served the finest in Continental cuisine. Even the waiter seemed to know him. In his navy dress uniform, Catherine thought he cut a striking figure. Catherine attracted attention, especially from the men who knew the commander.

"How long will you be in New York, Catherine?"

"As long as Michael is here, I'll be here. I came to see him off."

"Are you a college student?"

"No. I recently graduated from Bryn Mawr."

"Then you have a degree."

"Yes, Commander. My major was French language and literature."

"Do you plan to teach French?"

The question embarrassed her. "I don't know. My mother

doesn't welcome the idea of a career woman. I've set aside deciding for now. I expect I'll be considering it again now that she's in Arizona and Michael will be going overseas."

"I guess we've neglected Catherine's future, Commander," Michael interjected.

The commander's response left little doubt how he felt. "I agree with you on that point, Lieutenant. Victorian women were expected to stay home. The war has changed all that. Women have taken on many jobs that were once held by men. Your sister has a very special talent and should be allowed to use it. She'd likely be in demand at the very highest levels."

Catherine's interest in Commander Fields instantly grew. He wasn't talking about classrooms. Changing the subject, Michael asked about his duties at the navy yard.

"You'll get a physical tomorrow, probably from the captain. Orders could arrive as soon as tomorrow, next week, or next month. Until then, you'll be part of my staff. I'll explain when I see you tomorrow."

The commander didn't want the war to enter the conversation. They were at Delmonico's to enjoy the evening, not to discuss the war. He steered the conversation to Catherine's future. He was more interested in her future than in Michael's. He spoke of it again just before they returned to Kew Gardens.

"Miss Morris, you should be using your talent. Something should be done about that."

"The idea never entered my mind in the way you suggest, Commander." Catherine suspected he had something in mind and was intrigued by what it might be. His interest seemed genuine. No one else had expressed real interest in her future. Michael and John cared for her, yet they'd never asked her about her future. She was the youngest. A girl. In her family, these were handicaps. Her mother actually presented the greatest obstacle to her future. Other than marriage, nothing else was ever discussed between them. She loved her mother in spite of her objection but felt it impossible to make plans without upsetting her.

The commander's idea made sense. Given a chance, she was perfectly capable of contributing her talent. She'd certainly overcome doubt if there was a doubtless direction to head. Before she could respond, the commander spoke again.

"Your brother will be busy getting acquainted with the staff at the hospital. He's got to take a physical. Miss Morris, I'd like to bring you back to the city tomorrow. I know New York. We could talk about your future while I show you the city."

Any other time, such boldness would have embarrassed her. Tonight, it appealed to her. She looked at Michael to see his reaction. It would be too bold of her to agree without his assent. After all, she'd come to New York to be with him.

Noticing Catherine's glance at Michael, the commander added, "If the lieutenant agrees."

"Sure, Cath, go ahead. I'll be tied up. You might as well take advantage."

"Are you sure, Michael?"

"I'm sure. You won't have a chance to see the city with someone who knows it better than the commander. Don't worry about me. Go ahead."

"Commander? Will you come for me, or shall I have Monroe bring me to the navy yard?"

"If you don't mind, Miss Morris, I'll get you. Is ten too early?"

"Ten will be fine, Commander. Michael, I'll give the day to Monroe if it's all right with you. The poor man must be looking forward to some free time after the trip."

"I was going to suggest it myself if you didn't use the car. I'll give him my key."

It was settled. For a day, both her brothers would be set aside.

"I look forward to it, Miss Morris."

Monroe spent the evening in Kew Gardens. His room was in the rear of the house in a section normally reserved for a housemaid. Before going to Delmonico's, Catherine told him to make his dinner from anything he found in the pantry.

He couldn't find any bread or cheese. He found tea, a can of condensed milk, a few onions, and spices in glass containers. A top shelf held a variety of preserves in large jars with metal caps clamped firmly shut by wires snapped over the center of their lids. He found jars of preserved peaches, applesauce, and jelly. Behind the peaches were tomato preserves. Spaghetti stood in a tall jar topped with a large cork.

Monroe decided to make spaghetti. He used a whole jar of tomatoes. Several spices were available. He added basil, oregano, and a little olive oil. His mother had shown him how to cut onions without tears. He added a clove of crushed garlic and two tablespoons of the secret ingredient his mother once told him to add. He boiled the sauce and spaghetti. Spaghetti always made an easy meal that satisfied the hollow in a stomach, but tea didn't appeal to him.

He put his meal on a small table in the study, adjacent to the sitting room. Monroe found a decanter of white wine. The wine glasses looked small. He was forced to refill his before finishing his meal. He found a pen on top of the carefully polished mahogany desk. Paper in the center drawer lay next to assorted envelopes and stamps. Monroe decided to buy stamps at the post office. Using things without permission, in a house rented by the Michael, was not appropriate. Since there was nothing else to do, a bit of ink and paper wouldn't be missed. He was still composing the letter on a table near his bed when the Morrises returned. Hearing the door open, he laid the pen down and went to welcome them in a shirt and trousers. He'd put away Catherine's things. She'd asked him if he'd mind doing it, since she had no idea when they'd return from

New York. He told her he'd be glad to do it and should put it out of her mind. He was always there when she needed him. Every day, he became more indispensable.

"Hello, Monroe. Did you eat?"

"Yes, Miss Cath'rine. I had enough spaghetti to choke a cow."

"Good. I hope you'll be rested by tomorrow."

Michael interrupted. "Monroe, after you take me to the navy yard, I want you to take the day off. Catherine's going to New York with the commander, and we won't need you or the car. Use it if you like, but keep it on the island. Don't drive in the city."

"Okay, Mr. Michael. I don't mind waiting for you folks. Anyway, I'm not going to no New York! Too crowded. I seen enough cars in two days to last two months."

"I want you to enjoy yourself, Monroe," Catherine said. "Michael, I think I'll go straight to bed. I want to be fresh tomorrow. I'm too tired to stay awake. Good night, Monroe."

"Good night, Miss Cath'rine. All your stuff is put away."

"Thank you, Monroe. You're a great help."

"I guess I'll go to bed too," Michael said. "I've got a full day ahead. Will you be okay tomorrow, Monroe? Do you need anything?"

"Well … ah, not me exactly, Mr. Michael. But the Stutz could use somethin'."

Michael slapped his forehead. "I'm sorry, Monroe, I didn't mean to forget."

"That's all right, Mr. Michael. You've been busy thinking 'bout going to war and all. A lot of stuff goin' on inside your head."

Michael handed him fifteen dollars, the pay they'd agreed to for the weekend. He gave Monroe an extra dollar for gasoline. Monroe smiled. It was like getting three weeks' pay for two days' work. Every weekend they were here, he'd receive another fifteen dollars. Monroe couldn't refuse.

He hadn't made that much money all at once since the band's crap game in Baltimore. Everyone, including Kid Scratch, had faded his two-dollar bet. When the dice came up Little Joe, there was a lot of snickering. Little Joe was the hardest point to make. Boxcars showed up next and then snake eyes and more snickering. He'd rolled the highest and lowest points with his first two casts. The dice weren't talking to him, so Monroe started talking to the dice. He coaxed them with loving words, tenderly rubbing the dice in his palms. Little Joe turned up on the fourth cast. The moans and groans from those who'd bet against him still rang in his ears. The band couldn't remember anyone ever making Little Joe with that much money in the pot.

"Thank you, sir! Good night, Mr. Michael."

Michael went to bed unsure why Monroe was so enthusiastic about being paid. They'd settled the issue before leaving Guilford.

Michael's First Mission

MONDAY, JUNE 3, 1918, PROMISED to be sunny. A warm breeze came from the southeast despite crossing cooler ocean waters. Michael's medical examination began shortly after entering the navy yard hospital.

The navy wanted three copies of each form. Michael had trouble recalling his medical history. Each form asked for his name, address, and date of birth. One asked for his next of kin and the name of a beneficiary. The last requested that he list three choices of assignment in order of preference. The last form was irrelevant since there'd be no time for the navy to approve any choice he'd make for stateside assignment.

With Commander Fields off duty, Captain Turnbull, the officer who'd reprimanded the guard at the gate when they'd first arrived, conducted the examination. The exam mirrored the one he took when he enlisted, though the more embarrassing parts were done with less zeal. Michael's reflexes passed as before. His sight was good enough not to require glasses. His first eye exam hadn't amounted to much more than counting them and making sure they'd open and close. The exam ended with a physical stress test.

For several minutes, Michael jogged in place, increasing his pace at the captain's request. The test was exhausting. His blood pressure was monitored, and heart and respiratory rates recorded. It seemed irrelevant to Michael. He didn't think doctors needed to run around an operating table when performing surgery on sedated patients. However, as a doctor, he appreciated the thoroughness of the exam. Michael took a shower before getting dressed and reporting back to the captain's office.

At around quarter to eleven, a low rumbling sound came from the ocean carried by the wind up the mouth of Upper New York Bay. Its origin wasn't clear. The noise swept across the navy yard, loud enough to be heard from the Jersey Shore to Battery Park in Lower Manhattan. The sound was rhythmic, cycling high and then low, sometimes disappearing altogether. At ten to eleven, the phone rang in the captain's office. He was told to send a squadron to investigate the noise. The Coast Guard was put on alert, and sub chasers were dispatched immediately. The call informed Captain Turnbull to be ready in case casualties resulted should the noise prove to be coming from a hostile source that turned to fight. Michael's curiosity was aroused by the captain's response.

"What's happening, sir?"

"They don't know, Michael. We'll dispatch some boats to look into it. It could be a freighter with engine trouble or a submarine charging batteries."

"Sir, is the navy yard sending boats out?"

"Yes. We send whatever is available. Why do you ask?"

"I'd like to go with them, sir, as an observer. If anyone gets hurt, I could handle it right there. I'd get some firsthand medical experience."

"Those boats could be out there for hours, Lieutenant. You're scheduled to tour this facility after lunch." The captain's tone didn't completely close the door on Michael's request. Searching Michael's face, a sigh barely escaped his lips. Grudgingly, he uttered, "All right! But you'd better hurry! Those boys don't waste any time. Their boats are in the water and warming up engines. Come here. I want to show you something." The captain led Michael to the window and pointed to the area of the navy yard where the boats were docked. "You see the shack over there with the radio tower alongside?"

"Yes, sir."

"Get there as fast as you can. I'll let them know you're coming, but they won't wait for you. You'll have to take your chances. And keep your fool head down! If it's a sub, the bastards may get a shot off before they go under."

Michael barely heard the warning. The door to the examination room was still swinging closed as he ran through the front entrance.

The captain simply shook his head, muttering, "Youth! They always jump first and then look!" Remembering his own youth, the captain smiled.

Michael crashed through the hospital entrance and began to run the quarter mile to the radio shed. He knew he'd be late. Luckily, the guard who'd stopped them at the main gate was driving toward him. Michael yelled for him to stop and jumped inside.

"Can I take you somewhere, sir?"

"Get me to that radio shed, Sergeant, and make it fast!"

"Yes, sir!" The guard pushed the accelerator pedal to the floor and was there in less than half the time it would have taken Michael to run. Before the vehicle came to a stop, Michael jumped out and ran the last few yards.

The dispatcher looked up as Michael flew through the door. He was just hanging up a telephone.

"Are you Lieutenant Morris, sir?"

"Yes."

"That was quick! Follow me, sir."

The dispatcher led Michael outside and pointed to a pier where four small boats were warming their engines. Michael ran to the nearest, gave its young captain his name and status, and asked permission to board on the authority of Captain Turnbull.

"A medical officer! I hope he isn't expecting the need of a surgeon. Come aboard, Lieutenant. We don't have time to chat."

Michael jumped the gap to the deck.

The officer turned to his crew chief and yelled, "Cast off!"

Engines roared, and a huge surge of water gushed behind the propellers as they followed the others to the center of the East River. On the river, the captain called for three-quarter speed, and Michael felt a surge of power that caused him to grab the edge of the boat to catch his balance. The captain ordered his steersman to pass the other three boats and take the lead. They passed the others under the Manhattan Bridge, and all four threw up bow spray as their keels bounced on the rough river surface.

Passing the Brooklyn Bridge, the keel began to level off. The boat was doing over twenty knots, threading a course between merchant ships on either side of the shipping lanes used to enter the East River piers. Occasionally, the commander pulled a lanyard, and the boat's horn sounded, warning of its approach to slower vessels.

"What do you think is out there, Commander?" Michael shouted over the roar of the engines.

"Harrison, Commander Robert Harrison. Could be a ship testing its engines or a submarine charging batteries. We won't know 'til we get there, Lieutenant. Sit back and enjoy the ride. The wind's been blowing inshore all morning. It could be carrying sound for miles. I didn't get your name, Lieutenant."

"Morris, Lieutenant Michael Morris."

"Welcome aboard, Lieutenant."

The squadron sped between Governors and Ellis Islands. The statue that brought tears to Catherine's eyes yesterday was off the starboard bow. Sighting it brought a wholly different feeling today. Its up-stretched hand seemed to hold a torch of battle, not the torch that promised freedom to the huddled masses.

As the boat approached the mouth of the bay, the commander called for full speed. The pitch of the engines grew high and strained. The bow of the boat slapped hard on the bay's waves, sending showers of spray over the foredeck when it hit a swell. The boat's speed impressed Michael. Wind generated by its speed was strong enough to make a man lose balance.

"What's our speed, Commander?"

"We should be doing close to thirty knots, Lieutenant. We're not as fast as a hydrofoil. But if it's a sub, we'll catch it. She'll stay on the surface as long as possible. They make seven or eight knots submerged. They can manage about seventeen on the surface. If it sees us, we may only get off a shot or two."

Michael noticed the small cannon near the bow.

The boat entered the open sea. Judging by his orders, the commander had done this before, possibly in anger. Michael had confidence in him and tried not to distract him. The commander told the radioman to ask for the positions of other squadrons responding from as far south as Sandy Hook. A minute later, he was told his squadron was in front. They'd be the first to discover the source—and first to shoot—if it were a U-boat.

In Kew Gardens, Monroe asked, "You sure you don't need me, Miss Cath'rine?"

"Yes, Monroe, I'm sure. Where will you go today?"

"A beach south of here. My friend told me 'bout it. Said go and see if I ever got up here.

He said I'd be surprised. I guess I'll know when I get there."

Monroe left for Coney Island at about nine. On the beach, with paper and pen from the study, he found an abandoned daily newspaper on a bench that would make a nice desk to finish his letter to Kid Scratch. The Kid was a member of their band in Baltimore. Monroe had promised to write to him about the trip to New York.

Monroe loved to write letters to his friends. He liked to imagine the expression on their faces as they read. To make his letters more interesting, he embellished his more mundane news with bits of fancy and exaggeration. He'd written a little over a page by the time the noise from coming from the ocean disturbed his concentration.

Kid Scratch, June 3, 1918, Coney Island

THINGS ARE FINE AND DANDY here. I am feeling very good after my trip. It was a somewhat successful trip. I only had one flat tire and made better time from Phila to New York City Sunday than I made from Balto to Phila Saturday.

Monroe, old pal, I really am indebted to you for your kindness, and I hardly know how to express my thanks. Did you leave the bass drum with Young or didn't Tinner tell you?

I spent the day at the Brooklyn Navy Yard, and you would be surprised to see the strange events there. Of course, we are only three miles from there, and we can easily reach there. I didn't care so *damn* much about it, because I was under a guard all day. You know Miss Morris's brother is some kind of high medical inspector there, and we carried him there. Otherwise, we would not have been admitted near the death trap.

In adding the words Michael had spoken the day before, he didn't explain the source of the comment. The oversight was unintentional. He hoped the words would inspire curiosity in the Kid. Indeed, the things he wrote didn't always hold to fact. The noise from the ocean caused him to lose concentration. He decided to finish the letter later. He contented himself to rest on the beach, amazed at seeing whites and browns swimming in the same ocean.

"There, Commander! Two points off the starboard bow." The boatswain's mate pointed off the bow at a dark object floating on the surface at least a mile away. At first glance, it had the outline of a channel buoy, which posed an obvious question. The channel was six miles behind them. Unless a buoy had broken its moorings, its shape also suited a conning tower.

"Hand me those binoculars, Lieutenant."

Michael retrieved the binoculars hanging near a console. He handed them to the commander.

The commander's eyes never left the object. Whatever it was, they were gaining on it, though not as fast as if it were still. He sighted the binoculars, focusing each lens and studied the object for only seconds.

"It's a German submarine! U-31 class. She's doing about twelve knots and hasn't seen us yet. Hold this bearing! Radio! Signal all boats we sighted a German submarine. Tell them to fall in behind me. If she turns, tell them to fan out and fire as the target bears."

The radioman signaled the other boats. Michael watched as each one disappeared behind the other, creating a single file and giving the U-boat less to see. It wouldn't know the strength of the squadron until they were on top of it and might stay on the surface to fight.

"Gunners, man your gun! Fire on my command! Radio! Signal base. Give them our position. Tell them to verify the contact to the other squadrons."

The gunners acted quickly and efficiently. They ran to the foredeck where the cannon was mounted. Seconds later, it was loaded and aimed, and they awaited the command to fire.

Michael watched it all, transfixed by an odd combination of fascination and dread. His heart began to pound. Watching their calm efficiency astounded him. They showed no anxiety. The commander's orders were carried out with a methodical precision. Not a single crewman seemed concerned about the presence of an enemy submarine.

"Damn! I think they spotted us. Commence firing!"

The cannon blast shook the boat and made Michael flinch. His heart beat faster than when he'd entered the radio shed. The back of his neck grew hot. Sweat from his brow stung his eyes. His skin felt prickly, and his stomach took on a life of its own. As a doctor, he knew a sudden surge of adrenaline caused his response.

Before the first shell hit water, three explosions from behind shattered the interval between shots. The other boats had opened fire. Their shells hissed overhead. The gunners on the foredeck fired again.

"She's submerging. Bow planes in the water. Engineer! Get me more speed!"

"Sir, we're already running hot. We can't maintain this speed much longer."

"Maintain it, damn it, and get me some more!" Angry over being spotted, Commander Harrison demanded speed. "I want all the speed you've got! I want it now, sailor!"

"Yes, sir!"

The squadron got off six rounds before the U-boat disappeared under the waves, leaving a boiling wake. A minute later, they were near the spot the U-boat was last seen. The entire event lasted fewer than five minutes. To Michael, it had seemed much longer.

"Engineer. Dead slow."

The engineer repeated the command, and the boat slowed to coasting speed as the tortured whine of the engines subsided, leaving sooty smoke swirling over its wake. Michael's nerves reacted in unison with the engines, calming with the engines.

"Radio. Signal the other boats. Tell them to fan out and circle the area. Thousand-yard sweeps. Five hundred feet apart, bearing on me. Crewman, what's that white speck floating on the surface over there?" The commander pointed out the object.

A crewman near the bow leaned over the rail for a closer look. "Looks like an unlit cigarette, sir."

The captain smiled. "We didn't give him enough time to light it, crewman."

Proud at the implication in the captain's statement, the entire crew laughed.

"All right, men, back to your stations. Keep an eye out for a periscope. I don't think they'll resurface, but they might want to have a look at us."

Though the queasiness in his stomach left the minute the submarine slid out of sight and the cannons stopped firing, Michael's heart rate was still fast for a man who'd been standing motionless for two minutes.

"Do you think we hit it, Commander?" His dry tongue was fit more for the inside of a shoe than his mouth. The commander noticed the uneasiness in Michael's voice.

"I can't be sure. We might have scratched it with our third shot. They got a welcome they weren't expecting, Lieutenant."

The boats continued to circle for another hour. By then, others boats joined the search. The U-boat never resurfaced. The commander assessed the situation aloud for his crew.

"If its batteries aren't fully charged, it won't come up again until dark. They're safe submerged. I don't expect we'll see it again today. Good work, men!"

"Won't he use his periscope to see if we've gone, sir?" Michael asked.

"It's unlikely. We might spot it. It could sink one of us, but he knows it won't do him much good. He's looking for bigger fish. The sub chasers are never far behind. We'll see them on the way back. Grab a seat, Lieutenant. You look a little frayed around the edges."

The ever-widening search pattern took them several thousand yards from the center of the action without seeing so much as a tailfin. If Michael hadn't witnessed the action firsthand, it would be difficult to convince him anything had happened.

The commander returned to his console and put the binoculars back in the spot Michael had found them. He rubbed his eyes with bare knuckles.

"A little water will help, Commander. It'll wash the salt out."

"Thanks, Lieutenant. I'll be fine. What do you think, Lieutenant Morris? Did we keep you entertained? The crew wouldn't want to get a reputation for throwing a dull party."

The crewmen nearby laughed. Michael did too. His tension was finally gone, replaced by the nagging thought that a submarine could be lurking underneath their keel.

"Anything but dull, sir. I won't say I'm disappointed that your guest decided to leave early! I'd be more careful who I invite to these parties, sir."

The commander smiled.

Michael's comment again brought laughter from the crew. For the first time, Michael felt he belonged. Up to then, the men had attended to business. Michael hoped it was the last time he'd ever see that sort of business. He'd had time to digest his reaction. Under the circumstances, an increase in adrenaline was normal. When the submarine was sighted, the danger of its presence hadn't registered until it submerged. What he hadn't expected was his stomach's reaction to the event. That had nothing to do with the chasing a submarine on uneven seas, the blast of a deck gun, or the odor of burned gunpowder. Only one thing remained.

Michael had witnessed the highly methodical and efficient procedures that led to taking life. The process sickened him. It was professional but impersonal. Crewmen used terms like Huns to define the enemy. They'd condensed their enemy to a single term, allowing procedure to drive them and work the process. The generalization of the term allowed them to be insulated from any feeling toward the men in the submarine. Harrison's crew had tried to sink a submarine. The crew inside meant nothing. Michael thought war might be harder to wage if the men who fought didn't classify their enemies using names like Huns, Fritz, Boche, Tommie, Mick, or Yank. Harrison's crewmen were trained. Their training circumvented feelings for the men they fought. The procedure became cold and mechanical. For Michael, it defined war. Procedure turned killing into a profession, and war turned men into professionals.

Michael had taken an oath to save lives with all the knowledge and talent he had. When he saw what war was like and had witnessed the process that opposed his oath, war was revealed to him more clearly than he'd ever described it to himself. The profession Michael chose was right for him. His craft was to repair bodies, not make bodies of men. He was yet to practice his profession. At a base hospital in France, he might be close enough to hear the sound of cannons but not close enough to feel them shake the ground. But like the men on board, other professionals would decide where he'd serve. The navy would send him where needed. He knew that before he volunteered. He knew that once he arrived, the wounded would come. He'd try to mend what remained of them, and, if necessary, remove whatever their wounds made impossible to mend.

Today, he'd seen war. He'd seen its cold efficiency, its military nature, and its incredibly disciplined execution. He'd seen war at its most basic level. Whether fought over religions, politics, geography, or power, war boiled down to a determined, systematic profession to turn living men into dead men.

Considering Catherine

COMMANDER FIELDS WAS A MAN who kept appointments, particularly with women. At ten o'clock sharp, his Type 22A American Underslung stopped in front of the house in Kew Gardens. He reached to squeeze the rubber orb that honked the horn but thought better of it. Catherine wasn't a woman to be summoned by honking. She had intellect and manners. The night before, she had been the most beautiful woman in the restaurant. A lady. He left the car and walked toward the house. When Catherine came out to meet him, he was forced to rethink that impression.

A pleated navy-blue skirt barely covered her knees, revealing softly curved calves covered by black stockings. She wore a white blouse open at the neck and a partly buttoned red vest that accentuated a tiny waist under ample breasts. A dark blue full-brimmed hat, nearly old navy-style, adored her head. She'd tied red and white ribbons around its crown. The ends fell over her shoulders. The sophisticated woman he remembered the night before had become an innocent young girl. She looked like a poster girl for coeds dressed in red, white, and blue.

Her hair caused his eyes to widen and made his lips part. She'd tied braids from her temples behind her head. What remained fell behind her back in a cascade resembling a light-brown waterfall that almost reached her waist. She was stunning, a fully grown woman in a girl's costume. She smiled at him. At a loss for words, he finally managed, "You look positively radiant, Catherine! It's an amazing outfit. I didn't expect anything like it."

"Thank you, Commander. I hope it's not too girlish. I'm glad you wore your uniform. Shall we go? Would you prefer a cup of tea first?"

The invitation didn't seem to register at first. He was captivated by her appearance. The word "tea" finally penetrated his sensibility and restored focus.

"Tea? Yes. Thanks. That would be nice." At this point, he'd agree to anything she wanted. In the few hours since they'd met, she'd transformed from reserved to beautiful to totally free.

Catherine was at home serving tea. A family tradition inspired by her English-born mother, her practiced style of serving had earned her a reputation as host of tea parties in Baltimore.

Commander Fields noticed the elegant way she handled the simple task. Her movements reminded him of the ritual Japanese tea ceremony he'd witnessed it as a young ensign. President Roosevelt had ordered a fourteen-month tour of the Great White Fleet to demonstrate American naval power to the world.

"I was thinking about the cruise Roosevelt sent us on in 1907. I'd just joined the navy. We anchored in Tokyo Bay. I had a chance to tour some local villages. I had a chance to be treated to the tea ceremony practice by Japanese ladies," he explained.

Catherine became aware of his close observation.

"Am I doing it as well as they, Commander?"

"You're doing fine."

"So, you sailed with the Great White Fleet?"

"Yes. You must have been barely in your teens!"

"I was. I admit I had no personal interest in it. Father followed the voyage in the newspapers. It was all he talked about for weeks. John, my older brother, was thinking of becoming a sailor then. He changed his mind by the time he graduated. He's flying for the French now."

Her voice softened when she spoke of John. The commander noticed. Her concern for her brother was obvious.

"I see. You have two very interesting brothers, Catherine. John thinks navy and joins the air service. Michael becomes a doctor and joins the navy. I wonder what's in store for you."

Catherine smiled. Their tea finished, she put the empty cups in the sink. "I couldn't see much of New York last night. I'm glad you invited me today."

"You're more than welcome. I hope you enjoy it as much as I will."

Fields helped her into the sporty car. The top was off the two-seat Underslung, and there was no windshield. Had she done her hair the way she'd done it in Baltimore, the wind might well make a mess of it. The commander handed her a pair of goggles to help keep the wind out of her eyes.

"Do you own two machines, Commander? The one last night was larger."

"No. I wish I had a closed car. This one's mine. The other belongs to Captain Turnbull. The man amazes me. He's in his fifties, yet all three of his girls are in high school! I admire him, but I don't envy him. They're all active and brilliant. He claims most of the credit, but I imagine Mrs. Turnbull played a part." He glanced at her. She laughed.

Midmorning was sunny and warm. To save her any discomfort, he drove slowly.

"I noticed its name on the grille. Why is it called an Underslung?"

"To be honest, I haven't a clue. Sounds more like an illegal baseball pitch."

Traffic near the river grew heavy. It took longer to reach the bridge than it had the night before. Catherine was familiar with the route, but the novelty of crossing the bridge remained. The view of the city was spectacular from the bridge.

"Over there, Catherine! On the river! Do you see those boats coming toward us? They're from the navy yard."

Catherine saw four fast boats leaving long wakes, easily passing larger boats on the river.

"Why do you say they're from the navy yard?"

"They're pursuit boats. Probably on some exercise. They drill every week or so to keep themselves sharp. Strange, though. They usually go out Fridays, not Mondays."

Many New Yorkers couldn't hear the noise from the ocean. Those in Manhattan who did thought little of what they heard. The sounds of the city and clatter of horseshoes on pavement were enough to absorb the low rumbling of a U-boat's diesel engine. As for Catherine, the last thing on her mind was Michael as his boat passed under the Brooklyn Bridge.

Across the bridge, the commander drove north on Broadway, a street that cut the island in half from Times Square to Seventh Avenue. He turned east and parked the Underslung near the Plaza Hotel on Central Park South, better known as Millionaire's Row. He walked around the car and took her hand to help her out.

"You mentioned a park in Baltimore last night. Druid Hill, wasn't it? I thought you might enjoy a ride in ours. We'll get a hansom cab."

"Central Park, isn't it, Commander?"

"Yes. If you like parks, I think you'll enjoy this."

Fields took her arm, and they walked to a row of cabs waiting in a line along the curb. The drivers all wore livery. The horses were well groomed and decorated in finely crafted leather harnesses studded with bells. He chose the first in line.

"Take us through the park, please. We may want to stop along the way."

"Yes, sir. Is there somewhere you want to stop in particular?"

"I haven't decided. Take the west side to the lake."

The man simply lifted and lowered the reins, sending a leathery wave down the back of the horse, which responded by walking. Immediately, the bells on the harness came to life. As they turned into the street, another wave of the reins brought the horse to a trot. The sound of its hooves on pavement became rhythmic, matching the jangle of the bells on its harness.

"Catherine, I didn't want to say anything last night because of your brother. I wish you'd call me Bill or even William. I'd like to be your friend. My friends call me by my first name."

Catherine smiled. "I'd be happy to call you William. Somehow, Bill doesn't suit you."

The commander smiled and said, "Kate wouldn't suit you."

For a time, they were silent. The air in the park was more refreshing than the city streets, and the relaxed pace of the horse-drawn hansom cab found them content to look at the passing scenery. Catherine enjoyed the pace. It carried her back to the tranquil time before the war. Taking her hand seemed natural. She made no effort to remove it.

"It's peaceful here," she said, "something like Druid Hill Park, but with more trees."

"Catherine, I wanted to speak to you about it since last night. I didn't think it appropriate to get into the subject deeply, and I don't mean to impose on your personal life where I may not be welcome."

"You're talking about my future. Am I right?"

He was surprised she remembered.

"Yes, exactly. Do you mind my talking about it?"

"No. You spoke of it last night and hinted at it this morning. It's been on my mind much more lately. I was wondering what you thought last night."

"You have an unused talent, Catherine. I took the liberty of speaking to Captain Turnbull this morning. He agrees. If you're willing, he said he'd call a friend in Washington. The State Department sent out a request for a woman who's fluent in French but without much luck finding the right person. They were either not the age they wanted or too busy with family. The few who qualified wanted to work close to home. Would you be interested in working for the State Department?"

His question stunned Catherine. The magnitude of change it would bring to her life was breathtaking. She'd pledged to learn more about the war. Where better to learn than the State Department? It made perfect sense. She knew French. They needed people who knew French. She was certain Michael would agree. The opportunity would give her a chance to contribute to the war effort in the only way she could.

"Yes. I'd be very interested. Very interested indeed!"

As soon she spoke, the fear of being alone in Guilford vanished.

"That's the spirit! I was hoping you'd say yes."

"To be honest, I didn't expect this. I can't tell you how happy I am to know that someone is concerned enough about my future to actually care."

"You're the one who'll be helping, Catherine. I'll tell the captain tonight. He'll let you know what to do. It may take time, but I don't foresee any difficulty with Captain Turnbull on your side. Let's walk through the park. Are you up to it?"

"Yes. It's too much to take in from a cart."

"Driver, stop here, please."

The cab stopped near the lake. William told the driver they wouldn't need him anymore and paid the man full fare. They began walking east toward Seventy-First Street with Catherine's arm in his.

"Tell me about Bryn Mawr, Catherine."

"There isn't much to tell. When Wilson was elected, the college gathered as much information as possible about his lectures there."

"I don't mean Wilson. I mean you. What sort of life did you have there?"

"Well, I studied French, of course. I joined an English literary club and wrote a little poetry. They published one in a small poetry pamphlet. Nothing unusual."

"You've written poetry? In French?"

"Oh, no! In English. I had more than enough French writing to do."

"Do you remember the poem you wrote? I mean, could you recite it? I'd like to hear it."

"I'm not sure, William. It's been a while since I wrote the poem."

"Try, Catherine. Believe it or not, poetry is a secret passion of mine. I don't write it, of course. I enjoy reading it. Vachel Lindsay, Robert Frost, and Whitman are my favorites."

"Let me think. Promise not to laugh!"

"Catherine, you're stalling. I wouldn't laugh at your poem."

"All right. I visited the ocean a few days. I enjoy walking on the beach. The sunset is so beautiful. I remember it all. I called it 'At Dusk by Sea.'"

Reciting poetry, especially her own, was not her forte. Poetry was rooted closer to her soul than her mouth. The poem was a favorite, written after she'd left the beach that evening. Embarrassed, she spoke its verses very softly.

An iced-orange sun was
melting by degrees into the sea,
leaving its liquid light
on the rough-road sea surface,
dead-ending where the waves
stumbled onto the shoreline to
shatter in a muted explosion of orange sparks.

Behind, the beach was an unmade bed,
seasoned by the sodium seawater,
waiting for the wind to pull tight
its salty sand blanket.

Standing there, where the two met,
I could only wonder
at the power of the living ocean,
pushing and pulling
at the lifeless land as would hands
kneading a lump of dough—
plying it malleable.

Which would last longer?
Water or land—sea or sand?
Innermost feelings found
comfort in the hopeful answer ... neither.

The commander stood still for a moment, pondering its meaning. The struggle between sea and land could easily be compared to the tides of war. For a while, they walked along the path arm in arm, following it as it bent southward. As they approached the zoo, Commander Fields finally broke the silence.

"Catherine, your imagery is beautiful but also profound."

"I was simply trying to describe my mood, William."

"I still say it was beautiful and profound."

Catherine blushed.

They entered the zoo near the southwestern corner of the park. She watched the caged animals behind iron bars. It made her sad to see their confinement. They didn't stay long.

"Are you hungry, Catherine?"

"Yes ... a little."

"Let's get back to the car."

After eating lunch in a small restaurant in Little Italy, they spent time walking. They explored shops that caught their interest. Avenues in the old section of New York passed by like so many pages in a travel brochure. They would have enjoyed being together as much had they been walking in the desert. William was careful not to stray too far from the car.

"Are you getting tired, Catherine?"

Catherine's attention was elsewhere at the time.

"Look, William, it's my name."

A street sign had "Catherine" printed in bold letters.

"I see it, Catherine. You must be a famous poet in New York. They've named a street after you!"

"Don't be silly, William. It's a wonderful day, and I've enjoyed every minute. But I am getting a little leg weary. Perhaps we ought to start back."

Time had flown. It was late in the afternoon. The commander apologized for keeping her so long.

"Please, really, William. I've enjoyed every minute."

"Catherine, I've learned something about you I never would have expected."

"What's that? You aren't going to embarrass me, are you?"

"No. But if you prefer, I'll say nothing more about it to be on the safe side."

"William! That's not fair. Don't tease. Father always said you should finish what you start."

"Well … you're definitely not the young woman I first met. You're not only beautiful, you're thoughtful, and your feelings run much deeper than I'd imagined. I'm glad we're friends. I'd like to do this again. I hope that doesn't embarrass you."

Watching her reaction, he noticed she was blushing. He kissed her cheek.

"I'm glad you like me, William. Shall we go on?"

They walked in silence to the car, hand in hand. He drove to the house in Kew Gardens.

"You didn't answer my question, Catherine."

"What question?"

"About seeing you again."

"Yes, William. I'd like that very much."

Her look caused his heart to beat faster.

"I wasn't sure how you felt. I mean, whether you thought I was being too forward."

She stopped long enough to say, "Now you know, Commander William Fields."

Again, he kissed her on the cheek. She kissed him lightly on the lips.

"Who's being forward now?" he said. He followed an impulse to hug her, and changed the subject. "It may be a while before Turnbull has anything. I'll let you know."

The commander started the car. As he drove away, he squeezed the horn.

She watched as he drove the Underslung away, waving good-bye.

Monroe Finishes His Letter

WHEN CATHERINE ENTERED THE HOUSE in Kew Gardens, she was surprised to see both Michael and Monroe sitting in the study. They looked as though they'd been waiting for her. All three had stories to tell.

"Michael? I didn't expect you back this early. And Monroe, I thought you'd still be at the beach! Why are you here?"

Monroe stood up as if to make a speech.

"Well, miss, there was so much carryin's on out there." Monroe looked at Michael. "The beach was too noisy, miss. Too noisy, right, Mr. Michael? Maybe it'll be better tomorrow." He looked at Michael, trying to yield the storytelling to him.

Having had firsthand experience, Michael should be the primary storyteller.

Michael wasn't sure the chase on the ocean would shock her. Monroe, on the other hand, found it hard to restrain himself and quickly grew impatient for Michael to speak. Keeping folks in suspense was easier for Monroe when he was the primary storyteller.

"I'm glad you're back, Catherine. Did you and the commander enjoy yourselves in New York?"

Monroe's eyes turned upward. Monroe was never good at hiding his nervousness. He began to rock side to side on his feet, hands behind his back.

"Yes, Michael. It was wonderful, and I have news. But why are you here?"

Monroe stopped rocking. The time for Michael's story had arrived.

"News? What news?" Michael thought her news might be connected to his. It was possible the commander had heard about the U-boat before leaving the navy yard. Everyone at the navy yard heard the rumbling of diesel engines.

Monroe thought otherwise. She'd have said so if she knew. A spectator to their conversation, patience wasn't Monroe's strongest virtue. Putting off a good story was the tactic he'd pulled in Philadelphia to surprise people. Was Michael doing that now? Why was he waiting so long to tell her?

"Yes, well, tentative news. I can tell you about it while we eat. We walked most of the afternoon, and I feel a little sticky. I need to freshen up. Do you mind, Michael?"

That's too much! Monroe thought. Now, Miss Cath'rine was going to go wash up and put off her telling her story! He'd waited an hour for this! Working for white folks could be plain exasperating sometimes. Monroe's rocking renewed. He looked at Michael with a worried expression. Michael just winked at him! Monroe stopped rocking. Maybe storytelling time had finally come.

"Of course not, Cath! Actually, I was thinking of other news. For a moment, I thought you knew what it was."

Monroe started to rock again. Why didn't he just tell her!

"I don't understand, Michael. What are you talking about? Monroe, why are you rocking back and forth? You keep fidgeting."

Monroe stopped rocking.

Fidgeting wasn't the word for it. He was about to explode!

"It's nothin' much, miss. I jus' been waitin' for you folks to decide who's gonna say what to who! Maybe if I go to the kitchen an' make some tea, you folks'll finally start tellin' your stories!" He crossed his fingers behind his back and waited for one of them to speak. The rocking started again.

Puzzled, Catherine turned her attention to Michael.

"Michael, what's he talking about?"

Monroe's rocking stopped. It was storytelling time!

"Are you sure you don't want to freshen up first? I could tell you over dinner if you like."

A deep sigh escaped from Monroe. "I gives up!"

"What's wrong, Monroe?" she asked.

"Well, miss, I jus' wish one o' y'all would start sayin' somethin' about somethin' to somebody and quit whippin' a dead horse! If y'all got anythin' to say, y'all oughta go ahead and say it!"

"All right, Monroe." Michael's words brought a sigh of relief. Inexplicably, Michael shifted the floor to Monroe. "I don't know where to start. Monroe, why don't you tell her what you heard on the beach?"

Monroe wasn't expecting to be the one to start, but it was just as well. If he didn't, the damned story would never get told.

"Well, miss, I was on the beach writin', and this rumblin' noise comes up outta the ocean. I bought an extra on the way back here and read 'bout it. Now, Mr. Michael should be the one to tell you about it. They went out to find out what it was about."

Catherine was a confused. "What noise? What's this about, Michael? What's he talking about? What does he mean that you went to find out about it?"

"Go on, Monroe. You're doing fine," Michael said. After another sigh, Monroe continued.

"Yes, sah, Mr. Michael. Anyways, I was on the beach like I said, miss, writin' a letter to a friend, when this mighty roarin' comes off the ocean soundin' like a rumblin' noise. Made me put my letter down. That's about all there was 'til I got that paper. I went home, and Mr. Michael came back. Now, can I get you folks some tea? I'm gettin' powerful thirsty doin' all the talkin' here."

Monroe had done his part. It was Michael's turn.

"Thanks, Monroe. I'll have a cup. How about you, Cath?"

"Do you mind, Monroe? After all, it's your day off."

"I don't mind, Miss Cath'rine. I'll start the water. I want to come back to hear Mr. Michael finish this story. I been waitin' since you got back." He left to start tea.

Michael began with the examination room, since that's where it all began. He mentioned his dash outside and told her about the gate guard taking him to the radio shed. "If the guard hadn't been there, I'd have missed the boat."

"You were on a boat, Michael?"

"Yes, Cath. On one of the four fastest."

Catherine thought back.

"Commander Fields and I were crossing the bridge this morning. He pointed out four boats on the river. He told me they were from the navy yard. I didn't think anything of it at the time. You must have been on one of them. Where were they going?"

"The noise. We went to investigate the noise Monroe was talking about. I went along out of curiosity and in case anyone was injured. You wouldn't believe how fast they are. We were practically flying! Got to the ocean in minutes."

Monroe came from the kitchen with a tray loaded with a teapot and three cups. Michael finished the story. After serving them, he poured himself a cup and sat in a chair near the window. Monroe watched for Catherine's reaction.

Catherine was astonished by what she'd heard. Except for the queasiness he'd felt in his stomach, Michael had told her everything. He hadn't mentioned it to Monroe.

"I'd no idea, Michael. The commander and I heard nothing at all. I'm sure he's only learning about it now. It frightens me to think what could have happened!"

Michael sensed she may be blaming herself for spending time with the commander while he was in danger.

"It was nothing like that, Cath. John's in more danger than we were. The men handled it. It was over in a few minutes. We circled for a while and then came back. That's all it was."

The comparison between him and John didn't help. It served to remind her of the danger their older brother faced. His next question took her mind completely off the subject.

"It's your turn. What about New York? What's this news you were talking about?"

Her concern for Michael vanished. Her story changed everything. She was confident and a little proud, two feelings she hadn't had since graduating.

Monroe sensed the conversation was becoming private and rose before she spoke.

"If you folks'll excuse me, I should be thinkin' 'bout what we're goin' to eat for dinner."

"No, Monroe. It's your day off. Don't worry about Catherine and me. I'm taking her out for dinner."

"I don't know 'bout dat, Mr. Michael. The extra said there was goin' to be a blackout tonight. You folks won't see where you're goin'."

Michael smiled. Still, Monroe's comment gave him something to think about.

"That might be a problem, Catherine. If we leave soon, we needn't worry. We'll be home before dark. There's plenty of daylight left. I saw a little restaurant not far from here. Shall we go?"

"All right, Michael. Monroe, thank you for offering dinner, but I'll go with Michael. I've got to talk to him about something, and I want to hear more about this business on the ocean. Will you be all right?"

"Yes, Miss Cath'rine. You go on. I'll be jus' fine and dandy." Actually, Monroe felt a bit uneasy about being alone. If they were late, he'd be alone in a blackout.

"We won't be long, Monroe," Michael assured him.

Once Catherine freshened up, they walked to where Monroe parked the Stutz, leaving him to provide for his dinner a second time. Monroe wasn't thinking about dinner. After they left, he changed his mind about waiting to finish his letter. He was more interested in writing than eating. Writing would take his mind off blackouts.

Letter in hand, he went to the study and put it on the desk. He sat where Michael had been sitting behind the desk. Good letters took time to write, and he had a lot to write about. The hurry came in mailing it once it was finished.

Before continuing, he changed the three in June 3 to a four. It made sense to him. He wouldn't mail the letter until tomorrow morning, June 4. Of course, the main reason to mail the letter tomorrow was the thought of being caught outside in a blackout. Besides, he didn't know where the nearest post office was and would never find it in the dark. Tomorrow morning was soon enough to mail a damned letter.

To get back in letter-writing mood, Monroe picked it up and read as much as he'd written. After the part "Monroe, old pal, I really am indebted," he wondered if Kid Scratch would know he was quoting what Michael had said to him. He wanted Kid Scratch to read his exact words. So far, that was the best part of the whole damned trip. If the Kid didn't get it, that was okay. Monroe decided to leave it the way it was. He liked what Michael had said, and it sounded just fine to him. It would keep the Kid in suspense. He'd explain it later.

Satisfied he'd solved the problem, he started writing where he'd left off, barely able to wait to see how it would turn out.

> Yesterday morning about twenty of eleven we were very much worked up over an awful roaring which came from over the ocean, and hydroplanes and chasers soon were in squadrons going in the direction, and six hours later returned, and in less than two hours, extras were out stating that German submarines had been fired on by the Coast Guard a few miles off the Delaware capes, which is in easy reach off New York City, and tonight the city is in darkness and will be until further notice, and oh boy, I wish I was home. It makes you feel a sort of shaky.

> There's plenty of browns here, and you can go anywhere white people go. They even bathe in the ocean together, and it seems so cold I take mine in the tub where there's not so much water and hot at that.

> Remember me to all the boys, and give me their addresses so I can write them.

> Respectively,
> Monroe

There, it was finished. Monroe folded the letter in the middle twice, making a neat rectangle that just fit into a small envelope he took from the desk. He wrote the Kid's address using his given name, Frederick T. Lincoln II. The *T* stood for Taliaferro.

The Kid told him he was named after three men—Frederick Douglas, Booker T. Washington, and his grandfather, who was named after Abraham Lincoln by Yankee soldiers when he was freed. Frederick preferred Kid Scratch. He told Monroe the name Scratch came from earning everything he had from scratch. Most of what the Kid said was true. He was named after three famous men. But his nickname was earned in a poolroom from sinking the cue ball too often. The name stuck, so a new story was made up for reasons of pride to convince his new friends. A low nickname became a proud one—at least for those who'd never seen the Kid play pool.

At the restaurant, Michael and Catherine neared the end of their meal. Michael was beaming about Catherine's chance to become an interpreter. He wished her luck.

"I think it's a great idea, Cath. A big concern off your mind. I wouldn't worry about Mother. She managed well enough after John left. This is nothing like that."

"It's not as if I'd be doing anything like you or John. I suppose I'll be assigned an office somewhere in the State Department, if all goes well. I'm not sure about anything yet."

"Don't worry, Cath. It's perfect for you. Who knows? You might get involved in things more important than John or I ever dreamed."

"Michael, don't exaggerate! I just wanted to have a small part in what you and John are doing. This position will help me do that."

"I'm proud of you. They couldn't find anyone better. They'd be foolish not to take you. I hope I don't leave before you know. If I do, let me know how it went."

Michael saw something in Catherine change. He liked what he saw.

They returned to Kew Gardens. Monroe was cleaning pots and dishes in the sink. He'd warmed the leftover spaghetti from the night before and didn't care if he saw another spaghetti noodle for a month.

Catherine went to the kitchen and saw him cleaning up. Seeing Monroe wash dishes was odd. She'd always seen him do more manly chores. He never did dishes in Guilford. Before her mother went to Arizona, she'd always helped with the dishes. Monroe seemed out of place in front of a sink full of unwashed dinnerware.

"Monroe, let me do those for you."

"Oh, no, Miss Cath'rine. I'm pretty much done here. You go on and talk with Mr. Michael. I'll bring some hot tea soon as I finish."

"Thank you, Monroe, but I haven't room for another thing after dinner. I'll ask Michael if he'd like a cup."

Michael overheard and called from the study.

"No, thanks, Cath. I'm fine." Michael finished a short letter to his mother that didn't mention his adventure on the ocean. No harm had come of it. It wasn't necessary to worry her. Catherine entered the study to ask him whether he'd heard anything new about his departure.

"No. I didn't get to tour the hospital. I'll let you know as soon as I hear anything."

"Michael, I'm tired, and I need a bath. I'll say good night."

"Go ahead, Cath. I won't be very far behind you. It's been a busy day for both of us."

Monroe came into the study with a small pot of tea.

"I thought one of you folks might want some, anyway, Mr. Michael. I made enough for everybody so's I can sit with you awhile, if that's all right."

"Okay, Monroe. Thanks. I can use the company. Catherine's going to bed."

Monroe picked up the newspaper he'd bought that afternoon to look for news about James's unit. Michael was lost in thought. Monroe paused to read news about a submarine. The paper mentioned two recent sinkings. A steamer called the *President Lincoln* and a schooner named the *Edward H. Cole* had been sunk.

"What's a schooner, Mr. Michael?"

"A schooner? It's a two-masted sailing boat. Why do you ask?"

"Says here they sunk a schooner off the coast yesterday. *Edward H. Cole.* They got another boat called the *President Lincoln*!"

"Sailing is more dangerous today, now that we're in the war. Have you seen anything about Château-Thierry? I was wondering whether we managed to hold on to it."

Monroe saw the article in the center of the front page.

"Says here the men from Third Marines held 'em south of the Marne. Says they was supported by the Second and the Twenty-Eighth. I guess our boys showed 'em where the line was drawn, Mr. Michael."

"Sounds like it. I don't think the Germans are finished just yet. They'll probably regroup and try again. There's still plenty of war left, Monroe. It's not even close to being over."

"Yes siree. They might do that, Mr. Michael. Always up to no good."

Monroe put the paper down, his thoughts turning to his son, James. Monroe was worried. Michael was right. The ground fighting wasn't over. Attacks. Retreats. Battle followed battle. It made little sense to him. Millions were dead, and millions more might die. Nearly four years had passed, and the front lines had hardly moved since the first trenches were dug. The paper made no mention of his son's outfit. The news was dominated by today's events on the sea.

"Well, I guess I'll go on to bed, Mr. Michael. I'll take your cup if you're done."

Monroe's voice lost the power it usually had. Michael noticed the change but thought he was just tired. Monroe was troubled that he couldn't find anything in the news about James's unit. Letters from his son were all he had to tell him what James was doing. Censorship prevented him from knowing where his son was. Before he left, Michael thought he'd mention Catherine's situation.

"Monroe, there's a chance that Catherine will be sent to Washington. It's nothing definite, but I want to you know that as long as the house is in the family, we want you to stay and take care of it. I'll let know you as soon as anything becomes certain."

Michael's comment turned his thoughts from James.

"Yes, sir, Mr. Michael. After all these years, I don't plan on goin' nowhere. I owe it to your father from times when you was just a boy. The Lord's got him now. He'd want me to stay and watch over Miss Cath'rine. I'll be there as long as you say."

"Thanks, Monroe."

Michael rose and offered his hand. Monroe took it and then went to bed. He stared at the ceiling. His thoughts returned to his son. He imagined the guns, bombs, and death. A stream of unanswered questions floated through his mind until he was asleep.

The next day, they learned that several U-boats had been very busy the day before. Nine ships were sunk along the coast, and mines were discovered off Delaware Bay. Michael wasn't going anywhere until the shipping lanes were declared safe. On June 4, 1918, the ports in New York closed.

The Morrises Are Assigned—1918

IN KEW GARDENS ON THE morning of June 7, 1918, newspapers carried more of the story about the German mines found off the coast. Catherine had read most of the first page.

"Michael, do you think the submarine you saw put the mines in the bay?"

"I don't know. Frankly, I didn't know they could lay mines until I read about it. I thought they carried torpedoes, not mines."

"It says here minesweepers have cleared them, at least those that were reported. I suppose the navy will declare the bay is safe for shipping soon."

"True. Still, ships leaving port will have to be alert. Anyway, what should we do this weekend, Cath? See the sights?"

She heard but continued to read. The headline story said Americans were fighting in Belleau Wood. Their first attack against Hindenburg's strategist, a man named Ludendorff, was under way in a wooded area west of Château-Thierry. The outcome was still in doubt.

"Michael, it says our marines attacked a wood without a barrage. What do they mean? Is a barrage needed to attack? What are hand grenades and mortars?"

He ignored her questions, returning to his own. "Would you like to go to New York when I come back tonight? We really should decide what we're going to do this weekend."

"I know, Michael, but tell me about these. I promised myself to learn more about this."

Her interest in the details of battle was not like Catherine, but her tone was insistent. He kept his response brief and to the point.

"Oh, all right. An artillery barrage destroys things like barbed wire and chases the enemy to the rear. The attack usually follows the barrage. When did you get so interested in how war is conducted? Do you really want to know about that?"

"Yes. If I'm going to the State Department, I should learn as much as I can. Go on, Michael."

She was serious! He either must continue or risk antagonizing her by trying to change the subject. Her attitude had certainly changed, and Michael wasn't sure what the State Department had to do with it.

"Okay. Mortars are like artillery. They have a high trajectory and don't carry as far." Michael stopped. He didn't see the need for this and hoped she'd drop the issue.

"Well, what of hand grenades?"

"Really, Catherine? All right! They're small hand-thrown bombs. Are you satisfied now?"

A moment of silence fell as Catherine thought about what he'd said. A puzzled expression came over her. Having watched her expression change, he grew curious.

"What now? You look puzzled."

"The newspaper says the marines attacked without mortars or hand grenades. From what you've just told me—"

Michael interrupted. "That's strange! They normally do! Especially before attacking wooded areas." Michael's own puzzlement peaked over the apparent lack of preparation for the attack. He crossed the room.

"The article says there was no barrage," she noted.

"That can't be right. Let me see that."

"Really, Michael, I know how to read!"

She handed the paper to him, certain that she'd read correctly.

"You're right! That's not usual. They must have wanted to surprise them and take the place quickly. I don't think either side has done it that way, Catherine. I guess they didn't want to give the Germans time to prepare a defense. But according to this, casualties were high. They're still fighting."

Michael forgot about the weekend. His mind filled with visions of wounded men lying in the woods. He could be treating them if he were in France. He became upset at the delay in his posting and the debatable leadership that may have caused so much suffering. He decided to return to the hospital.

"Catherine, I'll ask Monroe to drive me to the hospital. Maybe they know more."

When he arrived, he asked Monroe to wait. He was immediately called into Captain Turnbull's office.

"I'm glad you're here. It saves me the trouble of calling you. Have a seat, Michael. I have a piece of paper you'll be interested in reading. It explains why I wanted to see you."

Captain Turnbull handed him a copy of his orders from the Department of the Navy. Plans were made for Michael's weekend.

By order Department of the Navy   NO: 16857-PD-OSN
Issuing authority: Secretary the   Attention: Captain John Turnbull
Honorable Josephus Daniels   Brooklyn Naval Yard (BNY)

RE: Lt. Michael Ryan Morris   Date: 5 June 1917
                        Subject: Disposition of Personnel

Status: Extremely Confidential   Effective Date: Immediate

Attention to orders:

1. Pursuant to Naval Regulations the following Naval Order is issued above date.
2. Lt. Michael Ryan Morris will proceed to a port of embarkation earliest transport. Destination France. Lt. Morris will report to General Headquarters, Chaumont, France, within 48 hours after debarkation.
3. Directly reporting to Col. George C. Marshall Jr. (GHQ, AEF), Lt. Morris will be temporarily assigned to the Allied Expeditionary Force (AEF) as directed.
4. This NO# 16857-C is approved under authority Josephus Daniels, Secretary of the Navy, Adm. William S. Sims, Commanding Officer, Fleet Naval Operations pursuant to orders of Capt. Winton C. Kenwood, Assistant Chief, Naval Operations, Department of the Navy, and under authority of Gen. John J. Pershing, Commander in Chief, AEF.

Cc: US Naval Dept, Records Div., Col. G . C. Marshall Jr., Capt. John Turnbull,

Lt. Michael Ryan Morris, and respective commanders.

"Michael, the next convoy gets under way tomorrow afternoon. Your orders are your travel voucher. The ship is scheduled to sail at 13:00 from Montauk Point on Long Island. You'll be told the name of the ship tomorrow morning. I'm afraid you won't be able to tell Catherine when you're leaving. Normally, it would be okay. Some VIPs are sailing on the same ship, and the Department of the Navy insisted on secrecy. They don't want to risk a rumor that may alert German U-boats."

Michael was speechless. He'd be sailing to France tomorrow! "Yes, sir. I knew the navy would assign me. I just never thought I'd be reporting to an army officer."

"The orders come from the navy, Michael. General Pershing has immediate need of qualified surgeons. I suspect they'll assign you to a base hospital. On the ship, you'll be temporarily attached to the ship's medical staff. Take a train or bus to Chaumont, whichever is faster."

"Yes, sir. I was hoping I could tell Catherine when I'm leaving. I can't just go without—"

"Michael, I suspect if I checked, they'd say no. So, I'm not going to ask. For Catherine's sake, as long as you don't give her the name of the ship, I think we can bend that part of the orders. I'm sure she wouldn't tell anyone. It's bad enough she won't be able to see you off. Use the rest of the day to get your gear together. I know your sister will want some time with you. I'll have Commander Fields take you back to Kew Gardens. Under the circumstances, it'll be quicker than calling your chauffeur back."

"Thank you, sir. Monroe might take Catherine to the beach to shop."

"If you need anything, tell me. I might be able to get it before you sail. To be honest, I wish I could go with you, but they need me here. My requests for transfer have been denied. By the way, when you first came I remember saying that I'd tell you about your father. I met him in 1911, after the Triangle Shirtwaist fire. I learned a lot about treating burns from him. I never saw a man work so hard for so long. He volunteered, you know, and never took a penny for it. I was very sorry when you said he died."

"Thank you, sir. He never spoke about his work at home."

No one answered the phone in Kew Gardens. Michael talked with Commander Fields about his assignment before walking to the hospital for midday rounds.

"I'm glad you came, Michael. Captain Turnbull just called. He wants to see you and Catherine before you sail. I'll come get you tomorrow morning before ten. Give my regards to Catherine."

Michael found Monroe waiting for him as asked.

Michael laid everything he needed on the bed. He packed his spare uniform and essential clothing and sorted through personal items he wanted to bring. He'd ask Monroe to take the rest home to Guilford. By the time Monroe brought Catherine back, he'd finished. He shut the bedroom door so as not to surprise her and asked her to come to the study.

"Michael! Why are you home at this hour? I thought you were at the hospital. Is something wrong?"

"Nothing's wrong, Cath. I was given some time off."

From his expression, she knew something was on his mind. She asked Monroe to put her purchases in the hall closet. When Monroe left, Michael told her the news.

"Orders came today, Cath. I'm sailing to France tomorrow. It came a bit sooner than I expected." He looked for her reaction. A silence fell over her as the full meaning and its implications settled around her like a dark gray cloud.

"I hope you understand, Cath."

Monroe had strained to overhear Michael. He returned to the study, concerned about Catherine. She'd sat down by the desk, her hands covering her tears. Monroe told them he'd overheard and spoke to Michael in hope of easing her sorrow.

"Bless my soul, Mr. Michael. You'll be close to Mr. John. Yes, sir, you and Mr. John'll be able to see each other again."

"Monroe, you have to keep this to yourself. You weren't supposed to hear."

"Don't you worry none, Mr. Michael. These ears never heard nothin'!"

No matter how she'd prepared herself, the news came unexpectedly. Her future suddenly looked decidedly lonely. More than ever, she felt the need to be involved in something that would dispel the feelings of loss and loneliness. She desperately wanted to call Commander Fields to ask if he had any news. The thought of living alone in an empty house, even for a week, was too horrible to contemplate. She hadn't heard from the commander, and her disappointment was deep.

"So soon! What ship do you sail on? Where will it take you? Where will you be stationed?" Her voice was tinged by resignation. In spite of herself, the feelings she'd been fighting so well immediately returned and would not go away.

"All I can tell you is that I must be at the navy yard tomorrow morning. Captain Turnbull wants to see me before I go. My orders don't allow me to say much else, Cath."

"But, Michael, we both saw John off when he left! You wouldn't say that if it weren't true, would you, Michael?"

"Of course not, Cath. I'd tell you everything if I could. This much I'll tell you. Captain Turnbull said some bigwigs are sailing on the boat. They want to keep it secret. You and Monroe must say nothing about this to anyone, not for at least three weeks."

"I understand, Michael. But it's so unfair! We've come all this way. I wanted to be with you and to see you off. It's not fair!"

"I'm sorry, Cath. My hands are tied. I'll write to you as soon as I can, honestly. I'll mail a letter as soon as I arrive. I'll tell you everything I can, I promise."

Again, Monroe tried to ease the situation. "I'll make tea, folks. Do y'all want some tea?"

"Sure, Monroe. Tea is exactly what we need," Michael said. "Okay, Cath? Oh, by the way, Commander Fields said to give you his regards. He'll pick us up by ten."

Before she could ask, the telephone rang. Catherine was nearest. "Hello?"

Commander Fields was on the other end. Michael heard only her side of the conversation.

"Yes …yes, a few minutes ago. You must have just gone. I'm sorry I missed you …Yes, he told me … It isn't fair. I wanted to see him off. What news? … Are you sure? … When? … Of course I can! I didn't expect it so soon! You didn't call and … Yes, that's wonderful! … No, I'll just need to dress. I don't know how to thank him! Good-bye."

"Was that Commander Fields?"

"Yes. Michael, you'll never guess! He asked if I would meet Captain Turnbull tomorrow morning. The captain's gotten me an interview in Washington and wants to give me details. It's wonderful, isn't it? I could go straight to Washington! I could be doing my part before you even arrive in France! It's wonderful. I'm so excited!"

Catherine was finally happy about her future. In the space of a single telephone call, all her worry and loneliness evaporated. The call from Fields transformed her into the person she hadn't been since her father's death.

"Well? What do you think, Michael?"

"It's terrific, Cath. I'm happy for you. You deserve to be happy after all you've been through this past year."

Monroe returned with hot tea, amazed that her mood had changed so quickly. Something good must have happened while he was gone, and he wanted to know about it.

"Man, oh man! What's goin' on in here? I go to the kitchen an' make tea to cheer you folks up, then I comes back, and you're already cheered up! Makes a man wonder. Does tea do all that?"

"It's Catherine, Monroe. She'll be going to Washington. If the State Department wants her, she'll probably become an interpreter for them."

"State Department? What's next? First Mr. John, den you, and now Miss Cath'rine! Things is movin' awful fast 'round here. Too fast, if you ask me! State Department! What's a interpurder, Miss Cath'rine?"

"I'll explain later, Monroe. Oh, dear! I'll have to tell Mother. You know how she feels. I'd forgotten about her."

Michael thought and then suggested, "Let me tell her, Cath. I have to write to her anyway. It's best she gets all the news all at once. By the time my letter reaches her, you'll be in Washington, and I'll be on the way to France. All she can to do is wish us the best."

"It might be easier, Michael, but no. It's not honest. She already knows that you're going. It's my place to write. I'll tell her you've left, as well. She'll get one letter. That's that, Michael! Don't argue with me. I know when I'm right."

Michael laughed. "Okay, Cath. Mine might not reach her for weeks. By the time she gets my letter, she'll know I'm writing to her from France."

The next morning, Catherine and Michael went directly to Captain Turnbull's office with Commander Fields. Monroe was given the morning off.

"Good morning, Captain Turnbull," greeted Catherine. Her smile was irrepressible.

"Good morning, miss. Lieutenant."

"Good morning, sir."

"Catherine, Lieutenant, please sit down." Turnbull sat behind a worn oak desk stacked with papers. A family photo was perched on one side. The walls were decorated with photos of naval vessels and scenes of the navy yard.

"This won't take long. I'm sure you'd like to have an hour or so together before it's time for Michael to go aboard. I'm glad you're both here. It makes this easier. Michael, we'll lose the rank for now. I asked you to come by to wish you luck and to tell Catherine, in your presence, that she will be interviewed in Washington either by the assistant secretary of state, Frank Polk, or his secretary if he's busy. The State Department's been screaming for someone competent in French for weeks. No one's come up to their expectations.

"I took the liberty of calling your French professor at Bryn Mawr, Catherine. He recommends you highly. If you ask me, the secretary would be a damned fool not to take you the minute you walk through his door. I've already sent a written recommendation. If the interview goes well, they'll do a background check for security reasons. That's automatic at the State Department. I assume you've been a good girl, so there shouldn't be any problem.

"He'll explain your duties and assign you a desk. I was told to inform you that you could be asked to travel where the department may need your service. You could be asked to travel even overseas. Personally, I don't anticipate that happening, certainly not until you've settled into the job. Both you and Michael should be aware of the possibility. I mention this should either of you have concerns over that possibility. If you do, now is the time to speak up." The captain awaited a response.

Neither she nor Michael envisioned the prospect that she might be asked to travel. The possibility was enough for Michael to ask, "If that should happen, sir, I assume Catherine wouldn't be in any way exposed to the fighting."

"I can't imagine them putting her in such a position. Many women work in complete safety behind the lines—mostly nurses and volunteers. Their security is thoroughly considered. Anyway, at this point, Catherine needn't worry. I believe there's only a remote possibility that she'd be sent overseas. The danger would be in crossing the Atlantic. How about you, Catherine?"

"Oh, I wasn't worried, Captain. Michael was. I'm quite prepared to go if necessary. I expect to earn my wages, whether it's at a desk in Washington or wherever they send me."

"Miss Morris, I can honestly say that whatever doubts I had about that, you've just eliminated them. By the way, I prefer you to go to Washington escorted. Since your brother won't be here, I've assigned—"

"Captain. I'm quite capable of going to Washington alone."

"I'm aware of that, miss. I admire your spirit. I must insist. Consider it a matter of protocol. My duties here don't allow me to get away for weeks. However, I understand you are acquainted with Commander Fields. I've selected him to act as your escort, unless you have an objection."

Catherine was pleasantly surprised. "Very well, Captain. Michael? That's all right with you, isn't it?"

Her question was posed out of politeness. Her tone clearly indicated she wasn't asking for his approval, and Michael knew she wasn't asking.

"He'll be a good escort." Indeed, she'd matured, almost overnight. A few days before, she'd been uncertain. Her emotion and anxiety were exposed. The captain had changed that. She'd become a woman with a needed talent.

"Good. Then I expect you'll do well. Let me know how it goes."

"Of course. And thank you, Captain. Thank you very much."

Battles were said to be won or lost. Alone in Guilford, she would likely lose hers. Opportunity didn't win a battle, but it certainly stimulated the will to fight. Catherine was willing to fight. She'd won the initial skirmish. The battle remained to be won.

The Morrises and Monroe

CATHERINE, COMMANDER FIELDS, AND MONROE arrived in Guilford before noon, the day of her interview. Anticipating a positive outcome, she'd packed extra clothing for an extended stay. On the way to the capital, a cautious enthusiasm grew within her. When her father died, she realized that the future offered no guarantees. Her interview with the State Department was a challenge she must face alone.

"I hope I say the right things, William."

"Have confidence, Catherine. Everything will work out."

In the maze of cross streets, they found a quiet rooming house within walking distance of the State Department. If the interview went well, she'd lease a room. Her smaller problem solved, she became anxious as the time approached for her interview. No matter how it went, her new life would begin within hours. She hoped it would be the better of the two.

"Monroe, forward all the household expenses to me. I'll write to let you know. Oh … I may need to ask you to bring me a few things."

She gave Monroe the key to the house in Guilford and made him responsible for the safety and upkeep of the property. In effect, she'd promoted him to live-in caretaker. To Monroe, it was the same as becoming the master of Dr. Sam's grand house.

"Do what needs to be done, Monroe, and let me know how you're doing."

"Yes, miss. But it won't be the same there without you."

"I have faith in you, Monroe. Call me if you need anything."

"Yes, miss."

The commander escorted Catherine to the interview. To encourage her, he reminded her of Captain Turnbull's recommendation. "Good luck, Catherine. I'll wait outside."

The interview was conducted by Counselor Frank L. Polk, the assistant secretary, acting on behalf of Secretary Robert Lansing. It was over in half an hour, and she came out beaming. Fields smiled. On impulse, she ran to hug him. The counselor had hired her contingent on a background investigation. If convenient, her orientation could start as early as tomorrow.

Early that evening, Fields took her to dinner to celebrate. She was filled with anticipation and gratitude, and she spoke freely about the interview.

"William, please thank Captain Turnbull for me when you see him. If it weren't for him and especially for you, I don't know what I'd have—"

"Catherine, you won the position. The captain told me you were perfect for the job. As for me, I'd simply told him about your background in French. I'd like your permission to write to you, if you don't mind. When I come to Washington, I'd like to—"

"Oh, William. Men are so thick where women are concerned!

Really! Don't you know how I feel about you? Of course you should write! I'd be miserable if you didn't."

Staring at her plate, she began to spread bits of food around with a fork. A wholly different sort of excitement began stirring inside her. Her old shyness returned and grew stronger when they said good-bye in front of the rooming house. The commander noticed her expression. He took her in his arms and gently kissed her. It seemed the natural thing to do and didn't surprise either of them. The surprise came when the next kiss intensified and assumed a power all its own, with a meaning that went beyond a simple farewell. Somewhat stunned, she watched him walk away until he'd turned the corner and continued to watch once he'd left her sight. Though the night air was cool, the warmth she felt remained. She restrained an impulse to run after him. She'd never felt the urge to be that bold.

Inside the rooming house, thoughts of the interview brought her back to herself. She couldn't sleep for thinking about the incredible events of the day. In the interview, Polk had suggested that her work could easily go beyond translating French documents.

The following day, Polk began by accelerating her background check. Later, he gave Catherine the nickel tour of the State Department. She took it all in as she'd done when she'd first toured Bryn Mawr, though the atmosphere in Washington was nothing like Bryn Mawr. The war brought an almost electric suspense to the staff that permeated the building. Her desk was in a small anteroom off a reception area, adjacent to Mr. Polk's office. He'd assigned her directly to himself.

Within days, an interim clearance came, allowing her access to unclassified materials. Everything was new to her. But with Polk's guidance, it all fell logically in place. Relations with countries as near as Mexico and as far as Japan changed on a daily basis. Nearly every communiqué required some sort of immediate diplomatic response.

By far, the war effort dominated the work of the State Department. Every one of her coworkers was a professional. The counselor told Catherine that her work would center around issues that went beyond confidential clearance. When her top-secret clearance was confirmed, she'd have access to extremely sensitive documents. It came within two weeks. Polk immediately summoned her to his office to give her the news and wasted no time in offering her an insight into her assignments.

"Congratulations, Miss Morris. From now on, your duties may be expanded at the pleasure of Secretary Robert Lansing. Meanwhile, I'll be your immediate supervisor. If you have any questions, come directly to me. Your work will center around documents forwarded to this office by the secretary. My office routinely deals with relations with our allies. Documents sent by officials of the French government must be translated. Your expertise in French will be invaluable. Moreover, the president may issue directives, often in response to enemy action. From time to time, I may ask you to compose materials that reply to certain other entities. Your interest is required."

His last statement was unnecessary. Catherine was more than interested; she was fascinated. The significance of her expanded duties implied deeper involvement in the department's work. Polk wanted anything from translating to whatever she was assigned. Before handing over her first truly sensitive task, Counselor Polk said something he hadn't mentioned in the interview.

"Miss Morris, I cannot overstress the importance of your work. It's vital that the department know the minds of those who communicate with us. When given a communiqué, a simple translation may not suffice. Anyone can translate dispatches. That's important, to be sure. I want you to note any meaning hidden within the written words. Diplomatic language can be evasive. It often conceals intent. In particular, those we get outside of normal channels."

Polk's statement held importance beyond her first impressions of her assignment. He made her work all the more fascinating. In essence, how she interpreted dispatches may well have an impact on the secretary's response, altering actions he'd recommend, including those he may advise the government to take. It was an enormous responsibility.

Her first task was handed to her with a deadline of two hours—an untranslated letter to Lansing from the French ambassador. A summary reading of the document revealed a request for information concerning the status of the discussions between Secretary Lansing and Viscount Kikujiro Ishii, Japan's ambassador extraordinary and plenipotentiary. To his surprise, she handed the translation to Counselor Polk in less than half an hour.

"That was short work, Miss Morris. Wait here while I read this. I may have questions."

Catherine sat. She waited quietly for him to read her translation. She had not included any personal comments concerning hidden meaning within the communiqué.

"Hmm. No. This won't do; this won't do at all!"

"I beg your pardon, sir? Is there something wrong?" She was stunned by his apparent criticism on her very first assignment.

"No, Miss Morris. Your work is first rate. I was referring to the request of the French government. The secretary's visit was publicized as a thank-you for Japan's efforts. He doesn't wish the true substance of the mission known. Clearly, the French don't believe ... hmm ... Miss Morris, I want you to draft a reply. Suggest that the discussions centered on an inquiry about Japan's future war policy. Tell them that Lansing was seeking clarification of their position. Tell them that the discussions are still in progress, and we'll be happy to inform them if there's anything new to report."

"Yes, sir. Shall I use your name in the response?"

"No, Miss Morris. Word it as coming from the secretary. I'll ask him to sign it at his convenience when he returns."

"Yes, sir." Catherine immediately gained an insight into the workings of diplomatic life.

She had no idea why Lansing was in Japan. The counselor's words revealed that his talks involved more than Lansing's concern for clarifying Japanese war policy. What she knew of relations between nations was too general. Her knowledge of history was limited to her own country and to France. The machinations of diplomacy were entirely new to her. She'd taken every course offered in French language, literature, poetry, art, and philosophy. Her lack of attention to political matters was a severe handicap. She was working at the State Department and had no understanding of the forces governing French and European affairs. She planned to remedy that at the Library of Congress whenever she had time from work.

John had knowledge of these things. He lacked her proficiency in French. *How ironic!* she thought. Nevertheless, she had a new respect for her older brother and wondered how he was getting on in the Lafayette Escadrille. She wrote yet another letter to him about her new position and Michael's assignment to the AEF. It was one of a handful that actually reached him and to which he almost never replied.

As ordered, Michael arrived in France. He was told that a train was leaving for Chaumont, the headquarters of General Pershing and his staff. Chaumont was only 135 miles southeast of Paris, farther from the lines than he'd expected. On arrival, Michael was told to report to Major General James McAndrew, Pershing's chief of staff. Though not a naval officer, procedure dictated who welcomed him to Chaumont. After a brief meeting with the general, he was directed to the office of the assistant chief of staff for operations for assignment by Lieutenant Colonel George Catlett Marshall.

Michael's knock on Marshall's door brought "Come in" from the voice inside. Michael entered, closing the door behind. He approached the desk of a man he guessed to be his senior by barely ten years. Marshall was writing. He didn't look up at first. Michael stood at attention, his hat tucked neatly under his left arm. Soon, the ACS stopped writing. Michael saluted the officer. Marshall returned it. For a moment, he looked at Michael with a hint of surprise on his face.

"It's not often I get a visit from the navy, Lieutenant."

Marshall rose from his chair and walked to the front of his desk. Michael sensed the bearing of a man who'd been in uniform for most of his adult life. Marshall wore a Sam Browne belt— as ordained by General Pershing himself for uniformed officers. His short hair was combed straight back. Prominent jowls and a thin mouth gave Marshall a serious, almost pouting expression. Confidence shone through his narrow, penetrating eyes. Marshall's bearing alone marked him as a member of the general's staff. From head to boot heels, Marshall was pure soldier.

"Sir, Lieutenant Michael Morris, surgeon, reporting as ordered."

He handed Marshall his orders and personnel record. Marshall seemed puzzled at the presence of a naval officer in his office, apparently not forewarned. He assessed Michael, and Michael sensed that he was being assessed. After skimming through Michael's papers, Marshall smiled, transforming his soldierly image into someone more cordial.

"Ah, yes. I think your orders arrived by telegraph some weeks ago." He extended a hand.

Relieved, Michael accepted a very firm handshake with a single pump.

"Welcome to Chaumont, Lieutenant. As you might suspect, it's not normal to see a navy man this far from shore. Your first visit to GHQ, I presume."

"Yes, sir. First time in France. Chaumont is big, sir! Bigger than the Hopkins campus. I had to stop a sergeant to get directions to your office."

"I can believe that. I arrived not so long ago myself and also asked for directions. Be seated, Lieutenant. I imagine even a navy man needs rest after a long voyage and trip across France."

"Thank you, sir."

Michael liked Marshall. A true professional, Marshall radiated a warmth that belied his military bearing. Michael saw him as the embodiment of an officer and a gentleman, with accent on the latter. Michael wondered what was in store for his assignment.

"When did you arrive on the Continent, Lieutenant?"

"Earlier today, sir. The station in Le Havre was pretty busy. People were going in every direction. I was fortunate to catch the express."

"Things are getting busier here, as well. General Pershing's asked the War Department for over two million regulars and draftees. We're building warehouses, rail lines, and depots to move supplies to the front. The tonnage in rations alone might lower the coastline." Marshall had a sense of humor.

"Yes, sir. It's hard to imagine."

"And your voyage? Any problems?"

"Not really, sir. Well, one small incident, sir."

"Oh? What was that?"

"A lady passenger, sir. She came to the infirmary complaining of cramps. A big woman, sir. She'd missed her time and wasn't feeling well. I examined her, and ... well, sir ... she was pregnant! She didn't believe me when I told her she was within a week of delivering the baby!"

Marshall grinned, and he shook his head. "Didn't know she was pregnant?"

"No, sir. A few days later, I handed her the baby. She believed it then, sir. The last I saw her, both were doing fine."

"I'll have to tell General Pershing. He'd enjoy that story. Now, we need to talk about you. We have primary aid people, but surgeons are pretty scarce. I assume you didn't cross the pond to deliver babies, right, Lieutenant?"

"No, sir. That's not why I'm here, sir."

"Stay seated, Lieutenant. This may take a few minutes."

Marshall went back to his chair, sat down, and took time to read Michael's personnel record. Rubbing his chin with his finger, he thought about what to do with Michael. Several minutes passed before he looked straight at Michael and said, "Lieutenant, the army would certainly use you in an operating room in some base hospital in the rear. You'd be put under the command of the ranking medical officer and probably do some sort of internship. You'd agree, wouldn't you?"

"Yes, sir. It's what I expected."

Marshall hesitated before continuing. The idea he finally presented caught Michael totally off guard.

"I assumed that's exactly what you expect. Lieutenant, at an aid station, you'd get into the picture before that. I believe that's where they need the most help—an aid station near the front."

"I ... well ... I hadn't considered the possibility, sir."

"No. I didn't expect that you would. Lieutenant, most of our wounded men go through several stations from the field. The first devotes immediate attention to controlling the problem prior to transport. The next examines wounds more thoroughly. It may redress a wound if needed and then decides on the disposition of the patient. Some are transported to casualty-clearing stations. More serious cases are sent directly to a base hospital. Frankly, I believe too much time goes by before the badly wounded receive proper treatment, especially those needing immediate surgery. They come down with infections. The entire process begins at that first aid station. I believe the action taken there is critical.

I also believe we should attempt emergency surgery at the first station. For that, I need a surgeon in that station, right there, near the front.

"That's where I'd like you to come in, at least for a few weeks. We'll consider it an experiment in preliminary care. Your success or failure will give us valuable information. It'll also give you some firsthand experience and prepare you for later work at a base hospital. We'll talk again in a few weeks. I want to hear your thoughts. If you'd like to stay at the front, I'll find a spot for you. A Hopkins graduate will be welcome wherever he's assigned."

Michael preferred to perform surgery in a base hospital, where he assumed he'd have all the equipment and auxiliary personnel he needed. But Marshall was right. The experience would give him useful training and might well save lives. Michael agreed.

"I don't think an aid station is equipped to handle complex surgery, sir. But simple initial surgery seems quite possible, sir."

"I agree. The nature of an aid station doesn't lend it to difficult operations. Battlefield medicine hasn't progressed much since the Civil War. Aid stations are supervised by MDs. They clean and bind wounds. Transport the men to the next station. They should be more able to take immediate action to save lives. Can you handle that circumstance for the next few weeks?"

"Yes, sir. Immediate action in some cases is essential."

"Good. I'm sending you to the Champagne sector. It's a fairly quiet sector under the overall command of Major General Piarron Mondésir. You'll report to Major General Joseph T. Dickman, Commander of the Third Infantry Division. He'll assign you to a regimental aid station below the Marne. Your orders will be ready within the hour. Have you eaten anything?"

"Yes. I ate on the train, sir."

"Good. If you think of anything you need, let me know. That goes for any supply you think you may need at the aid station.

I'll see you get it immediately. I'll have a staff car take you to Dickman's headquarters."

While Marshall made arrangements on the telephone, Michael peered at a large map mounted on a wall. He followed the path of the river Marne through Château-Thierry. Roughly five miles southeast of the town, a pin on the map marked the position of the Third Division.

Marines had taken Château-Thierry on June 25, three weeks earlier. Since then, the area had been quiet. Michael wondered why he wasn't being sent to a more active sector, where his medical skills would be more in need.

"That's all, Lieutenant. Good luck. A driver should be waiting outside. He knows where to go. We'll speak again in a few weeks."

Marshall again extended his hand. Michael took it.

"Thank you, sir." He saluted Marshall and left the office.

Michael entered the waiting car and left Chaumont. The driver stated their destination, and Michael acknowledged.

In the countryside, Michael saw few signs of battle until they reached towns that had been shelled. Military traffic grew heavy. He wondered how close the aid station would be to the lines. Even quiet sectors took casualties. Patrols were common. Both sides raided trenches for prisoners, hoping to gain intelligence about their enemy's plans. He decided to write Catherine on his arrival to tell her that he'd been assigned. He couldn't tell her where, but her letters should reach him indirectly through Chaumont and channels used by the army's mail service.

Hours later, he arrived at General Dickman's headquarters and was told to report to Brigadier General Ulysses Grant McAlexander's Thirty-Eighth Infantry Regiment. The assignment came on July 13, 1918. The aid station was directly behind the main defensive line above Condé-en-Brie in the Surmelin Valley, the name given the water that ran through the valley.

As darkness fell, the officer in charge showed him the equipment used in the aid station and took him to his bunk in a drab tent. "It's late, Lieutenant. Get some sleep."

In the distance, the rumble of artillery shells echoed through the valley. He was glad the shelling was distant. Until he began to repair human flesh, Michael couldn't be sure how he'd react to the results such shelling. In moments, he grew accustomed to the drumming. Its cadence actually helped put him to sleep. Early the next morning, he wrote to Catherine. The letter was short and emphasized his assignment to a quiet sector. He omitted the fact that the assignment was an aid station. She needn't know he was near the front, and the fact would never survive the censor.

After breakfast, Michael dressed a wound for a soldier who'd exposed himself above the parapet of his trench. The bullet made an ugly blue hole passing through the soldier's shoulder, missing bone.

"The aid will give you a sling and an injection. Give the muscle time to heal. You should be able to lose the sling in a month." He sent the man to the next station for disposition.

Captain McKay had charge of the aid station. "Nicely done, Dr. Morris. Now that you're here, I feel better about requesting a transfer to the base hospital in Savenay. A serious problem has developed at the port. Is that where you landed?"

"No, sir, Le Havre. What sort of problem, sir?"

"Soldiers stationed around Saint-Nazaire are becoming casualties. I don't mean to make a joke of it, but too many of our men are lying down on the job, if you get my meaning. The hospital is treating dozens for venereal disease. Saint-Nazaire is a magnet for mademoiselles who engage in what the men are calling horizontal entertainment. Local powers wink when we mention the girls. It's gotten out of hand. Pershing wants it to stop! He doesn't need casualties before the men get to the lines. It either gets cleaned up, or he'll remove the brass from some officer's shoulders!"

Toward evening, it grew quieter. The few men they'd treated were taken to the rear. The aid station was empty. Michael added the final lines to his letter and gave it to the regimental mail clerk. He was told it may take three or four weeks to reach the States.

"The Tommies are lucky," the clerk said. "Their mail only has to cross the channel. Takes less than a week to deliver, sometimes a day or two."

Michael went back to his tent wondering where John was located. His escadrille often moved. Catherine had promised to write to tell John that he was in France. His brother might be within hours of this place. The thought brought a desire to locate him. He hadn't seen John for nineteen months. Michael fell asleep on his bed, still dressed. A long sea voyage, the train, and bumpy trip to the aid station finally caught up to him. He slept as though the war were happening in on a different planet.

At 11:45 p.m., Michael and everyone else in the Surmelin Valley awoke to the sound of a massive artillery barrage. Nearby batteries of the Thirty-Eighth Regiment were firing rapidly at German lines. Springing to his feet, he ran outside the tent to watch the flashes of heavy artillery pieces along the Allied line. They extended as far as he could see in both directions. Captain McKay joined him.

"What's going on, Captain? Why are they firing? I was told this was a quiet sector."

"It was, Michael. I'm not sure what's going on. They'd never fire this much unless we're about to attack. This isn't normal. I should have been told hours before an attack. They said an attack may come in July, a German attack."

Sustained shelling tore into the German lines. Less than half an hour later, the opening barrage of Friedenstürm rocked the ground along the entire valley. It signaled the beginning of the Second Battle of the Marne. By 1:10 a.m., German infantry began pouring across the river into the Surmelin Valley a few miles north of the aid station. Fourteen German divisions descended on a narrow front between Château-Thierry and the city of Reims. The French had discovered the time of the German attack. It accounted for the preemptive barrage by American and French forces.

Unaware of the scope of the attack, Michael quickly realized that his quiet sector had gotten very loud indeed. Captain McKay told him to expect wounded. Their aid station was the closest to the fight. They were not sure the aid station was in line with the German attack, but that soon became obvious. Michael's heart began to beat faster. He hoped that he was ready for what was certain to follow. He hadn't been on duty a day, and the battle wasn't far away. The same sickening feeling he'd experienced on the Atlantic, chasing the submarine, instantly came over him. He excused himself, unsure whether his stomach would retain its contents. He went inside his tent to lie on his cot and settle the anxiety. Those were the last few minutes he'd have time to rest. The next thirty-four hours brought him and McKay a continuous stream of men with wounds that ranged from simple to fatal.

John at Pau—December 1916

THE WINTER OF 1916 WAS the most severe in Parisian memory. The express train—*un train rapide*—made several stops nevertheless. As it rolled south, the cold followed. But the passengers did escape the constant reminders of the chaos on the western front. Pau lay four hundred miles to the south, near the foothills of the Pyrenees.

After giving the conductor his ticket, John drifted in and out of sleep. When awake, his mind wandered from training at Pau to the time spent with Michelle and her father. Time crawled. He had much to think about. He hadn't thought of home for some time, in spite of the Catherine's letters. When Elizabeth said good-bye from the entrance to the house in Guilford, she'd handed him a letter. This was as good a time as any to open it. He expected to read of his mother's anguish over her son's leaving for war. He was wrong.

My Son,

No matter what happens, you were my first. I
watched you grow into the man you have become.
Your adventures always brought a smile to your
father. Though you only saw my concern, I felt
a mother's pride. You were never dearer to me
than you are right now. I'm sorry I couldn't bring
myself to see you off. I didn't want to embarrass
you with tears. I hoped you'd change your mind,
but I knew you wouldn't. Once you set your mind
to something, I never knew you to turn back. You
got that from your father. I ask only one thing of
you. Be careful. Your courage sometimes blinds
you to risk. I want to see you again, just as I
remember you.

If you ever find yourself alone, know that I am
beside you always.

With love,
Mother

He put the letter away and cleared the lump in his throat. She
had never spoken to him like that before. Her love for her children
was implicit and had always been expressed in terms of their safety
or comfort. These feelings were a surprise. John enjoyed reading
letters. Responding to them was another issue. He didn't want to
seem carefree. He was at war! He didn't want to worry his reader,
and the middle ground had never appealed to him. He'd try to
write from Pau, where his training would provide the topic. An
awful thirst came over him. He decided to find the dining car.

Instead of choosing a direction, he retrieved his dictionary. He couldn't find a word for dining car, so he chose the phrase for dining room. They were close enough. The old gentleman in civilian clothes sitting across the aisle looked as though he often traveled by train. Surely, he'd know the direction of the dining car.

"*Pardon, monsieur. Où est la salle à manger?*" Pressing the fingers of his hand together, he guided them toward his open mouth. He'd pronounced the words flawlessly, except for the last, which he uttered in the way of the place Christ was born.

"*Pardon? Ah … la salle à 'mon-jeh',*" the gentleman corrected. "*C'est le wagon-restaurant. Là-bas, monsieur, là-bas.*" The man pointed toward the rear of the train. "*Deux voitures, monsieur.*" The old gentleman held up two fingers.

John recognized the word "restaurant" and knew that *deux* meant "two." He rightly inferred that *voitures* must mean "coaches." The rest was simple deduction. The dining car was two coaches toward the rear of the train. French was not going to be as difficult as he'd thought.

Triumphant in his deduction, John thanked the man, "*Merci, monsieur.*" The dictionary was useful, after all. He'd simply have to polish his pronunciation.

"*De rien,*" the gentleman said, smiling.

Since his reply didn't have the tone of a question, John nodded and began making his way through the maze of passengers standing in the aisle. Many were soldiers going home on leave. Some sat quietly on their bags, looking tired and without expression. As John entered the dining car, he heard English being spoken. Welcome sounds; they drew his attention toward two men wearing British uniforms.

John approached a small bar and bought a glass of wine. He walked toward the words that sounded more like home. The two men were obviously veterans. John didn't want to disturb them on the lame excuse that no one else on the train spoke English. He contented himself to stand nearby and listen to the conversation. From what he heard, the topic was the war. They spoke using the colloquial terms "Fritz" for Germans and "Tommie" for the British. What John overheard was disturbing. Discussions of tactical details in war were not in place on a public train.

To John's surprise, they noticed his uniform and asked him to join them.

"Lieutenant Martin Dowling here. That's Sergeant Harry Short. What's yours, Yank?"

"John Morris."

"We were just talking about the boxing match scheduled for the convalescent depot in Trouville."

"A boxing match? I thought you were talking about tactics. War tactics!"

"War tactics are old hat, Yank. Now, this fight is another story. In three weeks, it promises to be a proper battle. Fritz Harmon and Tommy Lews. They've come all the way from Manchester to put on a show for our boys."

"You had me fooled! I heard you mention Fritz and Tommy and then say something about a flank attack. It sounded like you were talking about an upcoming battle."

"I assure you it'll be a proper battle, John. Just not the type you were thinking. You should have seen your face! Harry and I can use a smile now and again. The look on your face did the trick."

Feeling at ease, John replied, "I'm sorry. I should learn not to make assumptions." John had already learned that was a risky business. He'd made another earlier that day at Mrs. Weeks's.

"Are you fellas going to Pau?"

"Only as far as Tours," Lieutenant Martin explained. "We're on leave. Wanted to see what a French château looks like before the bloody German artillery blows them all to bits. By the time we get to see some historic French building, it's a pile of stone. They say the Loire Valley is the place to go. Far enough away to see a few that haven't been flattened by the bastards—and without having to stick your head over a parapet to have a look."

When John heard the Loire mentioned, he couldn't resist. He hadn't thought of André during the trip until then. Much had happened. It seemed like weeks since he'd left Saint-Nazaire. He reminded himself to write to Michelle. She'd be surprised to learn that he was in Pau, closer to the fighting than she was.

"I understand Chenonceau is beautiful."

"Chenonceau? Right, we'll look it up. It's exactly what we're looking for, John. Thanks for the tip. I'm glad we had a chance to chat. I'm off to get some rest. It's been a while since I slept in a proper bed. Sleep in the trenches is nearly impossible. Fritz likes to throw things our way, and their fifteen-inch mortar shells could wake the dead."

"There's plenty of time for rest at the hospital, Harry. The men should learn to keep their fool heads down. John, it's been nice meeting you. I'm off, as well. Oh! Thanks for the warning, old man. We wouldn't want Fritz to get on to us."

"Hey, I'm really sorry about that. I hope I didn't spoil your lunch."

"Not to worry, Yank. It's nice to know there's a colonist on hand to see we don't lose the war on a bloomin' train."

They shook hands. After another drink, John went back to his seat. To kill time, he gazed out the window and thought of Michelle, barely noticing the passing scenery. By now, the bakery would be open. André would be teaching. Life went on, war or no war. André told John that his wife had died giving birth to Michelle. Michelle had been motherless her entire life. It must have been a lonely life for a girl in a port city. He couldn't imagine what it would be like to be raised without a mother. He was glad his was alive. She provided a comfort only a mother can give. His father always seemed to have things to do at the hospital and sometimes slept there overnight.

Officially, John was a private in the French army. Before leaving Paris, he'd joined the Legion Étrangère and taken an oath. At Pau, he'd focus on flying to honor that oath. John became conscious of the clatter of steel wheels on rails and the rhythmic rocking of the coach. His eyes closed, but his mind raced. It occurred to him that training was all that stood between life and death. Up to now, the nearest he'd been to an airplane was a magazine. He began to recall terms he'd read—joystick, elevator, aileron, rudder, tachometer, and altimeter. None of the books said anything about a pursuit plane, charging handle, or machine gun. To John, Lewis, Vickers, and Parabellum were names, not guns. Learning how to use a machine gun would come only after he learned to how to fly. As for how to kill, that was an education he didn't need to think about now.

At Pau, all the supply attendants were French. Nearly all understood English. He was issued a uniform that included a pair of calf-high leather boots with leather pulls, light brown riding breeches, and a thigh-length jacket of similar color with breast and pouch pockets. A ridiculously long woolen scarf came next, along with two shirts without collars. He thought they'd finished after they'd issued him two suits of woolen underwear and a French kepi, which he immediately donned to save space in his rucksack. This much comprised the standard military issue. The sack nearly loaded, he went to the next line.

His flying gear consisted of a pair of fur-lined boots and an insulated flying suit with a fur collar. He was given a fur-lined leather flying cap with earflaps, a pair of goggles, and a brimless metal helmet. The next man handed him a pair of insulated leather gloves and a heavy fur-lined leather flying jacket that buttoned up to the collar and belted around the waist.

"Is that all, Sergeant?"

"*Non*." The sergeant pointed to a third smaller supply building next to the cafeteria.

There, he received a small sewing kit, fork, knife, and spoon, and finally, a tin cup and bowl with no lid. He was told the mess kit was to be returned. It was on loan while he was at Pau. Fortunately, Mrs. Weeks had agreed to keep most of his civilian clothing until he had a permanent assignment with an escadrille. Even so, at something over ninety pounds, this ungainly bulk was difficult to carry in one trip.

He was quartered in a drafty barrack resting on a thirty-yard-long, ice-cold concrete pad. He saw at least four wood- or coal-burning stoves belching wisps of smoke along its length. The smoke helped mask the smell of unwashed men and clothing. He estimated that the barrack housed roughly fifty to sixty men with their wooden double bunks squeezed close together. His barrack was one of six such buildings in a row exactly like his.

By the time he'd stowed his things, daylight had gone. Tired, he stayed in the barrack. Many of the men were French. A few spoke English. Some were Americans who'd lived in France. He discovered that many were former ambulance drivers. Several had seen combat in army units and had asked to be transferred to flight school. All were in various stages of training.

John met Private Arthur Meurot, who'd transferred from the *156 ème Régiment d'Infanterie*. His father had immigrated to New York. Arthur's friend Private Peter Mackenzie was an ambulance driver. Peter came from Columbus, Ohio. Both had been training for nearly nine weeks. It hadn't occurred to John that Americans belonged to anything except the Lafayette Escadrille. They told him that many were already flying with other French squadrons. Nearly all spoke French well, and most had applied through the Lafayette Flying Corps founded by Dr. Edmund Gros, an American who'd volunteered for service when the war started. Gros had once directed a unit in the French ambulance service.

Arthur told John that Gros and William Thaw worked together to form the solely American squadron that became the Escadrille Américaine. Thaw and a man named Norman Prince were two of its original members. The squadron was called N. 124, named for the squadron's Nieuport airplanes.

"Prince died last fall in the hospital at Gérardmer," Mackenzie said. "He'd crashed when his landing gear caught a wire at the head of the field. His plane flipped. He was tossed out and died a few days later. We got word of it in Paris before coming to Pau, the day our transfers were approved. We'll be finished soon. We'll get a Nieuport, their most advanced fighter."

On graduating from Pau, they'd earn the winged armband of the Service Aéronautique and be sent to the replacement depot at Le Plessis-Belleville where they'd continue training in combat fighter drills until assigned to a fighter squadron.

"By the end of January, we'll be flying against Rumplers, Halberstadts, Aviatiks, Fokkers, you name it! It should keep us busy," Peter added.

"We've waited months for this," Arthur added. "It's better than the stinking trenches. I'd rather take my chances in the air. In the lines, you never know what or when the bastards are going to fire. A lucky shell can kill you while you're relieving yourself. Up there," he said, pointing skyward, "you've got a chance to get the bastard before he gets you. In the line, they'd just as soon dig your grave in the wall of the stinking trench so they don't have to risk taking you to the rear."

"I felt the same way," Peter said. "Anyhow, if you're shot down from three miles up, you'll dig your own grave where you fall. The engine digs the hole for you!"

With that, a French bugler played taps outside. It was nearly ten in the evening. In ten minutes, the barrack lights went out.

The news of Prince's death troubled John. He hadn't considered the possibility of dying while landing a plane. The thought of accidental death hadn't occurred to him. Given a choice, that's not how John wanted to die. His original view of flight training grew from simply learning to fly to learning how to survive landing. Anticipating his first day of training, the thought of dying left his mind. Death lay north in the skies contested near the Marne, 450 miles from Pau. Flight training started right here, the next morning.

École d'Aviation

On December 28, at five thirty in the morning, John was awakened from a deep sleep by the blare of a French bugle. Seconds later, an adjutant entered the barrack and yelled at the men to leave their warm bunks immediately, without the usual morning rituals of yawning, stretching, or scratching whatever itched.

"Allez! Il est cinq heures! Allez! Tout de suite!"

Several groans arose. One of the French soldiers at the far end of the barrack impishly responded, *"Oui, mon adjudant, tout droit!"* This was followed by muffled snickers coming from the same general area. The adjutant simply glared at them and yelled louder. Grudgingly, the men in the barrack got up, straightened their bunks, and set out to wash faces, brush teeth, and shave.

John was bunked near some men who spoke English. He didn't need to ask them what was happening. He'd just experienced French reveille. The word itself was French. But as this was his first full day, John wasn't accustomed to the morning routine.

"What happens when we finish here, Peter?"

Mackenzie, affecting a childlike, storytelling tone, divulged in more detail than John's simple question called for.

"Well, after we dress and make the barrack pretty, we all join hands and skip off to breakfast of a sort. Then comes roll call. After that, the instructors take us out to play with the airplanes. Around noon, we have a sort of lunch, then we go out and play some more, and at five, we eat dinner of another sort. We play outside some more until Mother calls us home. Then we all hop in our little bunks, and the adjutant tucks us in and reads us a fairy story. The lights go out, and they sing "Le Marseillaise" to help us go to sleep. We sleep like babies 'til morning. Then—"

"Thanks, Peter, I think I've got the picture," John interrupted.

The story brought forth a groan from Arthur Meurot, who modified Peter's description. "Well, that wasn't very concise, but it had the virtue of being accurate ... except for that last part. They make you stand at attention when they sing 'La Marseillaise.'"

Peter responded with a yawn.

Once they'd cleaned up and dressed, the three of them went to breakfast. On the way, John asked Arthur how the English-speaking men handled the language barrier.

"It's usually the mechanics who speak lousy English, John. You may have some trouble there. Whatever Frog you can pick up will help. They considered that hurdle, so they made a British officer our primary instructor. I hear the commander of the Lafayette Escadrille also speaks English very well. Being French, he'll probably give orders in English and cuss you out in French."

"Be nice, Arthur. Show a little less bias toward our great French ally."

"I was referring to their language, Peter."

Breakfast—of a sort—consisted of coffee, a thick slice of French bread cut from a round loaf, applesauce, a boiled potato, a hunk of salted cheese, and a tin of something Peter called "monkey meat," the same ration given to French infantrymen. On opening the tin, John decided the contents looked roughly equivalent to the canned food cats ate in the States. Peter noticed John's expression.

"Give it here, John. I know just what to do with it."

John didn't ask. He assumed Peter would use it as bait to catch something even less edible he'd seen scampering around the edges of the barrack before the lights went out.

"Do they ever serve eggs at breakfast?"

"Not so's you'd recognize them as eggs, John," Arthur said. "We think they use them in the bread flour. But if you want to see them staring at you from a plate, you'll have to buy them. I'll give you the location of a farm nearby. He usually has a few left after his deliveries."

After breakfast, John went to the barrack to get his flying cap and goggles. If he was going to fly, he'd need them in an open cockpit. On the way, he ran into Eugene Falman, a Texan, and Fred Morgan from Chicago. John had met them briefly the night before. They'd been in Pau for two days and were his classmates. John liked Eugene's Texan drawl. His ungainly, long-legged stride made him walk like a man balancing himself on a curb. He was friendly and always seemed cheerful about something.

"John, Lieutenant Rennard wants to see y'all for your entrance interview. Don't worry none. His English is pretty good."

"Thanks, Eugene. I'll join you guys later."

In the personnel office, Lieutenant André Rennard started the interview welcoming John to Pau and asking him about his home, family, and former occupation. John gave brief details of his family in Maryland and told the lieutenant that he'd once applied for a position at a local newspaper. The *Sunpapers*, a Baltimore newspaper, had offered him a job.

"Not long after that, a bomb blew up the munitions depot

on Black Tom Island in New Jersey. I called the editor to say I'd changed my mind. A friend of mine in college was killed in the explosion. I told him the war in Europe was more important. I couldn't accept. I thought I'd join the American Escadrille. I want to learn to fly, sir. I owe it to my friend and myself. That's why I came."

"A commendable choice. Pau understands the desire to fly, Private Morris. Your decision seems to come from a personal motivation. This editor ... when you said you could not accept, what did he say?"

"He said he was sorry that I couldn't join his staff, sir, but he understood. He wants me to send stories from time to time about my training and when I'm assigned to a squadron."

"I see. On the face of it, this seems a logical request. You told him you would do this? You would send to him these reports?"

"Not exactly, sir. I told him I'd think it over. He said the newspaper would pay for the stories, but he didn't offer a contract. He said they'd pay for what I sent."

"I understand, Private Morris. However, France is in an extremely sensitive position. French intelligence does not encourage such reports. They become nervous when those who wear our uniform write to the foreign gazettes. Wait until you return to America, when the war is over. Then such stories will not benefit our enemy."

"Yes, sir, I understand."

"*Bon.* I must ask you about your prior experience. Have you received any prior training in aeroplanes, and how well do you understand French?"

John admitted to knowing very little French. "As for flying, sir, I've read quite a lot about it, and I learn very fast, sir."

Lieutenant Rennard paused, looking straight into John's eyes as he spoke. Rennard was skeptical. There was no mistaking the tone in his voice.

"*Naturallement.* Reading is good. Nevertheless, you must become a proficient flier. We can help in that regard. However, passing the review board is your responsibility. You must demonstrate an ability in combat technique before you are certified for placement in a squadron."

"Yes, sir. I promise to do my very best, sir."

"*Bon,* Private Morris. The pilot who flies well has a chance to survive and will live longer than his enemy. Give this note to Adjudant Gaullét waiting outside. You may go to your class, Private Morris. *Bon chance.*"

"*Merci*, Lieutenant. Thank you," John said, not aware the redundancy in his remarks.

The lieutenant smiled, shook his head, and again offered John luck. He recommended that John devote more time studying French.

"Lieutenant Rennard, sir? Which way is my class, sir?"

"Adjudant Gaullét will take you to your class."

John saluted the officer somewhat clumsily. He'd seen others salute but hadn't closely studied the motion. The lieutenant returned his salute correctly. John instantly knew he was being taught how to salute. After all, this was a training center. John corrected his posture and saluted Rennard correctly.

"That will be all, Private Morris."

"Yes, sir." John left the office. Adjudant Gaullét was waiting outside. He approached the man and gave him the note.

"*Je suis* Claude Gaullét, *adjudant de camp. Ce n'est pas trop tôt. Allez.*"

John had no idea what the adjutant said, but he knew how to say yes and remembered the expression the French soldier used in addressing the adjutant who awakened them that morning.

"*Oui, mon adjudant.*"

"*Bon,*" the adjutant said. Fortunately, the man said no more.

He led John to a field where two men wearing different uniforms stood facing Eugene, Fred, and several other trainees. The French War Ministry had yet to standardize the uniform worn by men in the Service Aéronautique. The adjutant handed the note to the instructor in charge.

"*Voici l'homme. Il est de les États-Unis, mon capitaine.*"

"*Bon,* Claude. *Merci,*" the instructor said with an English accent. Thinly mustached, he wore the uniform of a British air officer. His eyes scanned the note.

John was totally captivated by what stood on the ground behind the officer. His instinct was to get a closer look at the airplane. Thinking better of it, John saluted the instructor, remembering the way Rennard had demonstrated the proper method.

The captain acknowledged it with something like a wave. He finished reading the note.

"Glad you could join us, Private Morris," he said. "I hope we didn't inconvenience you." Addressing the group, the instructor said, "For the benefit of newcomers, I'm Captain Mallory, lately of Saint Omer. Welcome to our little group of potential pilots. Shall we get this show under way?" Mallory signaled John to join the other students in line and moved toward the odd little airplane.

Standing next to Eugene, the Texan whispered, "Captain Charles Mallory was once a fighter pilot in the Royal Flying Corps. He got wounded over Ypres. The corps told him his wound won't let him fly anymore, so he joined the French to keep a hand in flying. They sent him here to teach us guys who don't speak Frog."

"Are we ready to begin training, Private Falman, or shall we start by telling stories?" Mallory revealed his impatience rather than displeasure. Nevertheless, Eugene felt the need to defend himself in the eyes of the group.

"Ready, sir. I was just telling John how lucky we are to have an instructor who speaks American, sir."

"For your information, Falman, I don't speak American. I speak the King's English. The fortunes of war brought me here. I can assure you that luck had nothing to do with it. Now let's get on with flight training, shall we? I believe that's the reason we're assembled."

"Sorry, sir. I only meant—"

"That's quite enough, Falman. Spring will be upon us before long! This is a training center, not a damned social club in Soho! Are we all agreed, gentlemen?"

The entire group responded in chorus, "Yes, sir!"

Mallory told them to approach the airplane. Viewing the airplane from the front, John understood the reason why he and the others were puzzled. The airplane's wings were too short. Three yards of wingspan wasn't enough for flight. Obviously, the machine wasn't built to leave the ground.

"Gentlemen, you see before you a modified Blériot of a type not dissimilar to the one in which Monsieur Louis Blériot, its designer, flew across the channel some seven years ago. Its puny three-cylinder Anzani had barely enough power to get him across. Once the war began, a similar model was used to observe enemy positions. However, it proved useless as a war machine. We've come a ways since the Blériot, but I'm afraid it's not enough. The painfully observant trainee will notice this bird's had its wings clipped to prevent impetuous trainees from flying off to the front, where they'd learn, to their dismay, that our enemy is currently flying the Albatros D.III or the new Fokker."

Mallory's comments had a wry sense of humor that brought a smattering of nervous laughter from the trainees. The comment obviously implied that at least two German fighters were better machines than those used by the Allies.

"The Albatros can fly circles around most French fighters. However, our little bird will serve its purpose well enough. Pay attention and learn! That, gentlemen, is the reason you're here. Later on, you'll be given a chance to display what you've learned in a Nieuport. The model eleven is a respectable machine. In the hands of a good pilot, it could well be a match against a Fokker."

His opening comments completed, they were invited to inspect the cockpit. There wasn't much to see. Mallory pointed out its temperature gauge and another that counted engine revolutions. The panel didn't have an altimeter or compass. He showed them the ignition switch, throttle, stick, and foot petals. Fuel was checked by dipping a stick into the small temporary tank mounted by metal bands under the tiny wing. Fuel was fed to the engine by gravity.

With difficulty, Mallory entered the cockpit. After demonstrating the rudder and elevator controls, he turned the ignition on and off to show them the switch's positions and advised them that ailerons had been installed. Climbing out of the cockpit, his injury became apparent. He decided to pacify their obvious curiosity.

"The right leg was shot through on a patrol. Its replacement is a nuisance, but it keeps me upright." He didn't go into detail on how the injury occurred. He reminded them to focus on their training. Otherwise, they'd be the recipients of a similar replacement.

Quite abruptly, he said, "All right, gentlemen, who's going first?"

After a short silence, John responded. "I'll try it, sir."

Going first was natural for John. From childhood, he was the first to try anything, especially a challenge. After climbing into the Blériot, he was a surprised to see the man who'd been standing near Mallory appear in front of the propeller. John had assumed the man was merely an assistant. He also assumed he'd be repeating Mallory's demonstration, practicing the Blériot's flight controls with a dead stick. He was wrong.

Mallory checked to make sure John's feet were positioned on

the rudder controls. They were. Again, he pointed out the throttle and ignition switch, showing John its positions.

"Very well, Private Morris. It's a simple exercise. I want you to take the machine down the field. As the propeller gains speed, she'll start to roll. Use the rudder to keep it straight. Hold the stick in the center. As you near the two men at the end of the field, throttle back. She'll roll to a stop. Leave the switch on. They'll pick the tail up and turn it around. Then, all you have to do is come back. Have you got that, Morris?"

John's mind was racing. This was the first time he'd ever seen an airplane, and he was about to take it down the field! His heart pumped faster, and the back of his neck grew hot in spite of the cold air sliding off the Pyrenees. He regained the resolve he'd developed as a boy whenever the time came to actually perform a novel stunt. His eyes focused on the controls, and he repeated the instructions Mallory gave in his mind.

"Yes, sir. Keep it straight and throttle down at the end of the field."

Mallory gave him final instructions for starting the engine. The procedure was simple enough, but the words used in the procedure were French.

"Listen to the mechanic. When he says, '*Coupe ... plein gaz,*' be sure the switch is off and pull the throttle all the way out."

John wanted to ask Mallory what the expression meant, but Mallory continued to speak.

"Once you've done this, repeat his words. He'll pull the propeller through to charge the cylinders. When he says 'Contact,' turn the switch on. Throttle back about halfway, and yell 'Contact' to let him know the switch is on. His next pull will start the engine. When he's clear, throttle the engine up until she starts to move. The machine is aimed at the end of the field. Keep it straight. Have you got all that, Morris?"

"Yes, sir, I think so. Coop plane gas. Switch off. Throttle out. Contact."

"Yell loud enough for him to hear you. If you get in trouble, switch the engine off and stay in the machine. A mechanic will come to straighten things out."

Though his instructions were basic, it seemed a lot to remember. Nervous and worried about his French pronunciation, John was willing to go through with the exercise. He grew eager with anticipation.

Several advanced trainees, lacking anything better to do, came over to watch. John saw them from the corner of an eye, standing behind Eugene. Their smiles contrasted with the blank expressions on Eugene's and Fred's faces. Breathing a sigh, John steadied himself. He worked the rudder back and forth with his feet, turning to watch it move. It reacted quickly. John faced the mechanic, nodded, and lowered his goggles.

"Any questions, Morris? Are you quite ready?"

"Ready, Captain."

"All right, then. Have at it, Private Morris!"

Tension grew not only in John but in Eugene and Fred. Even the advanced trainees seemed more interested, though they'd all been through the exercise weeks before.

"*Coupe! Plein gaz!*" The mechanic's words startled him.

In that instant, John forgot the switch positions. A glance reminded him. The switch was off. To be sure, he turned it on, then off. He pulled the throttle back and wondered what else he'd forget to do.

The mechanic waited until John replied, "Coop! Plane gas!"

Putting both hands on the edge of the propeller, the mechanic raised a leg and pulled down sharply. The propeller spun completely around once and kicked back briefly. Hissing noises emanated from an exhaust manifold. The odor of gasoline and castor oil was immediate. John felt his temples begin to throb.

"Contact!"

His fingers slipped on the switch. He got hold of it and turned the ignition switch on, quickly giving the reply, "Contact!"

Again, the mechanic positioned the propeller and gave a terrific tug. A series of loud blasts followed as the three cylinders, saturated with fuel, ignited. Black smoke swirled around the cockpit. The engine raced crazily. A blast of air rushed by John's face. The mechanic leaped clear as the plane immediately started to roll forward. John forgot to reset the throttle. He'd left it wide open. The Blériot's movement surprised him. For a moment, he froze. The machine gathered speed quickly. His foot instinctively pressed the right rudder control. That's where the brake pedal was in the Stutz. The intent was good. The result wasn't. The plane began to turn right. John's heartbeat intensified. His forehead grew wet with sweat.

Realizing his second mistake, he immediately pressed left rudder. Compounding the error, the airplane abruptly turned left and began hopping on its right wheel. John grew more angry than afraid. He was not only reacting like the amateur he was, but his mistakes were on display for the whole world to see.

He thought he heard Mallory yell something. Engine noise made hearing impossible. Anyway, he was too busy trying to bring the Blériot under control. In what seemed an eternity, which actually took him about ten seconds, he managed to straighten the airplane. The crewmen at the end of the field were off to his right. When he applied gentle pressure to the right rudder control, the machine slowly turned until the crewmen appeared through the swirling propeller. He centered the rudder. The airplane straightened itself.

About one hundred feet from the crewmen, John eased the throttle in slowly until it was almost closed. The engine idled down, and the Blériot came to a rolling stop twelve feet from where they stood. One of the crewmen raised both hands, as if giving thanks to the Almighty. The other just shook his head and muttered something. They pulled the tail around, facing the airplane in the direction he'd started his somewhat awkward sortie. Slowly, John opened the throttle.

The return trip went smoothly. He tapped the rudder gently from side to side to get the feel of the aircraft set in mind. As his starting point approached, he throttled down and switched off the engine. The propeller stopped spinning, no longer sending its wash on his face. The Blériot rolled to a stop not five yards from where it had rested when John had first seen it. Before climbing from the tiny cockpit, he breathed a sigh of triumph and no little relief that the exercise was finished.

Mallory approached with the expression of a man who'd just seen his dog shredding his favorite pair of house slippers. He stopped beside the airplane, shifting his gaze from John to the controls in the cockpit. The hint of a smile began to turn the corners of Mallory's mustache upward, transforming an initially sour expression into one of dry amusement.

"Going on exploration, Morris? You should have shut it down, you know. Try to obey instructions next time. However, the return trip was done well. All in all, not bad for a first time."

John smiled. "Thank you, sir. It was terrific!"

John's tension was left at the other end of the field. The others, who'd expected to see Mallory thoroughly dress him down, applauded. They patted his back as though he'd just scored the winning goal in a football match.

"I wouldn't characterize it as 'terrific,' Private Morris. Just be grateful that you didn't flip her over," Mallory amended.

John felt he'd passed his first test as a pilot, though the only thing that left the ground was his spirit. Any doubt lurking beneath his confidence was gone. More than ever, John felt he was destined to become a pilot in the Lafayette Escadrille. Of that, he was supremely confident. At the same time, the exercise left him with a sobering thought. He'd only just begun and had already made several mistakes, any one of which would have ended his life in combat. He had much to learn indeed.

Flier Training at Pau

THE REST OF A COLD and gusty winter morning was spent as each trainee in turn ran the Blériot up and down the field. By the end of the day, they'd all had several turns. The following day, the Blériot was moved farther downfield. The goal was to gain enough speed on the ground to make the tail lift, putting the Blériot in the attitude for takeoff. Its speed, lift, and direction must converge in the proper sequence. Anything less might cause an accident.

The importance of coordinating its controls became evident to the trainees. The straighter they kept the airplane, the faster it gained speed for lift. A crosswind made steering difficult, but greater speed demanded greater control—not easy in a crosswind.

"Control, gentlemen. Control in takeoff, in the air, and on landing. Without it, you can't hope to fly, much less compete with the Boche. However, take care not to over-control!"

Training was halted after Fred Morgan closed the throttle on the Blériot too late and overshot the end of the field. The airplane rolled into a gully, tipping forward onto its propeller. Fortunately for Fred, the Blériot was coasting at the time. Shaken, he received a cut lip and large bump on his head. As far as Fred was concerned, his embarrassment was more painful.

The airplane was righted and pulled from the gully. Close inspection revealed a crack in the propeller. A new one was mounted. Mallory used the incident to make a point.

"Poor judgment can lead to the sort of awkward position found by Private Morgan this morning. No one is immune from mistake. Had Morgan been going much faster, he wouldn't have come away as cleanly. More likely, his head would become part of the cockpit. I remind you all of the danger in bad judgment. Let it be a lesson to you. An airplane's a living thing. How you handle it decides who survives combat. No matter what talent a pilot may have, the deciding factor lies with the man who knows the limits of his machine. Know its virtues and faults better than you know your own, and you may stay alive."

The trainees accepted the advice at face value. Mallory spoke from bitter experience as attested by his wound.

"My BE2," he said, "was outflown by a single-winged Fokker that climbed more quickly than mine could. He made a loop and roll and then spun 'round with Spandaus firing. I hadn't enough machine to evade. His was the superior machine. Mine took two dozen balls through the upper wing and missed my head by inches. One broke a spar, causing loss of control. Another split my leg. He watched while I tried to bring it under control. Luckily for me, he thought I was finished or was low on fuel and flew home."

Mallory hesitated when the men insisted he finish the tale.

"Not now. Let's get back to the reason you're here." He didn't tell them that he'd received the Distinguished Flying Cross. The decoration read in part, "He engaged a larger enemy patrol in solo attack, destroying two enemy observation planes. Severely wounded, he was forced to disengage. He brought the crippled airplane to safety while under fire from enemy antiaircraft batteries operating in Passchendaele." Rumor had it that another British pilot observed the fight. As the Fokker broke for home, markings on its fuselage were seen. Description of the markings led HQ to believe Mallory's opponent was Oswald Boelcke, the famous German ace.

"The lesson learned is that a pilot can only be as good as his machine. It's a lesson to remember. Otherwise, you'll learn it as I did."

Mallory spent most of the morning talking about the limited performance of airplanes. He detailed each factor that made a difference in their performance, including top speed, rate of climb, altitude limit, engine reliability, the capacity to maneuver, the strengths or weakness of wings in a dive, and the rate of fire and dependability of machine guns. It was the most comprehensive segment in their instruction up to that point. He answered every question arising from the group.

The rest of the day, the trainees listened closely to Mallory's instructions. While sloppiness in their short flights was still discernible, all the trainees exhibited better control. No further accidents occurred. The day's training ended with Mallory returning to his original point. Ending his lecture, he offered a solution to the problem of limitations.

"One may offset his aircraft's limitations. God gave you a brain! Use it! It's all right to show courage in attack, but to attack without thinking is fatal. Stay alert! Look before you fight! Don't fly into a trap! Enemy fighters cover their observers from above, often with the sun behind. When you sight them, climb. Put the sun behind you. Attack with surprise from behind. If his advantage is number, attack the straggler, the wanderer on the side. Hit him hard and fast. Get out before the others react. These thoughts will be repeated throughout your training. Never forget them! Those who do pay with their lives. If you came thinking flying is glamorous, you are literally dead wrong. Flying is more dangerous than the trenches. If you survive your first fight, you'll realize that no part of it is glamorous. That's all. Group dismissed!"

His thoughts on fighting didn't appeal to John's sense of fair play. However, John didn't need to hear them twice. Mallory's words were engraved in his mind as clearly as the Ten Commandments. Fred and John stayed silent halfway to the mess hall.

Finally, Fred said, "He sure took a lot of the fun out of it."

John replied, "Yeah. But he's been there, Fred. He ought to know."

The following day was a repeat of the previous one, but the next, December 30, was different. The Blériot had sprouted wings! Using the same field, they were to perform essentially the same tasks as before, but with one notable exception. Once the trainees had achieved the attitude of takeoff, they were to ease back on the stick, briefly lift off, and then land and repeat the exercise to the end of the field. Two crewmen would turn them around, and they would do it again on return. The trainees became more animated. They'd finished playing at flight. Now, if only briefly, they'd actually fly.

"Full power for takeoff, men! You may feel like a grasshopper, but practice is necessary, gentlemen. Get used to controlling the plane in takeoff and landing. Throttle down if you get into trouble."

Fred Morgan went first. His run was only partly successful. At best, Morgan got the plane to rise a foot or so for a few seconds. Mallory suggested the others lift to an altitude of over ten feet before bringing the stick slowly forward. He cautioned them about moving the stick too sharply either to lift off or to land.

"If you pull back too fast, she'll shoot up like a flushed quail. It could come down on its tail. Don't push forward too fast, or she'll dive in headfirst. Work the stick gently. You're flying the real thing now. I want no accidents. All right, Morris, you're next. Buckle up. And, Morris, watch the throttle this time. We mustn't filet the mechanic. That would be bad form."

"Yes, sir."

The wicker seat creaked as he climbed into the cockpit of the Blériot and buckled the safety belt. Pointed into the wind, John faced the Pyrenees. The starting procedure was routine by now. He automatically set the throttle half-open on the mechanic's second pull.

As the engine caught and the mechanic stepped aside, John opened the throttle nearly full. The heavier Blériot began lumbering down the field. Its greater weight and full wings added drag to the aircraft, making it slower to gain speed. He was tempted to open the throttle all the way but waited for the plane to stabilize before opening the throttle.

At full throttle, John felt a strong prop wash on his face. The wheels bounced on the frozen field as he gained speed. Looking through the blur of the propeller, the Pyrenees seemed to rise as the tail came up. As it gained speed, he held the Blériot's tail up and level. The engine whined, sending exhaust gas past his goggles. He glanced at the gauge counting revolutions. Satisfied, he pulled gently back on the stick. Seconds later, the bouncing stopped. His elation peaked as the Blériot lifted off the ground. For the first time, he was airborne. He was more exhilarated than he'd ever dreamed of being.

The books he'd read hadn't described the rush of adrenaline in the reaction to flight. His heart seemed to fly higher than the airplane, and its beat increased with the pleasure of it. Halfway down the field, he realized how far he'd flown but was reluctant to push the stick forward. Conceding to orders, he eased the stick forward. The nose of the Blériot dropped, revealing the base of the Pyrenees once again. The wheels touched ground and began to bounce.

Immediately, he pulled back on the stick. Again, the Pyrenees disappeared below the engine. He'd pulled back too sharply. The engine began laboring and losing speed. He recovered as he eased the stick forward. The loss of speed brought the plane down on the field with a heavy thud. Its nose dipped for a moment, but he was lucky. Nothing was harmed but his pride. Mallory was right. A pilot must maintain control of his plane.

John trimmed the throttle, and the airplane rolled to a stop yards from the gully Morgan had hit yesterday. Two crewmen came running as it rolled past. They picked up its tail and turned it around to repeat the exercise. On reaching his starting point, John switched the engine off. For a moment, he just sat there, reliving the experience. He was sorry it had ended. Mallory's voice broke the reverie.

"I see we prefer flying over landing, Private Morris. You were airborne for nearly eight seconds on that first hop. A good exercise, but the field has limits. Next time, be more attentive."

"Yes, sir. Sorry, sir. I was a bit taken up by flying." John couldn't contain a grin at his unexpected pun. He added, "It was the most fun I've had since I was a kid!"

Mallory's expression remained neutral. "Morris, I understand your enthusiasm, so I'll excuse your nearly leaving the field on grounds this was your first flight." Mallory turned, scowled at the group, and yelled, "The next man who shows no concern for the length of the field will be grounded! I want no more accidents. They waste time and money, cause injury, and as this is the only airplane allocated for use by the group, your training could be interrupted for days."

It seemed a harsh judgment. The airplane wasn't damaged,

and he'd offered an honest excuse. However, he'd come close to repeating Morgan's mistake. That would have certainly halted training, so the entire group accepted Mallory's warning.

"At ease. Group dismissed!"

The men went to the mess hall for lunch, a building that resembled the hangars. Eugene Falman loved to talk about his father's cattle ranch outside Waco. Eugene told John that he'd come to France as a horse orderly for a cavalry unit. They'd given him the nickname "Outlaw." After months of cleaning and grooming, he convinced his captain to let him transfer to the air service. John liked him. He was friendly, outgoing, and generous. Outlaw had already made John promise to come to Texas after the war to see his father's ranch. They became fast friends. After lunch, they returned.

"We need to get in as much practice as daylight allows. You're next, Falman." Mallory briefed Eugene with the instructions he'd given about hopping the Blériot up and down the field. He reminded Eugene to handle the controls gently.

"Don't you worry none, Captain, sir. I been bustin' broncs since I was old enough to get it hard. Just turn me loose." Outlaw wasn't bashful.

Mallory had no immediate reply but saw the others try to hold back laughter without much success. By the time Eugene climbed into the cockpit, Mallory had formed a reply to Outlaw's remarks. A man of dry humor, Mallory moved away from the airplane and turned his head toward the group. His rejoinder was spoken loudly enough for Falman and all the others to hear.

"The stick in your hands is the one to handle, Falman. And the movement is backward and forward, not up and down."

No one restrained laughter at these words. Eugene laughed, as well.

"Yes, sir! I'm ready to get my spurs into this old nag."

Mallory made no attempt to reply.

Smoke shrouded Eugene as the engine started. Outlaw let the throttle out, yelling, "Yahoo!" He did two perfect hops to the end of the field and was turned around for the return trip. His next two hops were either too low or too short, like Morgan's were earlier that morning.

To compensate, he pulled the stick back quickly on his last hop. The nose shot up, climbing to thirty feet. The engine labored. Surprised, Eugene pushed the stick sharply forward and lost control. The Blériot's nose dropped at thirty-five feet. To the horror of those watching, it flipped and crashed. A fuel line broke, starting a fire. Seconds later, the fuel tank exploded.

A dozen men, including John and Fred, ran toward the wreck. Two mechanics reached him first and cut his seat belt. They grabbed his arms and dragged him from the burning wreckage. Falman's face was badly burned. His head was bloody. He barely managed to say, "Damnedest bronco I ever busted." Mercifully, he blacked out.

Mallory immediately ordered the men back to their barracks. Outlaw was taken to a hospital in Pau by ambulance. Mallory stayed with him and was with him when he died of a brain hemorrhage. Eugene never regained consciousness.

The following afternoon, he was buried in a cemetery just outside of Pau, overlooking a small French farm with horses grazing in a field. The entire complement at Pau, officers and men, witnessed the ceremony. Townspeople also came. A silence came over the gathering as Mallory read a handwritten eulogy. Though he held the sheet with both hands, the paper quivered.

"We assemble here to say farewell to Private Eugene Thomas Falman. Words cannot justify his loss. But surely, France welcomed him. By volunteering for a war that his own country has yet to declare, he dedicated his life to the service of France, as have many gathered here in this place. However brief his service was, it was enough. France can only hope for similar devotion from men native to France. We commend Eugene's body to the land he chose to defend with the certain knowledge that his spirit remains with us. May God comfort his family and keep his immortal soul. Amen."

The crowd echoed, "Amen."

Quiet prevailed after the eulogy. Among those gathered, women openly wept. A small band from the town began playing a somber tune that John didn't recognize. When the music ended, the commander of the École de Combat marched a squad of riflemen beside the open grave. They fired a salute as Eugene's wooden casket was lowered into—and covered with—the land he'd come thousands of miles to defend. Most felt the terrible futility of his loss. They all felt a pride for the man they had known too briefly.

Mallory's eulogy expressed the sentiment of those gathered in honor of a man from Texas. As the band played a last tune, the group began to disperse. Several townspeople laid flowers around the wooden cross engraved with his name. Seeing it, the trainees were reminded that they too were mortal and might hope for an end less traumatic than Eugene's. They'd all learned that death in an airplane didn't have to come at the hands of the enemy. The inscription on the cross said what remained to be said. It was as succinct as his life. To the trainees, its black letters seemed burned into the wooden cross. They were more powerful than Mallory's eulogy.

Eugene T. Falman, Pvt
Volontaire de l'Amerique
Mort en France
30 Janvier 1917

Training at the center had paused for the burial. While Outlaw's death was tragic, the leaders of the flying school considered his death the waste of a potential pilot. Many fliers were dying in the skies over France. Life expectancy in a French escadrille was less than four weeks, far shorter than the trenches. Pilots were being killed faster than they were trained. The loss of a single trainee was a waste. If it weren't for the RFC and volunteer pilots from America, Canada, and other countries, only Frenchmen would be flying over the western front. The war had stagnated into futile attacks to relieve the static squalor in the trenches. As long as America remained neutral, time was on Kaiser Wilhelm's side.

President Wilson was reelected by a single state, under the slogan "He Kept Us Out of War." Prospects for an end to the war were bleak to nonexistent. Hollow talk of peace didn't change the fact that while fighting had ended in Verdun, another German offensive was expected in the spring. Prime Minister Lloyd George ousted Asquith, anxious to pursue the war on a different front.

War in the air would resume as soon as winter weather cleared. German observation planes would again have to be shot down. Mallory joined his sullen students as they assembled near the place where Eugene's airplane fell. The earth was still black, and the odor of fuel still hung in the air. Mallory felt the men needed time to become themselves, time to refocus on training.

"We'll resume training tomorrow. A new Blériot is arriving. I believe Eugene would want us to tame this new bronco. We'll break it in for him tomorrow." Mallory had a distinctly human side. He walked away without formally dismissing the group. His comments were more appreciated than his eulogy and were perhaps a more fitting epitaph for Eugene. If he'd lived, that's exactly what he'd be doing in Waco.

Outlaw's death hit John hard. Having made Eugene a promise, he tried to learn more about him. Few of the men had spoken to him at length. One came to Pau on the same train as Eugene. Outlaw told him he'd been transferred from the flying center at

Avord and already had a week's training in an old Caudron. The news only made his death more puzzling.

When John asked Lieutenant Rennard for Outlaw's address in Waco, the lieutenant asked him if he was a relative or friend of the Falman family.

"No, sir. I just met Eugene a short time ago."

"Perhaps it would be better to let Grand Quartier Général notify his family through ordinary channels as protocol requires. What you want may come later."

John didn't argue the point. The lieutenant was following procedure established long before he came to Pau.

Sadly, Eugene's accident took away the one man John had met up to that point whom he really liked. Though they'd only spoken a few hours, John felt he and Eugene were more alike than different. They were not afraid to test themselves in new ways. Eugene told him he was his father's first and only son and was going into partnership with him after the war. Waco had lost one of its own. Many an unbroken horse would be tamed by other cowboys.

The evening Eugene died, the French bugler played taps twice—the only time John would ever hear him do so. The whole incident had a tempering effect on the men. There was still laughter, though none was heard the day of the funeral. Newer trainees weren't badgered as much by older ones. Pau developed a more purposeful atmosphere that replaced the casual attitude the men usually used to mask their fear. In short, they had matured practically overnight.

All the instructors noticed the change in attitude. Pilot trainees and instructors worked together more closely than before. They began to offer more advice on tactics and survival in aerial combat, much of it coming from their collective experience. The learning accelerated.

John learned that death could be quick and ugly. He learned

that a man like Eugene, a man much like himself, might be killed in an instant by making a simple mistake. The lesson came like a slap in his face. It made him aware that death came unannounced. He buried his cockiness in Eugene's grave. Any doubt in his own mortality was erased at the inquiry when he testified as one of the witnesses to the accident.

After describing what he'd seen, he added, "It could have happened to anyone, sir."

The chairman of the panel replied, "Private Morris, let's hope that the mistake made by Private Falman will never be made again."

The results of the panel of inquiry into the cause of the accident were made official days later. It bore out the testimony of Captain Mallory and those who'd witnessed the event. Eugene had overreacted to a mistake when the airplane abruptly rose. He'd thrown the stick forward, lowering the elevators to the extreme at the top of the arc. The tail flipped over. Had he not pushed the stick forward as much, the airplane would have fallen on its landing wheels, not its nose. His actions caused the airplane to fall nose down. A fuel line ruptured, spilling fuel that ignited on hot cylinders. The impact caused his head to be thrown forcefully onto the edge of the cockpit, causing serious head injury. Eugene died as a result of his injury.

An addendum to the findings of the panel stated that the burns received by the two men who'd pulled Private Falman from the wreck were treated. They could return to service when their hands sufficiently healed. It determined that the two men had acted quickly and unselfishly. The panel recommended that each receive a special award to be presented at Pau in a *prix d'honneur*. These findings were made final and part of the official record.

As for John and the rest of the trainees, the only finding that mattered was that Eugene was dead. They'd seen what had happened, and none would ever be quite the same again.

The Lafayette Escadrille—1917

ALL OF JOHN'S FLYING, FROM the time he entered Pau, was done solo. Two-seaters were not used to train fighters. Before graduating, a *pilote de chasse* attended gunnery classes at the École Nieuport, where the Nieuport 17 was flown, the plane he'd fly in combat. By the end of March 1917, John was ready for the final test. Mallory asked whether he was ready to take the final test. John felt he was ready weeks before. The test included sustained flight at six thousand feet, recorded by barograph, and every aerobatic trick he'd learned to date. He mentally reviewed his training.

After eighty hours of solo flight, he'd learned basic combat maneuvers—circling turns, or *virages*, figure eights, loops, rolls, dives, chandelles, and standing on the tail. Figure eights came easily to John. The control was rhythmic and repeated. The most physically demanding was the dive and sharp climb with the option to either complete a loop and descend in the original direction or level off and roll at the top and reverse direction. Mallory said these were excellent defensive and offensive maneuvers when properly timed. Without question, the more challenging aerobatics included the sideslip, the falling leaf, and dizzying horizontal spiral—tactical maneuvers designed to evade a dangerous combat situation. Entering and leaving a spin, or *vrille*, demanded the most nerve.

The maneuver was extremely dangerous. From four thousand feet, they were to initiate a dive, spin no more than four times, and pull out no lower than one thousand feet. If the dive became too steep or too fast, they were warned that the stress on the wings could rip them away as they pulled out of the dive. Mallory said, "The success or failure in performing the drill determines who continues here and who doesn't."

For the trainees, the drill was the most nauseating and most exhilarating. It was the only drill that cost John his lunch. The spinning dive brought John's stomach to his mouth. His heart soared as the airplane struggled out of the spin. By the time it leveled off, he could recognize the faces of those who were watching from the ground.

The École de Combat also required them to fly to three thousand feet, cut the engine, and put the airplane into an intentional vertical spin. They must restart the engine and pull out of the spin before crashing. Mallory made the technique sound easy, but the whole school knew the danger. Wing fabric could tear away from a Nieuport 11 from drag in a steep dive, turning the airplane into a projectile. Without engine power, pilots had been known to freeze at the controls. A crash had such force that the engine and pilot were often buried several feet below ground.

Mallory constantly reminded the trainees, "Your reflexes must be automatic. A good pilot learns to fly his machine instinctively. You have no time to open the book on aerial tactics and not very much to think. React instinctively. Flying should take no more thought than you'd need to put on a scarf. Stay alert to the enemy. If you anticipate your enemy's reaction, you will survive."

At noon on Tuesday, March 27, 1917, Mallory approached John to ask him the question trainees were most anxious to hear. It marked the turning point in their training and could decide their future as a pilot or ordinary *poilu*.

With the group assembled, Mallory said, "Private Morris, you've done well over the past few weeks. The gunnery instructor tells me you've got better-than-average accuracy. Your aerobatics have proceeded well and without incident. In my opinion, your record meets the standard for pilot training. In short, how do you feel about taking your flight examination?"

The question made John the first in the group to be asked to attempt the approval of the review board. However expected the question was, answering it never failed to produce a faster heartbeat, whether the pilot was ready or not.

"I've thought about it for a week, sir. When do I start?"

The group cheered.

"Good!" Mallory issued John two invitations. "The monitors will be ready to critique you at two this afternoon. Would you care to take lunch with me in my office? We can discuss the test and answer any questions you may have. I think I can promise you a meal at least as good as you'd get in the mess hall."

John hadn't anticipated an invitation to lunch and was honored to accept. "Thank you, Captain. I'd be happy to join you."

Mallory dismissed the group earlier than usual. "Let's get going. Eating a bit early is better than waiting 'til the last minute. It's not uncommon for fliers to get queasy taking the exam."

"I get your point, sir."

Mallory's office was homier than John expected. A picture of a smartly dressed woman rested on one side of a cluttered desk. She was holding a small child. Both were smiling, almost out of place on Mallory's desk. It was a side of the man John was surprised to see.

"A boy, sir?"

"Yes. Evan ... oh, damn! That reminds me. He's four today! Dashed if I didn't forget his birthday! Thanks, John. Have a seat. I'll tidy up a bit. Amazing how much mess a desk can hold."

That was the first time Mallory addressed him by his given name. Another surprise!

Mallory removed the jumble of papers and heaped them on a nearby filing cabinet. He carefully wiped the desk with a bath towel and then spread it for a tablecloth.

"There. That will do." Mallory lifted a field telephone and asked for the mess sergeant. He spoke to him in fluent French. Obviously, he was ordering lunch, but John couldn't follow the menu.

"It'll be a few minutes. Marcel owes me a favor. I think you'll enjoy the meal."

Mallory opened a lower drawer to support his artificial leg. He noticed that John had made a conscious effort not to look at it. The privacy between an officer and enlisted man was sacrosanct. Oddly, it was Mallory who broke the unwritten covenant.

"Strange, isn't it?" Mallory said. "I could swear the real one was still there. A lucky shot. The Boche bastard had me in his sights a few seconds. Oswald Boelcke. He'd compiled a hell of a record in his day. Forty kills. I was his last victory. He died when one of his own crashed into his plane. The fortunes of war, John. Shoot a man down one day, die the next. I'd prefer a bullet in the brain to his death. He had time to suffer. A great tactician, Boelcke. A shame he was on their side. We could have used a man with his ideas in the early days. Our chaps were biting their fingernails expecting him to pop out of a cloud. Boelcke inspired their latest tactic. Formation flying. It's best he's gone, for our sake."

Boelcke was his opponent! Mallory had touched on how he'd been injured but had said little about the event and nothing about his opponent.

"I'm glad you told me, sir. It confirms the rumor that you fought Boelcke. Was he flying the new Fokker at the time, sir?"

"Yes. Fokker Eindecker. It had Fokker's synchronized machine gun. Shot straight through the airscrew. My machine wasn't much of a match for him. The Morane had deflector plates to keep the Lewis gun from chewing the blades off. His had less speed but was more maneuverable. In close combat, in Boelcke's hands, a dangerous machine indeed. A Morane is hard to maneuver at speed. You'd throttle back after chasing down an enemy plane and give it full throttle to escape, usually by diving.

"Against Boelcke, that was a mistake. I went straight for him. Had I left the throttle open, I'd have shot past with enough speed to climb. An ordinary pilot should be expected to sideslip and run home to Germany. As it was, it took him only seconds to get behind.

"He pulled the maneuver named for his rival, Max Immelmann. I'd never seen it done that well before. A steep climbing loop with a half roll at the top and another in descent. He was above my wing before I knew it. Had a free shot." Mallory patted his wooden leg. "Hell of a pilot, old Oswald. I should have liked to take him on again. I sorely wanted a rematch. That never came."

John was impressed by the detached way Mallory told the story. He referred to Boelcke with grudging respect, as though they'd met as opponents in a tennis match. Yet Boelcke was the man who'd caused the loss of his leg, doing his best to burn him alive in his airplane.

"It's a fascinating story, sir. I don't know if I could be as matter-of-fact about it if I were in your shoes."

Mallory grinned. "Well, thanks to good carpentry, I can still put two of them on, John."

"Sir?"

"Shoes, man, shoes!" Mallory laughed as he pointed to the foot on the end of his propped leg. John cautiously joined Mallory's laughter, which ended as someone rapped on the office door. John rose to open the door. Lunch had arrived. Marcel entered pushing a small cart accompanied by the clatter of tin lids covering several plates on two trays. Mallory greeted him in French. Marcel put the trays on Mallory's desk and removed the lid from the largest plate. A cloud of aromatic steam arose. Marcel spoke in accented English interspersed with pure French.

"*Voici, mon capitaine.* Fried potato, sausage, fresh bread, cheese, dessert, *et pour la grand finale, vin Mouseaux.*" Marcel's speech was laced with pride and spoken with a self-satisfied smile.

"Marcel, you've outdone yourself. *Tres bien! Merci, mon ami.*"

"*De rien, Capitaine.* For you, the best. *Bon appétit, messieurs.*" Marcel left as quickly as he'd arrived, leaving behind the aroma of hot food.

"Help yourself, John. The sausage is good. Can I pour you a glass of wine?"

"Thank you, sir. I can't help thinking how surprised Peter would be if he saw this, sir," John said, referring to his former barrack companion. Peter had graduated from Pau two weeks before.

"Who, John? Peter who?" Mallory asked, lifting lids from the plates.

"Mackenzie, sir. He was here before I came. He liked to refer to our meals in the mess as breakfast or dinner of a sort. I was wondering what he'd say if he saw all this."

"Ah, Mackenzie. Graduated not long ago. He got the blighty wound, last I heard. In England by now, I should think."

"The 'blighty wound,' sir?"

"Slang for a wound that's bad enough to send you home in

as few pieces as possible. The boys in the British trenches use the silly term. The report said he was hit his first time up flying offensive patrol in the same sector I was hit. Nothing too serious, I understand. The ball broke his shoulder, tore the muscle. His flying days are likely finished."

"I'm sorry to hear that, sir. He and Arthur slept in the bunks next to mine."

Mallory leaned forward, looking at the food. He remained quiet for about half a minute before saying, "Arthur Meurot. Many have come and gone too quickly since you came. Classes are up to ten men or more today. They have two Blériots now on the same field you trained."

"Have you heard anything about Arthur, sir?"

Again, Mallory went silent. He poured wine into John's glass.

"Yes, I have. I try to keep an eye on the men we train. A nice chap, Meurot."

That was all he said. Mallory began eating fried potatoes. John took a sip of wine, waiting to hear what Mallory had heard about Arthur. Mallory swallowed and glanced at John.

"How's he doing? He wrote to me saying he and Peter were assigned to the same unit. They were close friends."

Mallory took his glass and filled his mouth with red wine. It took two swallows to drink it all down. Again, he looked at John and paused before speaking in lowered tones.

"John, Arthur died last week. One of the papers on my desk was a copy of the report from his squadron leader, Commander Vincent. I asked him to keep me informed should any of our boys join his unit. I'd flown with Paul. He's a damned fine pilot and leader. Always asking me about the caliber of the new trainees. I was hoping I wouldn't have to tell you about Arthur before you went up this afternoon. I was aware you and Meurot shared the same barrack. I wasn't certain how well you knew him."

"What happened, sir?" John hoped Arthur's death didn't involve flames, like Eugene's had.

"They'd just got their planes, he and Mackenzie. The mechanics put them together literally fresh out of the crates. Arthur and Mackenzie were in the same patrol. Vincent led. He spotted a two-seater taking photos over the lines. Vincent waved them on, leading the attack himself. His report states none of them saw enemy covering above. They were hit by a wave of German Albatros coming straight out of the clouds. Seven of them. Ambush—the favored tactic of the Boche. They lay in wait for just such an opportunity, the bloody bastards.

"Mackenzie was highest in the group. Three of the Boche went for him. He was hit on their first pass but engaged without waiting. Arthur saw him and climbed to help. Vincent was ahead and below, turning to hit the observer and too low to come up. As Arthur climbed, four Boche came down on him. His engine caught fire almost immediately. Peter said he side-slipped to escape the flames. The Boche followed him down and shot a wing off Arthur's plane. Already in flames and they shot off a damned wing! It was a bloody rotten thing to do! The bastards! Damned leg! If they'd only let me fly again! Vincent got the observer. The others fought 'til the Boche flew away."

Mallory went silent once more. Peering at John, he said, "I'm sorry, John. I was going to tell you after the exam. Arthur was a good man. A promising pilot."

For a time, both sat quietly, picking at food. Mallory refilled his glass and took another long drink. Without comment, John followed his example, recalling the first time he'd eaten breakfast with the two men. Mallory broke the silence.

"John, no amount of training ensures survival. The old days are gone. The chivalry that existed up there before you came no longer exists. Don't let it harden you the way it does most men. The war will end someday. You should try to return to those you love the same man as when you left."

Mallory looked at the picture he'd put on the desk. "You will be tested up there, John. Don't let the war ruin your life. Family is more permanent than war."

"Yes, sir," John said, wondering if Mallory was speaking for himself, as well.

"You've got some flying to do today, and I expect to see nothing less than your best."

The difference in their ages was negligible, yet Mallory was indeed much more mature than John. John began to understand why. Keeping track of his students inevitably led to getting reports like the one Commander Vincent sent. For all the hardness in his veneer, Mallory cared about the pilots he taught. Through them, he continued to fly. It weighed on him to love flying so much that he was limited to reading about the lives and tragic deaths of his students even as he knew there was nothing he could do for them once they left Pau.

As they finished eating, Mallory said, "I wish you good luck today, John, and even better luck when you fly against the Boche."

"Thank you, sir. You've taught me things I won't forget."

The words seemed trivial thanks for the man who'd taught him more than how to fly. Mallory's smile reflected his confidence in John. On leaving the office, the memory of Arthur came to John again. He and Peter were close friends at Pau. They were lucky to get the same assignment. As it turned out, they were also unlucky for precisely the same reason.

Later that day, Mallory, one of the monitors who'd assess John's performance, waited for his final landing as a student. Mallory greeted him as he stepped from the Caudron G.2 trainer used for pilot examinations.

"Good show, John. The others agree. I'm tempted to say you've passed with flying colors, but it's a bad pun. How was it up there? I didn't see any problem from the ground."

"I felt an urge to fly to Orly to stop at Mrs. Weeks's. I'm really anxious to join the escadrille, sir." John was elated. He'd reached his goal. Mallory hadn't followed his reference to Mrs. Weeks.

"Mrs. Weeks?"

"Yes, sir. She put me up when I got to Paris. Her son was a legionnaire. When he was killed, she became mother hen to the men. I promised to visit her again."

"A generous woman. Perhaps I'll have a chance to meet her myself. Well, then, your flight test has earned you your wings. There won't be a formal ceremony, as you are the only one to pass today. However, Lieutenant Rennard will present your wings. Have you ever been kissed by a French lieutenant?"

"No, sir!"

"I didn't think so. It's a French custom. A bit like your pat on the back. Harder for some than taking the exam. Courage, old man. You'll survive."

"Captain Mallory, sir."

"Yes, what's on your mind?"

"I've been trying to think of a way to thank you for the help you've been to me here at Pau. I really appreciate—"

Mallory interrupted, "Damn it, Morris, that's why I'm here. I get paid to do that. You've got to help yourself from now on. I only hope I've crammed enough flying into you to give you a decent chance. The thanks I get come when you stay alive and shoot down bloody Boche. Now, your wings are waiting for you in Rennard's office, along with promotion to corporal. They're doing up your identity card and typing your release papers now. By the way, congratulations! You're officially a fighter pilot now, and never forget the operative word—fighter! I expect you to fight to win!"

In farewell, Mallory shook John's hand firmly. John knew

Mallory would be following his progress in the escadrille and hoped he wouldn't be disappointed.

"Yes, sir. That's a promise."

"A promise appreciated. Fight! Just be sure to look around before you charge into the fight."

Mallory's smile vanished as he turned and walked toward a group of nine trainees waiting near the hangar where two Blériots with clipped wings stood. He stopped before them, and John heard him say, "All right, gentleman, you see before you the famous Blériot"—the comment he'd once used to introduce the plane to a smaller group of prospective pilots. It seemed to John that he'd heard those words months ago. He wondered if the newer men would ever know what sort of man Mallory was behind his subtle wit, his crusty British bearing, and the mantle of an instructor.

Most graduates of Pau were sent to the replacement depot at Le Plessis-Belleville for reassignment at the pleasure of French authorities. John's assignment came thanks to his letter to Captain Thénault with the assistance of Ambassador Sharp. The assignment was contingent upon John's success at the flying school in Pau. John had met that obligation. In a private ceremony, Lieutenant Rennard gave John his orders after pinning shiny new wings on his tunic and handing him the chevrons of a corporal. Rennard wished him well. He believed John would be a credit to the Service Aéronautique. John winced but bore no scars from the French custom Mallory had warned him about. His orders directed his immediate departure to Paris.

Before they finished eating, Mallory mentioned arrangements he'd made for John. He'd called Captain Thénault. Thénault would meet John at Mrs. Weeks's house in Paris. It would give John the opportunity to get acquainted with his new commander and provide him with a measure of comfort in transport not normally afforded military personnel traveling to their posts. Thénault owned a motorcar and could take John directly to the airfield, avoiding long walks in the snow from train station to bus stop. The winter of 1917 was one of the worst on record.

By the time he reached Paris, John had nearly removed the luster from his wings in handling the new insignia. Tense but eager, he got off the train in the afternoon of March 29 with orders and a new identity card in hand.

Mrs. Weeks's house still felt warm and friendly. In the sitting room, where he'd embarrassed himself in front of the sergeant with a missing foot, several men were seated. One of them wore the unmistakable uniform of a French officer. Captain Georges Thénault, the commander of the Lafayette Escadrille since its inception in April of 1916, was speaking to a soldier wearing the cleaned uniform of a French infantryman.

John noticed the captain's thin mustache spanning the corners of his mouth. His dark hair receded at the temples. As he came closer, the captain saw him and stood. A German shepherd resting near his feet also stood. Thénault was average in height, thin, and not much older than John. He wore the tired expression of a man who bore the weight of great responsibility.

"Sir, my name is John Morris. I assume you are Capitaine Georges Thénault. It's a pleasure to finally meet you."

John saluted and extended his hand. The captain took it and formally introduced himself. He had a decidedly French accent, but his English was impeccable.

"Happy to meet you, Corporal Morris. May I introduce you to Fram, my four-legged companion? We should depart at once. Saint-Just-en-Chaussée is more than one hour away. Ravenel is not far from that town."

"Yes, sir. I hoped we might start soon. Lead the way, sir. I'll follow you."

"*Bon!* Perhaps you will be the exception."

John wasn't sure what he meant by that. He gathered his bags and followed the captain to his car. Fram walked beside his master's footsteps. He seemed docile for a German shepherd.

John threw his gear onto the rear seat of Thénault's side-flapped touring sedan. Fram sat on the front seat, next to Thénault. The three of them, Thénault, Fram, and John, began the forty-four-mile trip to the base. North of Paris, Ravenel was the fourth aerodrome to be used by the squadron designated N. 124 by the French. The world knew it as the Lafayette Escadrille.

John's mood reflected a mixture of pride in recent achievement and an unknown future. The more prominent mix was the latter. None of his training had come close to simulating combat. He wondered if he'd be good enough, brave enough, or simply lucky enough to survive. His test flight had been a joy. He knew his next flight could be his last. Arthur Meurot's death had proved that.

To Ravenel—March 1917

RAVENEL WAS ROUGHLY THIRTY-SIX MILES north of Paris. The outskirts behind, Thénault was forced to slow the automobile to a crawl. They shared the road with thousands of plodding men, horse-drawn caissons, and military vehicles belching acrid exhaust. An endless stream of men labored north, marching under the weight of supplies, ammunition, field packs, and rifles. Every man belched fog into the frigid evening air and swirling snow. At the sound of Thénault's horn, men cursed and then moved grudgingly into the deeper snow near the side of the road to make room for his automobile to pass.

Thénault told John that General Ludendorff was shortening the Germans line by eliminating the bulge between Bapaume and the Chemin des Dames ridge. They were withdrawing to the Hindenburg Line. The French were following to probe the new boundaries and rebuild defenses in areas they hadn't occupied for a long time.

During the slowest part of the ride, the conversation centered around John's questions about the escadrille. Thénault sketched the pilots' routines. He mentioned the sectors the escadrille had occupied. His account finally reached Cachy, the field N. 124 used before going to Ravenel.

"Groupe de Combat Treize joined us in Cachy last October, twenty-five miles north of Ravenel. Group Twelve was in the field nearby. Guynemer's squadron, the Storks, was the best.

"Georges Guynemer? The French ace?"

"Yes. Twenty-two years old, and already he has eighteen victories. René Fonck and Guynemer are the terrors of the Boche. Guynemer inspired a rivalry among the men. They became better fliers. After Cachy, we came to Ravenel. The weather is terrible now, worse than ever. They are like caged animals. I think the cold and snow has frozen their spirit."

John learned a lot about their former fields but little about his commander. Thénault admitted to being twenty-nine, only three years older than John. He said he graduated from the elite flying school at Saint-Cyr, but that was all. Once they'd passed the marchers, they rode in silence.

Passing villages recently under German occupation, John looked with astonishment. The villages had been destroyed. Whole orchards were cut down, buildings were in shambles, churches torn apart. Even the graves in the cemeteries had been ransacked. The senseless destruction sickened him. He couldn't associate what he saw with the acts of civilized men. Obviously, most of the destruction wasn't simply the misfortunes of war. The destruction looked thoroughly organized and methodically carried out over a span of weeks and months.

The anger in his voice obvious, John asked, "How can anyone do this, Captain? It's incredible! Trees cut down, churches burned, even the graves are dug up!"

"Churches have steeples. Observers use them. From the caskets, they steal lead to make ammunition. They destroy our villages. They are criminals. Animals. That is their war. They will be made to pay for their crimes. They will pay in full!"

It took time to reach Chantilly. After passing under a railway bridge, Thénault turned right.

"As long as we are here, I want to show you something."

Beyond the Grand Condé Hotel, he followed the Boulevard d'Aumale to a large house, part of a complex of buildings. "Joffre no longer lives here since becoming a marshal of France. Foch and high command use it now."

"Is this GQG, Joffre's old headquarters? Is he back in Paris?"

"*Oui!* Paris is where he belongs," Thénault said with relief. "Thousands followed his call for élan. He became a big hero—a hero with blood on his hands. Galliéni was a real hero, a great general! He threw the Boche back across the Marne. He was a fighter! Paris owes its life to him. Joffre should be dead, not Galliéni. We need leaders like Galliéni. No more Joffres."

Retracing their route, they crossed the river Oise at Creil five miles north of Chantilly. John asked a question he'd deferred.

"Captain, when we left Mrs. Weeks, you said something, and I wasn't sure what you meant."

"What was that, Corporal?"

"You said I might be an exception, sir."

"Ah … yes. I remember. Perhaps a small background will explain. In April, we came to Luxeuil to form the escadrille, six pilots and myself. We had trucks, workshops, and good mechanics. We had pavilions for the pilots and hangars for the planes but not a single aeroplane on the field. We could only curse our enemy."

"They hadn't issued airplanes to your group, sir?"

"No! In Fontaine, I asked for their training plane. The first pilot crashed into a hangar. Again, we could only curse the German observers.

"Two weeks later, six Nieuports arrived packed in crates. The mechanics put them together. There was ammunition for only two. In spite of this, the men wanted to fly. They came to my office. I told them we will fly our first patrol. I told them to stay close to me. Two broke formation to chase a German aeroplane. Two without ammunition! They risked their planes for nothing. You said you will follow me. That is why I said you may be the exception. Perhaps you will follow my instructions and take no foolish chances."

"I see. But they must be brave fliers, Captain."

Thénault paused. Passing through Clermont, he dodged the remaining horse-drawn artillery. Eventually, he responded to John's observation.

"They are legionnaires. They are brave. Sometimes too brave. Only three of the original pilots remain, and I am one of those three. They are too stubborn for their own good. They forget the Boche pilots are also brave."

Thénault grew quiet, busying himself with avoiding muddy ruts and weary French soldiers who wandered in front of the car. His last comment had the tone of advice. Now, John knew the odds in the escadrille weren't much better than the odds of others he'd heard about and were worse than he'd hoped. He felt the urge to reply to the question posed by Thénault's comment.

"I'll do my best, Captain."

"Good. The fire exists in you as it does in them. If you are less careless than the others, you may have a positive influence on them. They watch the new ones closely."

Thénault was right to ponder how a new pilot might react to his orders. In the air, a pilot had complete control of his plane. What any pilot did on his own impacted the entire squadron.

A few miles east of Saint-Just-en-Chaussée, Thénault pulled the car onto a dirt road that ran past a group of hastily built hangars.

Snow piled along their sides, giving them an undeserved look of permanence. On a dark and desolate field, he parked near a row of wood-framed huts covered in tarred canvas that served as living quarters for the pilots of N. 124.

Wood smoke spewed from stovepipe chimneys that skewered each hut to the frozen earth. Shifting winds swirled smoke and snow between the huts in patterns that defied gravity. The huts were dark, cold, and barren. It was as gloomy a winter scene as men ever inhabited. Still, he was glad to be where his training had brought him. More than anything, he'd wanted to be here. However cold or desolate, he was the newest pilot on the airfield of the Lafayette Escadrille.

"Your hut is there. The last in line. Two weeks ago, there was a casualty over Flavy-le-Martel. Pilot James McConnell. He was a good man. You will take his place."

John got out, retrieving his things from the rear of the car. Fram moved to spot warmed by John. Thénault's voice revealed emotion even through his accent. He hadn't become jaded by the losses his squadron suffered. Leaving his car, Thénault wished John luck.

"Sir." John saluted. Thénault, not expecting a salute, stiffened and returned the salute and turned toward his hut at the head of the row, closely followed by Fram.

Already shivering, John walked briskly to the last hut. Putting his bags down, he began to reach for the door. The door flew open, and Gervais Raoul Lufbery, a five-foot-seven-inch American of French heritage, fell over one of John's bags on his way out. His eyes, unaccustomed to the dark, Lufbery didn't see John or his bags. He was in a hurry to use the latrine.

"Damn, Corporal, that's a hell of a place to put a goddamn bag. A man could break his neck going to the damned crapper."

"Sorry, sir. I was just about to open the—"

That was as far as the conversation got. John's first encounter with America's first ace was short but sharp. Lufbery had an urgent appointment and no time for idle conversation. John picked up one of his bags and entered the hut. He turned to retrieve the other. Blasts of cold air and snow blew through the open door.

"Hey, Luf! Close the damned door! It's cold enough in here as it is," an impatient voice yelled from inside, his face hidden by a newspaper.

"Sorry, sir. I'm all in now." John had just arrived, and he'd already had to apologize to two of his mates. It was the most inauspicious reception he'd ever experienced.

Coming in from the dark, John's eyes adjusted to the dim light inside the hut. His unfamiliar voice animated the man reading the newspaper. He looked up in time to see John shut the door. The reader was Ted Parsons. He wasn't alone. Two others stood nearby.

"You're the fifth in a month. They must be planning something big," William Thaw said.

"Sorry about the door, sir. Had to get my bags. The other fellow tripped over the one outside. He didn't stay around long enough for me to explain."

Edmond Genêt punctuated John's words with "Lucky you! That other fellow? Let's just say his fuse gets lit quick sometimes … especially when his arthritis is acting up. This weather hasn't helped much. Anyway, I don't see any bruises, Corporal. What's your name?"

"John Morris, sir. I just got in. The captain was kind enough to meet me at Mrs. Weeks's house in Paris. Sorry about the door."

"The captain's a good man. He can use good fliers," said Edmond Genêt.

John walked toward the warmth of the stove. His eyes were drawn to the profile of a Native American's head painted on the wall behind the stove. Complete with war bonnet, the Native American's mouth was frozen in the snarl of a war cry.

"Ed Genêt. Welcome to our cozy hut, Corporal. You like our insignia? Painted it myself after they finally got around to building these huts. Worst quarters we've ever had, but they're better than the holes in the ground we had to dig when got here."

Genêt decided to act as host. He introduced John to the men near the stove. "That's Ted Parsons. Bill Thaw's reading the paper. Where were you trained?"

"At Pau, sir."

"We know about Pau, Corporal. Not a bad school. Nothing like the terrain we fly over here."

The other men remained seated near the warmest spot in the hut. Understanding their desire to stay warm, John stepped over to offer his hand.

The formalities observed, Genêt said, "By the way, that was Raoul Lufbery outside. Luf's known for his temper. Gets the best of him at times. Got him arrested once. A conductor tried to keep him from getting on his train without papers. He made the mistake of grabbing Luf and lost a couple of teeth for his trouble."

"I guess I'd better keep my bags out of his way, sir."

Genêt grinned and nodded.

William Thaw, an original member of the American escadrille, broke into the conversation.

"Hey, Ed, Luf's okay. He gets edgy when he's not flying. He's the oldest and likes to look after the new boys. He only gets mad when he's pressured or one of us gets hit up there. I'd hate to be flying a German plane in this sector when that happens. He's got seven so far, John. Two of 'em on one patrol. Luf's a pro. He's okay when you get to know him."

"I'm glad he's on our side, sir," John said. Warmer blood began to relieve the sting of cold in John's hands and cheeks. Fifteen feet from the stove, he was still exhaling fog. He moved closer to the stove.

The door opened again, and Lufbery came inside heading

straight for the stove, his hands under his armpits. "It's cold as all hell out there. You the new guy?" Lufbery approached John.

His frozen expression was hard to read. John couldn't tell if he was about to shake his hand or break his jaw. Lufbery was still shuddering from the cold.

"What's your name, Corporal?"

"John Morris, sir. I'm sorry about the bag. I'd just put it down to come inside and—"

Lufbery grinned and interrupted. "No harm done, Corporal. It's nice to know my reflexes still work in this damned cold. Did you come from Buc or Pau?"

"Pau. The captain brought me in from Paris. His German shepherd sat between us."

"Fram doesn't care who he sits next to. Fram's the only German we allow around here. He's a lot tamer than the sons of bitches flying Fokkers. Pau's a good school, Corporal. I hope you learned something about flying. Welcome aboard."

Lufbery offered his hand then edged closer to the stove. Feeling more welcome, John had a question for Genêt.

"Sir, can you tell me where McConnell's bunk is? The captain said I should use it."

When John spoke the name of the dead pilot, every head in the tent turned to look at him. For a moment, the only sound was the wind wailing against the walls of the hut.

Genêt picked up one of John's bags. Controlling his emotions, he said, "Follow me."

John wondered how McConnell had died. It was obvious he was missed. Genêt's face was filled with small scars. Curious, and to change the subject, John asked him about them.

"Sir, if you don't mind my asking, how'd you get those cuts?"

Genêt smiled. "Look, John, around here we don't normally call each other 'sir.' That's reserved for the captain. As for the scars, I got hit about a week ago. The swelling's down now. The weather's been too lousy to patrol since then. When it breaks, the orderlies will wake us, yelling, '*Monsieur, il fait beau!*' It gets cold up there. We drink a lot of hot coffee. Parsons got frostbite on his toe. He couldn't walk for a while. Grounded him for a week. Still bothers him. I was lucky. When you go up, be sure to wear every stitch of wool you own under your coat, or you'll freeze. Hopping clouds at ninety-mile-an-hour at ten thousand feet, the prop wash will freeze any exposed skin in no time. I put a heavy cream on my cheeks below the goggles when I go up. I'll give you some."

"Thanks. I saw smoke coming from the hangars. Where do the mechanics sleep?"

"They've got their own hut. They cut down empty fuel cans and build fires in them. Otherwise, we couldn't start the engine. Heat keeps the oil from freezing. When it gets too thick, the mechanic can't spin the propeller fast enough. Here it is, John. This was Mac's bunk. We'll talk later, after you've had time to get your stuff organized."

"Thanks, sir. I mean, *Ed.* I won't be long."

John spread his things on the bunk, putting the smaller ones on the wooden shelf behind the bunk. His clothing went into a wooden trunk at the foot of the bunk. Sitting on McConnell's bunk, he felt an urge to write. He'd written home once from Pau after Eugene died. Addressing the letter to both Catherine and Michael, he'd kill two birds with the same stone. John hated to write and decided not to mention McConnell. McConnell's memory should remain with those who flew with him. Until John was accepted as one the pilots, he wouldn't ask about McConnell.

Weeks would pass before he learned that Genêt's wounds were caused on McConnell's last patrol. Genêt blamed himself for McConnell's death and refused treatment for his wounds. McConnell had disappeared into a cloud as they climbed toward a couple of German observation planes. Genêt climbed to engage one. The observer in the two-seater was a marksman. The strut he hit exploded, sending hardwood splinters into Genêt's face, streaming blood into his eyes. A coupler snapped, adding to his injuries. In the severe cold, the pain was hard to bear. With bullets continuing to punch holes in his wings, Genêt turned into the clouds. He never saw McConnell again. After looking for him in vain, he returned to the field utterly dejected. McConnell never returned to the base and was assumed to be lost or killed.

John wrote about the cold and how flying was all but impossible due to thick layers of snow clouds. A pilot might as well fly in a fog, unable to see anything, or for that matter, to discern up from down. John had experienced the phenomenon during his last week at Pau when he came out of a cloud, surprised to see his plane headed down and banked in a sharp turn.

Addressing the letter to Catherine, John tried to keep it light, mixed with news of Pau and his arrival at Ravenel. He tried to describe what flying was like.

> The only canopy is the sky. The wind never dies when you fly. Do you remember when we were kids? We used to go to Electric Park to ride the roller coaster. That's as close as you can get to the sensation of flying on land. It's a shame they tore it down. We had a lot of fun there. I wish we could do it again someday.
>
> I'm not sure when the weather will clear. It's colder than I can remember at home.
>
> Snow is packed along the side of the hut. It helps to keep the wind out. The huts aren't very

airtight. Wind still gets under the eaves, bringing in snowflakes. That's all for now. When I get back, we'll see if there's a coaster in Pennsylvania.

Take care, and say hello to Mom and Dad for me.

John

He put the Guilford address on the letter and returned to the clubroom to get warmer. The sun hadn't shown itself all day. As he sat watching the other pilots, a huge cat padded up and unceremoniously plopped down on one of John's feet. Its head was abnormally large and definitely of the feline species. It was a lion!

"Looks like Whiskey's taken a liking to you," said Bill Thaw. "Soda should be around here somewhere. Probably asleep under someone's bunk."

"You mean there's another lion in the hut?"

"Yup. Whiskey got lonely. Needed company. Besides, he was getting a little frisky with the mechanics' dogs. They're good mascots. Especially in the cold. They'll keep your feet warm if you're lucky enough to have them park on 'em like Whiskey there. You should feel honored, Corporal. He doesn't usually do that for a new guy."

"I'm not sure honored is what I feel, sir," John responded, wishing the honor had fallen on Thaw's feet instead of his. The only lions he'd ever seen were in zoos and safely caged.

"You'll get used to it. Listen, John, we like to use first names around here. If you stop calling me 'sir,' I'll stop calling you 'Corporal.' Is that a deal?"

"Yes, sir. I mean, sure, Bill. Whatever you say."

"Good. We don't worry about rank around here. You're welcome to use whatever amenities we have, like that gramophone over there."

John hadn't noticed it tucked away in a corner of the hut. A small table held a crank-handled gramophone near a roulette wheel. Lufbery was cranking the gramophone. He placed a record on the turntable. A ukulele began playing a tune called "My Honolulu Girl." Raoul had a wistful expression that said, *I'd rather be there than here.* Compared to Ravenel, Hawaii was a furnace. John hadn't seen a girl since he'd left Saint-Nazaire.

He left Lufbery alone, remembering what Ed had told him about Luf. Besides, Whiskey was lying on his feet and had started to gnaw playfully at a corner of his boot. Just as his feet began feeling warmer, Genêt bounded in from the cold darkness.

"John, the captain wants to see you. Do you know which hut he's in?"

"Yes. The one at the other end of the row. Thanks, Ed."

As John tried to stand, Whiskey gave an irritated growl, indicating that he wasn't happy to let go of John's boot. John had to disappoint him. Some things took priority over a mascot.

"Sorry, Whiskey. Got to go see the captain."

"Don't worry, John, he'll start chewing it when you get back," Bill Thaw advised.

John hoped he was wrong. He was wearing his fur-lined flying boots and needed them in one piece.

He went to his bunk to get his wool-lined jacket and gloves. For ear protection, he had a leather pilot's helmet with earflaps or his long scarf. The wind blew so hard, he could swear he heard the hut's canvas humming. He decided on the scarf.

On the way out, a gust of wind blew the door out of his hand and wide open. John turned and forced it closed. Moving quickly, he turned and jumped off the step. His next stride was supposed to be the first in a series intending to dash through the snow to Thénault's hut. As luck—or the lack of it—would have it, he knocked an unseen man flat on his back. John was shocked to see

Lufbery outside and on the ground again. His neck reddened with embarrassment, but the urge to laugh was strong. He immediately thought better of it. Lufbery wasn't smiling.

Raoul's face showed more surprise than anger. He threw an arm behind his back to help him spring quickly to his feet. Recognizing John, he let go, fell backward, and began laughing as he hit the snow. John was surprised by his reaction.

"If you could only see your face!" Luf exclaimed through laughter. He rose more slowly than originally intended. "Okay, so you didn't do the job right the first time and decided to do it better this time. I admire your tenacity. Your expression saved you this time."

"I'm really sorry, sir. I didn't see you. The captain asked me—"

"Okay, okay, but two times is enough for one night. Everyone calls me Luf, Corporal. What's your name, again?"

"John Morris. Really, Luf, I didn't see you. Honest! The door flew open and I—"

"Take it easy, John. The only thing we apologize for around here is not taking a Boche off a buddy's tail." Lufbery's point was well taken.

"I've got to run, Luf. I'll see you when I get back."

Lufbery wasn't ready to let John go just yet.

"Tomorrow morning, John. I'm going to hit the sack. If the weather clears, I'll be up before sunrise." He put a hand on John's shoulder. "Hey. Watch where you're going next time, okay? I'd hate to have to scrape myself off the ground every time we run into each other."

"Okay, Luf. I'll be more careful. Especially now that I know you might be wandering around with a bladder problem." John ran as Raoul faked a punch. For a loner, Lufbery had a sense of humor, though he hid it well behind his supposed temper.

John knocked at the captain's door before entering. Thénault sat behind a large, crude wooden table on which a map and other papers were scattered. A handwritten chart hung from nails on a wooden wall, its columns and rows labeled in French. His interest aroused, he looked closer. The first column listed pilots' names followed by rows of mostly empty boxes under labels marking the days of the week. Boxes that weren't empty had check marks in them. It was a duty roster.

"You wanted to see me, sir?"

"Yes, Sergeant Morris."

"*Sergeant* Morris, sir?"

"*Oui*, Sergeant Morris. In N. 124, the flier's rank is my responsibility. I promote the pilots of N. 124. Your record at Pau and graduation from the École de Combat is evidence of your flying skill. You were praised for having the quality of leadership, a rare compliment from Pau. This is the primary basis for your promotion. Your new insignia, Sergeant. I leave the privilege of sewing them on to you. Do so tonight.

"This is not the main reason I have called you. First, I welcome you officially to the Lafayette Escadrille. The escadrille is a unique unit, as you know. We are in the public eye. The conduct of pilots is therefore observed by all sides, not only GQG, but by your countrymen and mine. Our record is our reputation, whether we fly or visit a town for pleasure. The Boche themselves take special interest in us. Therefore, we have a simple policy.

"First, I must warn you against consorting with ladies of a certain, shall we say, ancient profession. Moreover, the escadrille does not tolerate drinking to excess, as this not only endangers you but those with whom you patrol. Your conduct must meet the highest standards. These are set by GQG and must be observed without exception. I enforce all of them.

"I ask you not only to become the fighter of your expectation but of my expectation. While on patrol, you will follow the directions of the patrol leader without question. Each pilot must carry out his duty and help the others when necessary. Your assignment gives you the opportunity to serve France as well as fly with the escadrille. Prepare yourself and your aeroplane for whatever comes on patrol. But, beyond this … never forget why you are here. An airplane can be replaced. A pilot must be trained. Do you understand?"

"Yes, sir."

"Good. You may return to your quarters."

"Thank you, sir." John saluted and returned to the cold night. Most of the others had gone to bed. News of his promotion could wait. After sewing on his new rank, John slid into his bunk. His thoughts kept him awake.

Up to his last statement, nothing Thénault said was accompanied by facial expression. In making his last point, his eyes hardened and seemed to stare through John. There was no denying his meaning. John's duty was to kill the enemy. John had tucked that idea away in the recesses of his conscious thought. Thénault brought the idea squarely to the forefront. John was taught to fly and to shoot down enemy airplanes. Thénault expected him to shoot to kill. Killing the men who flew, even his enemies, provoked a more visceral feeling.

Though the cold was outside, an involuntary shudder coursed down the length his spine that had nothing to do with the cold. John hadn't felt a shudder like that since he was dared to do something new and risky as a child. He'd always accepted a dare. An hour's worth of wind and snow blew past the hut before his eyes finally closed.

AM at Ravenel

EARLY THE NEXT MORNING, THE weather was worse than the night before. The escadrille remained grounded. John hadn't slept well. Excitement didn't encourage sleep. The first place he went was a dark hangar where Thaw had told him his airplane was housed. Lit by lanterns and the fire from oil drums, the Nieuport presented a dark but impressive silhouette resting on the dirt floor. Its nose up, it appeared to be flying. Closer inspection revealed its newness. It wasn't completely assembled and still reeked of uncured dope. It lacked insignia and armament. He felt glad that the weather was bad. Otherwise, he could only watch others go on patrol. His mechanic was on leave, expected to return when the weather cleared.

In spite of the weather, anticipation among the pilots arose from recent headlines. On January 31, 1917, Count von Bernstorff, the German ambassador in Washington, told the US State Department that his country would renew unrestricted submarine warfare the following day. Wilson had often warned Germany against such a change in policy. Nevertheless, U-boats resumed sinking ships without warning on February 1. Two days later, Wilson ended Bernstorff's tenure, and America severed diplomatic relations with the German Empire. It wasn't a declaration of war, but it was as close as Wilson had gotten to ask Congress for a declaration of war.

Wilson warned that if German U-boats committed any overt acts against American ships at sea, he would ask Congress to declare war. He told Congress to arm merchant vessels. Kaiser Wilhelm returned threat for threat. If merchant ships fired on German boats, Wilhelm would sink all armed merchant ships and detain every American presently in Germany.

In February, the *Housatonic* and the Cunard liner *Laconia* were both sunk with loss of American lives. The sinkings raised speculation among the pilots. Would Wilson finally keep his promise? For days, hopes ran high at Ravenel. The talk faded when Wilson failed to carry out his threat, even as the kaiser added fuel to the fire. On March 1, news came that a message from Arthur Zimmerman, the German foreign secretary, to Count Bernstorff was intercepted. It suggested that Mexico be convinced into war with the United States. An America engaged in a border war would not send its army to Europe.

The note erased any doubt about German motives. American isolationists lost credibility. Even then, Wilson didn't ask Congress for war. In disbelief, the pilots' grew disgusted. They argued the issue to death. The topic in the huts returned to weather. Though still cold, the skies were beginning to clear. Thénault warned them to keep their airplanes in flying condition.

The prospect of a new land offensive was raised. French *poilus* were being transported to areas destined for attack. Several pilots flew single missions. John's airplane was nearly ready. A second coat of dope was applied to its fabric and had nearly dried. With clearing weather, Thénault choose from three types of patrol. Unless he had orders from Commandant Philippe Féquant assigning the squadron a specific task, Thénault made the selection himself. At the end of March, Thénault had no such orders. The choice was his.

On defensive patrol, the fliers remained over friendly territory, preventing enemy planes of any type from penetrating the imaginary wall that extended upward from the front lines. An offensive patrol sent the pilots through the wall. They became *pilotes de chasse*, hunters of enemy airplanes.

His third choice was reconnaissance. Observation planes normally used for the purpose were slow in bringing intelligence to Grand Quartier Général, GQG. Thénault normally informed the pilots of his choice the evening before the patrol. That evening, he called them together.

"Gentlemen. In the morning, weather permitting, Lieutenant Thaw will lead a reconnaissance patrol. In the afternoon, Corporal Genêt will lead an offensive patrol. Select your pilots, gentlemen. Good luck, and good hunting."

Both patrols would bring the pilots over German lines. Of the two, the morning patrol was by far the more dangerous.

Thaw conducted reconnaissance at low altitude. His patrol was not only subject to attack from above, the position sought by enemy fighters, but from below, in range of antiaircraft, machine gun, and even rifle fire. If the patrol flew through a valley, hostile fire could come from hilltops, directed downward on the hedgehopping planes. At low altitude, precious little time existed to glide to a safe landing. A crippled plane had seconds to fall. Thaw was a specialist at these patrols, and Lufbery liked to fly as his cover.

Saturday morning, a week after John's arrival, the clouds scattered. The morning patrol was already in the air. Lufbery and Thaw were well beyond the Somme. To his surprise, Edmond Genêt awoke John at six thirty that morning with a question.

"My hunting license takes effect this afternoon, John. How do you feel about flying? Ted Parsons and Harold Willis are coming." John had been ready since the day he arrived. His airplane was also finally ready. Parsons's mechanic had installed its armament the day before. Félix, John's mechanic, had finally arrived late the night before. Since Félix had gone directly to bed, John had yet to meet him.

"When do we go, Ed?"

"One o'clock. Right after lunch. You coming?"

"I'll be ready when you are. I'd rather be up there than waiting down here."

At the prospect of his first combat patrol, adrenaline instantly caused his hands to quiver. He decided to eat breakfast and skip lunch. Mallory's advice about nervous fliers crossed his mind. Though his Nieuport 17 was ready, he was anxious to verify the fact with Félix. John wasn't aware whether Félix spoke English or only French. He certainly hoped he was bilingual. John had yet to master even basic social dialogue in French. He couldn't possibly engage Félix in a detailed discourse concerning his airplane's motor, rigging, or armament in French.

After a breakfast that included enough hot coffee to float a seaplane, he headed to the hangar for another look at his biwinged fighter. As always, the hangar smelled of castor oil and gasoline, the fuel mixture he'd become accustomed to smelling at Pau. In the closed hangar, the odors mingled with the smell of curing wing dope, still strong enough to make him dizzy.

He marked the improvements over the Nieuports he'd flown at the École Nieuport, where he'd piloted the Model 11, called the Bébé. The Nieuport 17 had the nickname Superbébé. The addition of a 110 horsepower Le Rhône engine gained 30 horsepower. Greater power under the cowling increased its rate of climb, making it faster than the Fokker E.IIIs. Its top speed was 102 miles per hour, five miles faster than the Bébé. To make the greater speed effective, the lower wing was strengthened, ending its tendency to break off in a high-speed dive. Important advances in design, they gave the pilots an edge they had not enjoyed over their German opponents for months.

Most of the squadron favored retention of a single Lewis machine gun mounted above the upper wing. Its muzzle was above the arc of a spinning propeller to avoid hitting the blades. The synchronized Vickers in front of the windscreen on the cowling was known to shatter the wooden propeller when its timing gear loosen and failed. Nevertheless, John wanted both guns. If one failed, the other was used. To be sure, he wanted to test both with the engine running before taking off that afternoon.

He inspected the Nieuport, proudly noticing the initials *JEM* painted near the tail. The Seminole war chief was also there, painted in profile near the center of the fuselage. Its red, white, and blue feathered war bonnet crowned its head. Its raging silhouette was an exact match for the one painted in the hut and added a purely American accent to the French aircraft.

John put his foot in the cutout at the bottom of the fuselage to climb into the cockpit. The odor of dope still curing on the wings was strong. The Nieuport's instruments shone brightly. Not a hint of wear showed on the control stick. John was about to step over the padded leather roll around the cockpit when a bearded man wearing a French beret and a smile walked toward him. If it hadn't been for his fur jacket and boots, the man could have passed for a French farmer. John heard his words but understood few of them. Félix did not speak English.

"Bonjour, monsieur. Félix Henriot, mécanicien. Et vous?"

His disadvantage complete, John made an attempt to communicate in tortured French.

"Ah…jay swee John Morris. How is … ah … la airplane. Is it okay?"

He knew he'd failed when the man's eyebrows rose in astonishment compounded by confusion. At Pau, with Arthur's help, John had learned a saving French phrase. This was as good a time as any to use it: "Jay no parlay pah la Fron say."

At some point, Ted Parsons had come into the hangar. Ted wanted to check his Nieuport before the patrol. John didn't know how long he'd been standing there but was glad Parsons offered to help. Ted spoke French fluently.

"That was an interesting speech, John." Parsons found it difficult to restrain laughter and was sorely tempted not to make the effort. He gave Félix John's name and explained that the Nieuport was John's aeroplane.

"*Félix, mon ami, il est John Morris, un pilote de chasse. Le Nieuport, c'est à lui, oui?*" He turned toward John and said, "He wasn't sure who you were, John. Your French had him confused." Turning back to Felix, Ted continued, "*Je lui parlerai, Félix. Il est innocent. Seulement Anglais, oui?*" Ted explained John's obvious language handicap.

"*Ah, bon.*" Félix said with a shrug and a sigh.

"Felix didn't know you only spoke English, John. I'll ask him about your plane. *Le Nieuport, Félix. C'est bon?*"

"*Oui. Bon état, monsieur.*" Félix added that he was about to finish his preflight checks and add fuel when he saw John climbing into the cockpit.

John stood there, wondering what in the world these people were talking about. Ted asked Félix a crucial question on John's behalf.

"*Parlez-vous English un peu, Félix?*"

Felix said he spoke no English at all. Ted looked at John, "I'm sorry, John. He won't be much good to you." Ted had an idea that might solve John's problem. Addressing Félix again, he asked, "*Où est Charles?*"

If Charles Gallau agreed, John's problem was solved.

"*Sur le champ*," Félix said. Charles was on the field.

"*Rapporté Charles ici, oui?*"

"*Oui, monsieur.*" Felix walked out of the hangar to find Charles Gallau. If willing, Charles would solve John's language problem. He spoke English.

"Sorry to keep you in suspense, John. Félix said your plane is okay. He doesn't speak any English, I'm afraid. He can't be much help to you as your mechanic. I asked him to get Charles Gallau. Charles is my mechanic and speaks better English than the whole bunch. When they get back, I'll suggest we switch places. How does that sound?"

"Great! But you shouldn't give me your mechanic. It breaks up your team."

"I've only been here two months. It's not like Charles and I are married. Besides, I insist! You've got to be able to talk to your mechanic so you can explain the little quirks that come up in the engine. Sign language won't do when you're talking about carburetors and missing cylinders."

Ted was right. John didn't press the issue.

"Okay, Ted, if you're sure."

"I'm sure. We have a few hours before takeoff. Join me for coffee when Charles gets here."

"Okay. I've had plenty already, but it's awful cold out here."

"Cold? Wait 'til you get aloft!" Ted warned. "You can lose some toes up there if you're not careful." Ted wasn't joking.

Félix returned with Charles, and Parsons explained the situation. Charles said he'd be happy to service John's machine. It made no difference to Félix which Nieuport he was assigned. Both were good mechanics. To break the ice, Charles spoke to his new pilot.

"This forces me to speak English. I will learn more fast."

John thanked Félix and shook Charles's hand. Even with his accent, John understood every word. Charles went straight to work checking everything Félix would have checked.

"This makes things easier, Ted. Thanks. Let's get that coffee. I'm cold just standing around! I'll ask Charles to help me check the alignment of the guns before we take off."

The wood-framed shack serving as kitchen and dining room was located adjacent to the hangars. As they left, the mechanics began speaking in their native tongue and started to laugh.

"What was that all about?" John asked.

"Félix just cracked a little joke, John. It was harmless."

"Well, I guess I can blame myself for that. I wish I knew the language like my sister. Catherine could talk to them for hours and never pick up a dictionary."

"You've got a sister?"

"Younger brother and sister. Catherine studies at Bryn Mawr. A French major. For a while, we thought she might become a teacher. Michael graduates from Hopkins next summer. He wrote a while back to say he was going to volunteer with the navy."

"Johns Hopkins in Baltimore?"

"Yeah. Are you familiar with the medical school?"

"Not exactly. But Hopkins has a reputation. Is your family originally from Baltimore?"

"Yes. My great-great-grandfather Marcus Morris left England for Canada in 1813. A year later, he went to Baltimore to open a law office. Dad said he watched the British frigates fire on Fort McHenry in Baltimore's harbor back in 1814. How about you, Ted? Where are you from?"

"Holyoke, Massachusetts, just above Springfield."

"Is that near Boston?"

"Not very. Boston's a good seventy-odd miles east. Springfield's a quaint little town. I haven't been back for some time."

In the mess hut, pilots and mechanics crowded wooden tables. Ted and John poured coffee into tin cups and walked toward the stove to get warm. The odor of a spicy vegetable soup filled the hut, creating the aura of a kitchen in a French cottage. Their conversation remained light at first. Both complained about the cold. Paris came next. Ted gave John the names of two places the pilots frequented when away from the aerodrome. Ted was calm, nothing like Eugene.

"When did you come over, Ted?"

"Last year on the *Carpathia*, the ship that responded to *Titanic*'s SOS. Five years ago, I think. The same year New Mexico and Arizona became states. Time flies!"

"I remember. For a different reason. Dad took us to the Fifth Regiment Armory in Baltimore to hear Teddy Roosevelt. The year they elected him head of the Bull Moose Party."

"I often wonder whether we'd have been better prepared for this if TR were president instead of Wilson. Teddy didn't mind intervening in foreign affairs as much as Wilson."

"Dad liked him. I ought to write to my dad, but we don't have a lot in common. He didn't want me to come. It wasn't easy to convince him about joining the squadron. How did you get into flying?"

"I came on the pretense of being a veterinarian. I don't know a damned thing about horses. I asked for transfer into the ambulance service. When the squadron formed, I decided to switch. I'd already done some flying in Mexico."

"Mexico? How come? We aren't exactly on good speaking terms with Mexico these days."

"All in all, the reason we joined isn't too dissimilar, John. The paths we took are as different as night and day."

Ted began to tell John his story but stopped and sat perfectly still. He was listening to something over the noise in the hut. A low rumble from outside the hut suddenly ceased.

"Lufbery and Thaw are coming back."

"I don't hear anything," John said.

"They glide in. Cut their engines before landing."

John had gotten interested in Ted's story. "You were saying you flew in Mexico?"

"Yes. I trained fliers for Madero and a man calling himself Jeff de Villa. It didn't work out. The plane was junk when we got it ... an old patched-up Curtiss. The first day, I barely landed it with a student on board. The others ran off. They wanted nothing more to do with flying. Vamoosed like a covey of flushed quail.

"After that, I did a little reconnaissance for the general, but the plane wiped out. I went to Chihuahua for parts when a friend of mine pulled me up to his room. He said I should pack up and go home while I had the chance. Villa was heading for trouble with the States and didn't think I should get mixed up in it. I took the advice. He was a German agent and knew what he was talking about. That was all there was to it, John. I packed up and left."

"You're right. We sure got into flying differently. The men I knew at Pau had never flown before. A lot of them came from the ambulance corps, like you. Some from the infantry."

"Thaw and Rockwell were infantrymen before they switched."

"Rockwell? I don't think I've met him."

"No, I guess you haven't. He was shot down by a two-seater. The Boche used explosive bullets. Rockwell caught one in the middle of the chest."

"I hadn't heard about it."

"We lost a few like that. It's not easy to approach an Aviatik. Their only blind spot is underneath. It's not an ideal approach, but the rear gunner can't get his gun on you from that angle. Best to surprise them when you can ... out of the sun or cloud. Albert Ball does it like that. Flies underneath, tilts his Lewis gun up, and fires through the keel. Right up their backsides. Bit of a shock, don't you think?"

John's shoulders drew up, as if to avoid bullets. "I'll say! Gives you a funny feeling just thinking about it. Say, what time it's getting to be, Ted?"

Ted slid his sleeve past his wristwatch. "Damn! It's late. We should get back to the hangar. It's best to warm the engines and test the guns before taking off. Let's go, John. We've got enough time."

In less than thirty minutes, the pilots on fighter patrol, John's first, were in their airplanes. Wind blew hard and cold on the field. The pilots faced their planes directly into it, like ships at sea confronting the waves of a raging storm.

They waited for Genêt's Nieuport to start rolling, the signal to line up for takeoff. All four planes would leave the field in single file with Genêt in front, followed by Parsons, Willis, and then John. They'd climb and form in echelon. Genêt's plane would lead the formation at the bottom so those flying above and behind could see his hand signals.

As the last in line, John would fly at the top of the echelon. In theory, the highest plane had the best view to observe and attack anything below. Altitude was favored in attack. Having never been in the position before, John tried to think through the advantage. His mind kept reminding him that the upper plane in the rear of the echelon formation was also the most vulnerable to attack from planes at even higher altitude. He'd have to split his attention between what was going on below and above. He'd be like a goose at the tail end of a flight of geese, the most exposed to the claws of a diving eagle.

Waiting for Genêt to roll, John fought the image until it was replaced by something worse. As he lined up his plane, he couldn't escape the feeling that he was being watched from above. Directing his thoughts to the sound of the engine, its low, rhythmic drone dispelled the feeling for a time, but it returned. Some entity, hidden from view, seemed focused on him from a devilish place aloft. John didn't believe in premonitions and was fully aware this was his first combat patrol. He attributed the feeling to preflight jitters and forced the thought from his mind.

He cursed himself for having the nerves of a rookie. Then he smiled. He was a rookie! The only cure for that was combat. Up there, he'd be too busy staying alive to think about premonitions. To reassure himself, John looked up. Nothing was above but his wing and the cold, gray, windblown clouds. The heavens were empty as they took off from Ravenel. Whatever he sensed, it disappeared the instant the plane lifted off. Flying required undivided attention. He began by reading his instruments.

He spoke the numbers aloud while listening to his engine as the plane slowly rose. "Altitude 1,100 feet; 1,600 RPM; airspeed 74." The higher he went, the more he became conscious of the feeling in his stomach. It felt almost like a living thing, somehow separate from his other organs. His throat tightened. Every foot the plane rose added dryness to his mouth and fire to the back of his neck. The memory of the fate of Arthur managed to intrude during his climb into the cold, damp wind. He pulled his scarf tighter across his nose and focused on flying the airplane. "2,400 feet; 1,640 RPM; airspeed 78."

Mallory's advice entered his mind. John wasn't in training now; this wasn't Pau. He was flying a deadly French fighter over the Somme. Its guns were primed and ready. This was no exercise. This was real. He felt the nakedness of a green pilot, a man looking for or becoming prey. "3,200; 1,675; 85." The numbers became more like prayer beads than measurements. The plane's altitude slowly climbed—too slowly to suit John. Altitude was safe. The higher, the better.

"3,800; 1,690; 87." A flush of warm air puzzled him for

a moment. *At least the engine's gotten warm!* John adjusted his rate of climb to the formation. He'd risen too high, too fast. The temperature gauge read 205 degrees. It should be reading 180 or 190.

"Damn!" The curse came out of frustration. What was he doing? He was five hundred feet higher than Genêt and had to throttle back to avoid sliding ahead of Willis. Speaking to himself aloud emphasized the anger at himself. It was meant to snap him out of his awkward state of mind.

"That's how got Eugene killed! Calm down! Get hold of yourself! Think!" This time, he took his own advice. Hours seemed to pass before they reached an altitude of twelve thousand feet. Leveling off, John became calmer. He surveyed the sky above. He neither saw nor felt anything strange. His gaze shifted to Genêt, looking for hand signals. Nothing had changed. After a while, Genêt signaled a turn. The entire group banked to the east, heading toward a town called Ham.

P.M. at Ravenel

DURING THÉNAULT'S BRIEFING BEFORE THE patrol, he told Genêt he couldn't go with them. Thaw's reconnaissance report must be delivered to GQG. As it turned out, Willis wouldn't be going. Four miles from Ravenel, Willis fell behind, signaling engine trouble. Seconds later, his engine died. As John watched, Willis drew a finger across his neck. Willis's propeller slowed, turning from the force of wind. When cylinder compression overcame the wind, it stopped spinning. His Nieuport became a glider. Willis sideslipped out the patrol. He must try to glide back to the field. Waving to John, Willis banked his luckless plane south. John noticed a thin stream of smoke trailing behind the Nieuport as Willis circled, heading for the field at Ravenel.

An unlucky omen for the patrol, John hoped bad luck wasn't contagious. He craned to keep Willis in sight, making sure his Nieuport was gliding, not stalling or spinning. At this altitude, Willis should be able to glide back to the base for repairs. If the problem wasn't serious, he could rejoin them over Péronne, north of Ham, the town Genêt had selected for rendezvous if the patrol grew separated in combat. The three remaining planes continued to climb. Minutes later, they reached standard patrol altitude, lower than if Genêt had flown at full throttle and maximum pitch. Genêt decided it wasn't necessary. No enemy planes were sighted, and until they were well over enemy-held territory, there was no need to stress the engines.

The cold became bitter. John's engine ran well but radiated little warmth to his open cockpit. Parsons was right. Toes and fingers could easily freeze. The chill penetrated John's insulated gloves. His nose and feet were already too cold, and his fingers had little feeling left. John began to switch hands on the stick to beat his free hand on his leg and encourage blood to circulate. Freezing wind blew under his goggles making his cheeks sting. He shifted his scarf to cover them, wrapping it around his face twice, glad the scarf was so long. He tucked the ends into his flight jacket to keep them from tugging at his head in the draft streaming around the windscreen. He needed no distractions from the wind on his first patrol.

The patrol reached fourteen thousand feet over the Somme and headed northeast toward Saint-Quentin. Genêt began to gently slide his control stick from side to side to avoid flight in a straight line. The others followed his lead. The maneuver prevented an enemy in the rear from having a steady target in his gunfights. A normal procedure, especially on solo patrol, Genêt's irregular pattern was impossible to follow closely and forced the echelon to expand, trading tight formation for the benefit of defensive maneuvering. Tight formations were better. But at the start of combat, each pilot used his own judgment. Since clouds hovered above, Genêt's movement made sense.

The front lines were visible in the distance. John glanced over the side, anticipating a hand signal from Genêt. There was none. As they neared the front, John began to look carefully for enemy planes. He checked his position in formation by leaning the stick left, using his rudder to maintain course. The maneuver improved his view above and below. He scanned the sky overhead for enemy planes and saw nothing but clouds. Below, everything was vastly different.

Even at fifteen thousand feet, John saw ruin. Long stretches of the surface looked more like a scruffy moonscape planted with broken trees and saturated with craters from thousands of artillery shells. Layered in snow, the craters revealed crescent shadows. Some, capped with ice, reflected beams of skylight. A blanket of snow made short stretches of damage invisible. Snapping out of his gaze, he again looked for aircraft flying low. Snow on the field of battle made an ideal background for spotting enemy airplanes. John noticed nothing but the drone of his engine and the wind on his face. For an instant, he felt totally alone. To reassure himself, he checked the position of the others on patrol.

Forty minutes into the flight, Genêt switched to level flight and wagged his wings, signaling that he'd sighted an enemy airplane. Genêt pointed down on his port side. A raised fist signaled that he was about to attack. Parsons and John stopped maneuvering. Both looked, trying to spot the enemy airplane. John thought he saw a tiny shape flying in the mist that rose as high as five thousand feet emanating from a tributary of the Somme north of Ham.

Genêt began to turn. Parsons climbed to John's altitude to fly abreast, breaking the echelon. Genêt did not signal them to follow. He wanted them to stay aloft to provide top cover for his plane. Parsons searched above while John checked the flanks and then watched Genêt. Genêt didn't dive directly at the enemy plane. His turn was wide and nearly level. At full throttle, Genêt circled to the northwest to get sunlight trickling through the clouds behind his back. John admired the tactic but wondered if it would put the enemy out of range.

The German rose above the river's haze. John could see the plane clearly. It was a two-seater, an Aviatik C.III, maybe the same one that got Rockwell. The observer's seat was in the open, a few feet behind the pilot and upper wing. Genêt's attack would come from the front, making the observer's gun useless, but not the pilot's. A dangerous option, Genêt was trying for surprise.

Parsons signaled John to follow. Without accelerating or changing altitude, they banked left, staying close enough to Genêt to give him cover. Up to now, the German hadn't seen their planes. The light cloud concealed Genêt's descent. In minutes, he'd gotten ahead of the slower plane and was in position to attack. John observed in numbed fascination, watching a hawk about to pounce on an unwary sparrow.

Parsons waggled his wings and pointed due west. Three miles away and descending, a German fighter turned toward Genêt. It was an Albatros moving to intercept. Parsons signaled that he was going to engage the Albatros, and he veered to the right at full throttle on a direct course to intercept the intruder. Again, there was no signal to follow. John was left alone to cover both Genêt and Parsons. His responsibility had doubled.

John watched Genêt begin a shallow dive a mile in front of the Aviatik. The pilot of the Albatros saw Parsons's plane and banked sharply east, diving to gain speed. John had to look right to see Parsons, left to watch Genêt. With Willis gone, his duty was to help the flier in the most trouble. As of yet, both seemed not to need his help. Nevertheless, he began to circle toward Genêt.

The observer in the Aviatik saw Parsons's Nieuport. He reached a hand to get his pilot's attention. Distracted, the pilot turned his head to look seconds before Genêt began firing from sixty yards. The German veered sharply, reacting instinctively as bullets hit a strut between his wings. With Parsons and Genêt engaged, John did his best to monitor both at the same time. When chance presented itself, he looked briefly for other enemy planes above or below.

Parsons and the Albatros became a writhing tangle in the sky, performing crazy loops, rolls, and turns, each trying to get behind the other. Meanwhile, Genêt turned to get behind the Aviatik, firing whenever the plane came into his gun sights. The observer returned bullet with bullet. Again, John surveyed the sky above and below. No other planes seemed to be in the air. He began to feel left out of the action. As long as he was not under attack, his duty was clear. He stayed aloft.

The Aviatik went into a dive and turned back to the north toward friendlier skies. With Genêt in pursuit of the Aviatik, John turned and put his plane in a shallow dive to make a pass at the Albatros Parsons was engaging without success. He set the throttle wide open, and the Nieuport's engine responded by roaring and pressing him against the leather cushion behind his back. He tried to anticipate the next maneuver of the enemy plane. Halfway there, another plane caught the corner of John's eye, coming from behind a cloud to his left. The plane was on a nearly parallel course, well above and in front. It was about a mile away. Surprised, the new plane drew all of his attention as he tried to identify it. Cloud mist was thick. John couldn't discern its markings.

Until he identified it, caution dictated that he assume the plane was German. He searched for the French bull's-eye on the lower wing. It was there. No Iron Cross adorned its wings. His relief was instant. The tail, painted blue, white, and red, was exactly like his. He felt even better when the insignia on the fuselage took on the shape of a Native American's head. His heart, still pounding from the initial sighting, he said aloud. "It must be Willis. I guess the problem wasn't serious."

Satisfied, John looked ahead. Parsons and the Albatros had climbed and were heading northeast. He watched Ted slowly close the gap. Catching them now would be pure luck, for he could only match Parsons's speed. As it was the only combat in the air, John's appetite was whetted watching his comrade. Flying top cover no longer appealed to him. He turned to pursue Parsons, hoping to catch up to them if the German turned to fight once again.

The plane that had surprised him out of the cloud turned with John's. Its turn brought it directly in front of John a thousand feet above and half a mile in front. It began a slow dive toward him. Straight toward him! John was confused. Its attitude and course were right out of the textbook for frontal attack. It mimicked Genêt's attack on the Aviatik.

"What's going on? Willis, you idiot! Can't you see it's me?" Baffled, John watched like the proverbial bird hypnotized by the snake. The Nieuport kept coming, closing the gap at an alarming speed. John couldn't fathom it. He was certain that Willis would recognize him. Why was he coming straight at him like this? John wildly waved a hand to signal he was friendly and to ward Willis off. Willis kept coming!

A hundred yards away, the friendly Nieuport opened fire. Bullet holes appeared in John's upper right wing, tearing fabric and splintering wing framing. More holes appeared on the lower left wing, causing pieces of fabric to flap and tear off in the driving wind. John raised an angry fist as the plane flew overhead, still firing. The markings on both planes were clearly French! As soon as Willis passed, the holes stopped appearing in John's wings. John became incensed. He yanked the Nieuport's stick back hard and left. He gave it full left rudder, putting the Nieuport in a sharp turn with enough climb to drain all the power the Le Rhône could produce.

His only thought was to catch Willis and curse his blindness.

To be shot down by a friend was inconceivable! As John came around, he saw the Nieuport. Willis had turned east, still firing short bursts. John glanced ahead of Willis to see what the crazy bastard was shooting at. Only then did he see the Albatros banking and diving to the east to evade the line of fire. His anger instantly evaporated, and his stomach started to churn. The holes in his wings were German holes! He'd been flying in the gun sights of an enemy Albatros. Again, a shiver went up his back that had nothing to do with the cold. If Willis hadn't returned and seen the enemy plane on John's tail, if he hadn't run it off by firing at it, John would certainly have been counted among the dead on his very first patrol.

For a moment, his thoughts drifted to takeoff, when he'd felt he was being watched. His rookie premonition had developed substance. As he calmed down, he remembered where and who he was. Gaining control, he felt a mixture of anger at himself and terrible embarrassment. He'd not only become a witless duck in a German shooting gallery, but he'd blamed Willis. John scanned his wings. Although perforated, they were intact. The German had punched more holes in John's ego than his wings. John swore it would be the last time an enemy flier would get that close to giving him a permanent set of wings. An apology was due to Willis. He waved toward him, but Willis was more interested in the Aviatik than John.

The watch Parsons lent him before takeoff indicated that it was time to fly to the rendezvous. The others would wait for him, but only for a few minutes. If he didn't show up, they'd start to look for him. John turned his head to see the fleeing Albatros. A stream of smoke made it easy to follow. John guessed that the German would make it to safety. He gazed at the holes in his wings again and turned the Nieuport north, directly for the rendezvous point Genêt selected over a bend in the Somme, thirty-five miles northeast of the field. Genêt and Parsons were waiting for him when he arrived.

Willis was nowhere in sight. His tank refueled, he'd likely gone hunting on his own.

The patrol's tanks almost empty after nearly two hours of flying, Genêt turned toward Ravenel. Thick black puffs of smoke began bursting around the group. John's Nieuport began to jostle from the shock waves of antiaircraft shells. A German battery was trying to get their range. At this altitude, a lucky shell would send a Nieuport into the ground in twenty-two seconds. Genêt held the flight level to fly straight back to the field.

The trio landed in the wheel-rutted snow at Ravenel, sliding on frozen mud in easy succession. They taxied toward the hangars where Willis stood ready to greet them. John was surprised to see the tall Bostonian back at the field. He must have flown straight home. Hours before, John had spoken to Harold Willis at the briefing in Thénault's hut. They'd barely had time to get acquainted. Willis had graduated from Harvard. He was an architect. He liked to fly over buildings that took his professional interest, even beyond their sector. In time, John felt he could get to like him. John appreciated architecture, especially historic buildings, and France had many.

"Sorry I couldn't go with you. I was barely up long enough for the engine to get hot. Blew a cylinder gasket. The oil pressure dropped. I didn't want to ruin the engine, so I switched off. Good thing it gave out when it did, or I'd have had to land over the lines."

"You must have a great mechanic. He fixed it awfully fast," John replied.

"What? He's still working on it, John."

"You mean you didn't get the Albatros off my tail?" John's confusion was short-lived.

"I could hardly take on an Albatros from the hangar, John. You must mean Lufbery. He refueled and took off right after I landed. Said he wanted to see how the new boy was doing."

"Lufbery! I thought he was eating lunch! He went up with Bill Thaw this morning."

"I asked if I could use his plane, but he wouldn't go for it."

"I didn't see any initials on the tail. I thought it was you." John wondered why Lufbery would fly into combat a second time just to check on him.

"He's done it before, when he's not on patrol. Saved Parsons's neck once. It was Ted's first flight too. Luf went up right after he came off leave. Scared the hell out of three two-seaters trying to get Parsons in their sights. They were circling him like a Comanche war party around a solo Conestoga wagon. Luf went after 'em like the US Cavalry. He got his seventh kill. A lone Albatros doesn't have a chance against Luf. He's a great flier. He doesn't miss."

As Willis finished, the familiar sound of a Le Rhône engine idling down above the field drew their attention. Raoul Lufbery was landing. He flew the last three hundred yards at idle, throttling up to taxi into the hangar. Pulling off his gloves, Luf had a grin on his face as he sauntered toward the group gathered near the hangar.

"Seems I had you guessing up there, John. I thought you saw me come out of the clouds. Why'd you shake your fist at me? Did you think I'd changed sides?" Lufbery's directed his wry grin at John. He knew why exactly why John reacted. The others watched and listened. This was going to be good. Luf hadn't had a chance to needle John since he'd arrived.

"I guess I did, Luf. I didn't see the Albatros until I turned to follow you. He must have come out of the clouds above me."

Lufbery kept grinning.

"I see. Guess you figured I didn't know whether you were Fonck or Richthofen." His grin grew wider. The others began chuckling at the mention of the great French ace and the father of the Flying Circus in the same sentence.

John figured he had it coming after knocking Lufbery off his feet twice. Besides, Luf had saved his life less than an hour ago.

"I didn't know you went up again. I thought you were Willis." Embarrassing John served as the rookie's initiation. It was standard practice. John's comments gave Willis a chance to turn the needle.

"Hey, John," Willis mocked, "I wouldn't shoot you down any more than Fonck. I can't speak for Lufbery. He's always hunting stray planes to raise his score."

The others laughed to tease John and Lufbery. They knew Luf enjoyed hazing new fliers in the squadron. Dugan and Hewitt had arrived at Ravenel a few hours before John but had yet to go up. John was the only pigeon Luf could haze. Lufbery ended the initiation.

"All right, you guys. Lay off. You should have seen the expression on his face when I flew by. He was madder than an oversexed eunuch in the sheik's harem."

As the laughter died down, the crowd broke up. John caught Lufbery by the arm before he could get away.

"Wait up! You saved my neck up there, Luf. The least I can do is buy you a cup of coffee. By the way, did you get the Albatros?"

"No. He had a head start. By the time I turned, he was three hundred yards away and going for broke. Besides, my gun was empty. I could only throw rocks. I'll take you up on the coffee. Before we go, let's take a look at your plane. He had you cold. I was surprised he didn't send you down. Looked like he was measuring you for a flaming coffin. Another burst or two might've done it."

They went inside the hangar. John pointed out the Nieuport's wings. They were filled with holes. John noticed that an outer strut was hit badly enough to break in a dive. If Lufbery hadn't been there to scare the German off, he could have lost a wing trying to escape. Either way, he wouldn't be standing in a hangar counting bullet holes.

"I count twenty, Luf. Not bad shooting for a guy getting shot at. I'm sure glad you shook him off my tail. I never saw him. It won't happen again."

"You missed a couple, John. He came down on you. I counted six through the fuselage about midship. One only missed you by a few inches. He damned near shot your ass off."

John hadn't felt or heard those hits. Again, he grew angry with himself. He'd been a clay pigeon in a German skeet shoot. That had to change!

"That makes twenty-six, John. Lucky for you, not one of them was bad enough to take you down. Either someone is looking out for you or you're the luckiest damned rookie I've ever seen. Twenty-six. Not even a scratch on a cable!" Lufbery shook his head in amazement.

"Well, it's my birthday, Luf."

Lufbery looked at him with cocked eyebrows.

"What's your birthday got to do with it?"

"I'm twenty-six today. I guess the Boche was trying to blow my candles out before I cut the cake."

"I'll say! He blew 'em out good! Anyway, happy birthday, John. We'll call it my birthday present. Forget the coffee. I've got something stronger to drink for your birthday. John, I don't normally throw my advice around, but ..."

"What is it, Luf? I need all I can get."

"Next time you go up, look over your shoulder once in a while. Okay?"

"That's a promise."

"Twenty-six, huh! Maybe that son of a bitch knew it was your birthday. Trouble is, he blew your candles out without asking. Damned impolite, if you ask me, John. Some people just don't have good manners."

It occurred to John that he hadn't fired a single shot on his first patrol in spite of the fact that he'd seen three enemy airplanes. John was indeed lucky, though he didn't believe in luck. For that matter, he didn't believe in premonitions, though his had come true. The feeling of being watched on takeoff was a premonition. It had failed to prevent him from taking off. Nevertheless, John had to be more alert to his rear. Those German eyes had nearly cost him his life.

Lufbery and John celebrated over a bottle of French wine. Since it was Lufbery's bottle, John planned to drink more than his share. After all, he was celebrating more than his twenty-sixth birthday. He was celebrating the chance Lufbery had given him to celebrate his twenty-seventh birthday. Tonight, he'd write a letter to Michael. He could trust Michael to keep the story of his first patrol a secret from Catherine.

America Joins the Escadrille

Late Friday, April 6, 1917, John and Ted were listening to gramophone records and Général Robert Nivelle's preemptive artillery barrage when Genêt came in shouting, "We're in it, fellas! We're in it!"

"In what?" Ted asked.

"The war! Wilson asked Congress to declare war!" The war had become a truly world war.

Seven Americans had formed the American escadrille long before America decided to fight. The pilots were no longer the only unit of Americans at war. Nevertheless, they knew America wasn't ready to fight. Years of isolationism and two oceans had seen to that.

"When do you think they'll start coming over, Ted?"

"The army? I don't know. Maybe months. General Pershing commands the only units with any field experience, and he hasn't even tracked down Pancho Villa! If you mean pilots, we're it!

They're starting from scratch, John. It'll take months. The papers said the army is neither trained nor equipped, and the only reliable airplane we make is the Jenny. It's not a match for any enemy plane. Or French or British, for that matter. Could be a year before they make a difference."

Ted's thinking coincided with John's and that of the rest of the men.

"Well, at least the weather's clearing," John said.

To celebrate the declaration, Félix gave Ted Parsons a small American flag, the kind often waved by young and old boys alike on Independence Day. Parsons tied the tiny banner to a strut on his Nieuport 17 and left the field. His flight took him across the trenches. That small American flag became the first American ensign to fly over enemy territory.

The next day, the squadron left Ravenel for a new field in Eppeville, near the town of Ham. Recently, the field of a *jagdstaffel*, or *jasta*, the German squadron evacuated the field when its army fell back to the new Hindenburg Line, a line the Germans called the Siegfried Line.

The German army had been withdrawing for over two months, leaving behind a wasteland. On the way to the ruined aerodrome, the escadrille flew over piles of rubble where towns used to exist. Bridges were blown. Trees lay everywhere. Wells had been poisoned. When they landed, the stench of rotting flesh, animal and human, filled the air. It took two days for a French regiment to bury the dead around Ham. Even then, the odor of death remained in the air.

The squadron joined Air Group Thirteen and became attached to the army under the overall command of Général Robert Nivelle. Their mission was to provide intelligence on the new German lines across the Aisne River in anticipation of Nivelle's long-rumored offensive. Pétain had paved the way for Nivelle by retaking

Douaumont and Vaux near Verdun a year before. When Nivelle finished Pétain's work, he was promoted, replacing Joffre as the primary strategist at the end of 1916. Since then, he'd assured the Somme-weary British and the ever-changing French government that his offensive would crush the German army. He spoke so confidently that his plan raised little doubt until the Germans began to withdraw from the salient he'd wanted to attack. Without an exposed flank in the German lines, Nivelle scaled down his plan, combining his proposed assault with the British attack. No longer expecting a knockout punch, the attack became another headlong charge like those Joffre had ordered. Each attack had brought nothing but more dead Frenchmen.

The pilots had waited a long time for America to enter the war, but the only thing that changed was the weather and the number of holes in their Nieuports after a patrol. Nothing tangible came of the American declaration. The high spirits aroused in the squadron on the sixth were gone by the last week in April and were replaced by the hope that Nivelle's Aisne-Oise offensive would succeed as well as he had insisted.

Thénault told N. 124 that their patrols should focus on gathering intelligence in the area of Nivelle's attack. "Fighter reconnaissance will begin as we become familiar with this sector. Flights are scheduled for this very purpose. Tell your mechanics to warm up your planes. We go on patrol today."

No worse than Ravenel, the weather wasn't ideal in Eppeville. Their luck, however, turned worse than the weather. One mishap followed another. Before morning was old, an engine failure was followed by an accident causing a splintered propeller. Another plane broke its landing gear. Finally, one fighter flipped over after overrunning the field. Thénault had seen enough. Morning flights were canceled. John never got the chance to go up.

In the afternoon, Lieutenant Alfred de Laage, one of the

escadrille's original pilots, went up without incident and flew toward a group of Allied observation balloons, gathering intelligence. He noticed a lone Nieuport defending the balloons against several German fighters. De Laage attacked without hesitation. First one and then another enemy plane went down. De Laage changed the escadrille's luck and put N. 124 back in the fight. It also made him a knight of the Légion d'Honneur.

After repairs were made, Genêt took off. Lufbery and Thaw went up on reconnaissance. April 8 became a prophetic day for Raoul. He got his eighth victory that afternoon.

During reconnaissance, Thaw marked enemy positions on a map. When spotted, the enemy often moved quickly. The sooner his map got to headquarters, the faster artillery could be brought to bear. To shorten the time, Thaw landed on the lawn at head-quarters and handed his map over personally. Soon after, artillery was brought to bear.

Near dawn on the April 16, Nivelle's opening barrage was still hammering a thirty-mile front between Soissons and Reims with a gun placed every fourteen yards along the entire front. In Eppeville, forty miles west, the barrage was heard as a continuous rolling thunder. Early risers saw the horizon below Vailly glow crimson from the bursts of cannon and shell.

Standing next to Parsons in the cold and rain, John quietly watched the show one morning and asked, "Can anything survive that, Ted?"

With his blank expression looking toward the smoke-filled horizon, Parsons said, "I hope not, John. I hope not. If it doesn't do the job, they'll have hell to pay when the attack starts."

The start of Nivelle's attack signaled a welcome change in the squadron's mission. Reconnaissance flights ended. The escadrille became fighters again. It was the role they preferred. Fliers began shuttling from the field in teams of two. John paired with Parsons the day the French offensive began. At 12:30 p.m., their Nieuports lifted from the rain-soaked field.

Clouds filled the higher altitudes, but the German stronghold at Saint-Quentin was only eleven miles northeast of Ham, and a canal led straight to it. They couldn't miss it. Parsons decided to circle the field to gain altitude before starting toward Saint-Quentin. If they flew directly to the town, they'd be too low. At ten thousand feet, Ted finally headed northeast. With the Somme behind, they were still climbing as they crossed the front lines. John continually wiped drops of water from his goggles. The wispy clouds were heavy with water at twelve thousand feet.

Ted and John never got to the canal. Minutes later, they were sighted and attacked by three Albatroses crossing overhead coming from the direction of Soissons, where the front lines bent to the north. John hit the elevator and banked right toward the Oise to the south. Parsons's Nieuport was lower than John's. He broke north toward Saint-Quentin, where heavier clouds had formed at lower altitudes. He could use them to hide if he got in trouble.

Trying to rejoin Parsons, John continued to bank until one of the Albatroses cut him off. To allow for maneuver and put some yardage between them, John turned south again. The Albatros came on hard. At eighty yards, tracers screamed over John's left wing. He pushed the stick to the right as far as he could. The Albatros shot by on the left, expecting him to dive. John kicked the rudder left, and the Nieuport neither gained altitude nor sideslipped in the sharp turn.

The force of the turn pushed John deep into his seat and pinned his head against its thin padded roll. The result of the turn gave John a brief advantage over the enemy plane. As he came around, the Albatros was slightly below, attempting to climb again in a wheeling left turn. John quickly wiped his rain-speckled goggles and tilted the nose of Nieuport, anticipating the path of the Albatros. As it passed through his gun sights, he pressed the Vickers's trigger.

A stream of synchronized lead shot past his spinning propeller, holing fabric in the German's fuselage. The upper tail rudder support on the enemy airplane splintered. The German realized he'd already made two mistakes. A third might be fatal. He banked to the north, heading for his field. Escape was the German's only option. Its crippled tail created drag on the Albatros, slowing it down. He went full throttle and started a shallow turning dive to gain speed and get as far from John's gun as he could. Too steep a dive might peel the flapping tail away, causing him to lose control entirely and spin to his death. He was forced to make a cautious dive.

John turned with him. A hundred yards behind, he gained on the Albatros. He pulled on the throttle to be sure it was wide open. It was. Wind rushed by the support cables between his wings, causing them to hum like a badly tuned fiddle. John saw the Albatros was unresponsive to its pilot's control. He also knew the enemy pilot was heading for his field. If he let him escape, the man would surely get airborne again by tomorrow and become a threat once more.

John harbored no desire to kill the pilot. He preferred to force him down. If he shot the enemy's propeller, the pilot would be forced to glide to a landing. On the ground, John could easily destroy the plane. But a frontal attack was dangerous and would consume too much time. Mallory had sternly warned his trainees against such an attack, even when an enemy fighter was not so agile.

John remembered Mallory's words. *Frontal attack gives the enemy's Spandaus a free shot at you. Air combat is not the same as a gunfight on a street in Dodge City. Fighting an enemy airman is no gentlemen's game. The object is to kill him, or he will certainly kill you!*

Risking death in his Nieuport was not an option John

entertained. Falman had taught them that death can come painfully and quickly. John watched the pilot. Why didn't the German try to land? He had to know he couldn't outrun John's Nieuport! Landing was the sensible thing to do!

Gaining on the Albatros, John had to make a decision. He'd closed to fifty yards. Attack from behind would probably kill the pilot. John couldn't bring himself to pull the trigger. He'd never intentionally killed anything much larger than a mosquito.

Never forget why you are here.

Thénault's words came as though spoken through the clouds. The choice remained his, not Mallory's, not Thénault's. John must decide. His mind raced as fast as his airplane. Could he justify killing a man who couldn't defend himself? The German knew the risk of combat. He'd just tried to kill John! John's heart pounded. A knot grew in his stomach as the enemy plane loomed ever larger in his gun sight. What was it like to kill? He'd never know unless he pressed the trigger. John was neither cold nor dispassionate. The memory of Eugene's death was still raw. This was war. John was at war in the skies over the Oise. Even at thirty yards, the enemy pilot didn't evade. In minutes, he'd be safely home telling his friends the story of his close call with death.

He'd joined the escadrille to fight, hadn't he? War meant killing, didn't it? This was war. Merciless, cold-blooded war! He was at war! He'd seen its results in Le Mans. French soldiers bled even as they stumbled toward their ambulances. The soldier in Paris hadn't chosen to be footless. Mallory's leg wasn't shot off by mistake. Their wounds were real. The time for debate must end.

John's neck went hot, and his stomach churned as he made his choice. His emotions went blind as he fired. Bullets go where directed, reacting to Newton's laws of physics and the tiny specks of black powder Marco Polo brought to Venice from the distant lands of Kublai Khan. Bullets tore into the enemy fighter. The

German pilot received two of the twenty .303 mm Vickers machine gun bullets through his back. One severed his spine, paralyzing him from the neck down. John saw him slump over in the cockpit before his Albatros D.III erupted into a fireball of flame. By the time he'd flown past the burning plane, it was spinning toward the earth, leaving a spiral trail of smoke and burning debris. On impact, it disintegrated north of the town of La Fère, between Saint-Quentin and Soissons. Nothing remained but scattered pieces of plane and a column of boiling black smoke. Its loss was reported to Eppeville by a French artillery captain. John would be credited with its destruction.

A voice sounding much like Lufbery's spoke from the deep reaches of his soul. *Welcome to the brotherhood of killers, John Morris.* His belly spontaneously overflowed what was left of his breakfast and every bit of his lunch. It flowed on the floor of his cockpit. If this was what killing was like, he'd fought enough for one day. The Nieuport seemed to turn itself toward the field at Eppeville. John felt like a passenger in an airplane that knew its way home.

The thought of confirmation never entered his mind. John's only thought was he'd never again be the same man. Like America, he'd finally declared war and had finally experienced it. He learned what war was about. In taking the German's life, he'd lost a measure of his own, and he didn't like what it had done to him. His only desire was to live to see the end of it, the end of war, and the end of his internal war. He'd continue to fight, but he'd fight to end all war.

From that moment, John's cold passion became the destruction of the enemy who'd started the war. Only then would the rage boiling in his soul become calm. Both were battles he assumed all moral men who killed in war must fight. So long as he stayed alive, he had a chance to win the battles—the battle against the enemy and the battle raging inside himself. If his rage hardened and became pitiless, the battle outside would be hard and pitiless. He hoped not. The sooner the war was won, the sooner he could win his inner war.

Nivelle's offensive failed. Ludendorff knew of Nivelle's plans even as he withdrew his armies, creating ten divisions simply by shortening his front. Nivelle's barrage fell on empty trenches, pounding once solid ground into a morass of mud the French had to cross. When the attack came, over ten thousand German machine gunners sprang from hidden tunnels in ravines and along the ridges as if Nivelle's barrage had never happened. Told the Germans would never survive his barrage, the French had advanced confidently. Many carried their rifles at trail arms. In the rain and snow, the French attacked those positions. Whole companies fell in ranks as if a giant had swung his scythe through a field of ripe wheat. They attacked in formation, and they lay in formation, dead. Terrain too rough and too open was perfect for slaughter. French tanks were destroyed. The advance got as far as the rain, snow, the German guns, and the slopes and ravines of the Craonne Plateau allowed. German artillery rained. German grenades snowed. German machine guns spewed blizzards of bullets. The French went forward and died.

The victory Nivelle promised in a day became a debacle in ten and caused one hundred thousand French casualties. The heights weren't taken, and the morale of the French army dissolved. French élan died where they fell, machine gunned on the Aisne, in the ravines, on open plains, and on the murderous slopes to the Chemin des Dames ridge.

Nivelle did win mutiny in the French army. Too often, men were ordered in frontal attack against hundreds of entrenched machine guns. Soldiers were not bulletproof. Tanks were not fireproof. Nivelle was relieved of his command. His boasted plan had cost the French dearly not only in men but in the morale of the entire French army. Général Henri Pétain took over command. He became commander in chief. Marshal Foch became chief of the general staff.

Respected by his men, Pétain gave them what they needed—a commander who didn't throw away their lives in fruitless frontal attacks. Nevertheless, twenty-three thousand mutineers were court-martialed, and twenty-three of their leaders were executed. GQG dispensed justice with both a carrot and a stick. They served the purpose. The mutiny ended.

When John returned to the field, Parsons came to congratulate him on his first victory. John told him he wasn't in a victorious frame of mind. The same went for his stomach.

"His plane burned. I think he was dead, but I don't know. I hope he was dead. That's a horrible way to go."

"John, we've all felt that way at some point. Don't dwell on it. It's this damned war. Until it ends, nothing will make it any better. Get over it."

"I know. You're right. I'll be okay. It's just … well, he was the first. I've never really thought about … I guess it sounds stupid, but when I joined, I thought about shooting down enemy planes. I didn't think about their pilots. As he went down, I threw up in the cockpit."

"I did too. I'd be surprised if you didn't." After a brief silence, Parsons said, "It feels personal at first. It's just you and the guy in the other plane. In time, it gets impersonal. In better circumstances, we'd probably drink a beer with them. Up there is where it happens. That's all there is to it, John. You can't blame yourself. You can't even blame him. He's doing the same thing you do. He'd shoot you down tomorrow if he got the chance."

They walked quietly for a while. John asked, "How did you manage to get away?"

Ted looked at him and smiled. "You know, John, I'm becoming quite fond of clouds. Say, you look like you could use some coffee. How about it?"

"Sure. It'll take the sour taste out of my mouth."

Later that afternoon, Lufbery landed expecting to find Genêt waiting for him. They'd flown to Saint-Quentin shortly after Ted and John left the aerodrome. Genêt hadn't returned. Lufbery wandered around the field asking everyone the same question— "Did you see Genêt?"

"Not since this morning," Ted answered.

John simply shook his head.

"The batteries over Quentin had his range. I thought he turned for home. I followed for a while. He seemed okay, so I went back. I'd better tell Thénault. He can make some calls. Maybe he flew to another field. He oughta be here. He really looked okay to me."

Lufbery's concern obvious, Parsons tried to ease it.

"Sounds a lot like engine trouble to me, Luf. Maybe he landed on a British field. He's probably getting his Nieuport patched up. By the time Thénault calls the fields, he should be back."

All the same, Lufbery walked to Thénault's office.

In the mess hut, John settled down. The sickness in his stomach was gone. A lingering revulsion in killing a man remained. With the exception of sighting the Albatros, he'd been unafraid during the fight. He felt the need to explain it to Parsons.

"I was busy trying to get him off my tail. I didn't think about much else. Once I got clear and got behind him, it all sort of fell into place. Strange. It's just the opposite of what I thought it'd be like. I thought I'd be calm in the beginning and scared in the fight."

Ronald Hoskier came into the hut and sat with them. Hoskier knew Genêt. They talked about what could have happened to him. They were still there when word finally came.

Genêt was dead. They assumed he was hit by shrapnel from

an antiaircraft burst. He tried to make it back to Eppeville and either died in the air or passed out from loss of blood. Soldiers who saw what happened reported that his plane went into a spin at full throttle. The wings sheared off the Nieuport. It fell to earth like a stone. The engine buried itself in a roadbed. Nothing was left. What remained of Genêt was recovered. The entire mess hall went quiet on hearing the news. Hoskier reacted to the news first.

"Antiaircraft! Damn! What lousy luck! There's so much stuff to think about up there! Ground fire never really bothers anyone! You know how Lufbery will take this! I guess I'd better his stuff together for Thénault to send home."

"Ed was a good man, Ron," Parsons said. "Luf won't let this sit."

Edmond Charles Clinton Genêt, a knight of the Legion of Honor, a descendant of Citizen Genêt, was buried in a modest cemetery in the town of Ham. A member of the escadrille since mid-January, his friends remembered him as a man who'd weep when one of them was shot down. Many of them did just that. He'd be missed.

Not long after, Ronald Hoskier took up an old Morane Type L along with de Laage's orderly, Jean Dressy, as his rear gunner. He'd always wanted to fly the old plane. The Morane's eighty-horsepower engine was weaker than the Nieuports. Hoskier lagged behind. In combat, he was shot down, and both he and Dressy died in a long fall. The escadrille was winning its share of victories. Lufbery got his ninth shortly after Genêt's death. Other pilots in the squadron shot down three more enemy planes.

Moranes weren't finished with N. 124 just yet. A single-wing Morane, Type N, was still on the field. Few were still in production. De Laage decided to try the sleek-looking plane. To him, it was like picking the last apple on the tree. Word spread that he was taking it up, and nearly every pilot and mechanic on the field turned out to watch. It had a good rate of climb, and de Laage wasn't noted for being timid during takeoff. A sharp turn had to be made at the end of the field to avoid flying over Eppeville and disturbing the townspeople.

True to his image, de Laage attempted takeoff on the muddy field right after the tail came up. He pulled back on the stick and put the plane in a steep turn. The engine that sounded so good on the ground immediately stalled. He was killed in the fall to the field. Another needless tragedy struck N. 124 from the weaknesses inherent in a Morane fighter. De Laage's death rocked the escadrille. All were reminded that death needn't come at the hands of the enemy. One's own airplane could kill just as surely and more quickly. John recalled Mallory's lecture that a pilot is only as good as his machine. He wondered if the replacements coming in had been taught by someone like Mallory. Every day, his lessons made more sense and had already saved his life once. He wrote to Mallory, describing his first combat, and thanked him without explanation. There was no need. Mallory would understand.

The escadrille received replacements. One new pilot brought a British newspaper to the field. They learned that Wilson ordered Major General John "Black Jack" Pershing to France. His staff included Captain George C. Marshall, Captain George S. Patton Jr., and Captain Charles E. Stanton. It was the first sign that America was beginning to act on its declaration. Pershing arrived a month later, and Captain Stanton spoke the words many would credit to Pershing. Before a crowd of Parisians in Picpus Cemetery, Stanton said, "*Nous voici, Lafayette.*" The pilots felt good about his choice of words but couldn't help smiling at their irony. Lafayette himself would have been amused. At the time Stanton spoke, the Lafayette Escadrille had been in France for over a year.

The Aid Station—1918

STOPPED AT CHÂTEAU-THIERRY AND BOOTED from Belleau Wood, Ludendorff was ready to try again. Postponed from July 4, the "peace offensive," Friedenstürm, would begin eleven days late. Planned by Ludendorff himself, three armies under the command of Prince Rupprecht, von Boehn, and Prince Wilhelm would win the war by succeeding where the spring offensive had failed. Unlike the others, the plan called for a short opening barrage. The attack would fall between Château-Thierry and Reims on July 15, a day after Bastille Day. The French south of the Marne would be drunk from celebration. Once the drunks were overrun, the objective would shift to Paris and final victory for Germany. That was the plan.

The main attack would fall west of the Bois de Condé at the head of the Surmelin Valley, directly above Michael's aid station. Field Marshal Sir Douglas Haig's army would be lured into a counterattack, allowing Rupprecht to spring his trap and knock the British out of the war. Without British support, the French army would collapse. Without French support, the puny American army was helpless. The plan made sense. All it needed was surprise.

The groundwork for Friedenstürm was observed, and captured German officers confirmed the place and hour of the attack. Ludendorff's plan was known to Général Gouraud, commander of the French Fourth Army. Ever mindful of the fortune of war, Gouraud needed to plan contingencies. The 369th was part of his command. Privates James Jefferson, Josiah Williams, and an officer from the 369th were instructed to assist Général Degoutte's Sixth Army. Their mission was to map the terrain near Courtemont, a town that lay at the head of the Surmelin Valley on a neck of land just below the Marne. Courtemont was in direct line with von Boehn's main attack. If the Germans managed to break through, Gouraud needed a map of the area to plan a counterattack. Their new orders put James and Josiah within walking distance of Michael's aid station.

In anticipation of the German offensive, Gouraud issued an order of the day to the Fourth Army on the July 7. Every unit was given a copy. In part, the order said this:

> We may be attacked at any moment.... We are forewarned and on our guard.... The bombardment will be terrible. You will endure it without weakening. The assault will be heavy ... but your position and your arms are formidable.... No one will retire a single step.... Kill ... up to the moment when they shall have had enough ... it will be a glorious day.
>
> *Gouraud*

Since July 4, constant alarms wore on the men's nerves. Shortly before midnight on the evening of July 14, the alarms ended. Gouraud's guns opened fire in a preemptive barrage from thousands of artillery pieces along the whole line of attack. Less than two hours later, too late to change his plan of attack, von Boehn's artillery answered. For the Allies, it signaled the start of the Second Battle of the Marne.

Major General Ulysses Grant McAlexander commanded the Thirty-Eighth Regiment in the Surmelin Valley, west of Degoutte's weary French units. In the woods of the Bois de Condé, companies from Major General Muir's Pennsylvania National Guard supported the French.

Michael's aid station sat near a creek running north along the Bois de Condé to the Marne. Von Boehn didn't fire mustard gas into the valley's wheat fields. To do so would force his own assault troops to wear gas masks. Instead, his artillery fired high explosives on Courtemont and down the whole length of the valley.

In minutes, casualties came into the aid station too fast for Michael and Captain McKay to keep pace. They sent for bandages and orderlies. When told men could not be spared, the walking wounded became orderlies once their wounds were bandaged. The regular orderlies were told to explain how to dress lesser wounds. The sickly odor of Carrel-Dakin, a solution that killed bacteria, soon filled the aid station. The station's only supply of syringes was used up, washed in alcohol, and used again to inject the next man. The seriously wounded were stabilized and immediately transported to the hospital. Some died from shock and loss of blood.

All the early wounds were caused by artillery. Exploding shells drove shards of hot metal, stone, and dirt into their bodies. For those who survived, the last was the most dangerous to life. The highly cultivated farmlands in the area carried infectious bacteria. In some cases, to prevent infection, limbs were removed. Michael handled many needing immediate amputation. A macabre collection of bloody shirts, trousers, boots, and human limbs began to collect in a dark corner of the aid station. The two worked at a frantic pace. Michael's hands became less steady, less sure. The wounded were much worse off. His stomach began to feel uneasy. During the first ten hours, he excused himself only once to allow himself time to relieve its contents behind the tent. The injury that stimulated the urge was an abdominal wound.

Carried by two men from his platoon, the wounded soldier was fully conscious when brought to the aid station. His stretcher was placed on a table used to operate on those who needed immediate attention, those who'd otherwise die in transport. The soldier's hands firmly held his abdomen. Blood oozed between his fingers. His face reflected more fear than pain.

"They come out when I take my hands away, sir." The soldier winced at the effort to speak. Michael examined the wound. A long gash opened his abdomen.

"It'll be okay. I'll have to clean it and sew it shut. You've got to let go, or you'll die." Michael's words were frank and urgent. Others were pouring into the aid station. Their wounds had to be treated. His patient voice helped to calm the panicky soldier. He looked like a boy, barely sixteen.

"Where are you from, son?"

"Pennsylvania, sir. Intercourse. Near Lancaster."

"I know it! It's near Bird-in-Hand."

Michael recalled the trip his father had suggested the family take one summer weekend, one of several the family made to Pennsylvania. As a young boy, he laughed at the names of the towns. He wasn't laughing now.

"Yes, sir," was all that the boy managed. Removing his hands caused a groan. The boy's hands returned to the wound.

"I can't help you unless you help me. Your wound must be cleaned and sewn."

Michael's familiarity with the boy's home calmed him down. It gave him confidence in Michael, and confidence helped him overcome the fear of removing his hands.

"Okay, sir."

As he removed his hands, the pain caused the soldier to tighten his abdomen. Several feet of intestine spilled from the wound. The boy screamed, and more came out.

"Hold his arms down!" Michael yelled. Two orderlies grabbed the boy's arms. Michael saw a third orderly across the tent. "Get the ether! Now!"

A short time later, the young soldier was asleep, no longer in pain. Michael opened the wound to clean it. He removed dirt and bits of cloth, and he irrigated the wound. He cleaned the exposed intestine. Fortunately, it wasn't punctured. He replaced it and sewed the boy's abdomen closed.

"I want this man transported directly to the base hospital. He's lost a lot of blood and may need more surgery. Tell them to watch him closely for infection. His temperature should be taken every half hour. Report his condition back to me. I want to know how it goes. Can you remember all that?"

"Yes, sir," the orderly said. "I'll see to it personally!"

During the whole procedure, Michael tried to remain calm and focused. He did his work with all the talent he commanded. It was only afterward that he excused himself. When he returned, his face and hands washed, he was back in control. His work was not finished. Men's lives were at stake. For hours, they came two and three at a time. There seemed no end of them. He lost track of how many he'd treated. His hunger and fatigue no longer mattered. Time didn't matter. He lost track of that, as well. His focus entirely shifted to treating wounded men.

The artillery fragment that hit James Jefferson shattered his thigh. Josiah Williams, his friend in Saint-Nazaire, was nearby when the shell struck around a bend in the trench. Dug to prevent casualties when a shell made a direct hit, the bend saved Josiah. The force of the explosion threw Josiah against the trench wall. He temporarily lost his hearing and wind, but he was okay. Josiah knew that James was around the bend. He ran toward him, expecting to find him dead. James was alive. Josiah barely recognized him for all the mud and blood on his face. James was dazed, not yet in pain. The collapsed wall of the trench partially buried him. Josiah began to dig him out.

"I'm hit, Josiah. My leg. The lieutenant. Oh, God! There's nothing left of him. He was standing over there, where the wall used to be." James's face began to contort as his head cleared and the pain came. Josiah could barely hear him in the rain of artillery shells. A mound of dirt blown from the trench wall had partially covered his leg. Josiah saw blood but not the wound.

"Don't you worry none, Jim. I'll get you to the aid station. That's a promise! You hear? I'm going to get you outta here!" James couldn't hear. The shell blast numbed his hearing.

The effort to pull him from the mud caused James to scream. Josiah stopped and looked. James had fainted. Josiah dug the leg free. Pain no longer mattered. He grabbed James's right arm and hoisted him headfirst over his shoulder in a fireman's carry. He grabbed his left leg to support it. It was wet with blood. Part of his thigh was gone. Laying him down, Josiah tore a strip from his torn trouser leg. He tied it around the hemorrhaging wound. This done, he again lifted him onto his shoulder. With shells falling everywhere, Josiah went around the bend in the trench, practically jogging toward the communications trench. He knew that James could die without treatment. The communications trench was blown, blocking his way to the rear. Shells fell just beyond. He was cut off from the French aid station. He'd have to find another and quickly. The lightest shelling fell to the west, toward the Surmelin creek.

The Huns would be coming now that the barrage had died away. James posed no special burden to his powerful legs, so Josiah climbed the collapsed trench wall. French soldiers ran past him, taking their rifles to the second line of defense. He asked one where an aid station was located, but no one answered. They were too busy running to the rear. Josiah followed them, knowing they were headed to safer ground.

James was semiconscious. When he gave low groan, Josiah asked, "Are you okay, Jim?"

No answer. James blacked out from shock and loss of blood. Josiah continued to carry his friend, plodding along in the mud, trying his best not to lose his footing in the slippery muck. A hundred yards to his right, he saw two stretcher bearers carrying a wounded man along a railroad track. Others were crossing a nearby creek, going in the same direction. A few were walking wounded, going to the rear. Josiah knew that he'd made the right choice. Their aid station had to be in the direction they were going.

As the muscles in his legs tired, his pace grew slower. He'd promised James he was going to get him to an aid station, and nothing was going to stop him—least of all his own legs. Minutes later, the aid station came into view. In spite of his desire to go faster, his pace slowed. Every ten paces, he stopped to squat on a knee, still holding his burden. By the time he reached the entrance to the aid station, his thigh muscles were as hard as tree trunks. Barely able to stand, he was afraid to put James down. If he lost his balance and fell, he might wake up James. He went inside, not waiting for anyone to tell him differently.

"Captain, this man's hurt bad. Can you help him, sir? He's bleedin' real bad."

Captain McKay glanced at the new arrival, saw that the makeshift tourniquet had stemmed the flow of blood, and said, "All right, Private. Take the man outside. I'll see him as soon as I finish dressing this man's wound."

"But, sir, he's my friend. I promised I'd get him to the aid station quick as I can!" Josiah's legs couldn't take another step. "I got to set him down, sir."

Though he spoke English, Michael noted that Josiah wore a French uniform.

"I'm sorry, Private. I can't see him now. Take him outside. I'll get to him when—"

Michael interrupted, "I'm finished here, Captain. I'll look at him. Bring him over here, Private." The soldier with a freshly bandaged shoulder rose from Michael's crude operating table to make room for the wounded man.

By sheer force of will, Josiah brought JJ to the vacated table, relieving himself of his burden for the first time in twenty minutes. He legs recoiled from the lack of a load. He fell backward onto the floor, feeling light enough to float.

"Are you all right, Private? Are you wounded too?"

"No, sir. It's just my legs. I'll be okay, sir. My friend Jim is hit bad. His leg. I tried to—"

"It's okay, Private. Don't worry about Jim. I'll take good care of your friend. You wait outside. I'll let you know how he is after I've had a chance to look at him."

"Thank you, sir. He gonna be okay, sir?" Josiah struggled to get on his feet. Tremors in his thighs made his legs useless. He looked like a man who'd drunk too much wine. He grabbed a chair to steady himself.

"He lost a lot of blood. He could lose the leg. I think he'll live. Go outside and rest. Stay off those legs and massage them. They've done enough today. That's an order, Private. Don't let them cramp.

Keep massaging them until the tremors stop. What's your name, Private?"

"Josiah, sir. I'll go on outside." Embarrassed by his wobbly legs, Josiah left.

The man he called Jim was still unconscious. Michael cut the muddy trouser leg off. There was no need to remove the boot. The leg had to come off. The thigh bone was shattered. Only splinters remained. A large hunk of thigh was also gone. The man had lost a lot of blood, and unless Michael amputated the leg quickly, the man could bleed to death. Michael instructed the soldier he'd just treated on how to administer ether. Michael didn't want Jim to wake up during the procedure. Working as fast as he could, Michael removed the leg. When he was done, the stump was eight inches long–enough for an amputee to be fitted with an artificial leg. In time, he'd walk again. After dressing the stump, Michael began to clean mud and blood from the man's stump. Then, he wiped mud from the man's face.

His heart jumped when he realized that the man looked familiar. It was James Jefferson. James was in France! Michael had just removed his leg! The shock of seeing James, added to what he'd already seen and done, was too much for Michael. He excused himself and walked outside to breathe fresh air and clear his racing mind. He wasn't aware that James had joined the army and didn't understand how he'd joined the French army.

"Is he okay, sir?" Josiah's voice startled him. It took a few seconds for Michael to shake the raw emotion that had overtaken him.

"What? Oh. Yes, he'll be okay. I had to take his leg. I'm sorry." His apology was reflexive and came partly from a sense of guilt. It was difficult to come to terms with the fact that he'd just removed the leg of a man he'd known since childhood. James, the son of his chauffeur, a boy he'd never played with, who'd always been friendly, was on his table. He'd never gotten to know the man inside his aid station. Now, he was missing a leg. His struggle to survive had just begun.

Michael had also generally ignored his father. Monroe had served his family for as long as he could remember. He was a good man, as was his son. The emotions these thoughts aroused, combined with his mental and physical exhaustion, became too much for Michael. Tears welled in his eyes like the water of absolution. He wiped them away in abject shame. Never again would he look at someone and assume distinctions in race were acceptable or the inherent property of whites or blacks. Never again would he ignore the friendly faces and willing hands of Monroe or his son.

"You okay, sir?" Josiah's concern broke his thoughts and emotions.

"I'm all right, Private. Thank you."

Josiah wasn't sure. "You sure, sir? You don't look so good to me."

"Really, I'm okay. Thanks for bringing him in. Where did it happen? Why are you in this sector? You're uniforms are French."

Still wobbly, Josiah stood and told Michael the whole story, adding nothing about his legs. Both were cramping. His ears still rang from the concussion of the shell that hit the trench.

"Thank you, Private. I'll see that your regiment is notified. What's your name, again?"

"Private Josiah Williams, sir. The Fifteenth Heavy Foot outta New York." Josiah saluted Michael, the officer who'd saved his friend's life. Michael returned the salute, making the best he could manage. He shook Josiah's hand, thanking him by name, not by rank.

Under the leadership of Major General McAlexander, the Thirty-Eighth Regiment held its positions during the attack. The Rock of the Marne didn't yield an inch in the German assault. The attack failed. For the rest of the war, the Second Battle of the Marne turned out to be the last big German offensive. Michael's aid station was moved closer to the front.

Michael was finally relieved from duty after thirty-three hours of continuous cutting, cleaning, and sewing human flesh. He'd treated hundreds of wounds. Only two stood out in his mind. For the rest of his life, he'd remember a man whose name he didn't know holding his own abdomen. The other was James, the only man he truly regretted having to make an amputee.

The best base hospital was located in Savenay, northeast of Saint-Nazaire. Monroe's son didn't awake until he was on a train to Savenay. He remembered practically nothing. Michael promised himself to visit James when he could get away from the aid station. As a doctor, he wanted to see how this patient was doing. As a man, he wanted to talk to James before his therapy was complete and he was shipped back to the States.

That night, Michael had only one duty remaining before going to sleep. Sitting at a tiny wooden table lit by a kerosene lamp, he began to write a letter. It began, "My dear friend Monroe."

The letter finished, Michael's eyes closed before he could write to Catherine. The busiest day of his life had taught him more about living and dying than he wanted to know. Tomorrow might bring a renewal of fighting. In his memo to Josiah's battalion headquarters the next day, Michael referred it to Josiah's commander, Captain Arthur Little. He explained what Josiah had done and recommended that he receive recognition. Michael mailed the memo himself to be sure that it went out with the afternoon mess truck.

On August 1, the 369th assembled in a rear area. A ceremony was held outside French headquarters. The battalion formed in ranks. Josiah stood at attention in front of the men in his company. American and French officers presided at the event, representing their respective commands. Citations were read in turn. Josiah's was first.

"Step forward, Private Williams, and stand at attention.

"Section one: On the fifteenth of July, and while under heavy enemy fire, Private Josiah P. Williams, of the 369th Infantry, risked his life to come to the aid of a comrade, Private James Jefferson.

"Section two: Private Williams personally carried Private Jefferson for over a mile to an aid station behind the lines, thereby becoming instrumental in saving the private's life. In recognition of this action, he is hereby awarded the Distinguished Service Cross by order of Général Gouraud, commanding general of the French Fourth Army, and by General John J. Pershing, commanding general of the Allied Expeditionary Force.

"Section three: In recognition of his devotion to duty and gallantry in face of enemy fire, the Croix de Guerre with Palm is further awarded to Private Josiah P. Williams by order of Marshal Ferdinand Foch, commander in chief, Allied forces, France.

"Step forward, Staff Sergeant Williams."

Josiah though he misheard. He was a private. He stepped forward at Captain Little's urging. American and French officers pinned their respective awards to his uniform. After the ceremony, his platoon commander asked Josiah why he looked so embarrassed when the last award was pinned to his jacket. Captain Arthur W. Little, commander of the First Battalion, was standing nearby and overheard Josiah's reply.

"I don't mean no disrespect, sir, but it weren't no need for that French officer to kiss me in front the whole damn battalion! Anyway, it's not like he said, sir. I sure enough got Jim out of there, but I didn't do no gallivantin'! Hell, I couldn't go gallivantin' while I was carrying him, sir."

The platoon commander and Captain Little turned toward

each other. Little held his laughter, but the commander didn't. On hearing this, Josiah thought the officer hadn't understood him.

"It's true, sir! Wasn't nothing like that!"

"It's okay, Sergeant," said Captain Little. "We know you weren't gallivanting. You saved a man's life. The regiment is proud of what you did."

The ceremony ended, Captain Little gave Josiah a three-day pass and offered to pay his train fare anywhere he'd like to go in France.

Monroe Receives Michael's Letter

MONROE LOOKED FOR THE LARGE book called *The Pictorial Atlas of the World* in Dr. Sam's library in Guilford. Aside from James, Monroe was the only person outside of family allowed to use the library. James had mentioned the atlas to him long ago, saying that each country had a map with the names of cities, towns, and rivers. The trouble was that the atlas wasn't the only book in the library.

Dr. Morris's and Mr. Michael's medical books lined six shelves on two walls. Mr. John's history and journalism books and Miss Catherine's French books filled another wall. Many were Mrs. Morris's story books, filling spaces on the other. Among those stood the taller books.

Now that everyone was gone, Monroe had developed the habit of talking to himself aloud. An empty house was a lonely place. When worried or frustrated, his accent always returned. Anxious to find the atlas, it returned. The accent made him feel closer to his roots. It brought back memories of his mother's soothing voice.

The medical books had the most interesting titles. Monroe didn't understand them. Several included the word dermatology, another was called *Operative Gynecology*. Some sounded familiar, like the one called *Journal of Pharmacology*.

"Them doctors sure do spell funny. Like they was writing 'bout some fancy agriculture. This operatin' ginniecology don't sound too good! I hopes I never catches that! Don't ever want to be operated on. Never heard 'bout most of this stuff before. Now, where's that picture atlas at?"

"There's more 'cologies here than trash got flies. Let's see. JJ said that atlas was a pretty tall book." He finally found it on the shelf with the novels. It was too tall to fit on the shorter shelves above and much heavier than he expected.

"This got to weigh more than five pounds! Must be a powerful lot of countries out there."

He put it on the doctor's desk and began leafing through page after page to find the map of France. It started on page 124, halfway through the book. France took up two whole pages. Even so, the names were so small that he could barely read them. Printed in blue, green, yellow, and red, the colors didn't always line up with the items they identified. He used Dr. Sam's magnifying glass to read the small print. Without it, he'd never find the port the papers said James's unit was posted.

He reopened his son's letter that had come all the way across the Atlantic. The paper said that Saint-Nazaire was a port town on the coast. Starting from Dunkirk, Monroe followed the coast southwest. Saint-Nazaire should be easy to find.

Before long, the front door chimes signaled that the postman had come. Nowadays, he was the only visitor to the house. He handed Monroe an envelope that had Mr. Michael's handwritten military address on the outside. The letter came right after he'd gotten as far as Calais. The last person Monroe expected to get a letter from was Michael. Back in the library, he looked at the letter with Michael's writing on the outside. It had made him forget where he was on the map. Why would Mr. Michael write to him? Why did he address it *Mr.* Monroe Jefferson? Monroe guessed he was checking up on him. It could wait until he found James on the map.

He picked up the magnifying glass again and started again from Dunkirk. Happily, he wasn't interrupted again.

After side tours to Paris and Brest, Saint-Nazaire finally appeared on the west coast at the end of a long river called the Loire. Using his index finger as a ruler, he checked it against the scale in the upper corner of the page. Paris was farther than his index finger. He guessed that Saint-Nazaire was between five or six inches from the fighting in northern France. It made him feel a lot better knowing the port was nowhere near the front. Now that he'd found the place where James had landed, Michael's letter came back to mind.

"I best open this case, it's 'bout the house. But somethin' tells me Mr. Michael found out what Miss Cath'rine done, and I'll have to leave here and live back at my place. Means I'll have tah buy more gas for the Stutz or take the bus. How my goin' tah explain dat to Miss Cath'rine? Maybe Miss Cath'rine tol' him what she done. Every time somethin' good happens, it don't last long.   "Course,if I was to pretend like it never came, I could stay. After all, I'm doin' what needs doin' 'round here! Them folks oughta be glad I look after them whiles they're away. I ain't no Dr. Sam, but I know what this house needs, an' I takes good care of it! It ain't so easy doin' this stuff by myself."

In spite of his justification, Monroe was a little afraid to open Michael's letter. Inside, he knew either he was wrong or something else was wrong. Either way, something was wrong! If he was wrong, then what was this letter about? He held it up to the sunlight pouring through a window. The paper was too thick to see through, even in direct sunlight.

"You old fool! It's only a letter! It ain't gonna bite. Your name's on it, fool! Open the damn thing!"

Nevertheless, Monroe was in no hurry. Michael wasn't here, and there was plenty of time to open a damn letter. It wasn't going to fly away. He laid it on the desk next to James's letter and went back to what he was doing when the postman rang. Michael's letter would wait.

James's letter said that the regiment left the port and went to a place west of Reims to rejoin the battalion. Soon, they'd start training under French instructors below the lines. JJ said he'd made a good friend named Josiah, and they'd gone to a town called Châlons-sur-Marne the weekend before training was to start. The news was many weeks old. By now, James might even be finished with training. The battalion could be anywhere. Again, Monroe looked at the map.

Châlons wasn't next to the front lines, but it was a lot closer than Saint-Nazaire. Maybe James was only guessing. Their training didn't have to start right away. War was filled with rumors, and James was only a private. He wouldn't know where they'd go until after training. Even if training started right away, it should take weeks before it ended. Even then, they'd have to wait for orders. There was no hurry. Schedules often got changed in war. Nothing was certain.

"Maybe they'll need to train a lot. Hell, the damn war might be over before he gets all that training. And maybe I'm foolin' myself. Least I'm not nobody else's fool."

Once again, Michael's letter returned to mind. "Anyway, Mr. Michael thanked me in Philly for getting that new tire, didn't he? He got real nice up the navy yard. Let me use the Stutz all day. So read the damn letter and stop worrying 'bout it!"

Monroe walked around the desk and sat in Dr. Sam's big black leather chair. Monroe admired that chair. "Just sitting here makes a body feel important."

He picked up Dr. Sam's silver letter opener and read the inscription stamped into the handle: Johns Hopkins University Hospital. The other side said, "In recognition of your pioneering work in dermatology." He'd waited as long as he could. With no other excuse to delay, he opened the letter very slowly and read. The opening surprised him.

> My dear friend Monroe,

"'My dear friend Monroe'? That ain't like Mr. Michael! He ain't never called me that! Maybe this was a good letter, after all. Maybe he'd stay in Guilford."

> It's July 15. Before I tell you what happened, I want
> you to know you have always been a kind and
> thoughtful friend to my family and to me. I may
> not have said so before. I think of you as a friend,
> one I often failed to appreciate but who was always
> there when needed.

"Well, now, what do you know! I'd better read that again in case I missed somethin'."

Monroe read it again, feeling a little choked by the sincerity of Michael's words. No one had ever said those things to him, not even Dr. Sam or his friend Tinner. This was going to be a good letter!

> I'm not sure where to start. I know you must have
> had good reason for not saying that James was
> in France. Before I go any further, I want you to

know that he is alive and will be coming home in a month or two.

When I arrived, I was assigned to an aid station below the Marne River. As luck would have it, I was in the only place in which I could be of help James. Last night, there was an attack. The fighting was hard, and men got hurt. James was one of them.

A man named Josiah Williams brought James into our station, badly injured from a shell explosion. Josiah had carried James for a mile to get him to the aid station. I think they'll decorate him for what he did. James had a bad leg wound.

Please understand, Monroe, I could not save his leg. It had to be amputated to save his life. When the operation was over, I washed a lot of mud from his face. Until then, I didn't know that James was in France. He hadn't said anything to the family that I'm aware of. I'm sorry to have to give you this news, Monroe, but I'm absolutely certain that James will recover.

He took the operation well. In time, with therapy, he'll recover completely. They'll give him an artificial leg and teach him how use it. Knowing James, he'll learn quickly, and they'll send him home. He's out of the fight, Monroe, in a hospital in Savenay on the Loire. Savenay is near Saint-Nazaire. He's safe there and has the best care.

Don't worry, Monroe. He'll be fine. I promise
I'll visit him at the hospital as soon as I can. The
orderly who took him to the train station said he
woke up saying he was hungry. That's a good sign
that he's okay.

Michael

Monroe was sad and relieved at the same time. James was
coming home, and Michael was special to him now. He'd saved
his son's life. Monroe read the letter again from the beginning.
Finished, he picked up the magnifying glass and focused it over
the town of Saint-Nazaire.

"I know where that is, Mr. Michael," he said softly and without
accent. Monroe wasn't anxious anymore, not for himself or for
James. His eyes followed the Loire a short way. There it was.
Savenay. Just like Mr. Michael said. When he'd found it, a tear
created a small lake near the town on the map. He quickly wiped
it away. James mustn't know he was crying.

Catherine Takes an Assignment

"COME IN, MISS MORRIS."

Mr. Polk had Catherine come to his office at ten every morning for a briefing. He'd usually give her whatever needed her expertise that day. It was her custom to knock to be certain that she wasn't interrupting. His reply meant that he was free. She entered, as usual, expecting to be handed yet another letter or some official French communiqué.

"On time again. I've come to rely on that trait in you."

For her part, Catherine had come to rely on his regard for her more obvious traits. She disliked his less-than-concealed glances, though he'd never done anything more than look. She withstood the glances and promptly steered the conversation to business.

"Thank you, Mr. Polk. I've completed the translation of the letter received from Ambassador Jusserand concerning the extension of the Arbitration Convention of 1908. My work on the Military Service Convention has only begun. I was hoping you might give me the afternoon to complete the translation."

Catherine's work had become vital to Polk but was less interesting to her than she'd hoped. She'd become all too familiar with protocols and diplomatic language, which bore little resemblance to her French literary study at Bryn Mawr. Couched in legality and dripping with deference to official titles and national policy, the documents she translated were uninspiring. Their legal topics were often unfamiliar, as were the diplomats or their assistants who'd signed them.

"Thank you, Miss Morris. The State Department is quite satisfied with your work here. That isn't the subject of our meeting. I need to discuss a matter of some importance to you. Please bear with me. General Pershing sent us an urgent memorandum from Chaumont asking the secretary to send him a special assistant. It seems he needs some sort of civilian liaison. Lansing believes we should refrain from appointing anyone who's been with the department for a length of time. He believes someone less traveled will not attract undue attention. I agree. Are you following me, Miss Morris?"

Catherine understood his words well enough. It was their meaning that lacked clarity. The question in her mind was, *What has General Pershing got to do with me?* At the moment, the question was inappropriate. Her bewildered expression and lack of a vocal response were enough to signal Polk to continue.

"I suppose you're wondering why I'm telling you this," Polk said, reading her mind. He began to pace slowly behind his desk, hands folded behind his back. Obviously, Polk was searching for words that would give her some substance without revealing the purpose of the appointment.

In observing him, Catherine instinctively felt that the matter must be unusually sensitive in nature. Remaining silent, she waited for Polk to define Pershing's request as it related in importance to her.

"May I be candid, Miss Morris?"

"Please, sir. I can't imagine what General Pershing—"

"Of course. Of course. I'll try to explain. As you may know, when the president appointed General Pershing to command the Allied Expeditionary Force, he was instructed to work closely with the Allies. At the same time, he was told to maintain the integrity of the American army. The president insisted on this. It was his view to keep our participation distinct from the Allies." Polk was hedging the issue.

"I understand, sir," Catherine said, "but I do not see how that affects me."

"Quite right, Miss Morris, quite right. First, correct me if I'm wrong. When I first interviewed you, I believe I asked whether you'd be willing to travel should the need arise."

"Yes, sir. Are you asking me to travel with the new assistant as translator, sir?"

Frank Polk stopped pacing and stared directly at her. This time his gaze was pure business. It was time to do his job as a professional.

"No, Miss Morris. They want you to be the assistant. I'm afraid the need to fill the position demands an immediate response." Polk watched for a reaction. He saw surprise.

Catherine still had only a vague notion of the assignment. She wanted to know more before committing herself. "I see! I hardly know what to say. Is it possible for you to be a bit more specific, sir? I admit, I'm at a loss. What sort of work is expected?"

"I'm sorry, Miss Morris. That can only be explained to you by the general and his staff. It would, of course, require you to travel to general headquarters in Chaumont. The option to go is yours. May I tell the secretary you are willing to take on this assignment?"

There it was. His question needed an answer now. Catherine

was still puzzled, and rightfully so. He'd barely hinted at what was behind Pershing's request. In fact, he hadn't really explained a thing. The terms "civilian liaison" and "assistant" could mean anything beyond merely translating for Pershing or his staff.

For a moment, she sat quietly, her thoughts racing. To turn down his request would simply mean she'd stay in Washington and continue her rather dull work. She'd longed for more direct involvement in events that shaped the world, something closer to her brothers. Chaumont was headquarters for the American army in France. No better place existed to become more closely involved. The idea of sailing to France excited her. But accepting the position was the only way to discover its purpose. To turn him down would mean disappointing Polk and herself.

To accept the offer without knowing what it entailed was bothersome. The deciding issue was a chance to be near her brothers, a prospect that mitigated her revulsion at being close to a war she hated, a war she blamed for her father's death.

"How much time do I have before leaving, sir?" The decision was made. She'd know the rest when she arrived at Chaumont.

"Good. Your vessel leaves New York in three days. I apologize for not giving you more advance warning. This much you should know. You may be in very different circumstances than you are used to here. Though you will be officially assigned to the embassy in Paris, you'll be under the direct authority of the military—either General Pershing or members of his staff.

"Ambassador Sharp is aware of the matter. He said he'd find someone to meet you when you arrive. If for any reason no one meets you, you are to proceed directly to the embassy. Your accommodations have already been made. I'll have your travel voucher and passport later today. Ambassador Sharp has a copy of your instructions and will communicate with Chaumont as soon as you arrive. This discussion is confidential, Miss Morris. As far as anyone else is concerned, you are being transferred to the embassy in Paris, nothing more.

"I'm sure you have questions, Miss Morris. They will be answered at the proper time and place. Is there anything I can do for you before you go?"

"Will I be able to stop in Baltimore on the way to New York, sir? I'd like to gather a few things for the trip, and I must inform our caretaker that I'll be out of town."

"I see no reason why you can't. But I suggest you begin as soon as your passport arrives. You must arrive in New York the morning the ship sails. If you do, it shouldn't be necessary to find lodging in New York. Your ship sails from the East River on Monday morning. This envelope contains a ticket, boarding pass, and your sailing schedule. Leave your current assignment with me.

"Before you go, Miss Morris, I want you to understand that you remain employed by this office. The secretary is merely loaning you to Pershing. The embassy in Paris will deal with your salary. Meanwhile, this envelope contains enough French currency to take care of your expenses and lodging for the foreseeable future. I believe that's all. Good luck. The department will be glad to have you back when you return."

"Thank you, sir." Catherine took the envelope and went to her desk to tidy up loose ends. After her passport arrived, she went to the rooming house and called New York. Her excitement was difficult to conceal.

"Hello, William. It's Catherine. You'll never guess what's happened!"

"I won't even try, Catherine," Fields replied.

Deferring to her promise of confidentiality, she told William she was being transferred to Paris to work with Ambassador William Sharp and added that she'd sail from New York on Monday. That was as much as she could say without breaking confidentiality. In any event, the nature of her assignment was unknown, so there wasn't anything more to say about it.

"I'll meet you at the station and take you to the dock when the time comes. The house in Kew Gardens is available if you need it. When do you arrive in New York?"

"I meant to ask you about the house, William. You're sure it's available?"

"I own the house, Catherine. It's available."

"You own the house! Michael never told me."

"I didn't mention it to him. When he said you'd insisted on coming with him, I suggested that you both stay at my house. I rarely go there expect weekends. I live at the navy yard. It's more convenient."

"I see. I may need to use it, William, if that's all right. I plan to arrive the night before the ship sails."

"Of course it's all right. I'm glad I can offer it. I want to see you before you go, Catherine. Do you know when your train arrives?"

"It arrives Sunday, late afternoon. I must stop in Baltimore to tell Monroe and make arrangements with the bank."

"Let me know which train. I'll wait for your call. I'm only ten minutes from the station."

"Thank you, William. I'll call when I know. Good-bye."

"Good-bye, Catherine. I'm looking forward to seeing you."

The idea of seeing William again was as exciting as travel to France. Her trip to New York with Michael was the longest she'd ever taken. She never dreamed she'd leave the country!

The department had placed a huge trust in her, and she planned to warrant that trust with General Pershing. She packed only the things she'd need from the rooming house in Washington and boarded the first train to Baltimore later that afternoon.

When the taxi arrived in Guilford, Monroe was finishing work in the flower garden. His surprise at seeing her made him speechless until he saw her carrying luggage and came to help.

"Miss Cath'rine! I declare! You're the last person I expected to see. Is everythin' all right down the State Department, or did they close the place up?"

"Of course they haven't closed the department. I'm on my way to New York and had to gather some things from the house. How are things? Any problems?"

Monroe became more confused after she'd mentioned New York.

"Miss Cath'rine, what's going on? First you go to New York. Then come back here. Then we go to Washington. Now you're back here and going to New York! Man, oh man! Must be something mighty important for you to be travelin' so much! Anyways, you want me to take you up there? I can get the Stutz ready, but them front tires are 'bout wore out."

"No, Monroe. Thank you. I'm going by train. Before I go, you must take me to the bank. I'll explain everything on the way."

"All right, Miss Cath'rine."

On the drive to the bank, she told Monroe what she'd told William. Monroe had mixed feelings about it but didn't prod. Once she'd made arrangements with the bank, they returned home. She asked him to find her spare suitcase.

"I got it for you, Miss Cath'rine. Do you know what all you're going to take? I can help you get what you need."

"No, Monroe, I'll do that. I'll need you to pick up my things from Washington." Monroe was puzzled. There should be plenty of people in France the ambassador could use besides her. He wasn't sure that Mr. Michael would like the idea of her sailing alone all the way to France, especially with submarines sinking all those ships in the war zone.

Concerned for her safety, he asked, "Does Mr. Michael know you're goin', Miss Cath'rine? France is an awful long ways from home!"

"No, Monroe. I only found out today. Don't worry, I'll be fine. I've arranged for the bank to pay all the household bills. Take them to the bank for me at the end of each month."

"Yes, miss. I'll get your stuff in Washington too. You can count on me!"

"I know I can, Monroe. You've been a great help to me, and I appreciate it. I've instructed the bank to send you a check each week. I've increased your salary. I hope you continue to stay here at the house. It eases my mind to know that someone I trust will be here taking care of it. From what I can see, you're doing a fine job."

Monroe's bubble of pride nearly burst.

"Yes, ma'am, Miss Cath'rine. After twenty years, I've kind of grown fond of this place."

She returned the subject to his earlier question. "To tell the truth, I hadn't considered how Michael might feel. Actually, I'm more concerned about Mother."

Monroe went quiet, and his mood changed watching her pack. He hadn't told her about James. Now that she was going to France, he felt he should tell her. Catherine noted his silence.

"What is it, Monroe? Is everything all right? Have I forgotten something?"

"No, Miss Cath'rine. It ain't nothin' you forgot. I don't know just how to say it, that's all."

"What is it, Monroe? You can tell me."

"I know, Miss Cath'rine. I need to show you a letter that Mr. Michael sent from France."

Catherine grew frightened, thinking some horrible news had come about John.

Monroe reached into his shirt pocket and pulled out a carefully folded letter. He handed it to Catherine. She looked at Monroe once more.

"Go on, miss. You read that first."

Catherine sat on the bed and read the letter. By the time she'd finished, she was crying.

"Oh, Monroe. I didn't know. I'm so sorry. I didn't know about James."

"Don't you feel bad, Miss Cath'rine. Mr. Michael said he's okay. They's goin' to send him home. Everything's fine. You know JJ wouldn't want you to cry."

Catherine wiped her eyes, stood, and hugged Monroe. The comments Michael made to Monroe had touched her.

"I feel like I've let you down, Monroe."

"Ain't no reason to feel that way, miss. The Lord works in His own way in His own good time. Everything is all right. Don't feel bad no more, else I'll feel bad."

Monroe's gentle reassurance touched her more than Michael's letter. She took his hands and took a step back. Monroe had a sorrowful smile. His heart swelled when she smiled. Tears welled in his eyes. Neither Catherine nor Michael was indifferent to him. Both she and Michael had said how remarkable he was, as was James in his own shy way.

"Thank you, Monroe. I'm proud of you and James. Will you tell him for me?"

"Yes, miss. I'll tell him you said so."

After calling William in the morning, she boarded a train to New York. Monroe waved good-bye to her from the platform, and Catherine waved in return. With Dr. Sam gone, she'd become more like a daughter to him than Mistress Catherine. As the train left, she heard his deep bass voice speak to her once more.

"You behave yourself over there, Miss Cath'rine. I hear'd stories about them Frenchies!" His deep laugh seemed to fill the station.

Before leaving, Catherine made a surprising decision. Her family's disintegration, her responsibility to the State Department, and the new uncertainty in her future all seemed to focus on her unexpected trip to France. The war had quickly brought changes in her life, changes that were absorbing her life. Looking back, she realized she'd once resisted the tug of change. The war had taken everyone she loved. Now, it was about to take her. In spite of her commitment to go forward, Catherine became a bit frightened. Nearing the station in New York, she scanned the crowded platform for William's comforting face.

She saw him as the coach ran by the platform. As promised, he was waiting for her when the train arrived. His presence made her calm. He understood her in ways that neither Michael nor John did. As she got off the train, an awful thought came to her. For a second, she wondered whether the war would succeed in separating her from William forever. She immediately forced the thought from her mind, choosing to recall the time he'd left her in the doorway of the rooming house in Washington. She'd watched him from the steps, hoping he'd turn and wave. He'd done just that. Soon, it would be her turn to leave. The regret she felt then returned. The thought of being with him, only to leave him again, brought on feelings she couldn't define.

"Over here, William!"

"There you are. I looked up and down the platform for you! It's good to see you again, Catherine. Let's drop your bags off and get something to eat."

"That would be wonderful. Before we go, I want to ask you something."

"Ask, and ye shall receive."

"Will you stay with me tonight?" The question seemed to leave her lips of its own volition.

"Of course, Catherine. I'll stay as long as you like."

"I'm worried about going away."

"We'll worry about that when the time comes. We have the entire evening."

Once again, he'd reserved a table at Delmonico's. She'd seemed happy, if not entirely relaxed. He attributed her distraction to the trip.

As the evening grew old, he said, "You must be getting tired. I'll take you to the house so you can get some sleep."

"William? You said you'd stay with me as long as I liked."

"I did."

"I meant all night, William."

Had he realized, he might not have agreed, but the urgency in her eyes caused him to hesitate. He'd misjudged how afraid she was about the trip to France. Up to then, he'd dismissed her concern as originally expressed. She needed assurance, and he was the only one close enough to her to give assurance. Nevertheless, as they returned to the house in Kew Gardens, William couldn't help but feel awkward. He'd invited other women before, but Catherine was different. The others needed to be persuaded or pretended to need persuasion. Catherine was the only woman to ask him to stay the night.

"You must be tired. After all, you're about to take a long voyage. Use the main bedroom, Catherine. I'll stay where Michael slept."

What she said next had the effect of weakening his knees.

"No. When you agreed to stay with me tonight, William, I meant *with* me."

When she'd first asked him to stay, he thought she meant for the evening, not the entire night. There was no mistaking her meaning now. She was sincere. Before agreeing, he looked deeply into her eyes. What he saw was desire. Speechless, he watched as she took his hand and led him into the bedroom. Nothing he'd say would make any difference to her. In the bedroom, his gaze fell on the bed. Catherine was a beautiful woman. His own desire overcame any further hesitation on his part. She undressed. He became conscious of her naked beauty, and nothing else mattered. At that moment, he would have done anything she asked. The soft curves of her breasts in the dim light invited touch. His only concern was that he not disappoint her. They had one night before she left, and he wanted it to last forever.

He also wanted the feeling of being inside her to last forever. He wanted to stay joined to her forever. Even forever wasn't long enough. Eternity seemed a short time. She responded to his every touch. Each movement he made brought some amazing reaction from her.

Catherine was the only one to get any sleep that night. William was content to lie beside an amazing woman. He discovered a calm he'd never felt for another woman. He looked at her lying there, naked, unafraid, and so close he felt her warmth. He dared not move lest she disappear. The spell would break, and he'd awake from some wonderful dream. He watched her for hours, hardly able to believe what had taken place. No man had a right to feel that warm, that loved. As the sun rose to announce a new day, he made up his mind.

When Catherine awoke, he said nothing. He simply kissed her. The fear he once saw in her eyes had left. It was he who harbored fear, a fear she might say no when he proposed to the woman who'd made love to him in the night, this beautiful, sensitive woman who'd just awakened at his side. William drew a finger across her lips. He had something to say.

"Catherine, I never dreamed I could be as happy as I am at this moment. You're so beautiful. I can't express my feeling for you. It's like some fairy tale. I'm the toad who's been kissed by the princess. Catherine, will you marry me? You needn't say anything now. I understand if you need time. I'll wait as long as it takes."

Catherine already knew. She needed no time.

"Yes. I'll marry you. If you hadn't asked, I'd have asked you. I love you more than you know. I've known ever since that first night in New York, when you told me I should be using my talent—and again when you left me in the doorway in Washington. I've missed you so terribly ever since. That's why I'm afraid this war might separate us. It's torn my whole family apart."

"Are you sure, Catherine? It's not just last night, is it? I want you to know I never expected that we'd—"

"Oh, William, I'm sure. After last night, you of all people should know. I never expected you to have a modest streak when it came to women."

He grinned. She'd read him as if he were no more complicated than a menu.

"So, I'm that transparent, am I? I'll need to work on that."

In more than one way, Catherine's life had reached a summit. Much had changed. Leaving Guilford, her mother and father, and her brothers, John and Michael, all that seemed past. She had William now and was no longer the uncertain girl she'd been only weeks before.

He'd watched her become a woman and gave her the chance to become that woman.

The trip to France lost its excitement. Catherine held back tears as her ship departed. There was no escaping the sadness of leaving him. The thought of their promise consoled her. She was leaving more behind than she was going to in France. Days later, the sorrow of going began to mingle with the intrigue of arriving. This time, she wasn't concerned by her mixed feelings.

Pilots and Planes

IN EARLY JUNE 1917, N. 124 moved to a different aerodrome near the town of Chaudun. The field was six miles southwest of Soissons, a town on the Aisne River named after a Belgian tribe known to Julius Caesar as the Suessiones. Occupied in 1914, the French had retaken the town. Soissons had always been an outpost guarding Paris, only fifty-five miles to the southwest. For two years, Soissons had been under the guns of German artillery from behind Hill 132 just across the Aisne. The old town was in complete ruin.

Three days after N. 124 arrived, Chaudun received news of a huge explosion near Ypres. On June 7, a million pounds of dynamite, which British sappers packed at the end of nineteen tunnels, was detonated. In an instant, ten thousand German soldiers were blown skyward, meeting their Maker in the air. The shock was felt in London 130 miles away. The report said the crater was large enough to bury three U-boats. The prelude for the Third Battle of Ypres was sounded.

News also came that the Nieuport was being replaced. A trickle of new planes began arriving at Group Thirteen. John was one of the lucky few to be assigned a new Spad VII. Made by the Société Pour Aviation et ses Derivées, the Spad took its name from its producers. It was tougher than the Nieuport17. The new Hispano-Suiza engine added forty horsepower, making it faster than a Nieuport. The Spad had a stronger fuselage and stronger wings, ending the problem of wings shearing off in a dive. It carried a Vickers machine gun that fired five hundred rounds through its propeller. Though less maneuverable than the Nieuport, its greater speed and rate of climb to higher altitude made it a more advanced warplane and helped offset the difference in handling. The result was that N. 124 became SPA124, and the pilots busied themselves learning to finesse the heavy new machines.

Lufbery was flying the new Spad when he darted under the top cover of an Albatros to make a single pass at a German observation plane flying at the side of its main group. He'd calculated that the Albatros would react too late to his attack. The observer was his tenth victory and made him a double ace, the first and only one in SPA124.

New pilots began to join the escadrille, one of whom was Sergeant Andrew Campbell, a swaggering man whose antics followed him from college. Thénault warned him against crowding the planes in formation to no effect. Piloting his Nieuport in a series of stunt dives, Campbell lost a wing and barely landed his disabled plane far from the field.

James Norman Hall, another new pilot, was a different matter. Hall didn't fit the mold of a fighter pilot. From the modest town of Colfax, Iowa, he was later to meet Charles Nordhoff of the Lafayette Flying Corps, and they would write three novels—*Mutiny on the Bounty*, *Men Against the Sea*, and *Pitcairn's Island*.

At Chaudun, his mission was to write the death warrants of the enemy across the Aisne. On June 26, 1917, the day Jimmy Hall flew his third mission, General Pershing came to Saint-Nazaire to greet 14,500 Americans landing at the port, the first American soldiers to reach France. Among them was Sergeant First Class Edward V. Rickenbacker, a man two years older than regulations permitted a man to become a flier. With his long experience in gasoline engines, his friend Captain James Miller asked Rick to become an engineer at the new flying and training school at Issoudun, a school built exclusively to train American fliers. Rickenbacker, a practical man with a bent for adventure, told him that an engineer should know something about flying. Rick had valuable connections. His doctor amended his age on paper by two years. Rick passed his physical. He was on his way to becoming a fighter pilot.

When scheduled missions were completed, John developed the habit of flying alone to acquaint himself with the new area and new airplane. It didn't take him long to become familiar with the controls. More powerful, the engine actually ran more smoothly than the Nieuport's rotary. One day, he decided to test the Spad and turned it toward the Chemin des Dames ridge, looking for the enemy. After the morning patrol and quick lunch, John took off from the field.

Twenty miles to the northeast, the ridge was in line with a part of the Aisne that ran east near the German-held town of Vailly. The ridge was typical of the front. Since the French abandoned it, the line had barely moved since 1915. General Nivelle's attack had practically wiped out the French infantry trying to retake the ridge.

On his way to the ridge, the destruction in Soissons again became visible on his left. Time and again, John saw tall, broken spires of churches standing out from the ruin and the rubble of French towns. Used for observation, they were targets for enemy artillery and bombs. The gutted towers of one cathedral stood like misshapen chimneys. A gaping hole in its roof opened the vault to its floor. Rubble littered the streets of Soissons, a town already rebuilt once after Julius Caesar's triumph in Gaul. Hardly a thing had gone unscathed. It sickened John to see the ruins from the air. He'd come to strike back at the artillery responsible for most of its destruction.

John enjoyed flying, up to the time he flew over ruins. Crossing the front lines, he wished he had eyes in the back of his head to go with the two the Creator gave him. To remedy the problem, John decided to improve his field of vision. After his first flight, when he'd thought Willis had attacked him head-on, he looked for a parabolic mirror like those he'd seen on some automobiles. He found what he was looking for in the town of Senlis, halfway to Paris from the field. Charles Gallau mounted it on the underside of the upper wing directly over his head. This was the first time he'd flown with it, and it often drew his eyes. He liked the fact that the mirror gave him a wide field of vision to his rear and didn't obstruct his view in front or above the Spad. Its only liability was that objects in the mirror appeared much farther away than they actually were.

North of the broken town, the flight over Soissons ended near the Aisne. He followed the river east, gaining altitude through scattered clouds. He'd reached a point that he could estimate his altitude by the chill in the air or when his ears popped from lower atmospheric pressure.

Antiaircraft batteries tried to find his altitude as he flew over Vailly. The blast of shells exploding closely created pressure waves that jostled the Spad. John pulled back on the stick to climb above the bursts. He moved the stick side to side in broken rhythm to spoil their aim. He'd become accustomed to "archie," as the British called it. Approaching the ridge, he climbed again to compensate for its height and made a turn to the north to reach its western end.

The archie grew lighter, but he noticed tracer rounds floating lazily upward from machine gun emplacements angled to fire at him. The Spad was too high for the guns. At seven thousand feet, he looked upward to see if any fighters were stalking him. There were none. He glanced into the new mirror and again saw nothing but smoke and scattered clouds.

To be certain, he turned his head left and then right. Nothing was behind, above, or on either side. Rocking the wings up and down, he looked below, not expecting to see an enemy plane below. The skies were his. As far as he knew, his Spad was the only plane anywhere near the ridge.

John had never strafed the enemy before, but the damage and confusion it could cause was well known. With no planes to distract him, the Germans who ravaged Soissons were about to feel the bite of his Vickers. John pushed the stick forward, diving on the ridge at full throttle. In less than twenty seconds, he was eight hundred feet above the ridge. The Vickers spewed its unbridled anger at German positions along the crest. He continued to dive until he could see their faces.

Gray helmets tilted upward, and at two hundred feet, John saw looks of surprise. Firing only when helmets appeared above his sights, at one hundred feet, he leveled off and turned sharply north. The Spad climbed a mile behind the trenches west of Corbeny. He paid no attention to the bullets following his Spad. He intended to retrace his path, though he knew he'd lost the element of surprise. Pausing to view the mirror, he saw a speck leveling off behind. A second speck appeared beside the first. The mirror was working. John turned to gauge their distance. Two Albatroses were a half mile behind. They misjudged his turn, assuming he would head for his home field.

Still at full throttle, John climbed at an angle he knew was the maximum before the Spad stalled. The Albatros followed, but John was above them. He'd learned his next maneuver accidentally as a student at Pau. The quickest way to reverse direction was to stand on the tail. He pulled the stick back, putting the plane in a nearly vertical climb. For an instant he hung motionless in the sky. As the engine stalled, he kicked the rudder hard right. Like a gate on a hinge, the Spad's tail swung skyward as the nose fell like a stone.

John regained powered flight in the dive that restarted his engine. At the same time, the leading Albatros was about to cross his gun sight. He pulled the trigger on the Vickers at a distance of fifty yards. The engine of the Albatros became a ball of flame that engulfed the pilot. The second Albatros appeared slightly over his cowling, firing at him. John saw the muzzle flashes of the German's twin Spandaus. Bullets cracked like whips around his ears, ripping fabric from the Spad's tail. John tilted the nose of the Spad upward, pulling the Vickers's trigger at the same time. A dozen rounds emptied the gun. It was enough. Several punched neat holes in the radiator of the Albatros, sending scalding hot water into the German's face. Its engine began to smoke. As John flew past, its pilot raised an arm to shield his face from a stream of hot water. His goggles became a useless blur. An overheated cylinder expanded and cracked, mixing hot engine oil to hot water. John caught a glimpse of the Albatros in his mirror making a perfect arch on its way to earth. He didn't stay to watch.

Crossing the Chemin des Dames ridge at 1,200 feet, he was greeted by rifle fire and Germans shaking their fists. John yelled, "You had it coming!" Yelling released the anger he'd stored inside for weeks. Eyewitness reports were slow in coming. The closest witness had watched from an observation balloon below Craonne, but his view was obstructed by ground mist. It wasn't until Lufbery landed an hour later that confirmation came.

Lufbery hadn't joined John for weeks. When told John had headed toward Soissons, Raoul flew the same route, straight over the town, but he didn't turn to follow the river. When he finally looked east, he saw a plane going down in flames. A second had just been hit. At half a mile, Lufbery recognized the bright colors of an Albatros going down, the red, white, and blue clearly painted on a Spad's rudder. He thought the Spad must be John's.

John was in the mess tent when Lufbery ambled inside. His hand shook from nerves, anger, or too much coffee, he wasn't sure. Luf poured a cup before joining him.

"What in hell were you trying to do? Win the damned war all by yourself?" Luf grinned at the sullen figure looking down at the table.

John hadn't even noticed the double ace until he spoke. His thoughts were internal. Slowly looking up, he managed a limp smile.

"Look who's talking! I haven't knocked down ten of them like somebody I know." Neither pride nor shame showed in John about what he'd done over the ridge. They'd gotten what they deserved.

"Hey, no kidding, John. What made you do that?"

"It's what they pay me to do, Luf—shoot the SOBs down."

"I'm not talking about that. We all do that. By the way, you got 'em both in less than thirty seconds. That's pretty damned good flying! I meant the ridge. Why'd you go after the Boche on the ridge?"

"You saw that too?"

"Yeah. I looked over the side when I crossed the ridge. Maybe twenty stretcher teams were carrying the wounded when I flew over. They tossed the dead out of the trenches. They'll probably collect them tonight. It looked like you'd declared war on the damn ridge. You really messed 'em up, John. I was just wondering what made you pull a stunt like that."

John looked at Luf and invited him to sit down. Lufbery took a stool opposite John, waiting for an answer.

"The spotters, Luf, the ones that direct their artillery. I've been flying over Soissons for weeks. Every time I'm over the town, I see more rubble. Soissons is historic, like Amiens and Reims. They were towns I read about in college. Some are older than Roman towns. At one time, I wanted to be an architect, Luf. I used to wonder what it'd be like to see places like that. Not in piles of stone. Seeing them torn apart makes my guts crawl. They shelled Reims! Wrecked the cathedral. I know what those places meant. The pride of the craftsmen who built them. Those towns represent years of French history. They're like monuments. Now they're monuments to the damned war. Piles of stone. Town after town. They're all gone. Anyway, I just thought the bastards should pay for it. That's all there was to it, Luf. I've been in a bad mood lately."

"A bad mood? Jesus! I'd hate to see you when you get mad! You made 'em pay, all right. They'll remember your Spad. Hell, you flew low enough to shake hands with the sons of bitches. They're probably reporting your tail numbers to the Boche aerodromes right now. And there's something else I wanted to ask you. I see you put a mirror on the wing."

"Do you remember the time you shook that German off my tail and saved my neck? Dad had one put on his Stutz back home. It works pretty good. I saw those two Albatroses coming up behind me. They looked about half their real size and twice as far away, but I saw them. Maybe you ought to try one, Luf. It covers the blind spot behind the plane."

"My neck's limber enough. Listen, John. You got to be more careful. If the sun gets behind you, the glare from that mirror could blind you a few seconds. You might need those seconds. Besides, I'd probably get too curious about it and get my ass shot off from in front."

"I hate to tell you this, Luf, but your ass is behind you. Anyway, I'll remember what you said. I hadn't thought about that. I'll tilt it up when the sun's behind."

"Okay, John, but that was still a crazy damned stunt. You ought to ask for some time off. Go to Paris for a few days. You've been at this since you joined. A few days' leave would take the edge off."

Lufbery had noticed the change in John. He was tired, angry, and distracted by his thoughts. What he'd done had exposed him to every gun on the ridge, even rifle fire.

John knew that he'd changed. He was close to burnout from constant patrols. His reaction was to go up by himself, to be alone with his thoughts. He was more focused when he was in the air. On the ground, he was restless knowing that his Spad was never more than fifty yards away, while the enemy was flying. Was the problem war, or was he the problem? Even Charles, his mechanic, had begun to notice the change.

A week before, John told him, "I want you to keep the Spad ready to go on short notice."

"How short, *monsieur*?"

"Fifteen minutes."

Charles was a good mechanic. But since then, he got nervous whenever John came to the hangar. He'd often have to tell John that the plane wasn't ready. Charles wanted his plane to be perfect.

The events of the day had drained John. "I'll see you later, Luf. I've got to check my mail. Maybe you're right. I'll ask Thénault for a few days. I've got some time coming."

He thanked Lufbery for his concern and walked to Thénault's office. Thénault was surprised to see him. He was about to call him into his office.

"Good afternoon, sir. I came to pick up my mail and ask if I might take a few days off."

"*Non!* Take a week. But first, I congratulate you on your

victories. I have recommended you for the Médaille Militaire and will be surprised if it is not approved. There is one letter."

Thénault took a letter from a small pile of papers and said, "It came today. You sister addressed this letter to me. She asked that I wait as you read it. I am honored by the trust your sister has placed in me. With your permission, I will do as your sister wishes."

John hesitated and then replied, "Yes, sir."

Thénault's speech mystified John. He couldn't imagine why Catherine would send him a letter under the care of his commander. John took the letter feeling uncertain, a trait he rarely felt and would never show in front of his commander. Briefly, he stared at the envelope. It was definitely from Catherine.

"Sit down. Take as much time as you need."

John took the chair near Thénault's desk and opened Catherine's letter. Military date stamps indicated the letter had gone to Eppeville weeks ago. The letter was dated the day after America entered the war. The sight of her handwriting had a comforting effect, but that didn't relieve his concern over its content.

April 7, 1917

My dearest brother John,

It seems nothing of the past remains. So much has changed. Yesterday, our dear father died quietly in his sleep sitting in his favorite chair. The doctor said he died too quickly to suffer.

John was noticeably shaken. His eyes closed for a moment, and he brought a hand up to cover them. His whole body seemed to sink lower into the chair in grief and despair. He lowered his hand and began to read once more.

Michael was wonderful. Without his support, I don't know what I would have done. Mother took it very hard, and her coughing became difficult to control. I will ask her to see the doctor. I worry about her. Michael promised to make arrangements for the funeral and has taken this entire burden on himself. He left the university and won't return until after the funeral.

My thoughts are with you, and my hope is that you will not suffer too greatly from his loss. Remember that we love you. Father would want you to go on as though nothing happened. Please let me know you are all right. You can be too brave at times, and I fear for your safety. I have asked Commander Thénault if he could give time to recover from this. Please do. This mustn't be on your mind as you fly.

Your loving sister,
Catherine

For some time, John sat in respectful silence. Despair was replaced with a forlorn feeling that he was not home and had not had a chance to talk to his father before he died. Most of his letters went to Catherine, telling her to reassure the family that he was safe and that his missions were routine. None of them told the truth. He saw no reason to worry his family with the truth. He routinely asked how things were going at home. They all were perfectly well before he left. It never occurred to him that his father would die before he did. John assumed the odds of surviving the war were very small, if not nonexistent. Sitting there, he became aware that Thénault hadn't said a word. When he looked up, Thénault spoke.

"Is there anything I can do?"

"No, sir. It was kind of you to wait. Did Catherine mention that my father died, sir?"

"Yes, in her letter. She is a remarkable woman, your sister. Have you a picture?"

John drew a wallet from a hip pocket. The edges of the photograph were worn, but Catherine's smile was radiant, and her beauty shone through the well-handled photo.

"Ah, yes. You must be very proud. Thank you. I am doubly honored by the trust of such a beautiful lady."

"That's what he used to call her, sir. 'Lady' was his pet name for Catherine. She must miss him very much." John cleared his throat. The impact of his father's death hit him a second time. John realized that he needed time away from war. "He was a doctor, sir. Well known in his field."

"Great sadness comes when one so near dies. The loss of a pilot is sad for everyone at home. I have written too many such letters. I sympathize with your sister. She must feel terrible to write this letter. I have learned in life there is also death. Those who live must go on. You will have seven days to reflect on life. It is your sister's wish and also mine.

"When you come back, you must fly with eyes open and a sharp mind. If you need more time, call me. I will give you as much time as I can. I am very sorry for your loss. It is terrible to lose a father. But I can assure you, it is much worse for a father to lose a son."

"Thank you, sir." John stood, saluted, and left. His anger had completely vanished. What remained was a deep feeling of humility, something John had salted away months before. Now, humility permeated every sinew. He was reminded how fickle life could be. His fire to fight was replaced by the lump in his throat. What made his father's death harder to swallow was the fact that had he taken his father's advice and waited until America declared war, he might still be home near his father. His father's death brought with it the realization of how much he'd changed. Sam Morris was dead. Nothing would change that.

A Time for Healing

In a supply truck headed for Paris, John quietly watched the trees of the Forêt de Retz go by on the road to Villers-Cotterêts. The sight of trees that still had limbs was calming. They proved that he was leaving the chaos of the battlefields. The driver was Senegalese, a bright-eyed young man who'd made many trips to the front, wherever supplies were needed. If John thought French was difficult, his driver's Pidgin English was as foreign to him as his West African country. John simply smiled or nodded at the man's comments. He sensed that the young man was being friendly. John's smiles were as much forced as genuine. They made him realize how tired he'd gotten since leaving Pau.

The road bent west through the town of Villers-Cotterêts, leaving Château-Thierry behind. Rubble still littered the town, but people went about their daily lives, walking on the streets and sidewalks, carrying on as though the war were a thousand miles away from Soissons, not twenty miles. Twenty miles wasn't far, but it made a difference. Here, the war seemed to have an end. A young girl smiled at him from the sidewalk as the truck ambled through the tiny town. She'd done such a human thing. John raised a hand and waved in acknowledgment. For the first time in nearly a year, John relaxed.

The truck reached Senlis, where weeks before, John bought the mirror on his Spad. To John, it seemed years ago. The street was free of rubble. Traffic grew heavier and slowed near the center of town on the Rue de la République, giving him time to see the damage wrought in 1914. Hollowed buildings remained as a testament to the visitation of war. The Court of Justice had burned, leaving behind a blackened facade. Sunlight beamed through broken windows from the wrong side. The cathedral's tower was still standing! Townspeople went about their business. The trip was better than John expected. The farther he got from the war, the more he relaxed. Paris was less than twenty-five miles to the south.

Every mile put between himself and the squadron allowed for more relief. The driver took John straight to Mrs. Weeks's house. Only then did John realize that Thénault had given the driver directions. Mrs. Weeks did her best to make her guests feel at home. John felt out of place. After writing letters to Catherine and his mother and with a week in hand, John headed toward the train station. British soldiers crowded the streets near the station. Something very big must be planned. They carried backpacks and rifles, and they all looked somber as they were directed to the freight cars by shouting sergeants. Their train was headed north, toward the front either to Amiens or Flanders.

For a week, John didn't have to be a part of any attack. Away from the killing and ruins of old French towns, he hadn't decided what to do or where to go. He wanted to forget the war but didn't want to be alone to brood over his father's death. When he left England for France, he'd accepted the idea that he might never go home again. The irony to John was that he'd outlived his father. A greater distance between him and the war was what he needed.

England was an obvious choice, the only place where English was spoken universally. It wouldn't be difficult to cross the channel and return within a week. Albert and Bertie had asked him to come when he had leave. John enjoyed Albert's endless tales of London, and Albert would want to hear what John had seen and done. There'd be more time for London after the war and no one waiting his return to duty. John bought a train ticket to the port on the west of France.

The young girl's smile made him remember Michelle. He hadn't written to her for a month. Saint-Nazaire was far from war. She'd welcome him. He recalled her vibrancy and the patience she'd shown teaching him French greetings and good-byes and how André had spoken so lovingly of the castles near the Loire. The Loire had not seen war. Perhaps he'd tour its banks. Michelle could come with him. The idea pleased him.

It was late when he got off the train. Saint-Nazaire looked very different to him. Everywhere he looked, American soldiers roamed the streets. Long warehouses near the tracks weren't there when he'd first arrived. As he walked outside, he almost expected to see André du Montrey. The way to the bakery was familiar. As he approached, the bakery was still busy. Several soldiers stood outside waiting their turns to go in. The crowd was so thick that he caught only glimpses of Michelle filling orders and warding off their constant playful advances. John squeezed past the doorway against the complaints of men of lesser rank.

Michelle didn't notice him. Inside, he stood by the shop window, watching her. It was near closing time. Soldiers complained when she told them that she had nothing more to sell. They'd bought everything on the shelves. She looked tired, but her voice still had the fire he remembered when they'd gone to the butcher shop in the heart of the town. As the shop emptied, sunlight shone through the shop window, making John a dark silhouette. When she saw him, she thought he was just another soldier.

"You must go, *monsieur*. There is no more. The bakery will be closed until tomorrow."

"Do you really you want me to go, miss?"

She responded impatiently. "Of course. The bakery is ..." She paused. Something in his voice sounded familiar.

"Jean? Is that you, Jean?"

"Yes."

She ran to the shadow in front of the window. He caught her in his opened arms and lifted her off the floor, feeling happier than he could remember.

"Can you close the shop for a few days? If your father doesn't object, I want to take you up the Loire." For a time, she stayed pressed against him, breathing deep sighs.

"Yes! Papa will say yes, Jean. He talks about you always. He says I am lucky to know a man who cares so much. He gets angry when I tell him of the towns in your letters. He says he will fight if the Boche come to town."

John believed her. Knowing how André loved his town, he'd probably fight.

Shortly after, André returned. He was surprised and happy to see John. He'd spent the day talking to some of his old students who worked in the rail yard. Their stories, he said, gave him news of the war he didn't find in newspapers. Approval to their outing was given, and André filled them with suggestions about where they should go and what they should see.

"Papa! I have lived here all my life. I have heard you speak of these places so many times I can see them with my eyes closed."

"You are right, Michelle. I talk too much," the old man said, feeling sorry that he couldn't go along.

"Stay with the store, Papa. The soldiers will be back tomorrow. Tell them I get supplies for the bakery."

The idea actually appealed to him. It would give him an excuse to talk to them. "I must go upstairs to wash. The depot was busy today."

John noticed the time and suggested that they eat and go to bed early. Michelle agreed.

The next morning, Michelle made breakfast. John was the last to rise but the first to be ready to go. He hadn't worn civilian clothes for months and was glad to be out of uniform. After packing a small bag, Michelle was ready. They said good-bye to her father and rode their bicycles to the bus station. John bought two tickets to Tours and had the bicycles tied to the roof.

Once the bus left Saint-Nazaire and passed Nantes, Michelle told him that it was as far as she'd ever been from town. From now on, everything she saw would be new to her.

"It's new to me too," he said. "I slept all the way to Le Mans when I left for Paris."

On reaching Tours, they ate in a local café. Their first destination was Chenonceau. It was exactly as André du Montrey described. Already late, they found a small pension in the town of Bléré. When the owner, a stodgy old man wearing glasses, asked if they were married, John was about to explain that he didn't speak French. Michelle pinched his arm. She answered the question before John spoke.

"*Oui, monsieur, une année. Avez-vous une chambre?*"

"*Oui, madame.*"

John knew enough French to know that *madame* was the term used to address a married woman. He looked at Michelle. She pinched his arm hard. The owner showed them the room, and she told the man that it suited them. She asked about the bathroom. He pointed to the end of the hall. She thanked him, and the proprietor left.

"Well ..." John began saying. Michelle grabbed his arm and put a finger to her lips to warn him to be quiet. She put her ear to the door until she heard footsteps going down the steps. Satisfied, she hurried back to John with a very pleased smile.

"I see we suddenly got married," John said with raised eyebrows.

"Tonight only. If he knew we are not married and you are American, the price is twice as much ... oo-la-la! We are married. Or you have no more money!"

John had noticed the tendency of French retailers to charge Americans much more than their French patrons.

"I hear the soldiers talking in my shop. They pay too much for everything," she said.

"It's the war, Michelle. People act as though tomorrow will never come. Besides, many of the things they sell are rationed and hard to buy."

"Perhaps. But tomorrow will come, war or no war. *C'est égal.* For the shop, the only change from war is the cost of cooking oil, sugar, salt, and flour. I had to make my prices higher. The soldiers pay more for everything because they are soldiers!"

He admired her sense of fairness. The truth was that he'd paid an exorbitant amount for the mirror in Senlis. But his need for it gave him no other choice. He'd paid gladly. No other shop had the mirror in stock.

John looked the room over. Among the furniture, a double bed rested against one wall of the modest room. It wasn't much wider than his bed in Guilford.

He gestured toward the bed, looked at her, and said, "Do you think we'll both fit?"

Michelle grinned and took him by the arm. At first, John thought she was agreeable. She led him to a modest three-cushion sofa resting against the wall opposite the bed.

"Jean." She giggled. "It looks too small for you. If only you were not so tall."

John sighed. "Okay. At least it looks more comfortable than my cot. I was just thinking ..."

"Oh? And what are you thinking?"

"Never mind. This will be okay."

Too late to ride bicycles, they decided to walk.

The first few days, they biked and spoke constantly. After the first few days, his advances became less subtle. She met them with varying responses, all of which meant no. It became a sort of game. He'd thrust. She'd parry. John rediscovered her intelligence and wit. She was his interpreter, explaining placards written in French. He was her escort to places both had only imagined. John often contrasted what they saw with places he'd been to in America. She would listen and respond with reverence for the things her country had accomplished, emphasizing the youth of America to the age of France. Michelle asked John to tell her about life in America. Between them, a familiarity grew. Something more than familiarity was also growing, but they were not aware of anything unusual. For her part, there were so many things to see. For his, it was a time to heal, a chance to cleanse himself of war.

Michelle noticed his mood changes. She could read his moods with uncanny accuracy. John noticed that she'd become attuned to his moods. To avoid telling her the truth, he'd sidestep her questions. But Michelle was not a woman who was easily circumvented. Her persistence made it difficult for him to evade her questions but easier for him to play tricks on her. At a sharp turn, he purposely steered his bicycle off the road and fell very near a large stone, pretending to be unconscious. She ran to him screaming.

"Oh no, Jean! *Mon Dieu!*"

Putting his head in her lap, she began to rub his forehead, repeating, "*Mon dieu! Mon dieu!*" He immediately grabbed her and rolled her on her back. She shrieked with surprise and scolded him for being so cruel. He kissed her, and something beyond intimacy became apparent to both. They grew more serious when speaking to one another.

Before the tour was over, he told her everything about himself, carefully omitting his combat experience. She laughed at his boyhood tales, told him about a headstrong little girl growing up without a mother, and how she had started the bakery. They were falling in love, and nothing they said or did either forced or prevented it. It was as natural as night following day.

One afternoon, they made love in a grassy meadow below an old château near the Loire. Before the week was over, Michelle asked him if he would marry her. John had thought about it long before she asked. Facing his boyhood dream, he wasn't sure how he should answer her question. He'd come to France with a very different goal in mind, a goal that had become more like a repeated nightmare. In any time except war, he'd have asked her the question first. Michelle was the woman he'd always imagined he'd marry. But John was engaged in a war that constantly reminded him of his mortality. His future was too uncertain to enter into a marriage. The thought of marriage, only to make her a widow, was unacceptable.

"Michelle, nothing would make me happier, you must believe that. But I'm past the time most pilots are killed, and I've got to return. All I'd think about is being with you when I'm flying. It's not fair to either of us. You've told me how hard it was for you to grow up without a mother. It wouldn't be fair for you to lose your husband."

"I don't care. If we have only a week together, it will be enough," she pleaded. Her eyes filled with sadness. "Don't worry for me. Just come back." She began to cry.

John held her tightly. "Wait for me. I'll come back. I'll marry you, Michelle. Will you wait?"

If he survived, he could fulfill a dream he'd never expected to realize. Only then could he give them a future. Michelle was like no other woman he'd ever known. She spoke her mind with courage and honesty. She was willing to risk her deepest feelings with him, unlike the coquettes he usually met at home—women who were more worried about how they looked or who their friends were. John didn't want to leave. He had to leave. He was engaged in war, not to Michelle.

She didn't answer. He repeated, "Michelle? Will you wait for me?"

Through her tears, she whispered, "*Oui, mon amour. Pour un moment, une année, ou la fin des siècles.*"

"Michelle, please. Tell me in English."

"Yes, my love. For a moment, a year, or the end of time."

He smiled. She threw her arms around his neck, afraid he might disappear before her tears dried. He held her tightly.

"Maybe we won't have to wait long," he said. He kissed her cheeks to dry her tears and kissed her lips until he was sure she'd never forget his promise to return. Hours later, they fell asleep in each other's arms. For the first time in his life, John felt whole, unfettered by the need to prove himself. His goal had changed. Once a fighter who took chances, his new goal was to stay alive.

Savenay

Months later, James was lying in the base hospital at Savenay, only fourteen miles from his port of entry at Saint-Nazaire. When he'd walked off the transport, he'd had two legs. Now he had time to reflect. He remembered how shaky his legs were as he descended the gangway to the pier.

Before he stepped on French soil, he tripped over one of the wooden cross boards on the landing platform, spaced to prevent wet boots from sliding. With his equipment on his back, he was lucky that he hadn't fallen off and drowned in the water beside the pier. He managed to grab the railing and steady himself. His rifle had slid from his shoulder, hitting the shin bone of the leg that was once made a pair of legs.

"Guess I won't be banging that leg anymore," he muttered to himself.

James was not doing as well as his doctor hoped. The pain had subsided, but not enough to let him forget. The stump was healing well enough, but not James. He hadn't healed inside. From the time Josiah reached him until he awoke in the transport train, he remembered nothing. On the train to the hospital, he had a lot of time to think. In the trench, a mound of dirt hid his leg, and for all he knew, it could have been saved. Now that it was gone, nothing he could do or say would ever put it back. He had very few good moments, and they became fewer each time he looked at the blanket on his bed and saw it resting perfectly flat where his leg should have been. In Spartanburg, he'd suffered a different sort of pain, racial pain. That pain had gone on the *Pocahontas*. The pain caused by his wound had not gone—neither the physical nor the mental pain.

He'd trained hard and come all the way to France to fight, but he lay in bed, half the man he was before the explosion. All that training, and he'd never fired a single shot in anger. He hadn't written to Monroe. Writing his father about his leg would force him to acknowledge that it was gone. James hadn't reached that point. He hadn't adjusted to the permanence of its loss.

Dr. Burns had brought him an artificial leg, showed him how to put it on, and told him what to expect when he walked with it. Until he was well enough to wear it, Dr. Burns told James to use his crutches. He quickly learned how to keep his balance with them. For short periods, he also learned to keep his balance without them. That had become necessary when it was time to sit on the toilet. But the thought of wearing an artificial leg was repugnant to him, as foreign to him as the place where he'd landed. He rejected the idea each time Burns presented it to him.

"No, sir, I don't want that thing on me. That's not my leg!"

Dr. Burns began to try the nurses. The door to the ward opened, and Nurse Elisha Denbow came in wearing her motherly smile. Elisha was the second nurse he'd tried. She was older than Marcia Waverly, the good-looking brunette that Dr. Burns first tried. As good a nurse as Marcia was, she'd only been a threat to James. His natural shyness and feeling of being only half the man he was combined to reject her pleas to use an artificial leg.

Marcia had suggested Elisha to the doctor. Elisha was more matronly. She tried to appeal to his maternal side. James wasn't buying any of it. His mother had died before he was old enough to remember what a mother was. Monroe had raised him, and he resented Elisha's maternal appeals. Nothing any of the nurses or his doctor did or said to him changed his mind.

On one of his better days, Lieutenant Jim Europe came to see him. Jim asked if he'd ever played an instrument. James admitted that he'd played a cornet in his father's band when he was in high school. Not sure that he remembered, James reminded the lieutenant that he'd spoken to him about his father right after the regiment landed in France.

"I thought that was you! You told me about your father's band. Listen, James, I want you to give me his address. I want to look him up when we get back to the States. Okay?"

"Gosh, Lieutenant, he'd be proud to meet you. He wrote to tell me to ask you if you'd mind meeting him sometime."

"I'll do better than that. What does your father play?"

"Drums. He hammers on the piano a little, but he's pretty good on drums."

"Well, if he can get to New York when we have our homecoming parade, I'll put him in the drum section. I'm going to need another drummer, and I wasn't sure I'd find one on short notice. Have we got a deal?"

"We sure do, Lieutenant, sir!"

"Good. Now while you're healing up, start practicing, because a good cornet player is hard to find, and I'm going to need a mighty big band when we march down Fifth Avenue. I want New Yorkers to remember that day!"

James cringed when he heard the word "march." He wasn't sure he'd ever walk again, much less march and play at the same time. The thought of marching was as remote as his missing leg.

"Yes, sir. I'll need to practice." The words came out in a lower tone as he replied, and Jim Europe took notice even though James's expression hadn't changed.

"Okay, James. Concentrate on getting yourself well. Damn! I almost forgot. I got something for you. I'll be right back."

In a few minutes, Jim Europe came back carrying the prettiest cornet James had ever seen. He handed it to James. James thought it was a loaner.

"I figured you might've left yours home, so you might need this. Good luck to you, James. We're gonna have a great parade. Everyone will be proud. Get yourself well, you hear? It won't be the same if you're not there with your father."

"I don't know what to say, Lieutenant. Thank you. I'll return it when—"

"Get well, James. That's enough for me. Got to go now. I'll look up your father when we get back home. That's a promise. You practice on that cornet. I need pure tones in my band."

What James didn't know was that Jim Europe took a chance that he might play an instrument and had loaded every spare flute and horn the band had on the truck. James was the only man he'd come to see. He'd been made aware of James by Captain Little, their battalion commander.

Two weeks had passed since then, and James had done nothing more than pick up the horn and polish it with a cloth. Several men in the ward asked him to play, but each time, he said that the noise would wake men in the wards. Playing wasn't the problem. The thought of marching was. How could he march on crutches and hold a cornet? For now, it was enough that he had it and remembered Jim Europe's promise to visit his father. It was going to take more than a promise and a horn to get him up on that damned artificial leg.

When Michael came to the base hospital in Savenay, he didn't rush to see James right away. One of Michael's concerns was that James may not want him to know he was in France. He'd feel compelled to explain why he'd never said anything to the family about it. On a personal level, he knew that James wasn't aware that he was the surgeon who'd taken his leg. He'd have to explain how James lost his leg. That could be a sensitive topic to James. Michael's main interest was as the physician who'd performed the amputation. On a professional level, he wanted to check with James's doctor to see how he was doing. By this time, Michael thought James would be well on his way to recovery. It never occurred to him that James hadn't really begun to recover.

"Dr. Burns, I'm Michael Morris, the surgeon who removed James Jefferson's leg. I came to check with you to see how he's coming along. I assume he's tried to walk without crutches by now."

"A pleasure, Dr. Morris. You certainly did a fine job saving his life. Unfortunately, we haven't been able to do much about his heart."

"I don't understand. Are you saying he's developed a heart problem?"

"In a way. You see, he doesn't want to wear his prosthesis. He's refused everyone—the nurses and myself. We've tried many times. For a while, we thought we had an ally when one of his battalion friends visited. That cheered him up for a while, but things seemed to get worse when the man left. I'm worried about atrophy. When his stump was well enough, he had the strength to try the leg. But since he won't use the prosthesis, he may never be able to walk without crutches. He isn't using his legs the way he should. If he doesn't start to, he may not have the strength to stand on it, much less walk. I've seen it happen with other amputees. They don't want to admit the injury to themselves. They're afraid to take the only step available to them to fully recover."

The doctor's words surprised and discouraged Michael.

"That doesn't sound like the James I knew."

"You must have a strong interest in the man to remember him so well and travel this far, Doctor. I wish there were more like you in those God-forsaken aid stations."

"If he's awake, I'd like to see him, Dr. Burns."

"That may not be wise. His leg preoccupies his thoughts as it is. He once told his nurse that he wasn't sure it needed to be amputated. If he were to come face to face with the man who'd removed it, we might lose him for good."

"I understand, sir. But James is the son of our chauffeur in Baltimore. I've known him ever since we were boys. I wrote to his father explaining what happened and promised to visit him."

Dr. Burns grabbed his chin for a moment. "I can see why you'd want to see him. Give me a moment to think about it. I'm about to make my rounds. You're welcome to come along, if you'd like."

"Yes, sir. I'd like that. It's kind of you to offer."

The hospital had wards on two floors. Michael followed Dr. Burns. He wanted to see James. He hoped that Dr. Burns would allow it. If he didn't, his only alternative was to accept Dr. Burns's reason and leave Savenay in the interest of James's mental state. The latter choice held no chance to see James and keep his promise to Monroe. As Dr. Burns was James's primary physician, Michael couldn't disobey him. He'd sworn to uphold the ethics of his profession. To see James in spite of his doctor's orders would amount to a court-martial offense. Dr. Burns saved the ward James was in for last. He stopped at the entrance to the ward.

"This is James Jefferson's ward. I've given it some thought. It might be worth taking the risk. As it stands, we've gotten nowhere. Nothing else has worked. You may be his last hope. Take it from here, Dr. Morris. Finish checking the ward. He has to confront the fact that he's lost his leg when he meets the man who took it off. I just hope we're doing the right thing for him."

Dr. Burns had indeed done some thinking during his rounds, and Michael recognized his valid concern for James's well-being. It was up to him now. The next few minutes might determine the rest of James's life, and Michael had to find a way to help him.

"Thank you, Dr. Burns. I'm pleased you've given me this chance. I'll do my best to earn that trust. I have a much better understanding of his condition now."

Michael took the medical chart from Burns and entered the convalescent ward. His strange face immediately brought stares from the men on nearby beds. His eyes stopped scanning the room when they saw James's bed. James was reading and hadn't noticed Michael entering the ward.

Michael looked at the names on the chart and started visiting the numbered beds as though he'd be doing it all along. A sergeant occupied the first. Caught in a mustard gas barrage, his eyes were bandaged, and he was having trouble breathing.

"When's the last time they changed your bandage, Sergeant?"

"Yesterday morning, sir," the sergeant stammered, gasping the syllables three at a time.

"You're due for a new one tomorrow. The chart says your burns are beginning to heal. How about your lungs? Are they feeling any better?"

"They're better ... than they were ... before, sir. Lungs ... aren't so good."

"According to this, you took a good dose before you got your mask on. They'll keep the salve around your eyes for a while. The scarring should look better in time. In twenty years, you can tell your story to your grandchildren." Michael noted the patient's comment.

James stopped reading and saw the back of a doctor standing about thirty feet away across the center aisle. He seemed familiar, but James couldn't see his face. New personnel came and went with regularity. His book interested him more than new personnel. He began reading again.

Michael moved from bed to bed without looking toward James and continued to do what doctors do making the rounds. The next patient was British. Private Willison was a balloonist who'd suffered a broken shoulder in an attack on his balloon. He'd fallen hard when his parachute was set afire by incendiary bullets.

"Private Willison, it says here you want to return to your company. Don't you like it here?"

"Well, sir, I was hit in the big push-up Fizzmees. I ought to be in Ruin. But me MO got me papers screwed up, and I winds up coming 'ere in an homme-forty. I understand, sir. He's just a Jock, you know. But if I don't show up pretty soon, the boys might think I came down with dugout fever or became a landowner. They're a good bunch of lads, sir ... call me the best balloonatic the company ever had."

Michael had heard accents before but was at a loss to decipher the words his patient was using. He continued the interview without asking for explanation.

"When were you wounded, Private Willison?"

"On the way down, sir."

Michael's face revealed that this wasn't the answer he'd expected to his question. The soldier understood.

"Ah! Right, sir, you mean what time! Around four in the afternoon, sir, above Fizzmees. They spell it F-i-s-m-e-s, sir, a ways up from Reims." Willison smiled. His explanation seemed sound to him.

"You said you ought to be in ruin?" Michael questioned the comment since the man's wound was healing well enough, and he seemed in good spirits.

"That's right, sir. It's where the Tommies hospital is located on the Seine, west of La Havre. Where we came to join up with the Frogs."

"Ah! You mean Rouen. Okay, let's see if I've got this right. Your medical officer made a mistake sending you here instead of Rouen, right?"

"That's it, sir. You've got it."

"Okay. But it doesn't say anything here about you getting a fever or owning land. I have no idea what you mean by that. Please explain it for me so I can finish my notes."

"Sure thing, sir. Dugout fever's when a man's idlin' in the dugout, sir. You know, sir ... he's afraid to raise his head and get it shot off. Now, a landowner, well he's one what's bought the farm, so to speak, sir. Pushing up daisies, feedin' worms, sir."

Michael finally understood. "I think I've got the picture now. When I see Dr. Burns, I'll ask about getting you transferred back to Rouen. Is there anything else I can do for you?" Michael was taking a semantic gamble but was willing to risk it.

"Well, sir. The bum fodder used around here ain't what you'd call cushy, sir. It's better than the trenches, but you might mention that to the doc, as well."

"Bum fodder?"

"Yes, sir, the six by four. You know. In the latrine? It's what we wipe our arses with, sir."

"Oh! Toilet paper!"

"That's it, sir. It's the same."

"I'll mention it, Private, but I'm not sure anything can be done. The British military requisitions its supplies. Maybe they'll have what you want when you get to Rouen."

"Oh, I dunno, sir. I'm sure I'll have to go before then, sir."

"I see what you mean. Well, when you need to go, you go right ahead as often as the urge hits you. Don't let the bum fodder stop you."

"Will do, sir! Pleasure to meet you, sir, I'm sure."

"Good luck."

Soon, Michael had seen everyone but James, who was so intent reading his book that he hadn't bothered to look up. Michael approached his bed with the chart in front of his face.

"Sergeant James Jefferson. That sounds familiar."

James immediately recognized Michael's voice. He put his book down.

"Mr. Michael? Is that you?"

As he lowered the chart, James saw a big grin. James was wide-eyed with amazement. He hadn't seen Michael since Guilford and wondered how he had magically appeared in front of him.

"It's me, James. I'm glad to see you." He extended his hand.

Instinctively, James moved to stand to take Michael's hand. As he swung his right leg over the side of the bed, the left didn't follow. He'd forgotten. He immediately became embarrassed at being unable to stand. Michael took his hand and shook it vigorously.

"How are you feeling?"

"I'm okay, sir. Sorry I can't get up. How did you know I—"

"I've known for some time, James. I was surprised to learn you were in France. You never said anything about it, nor did your father . Whatever your reasons … it's okay. I'm glad to see you."

"Mr. Michael, sir, I was going to tell you when—"

"Please, James, call me Michael. We've known each other since we were kids. I may outrank you, but drop the 'sir.' From now on, I'm just another friend."

"Yes, sir. Sorry. I guess it'll take some getting used to. I'm okay, Michael. It's been a couple weeks since this happened. The pain is mostly gone." James couldn't bring himself to say he'd lost a leg and had never used the term "stump."

"It's been longer than a couple of weeks, James. You lost your leg on the fifteenth of July."

"Yes, sir, that's right. I'm sorry … Michael. Can't seem to get that right."

The old embarrassment returned, and it showed. Pride kept him from wearing an artificial leg and fear from practicing for Jim Europe. Now, his leg was keeping him from standing to talk to Michael. For the first time, he recognized the full implications of his condition.

"How did you know?"

"I've known all along, James. You're going to be all right."

Tears began to well in James's eyes. In that instant, he finally acknowledged that his leg was gone. Michael waited as the binds that James had placed around his spirit loosened. James was finally releasing the anguish of losing a leg. Michael sat on the edge of the bed and put his hand on James's shoulder. He waited until James composed himself.

"I didn't want to face it, Michael. I don't know why. I don't remember anything after the shell hit. When I woke up, it wasn't there. I didn't want to believe it. I ignored it at first. I tried to put it out of my mind."

Michael waited to be sure that he'd said all he wanted to say.

"I've been a fool, Michael. They tried to help—the doctor, the nurses. I turned them away."

"Have you told your father?"

"No. Up to now, I couldn't even tell myself. I'm not sure how to tell him. He worries about me. I don't know how he'll take it."

"Okay. It's my turn now. It's time you knew. I wrote to Monroe about it, James."

"You wrote to him, Michael? How did you know?"

"I was on duty in the aid station when Josiah brought you in. I didn't recognize you. Your face was muddy. Your leg was shattered. You'd lost a lot of blood. The muscle was gone. I had no choice. I had to take the leg. It couldn't be fixed, James. It was the only way to save your life."

"You did it, Michael? You took my leg?"

"Yes. It was me. I amputated your leg."

The moment came Michael had worried about. How would he respond? For a moment, James sat in complete silence, thinking about what Michael had said. Then he looked at Michael.

"I'm glad it was you, Michael. Now I know it had to come off. I'm okay with it."

"I can't tell you what that means to me, James. I promise you, even if I'd known it was you, it would have had to come off. It was nearly off already. I just finished the job. When I found out you were on my table, I went outside. I couldn't look at you knowing what I'd done. What it meant to you. I was afraid you might think …"

"Michael, I mean it. I'm glad it was you. You saved my life."

"I was just doing my job, James. When I came here, I was worried when I learned you hadn't tried to walk without crutches. You can walk, James. Didn't the nurses help you?"

"To tell the truth, Michael, I didn't care much for them."

"Okay. Before I go, I'll find a nurse for you. I'm glad I came, James. I was more worried about what you'd say about amputating your leg."

Michael kept his promise. Nurse Anitra Nashri was from India. She was shy like James, and her tenderness and patience came highly recommended by Dr. Burns. Dr. Burns thanked him for giving James the heart he'd mislaid somewhere between the Marne and Savenay. Before leaving the hospital, Michael introduced James to his new nurse. James smiled a coy smile at him as Michael waved good-bye. He approved. Michael would have liked to stay, but his orders were to report to headquarters.

When he returned to Chaumont, Marshall was interested in Michael's impressions about the aid station.

"From what you've told me, there's room for improvement.

Unfortunately, treatment is often given too late to save life and limb due to the confusion on the battlefield. We need to get help to our wounded faster. It might mean putting doctors in the field."

Michael asked if he could continue working in an aid station.

"If that's what you want, I'll see to it today. Your experience gives us a head start in improving our medical response."

Saint-Pol-sur-Mer

IN PARIS, JOHN STOPPED BRIEFLY at Mrs. Weeks's house. He had a cup of coffee and made a phone call to Chaudun. The telephone rang many times at the field. His mechanic, Charles Gallau, answered the phone in Thénault's office. Charles told him that the escadrille had moved. He and several other mechanics had stayed behind to load spare parts and equipment into trucks.

"Has the captain gone to the new field?"

"*Oui, monsieur.* They go to the coast this morning. Capitaine Thénault, he tells me to stay in case you call. The fliers are gone."

"Where did they go, Charles?"

"Saint-Pol-sur-Mer, below Dunkerque, in Flanders. But you must come first to Chaudun, *monsieur.* The Spad, she is ready. The *capitaine* said you come as soon as possible. I wait for you. The trucks, they are loaded."

"Thank you, Charles. I'll be there as soon as possible. It may take an hour or so to get there. *Au revoir*, Charles."

"*Oui, monsieur.* I wait for you."

The bus would take him as far as Soissons. He'd have to transfer. When the next approached Chaudun, he'd ask the driver to stop and walk to the field. The bus was crowded. British soldiers outnumbered French civilians. John was the only pilot. He sat next to a British officer. Two civilians occupied seats in front of them—a young woman wearing the habit of a sister and a middle-aged man wearing glasses and a weathered beret.

The man had the demeanor of a minor official. As soon as the bus was under way, the two civilians began talking to one another using exaggerated gestures, speaking too quickly for John to catch any of it. Whatever the topic was, it wasn't good. The officer sitting next to him noticed John's puzzled curiosity. He assumed that John didn't understand French.

"Need any help with the language?"

"I can't follow it. It must be something they don't like."

"They're talking about funding a monument to commemorate some people killed by the Germans in 1914. A rather nasty affair, judging from their tone."

"I couldn't help wondering. The sister was really animated. I know enough French to order a coffee. I'm Sergeant John Morris of Maryland, sir. You?"

"Major Paul Eddington from Cambridge. A pleasure, John. I thought you might be American. But that's the insignia of a French squadron you're wearing, isn't it? Aren't Americans flying their own these days?"

"Frankly, America hasn't got much of an air service, Major. I heard they set up a training camp in Rantoul. Their main base is Issoudun, south of Paris. It's just starting to take shape. I joined after Wilson was reelected."

"I admire your spirit. By the way, it takes a while to get accustomed to the language. I assume you communicate well enough with our French compatriots."

"Yes, sir. It's an all-American outfit. The officers and mechanics are French. Most of the pilots either live in France or had French parents. I'm one of the few who doesn't speak French."

"What's the name of your unit?"

"SPA124, sir. Combat Group Thirteen. The Lafayette Escadrille."

"Indeed! That explains your early entry. They've got something of a reputation in France, and I daresay the rest of the world. Excuse me a moment, John." The major stopped to listen more closely to the two civilians. He'd also gotten interested in the conversation. Its intensity had grown.

"She said she didn't understand why the assembly wouldn't give them funds right away ... something about Joan of Arc saving the town and other such things—none of which I'm familiar with."

John remembered his history studies. An idea struck him about the life of the Maid of Orléans.

"They could be talking about Senlis, Major. Saint Joan saved the town from the English in the fifteenth century. The Burgundians captured her and turned her over to the English. She was eventually burned as a heretic."

"Ironic, isn't it? Here we are helping them fight the Germans, and they'd have been better off without us then. Gives one pause to wonder at the leanings in religion and politics.

"It seems the maid was mentioned to demonstrate the importance of Senlis to the assembly. The monument they want is meant for some innocent people the Germans shot in a local hospital. The gentleman just explained how they executed his brother and the mayor of Senlis. He thinks it's reason enough for Paris to give them the money."

The end of their conversation brought an end to the major's commentary. What he'd heard angered the major. An officer himself, he believed that German officers should refrain from harming civilians.

"I've heard enough, John. That's the most barbaric behavior I've heard up to now. Officers who behave like that should be summarily shot! We're going to get a crack at them soon. It's this sort of thing that fires up the men. You can jolly well depend on that."

"Yes, sir. I'll get a crack at them myself when I get to Saint-Pol."

Forty minutes later, the bus stopped in Senlis. The two civilians got off, still discussing their dilemma.

"Looks like you were right, John. They're getting off. You missed your calling, old man."

"Sir?"

"You should have become a history professor. I'd give it some thought after the war. Are you getting off, as well?"

"Yes, sir. I need to transfer to a different bus. How about you?"

"Amiens. A quick stop at HQ. After that, it's Flanders. Ypres. Good to meet you, old man. Stay alert. You've got a good head on your shoulders. I wouldn't want to see it lying in the muck."

John thanked Major Eddington and wished him luck. An hour later, the transfer neared Chaudun. He reminded the driver that he needed to get off. By the time John reached the airfield, a single truck remained. Charles was standing near the Spad with a dirty towel in his hands when John entered the hangar.

"Ah, you are here, *monsieur*. The others went a long time ago. You feel better, *monsieur*?"

"Yes. Thanks, Charles. I'm glad you waited. Is the Spad ready?"

"*Oui, monsieur!* She is good. I run the engine every day you are gone. She runs very well this morning."

"I appreciate your time and your work. Is there a map in the office … one that shows Saint-Pol-sur-Mer? I'm not familiar with that area."

"*Oui, monsieur.* Come with me. The *capitaine*, he has one big map in his office."

They walked to Thénault's office. The captain had left the map on a large wooden table. John spread it open. Before he could look, Charles pointed out the new base in the upper-left corner of the map.

"*Voici, monsieur.* Saint-Pol-sur-Mer. Below Dunkerque, *près du Canal Anglais.*"

"In English, Charles."

"*Pardon, monsieur.* Saint-Pol-Sur-Mer. It is near the English Channel. We must be going, *monsieur.* It is late."

A scale measuring kilometers was in the lower-right corner. John picked a scrap of paper and laid the edge along the scale. He made a small tear at one hundred kilometers. The base was almost exactly two hundred kilometers north by northwest. It was close to the Belgian border and adjacent to the English Channel. John began to think aloud.

"In a minute, Charles. A straight flight roughly follows the front lines. Amiens is a bit south of it halfway there. Is the fuel tank full, Charles? I don't want to run out before I get there."

"She is full, *monsieur.* But she has no more than two hours."

"Good. If you don't need this, I'll take the map with me. I'll head toward the old field near Ham to avoid the front and then follow the tracks to Amiens. From there, I'll head due north. I should make it to the coast by nightfall. I'm a little worried about fuel. The Spad is rated for two hours on a full tank. I'll be cutting it very close. If I'm not there by the time you arrive, tell Captain Thénault my flight plan. I don't expect a problem, but you never know. It's a new sector. Close enough for enemy fliers."

"*Oui, monsieur.* I will tell him myself. But you should go now, *monsieur!*"

John changed into flying gear, and together, they rolled the Spad from the hangar. Charles pulled the propeller to prime the cylinders. The engine started on the second pull. A cloud of black smoke shot out the exhaust as John opened the throttle to taxi to the end of the field. As the plane took off, he waved to Charles. He circled the field once, wagged the Spad's wings to let Charles know that the engine was running smoothly, and then put the lowering sun on his left. The compass indicated several degrees west of true north. It pointed straight for the field near Ham.

Having been out of the air for a week, the sensations of flying came back to him—the roar of the engine, the lash of the wind, the pressure of the seat at his back, the light-headedness from banking the Spad, and the heavy feeling of gaining altitude. The feeling of freedom also came back and more than made up for the other distractions. He'd forgotten how much he enjoyed flying. His only remaining concern was about the fuel. Was there enough for the flight? Or would the wind be against him?

As the horizon steadied, John did a four-point roll to test his sharpness with the controls. His heading hadn't changed when the plane leveled off. He was in control. From the look of the scenery over the Aisne east of Soissons, he'd also returned to the war.

In less than fifteen minutes, John saw Ham and banked to the left. The road directly below paralleled the tracks, and the tracks led directly to Amiens. He looked at the map to check for landmarks. The map showed that he should be over the tiny town of Nesle. Peering over the side of his cockpit, he saw a little town slide under his left wing. He was on course.

Even in friendly skies, it was best to stay alert for enemy planes, especially at his back. Nothing showed in his mirror. The skies ahead were clear. To his right and below the Spad, a formation of four French fighters headed in the direction of Péronne. John rocked his wings in recognition, and the plane at the rear of the formation responded in kind.

Above Marcelcave, he could barely see Amiens through the mist that hung over the ground. He descended to nine thousand feet for a better look and caught a glimpse of a lone two-seater Aviatik heading northeast about two miles to his right. Strongly tempted for a moment, he decided against pursuit. Even with a full tank, he needed all of it to get to the new base. If he engaged an enemy, the fight could consume too much. Beyond that, John wasn't mentally ready for combat.

Amiens was a handsome city on the Somme. John noticed only scattered destruction from the air, though the rail station looked demolished. On the western end of the city, the road swung to the north, and John changed his heading to follow it, crossing the Somme for the third time. The ground became dark as the sun began to settle on the western horizon.

Saint-Pol-sur-Mer was eighty miles to the north. With good weather and a favorable wind, he'd reach it in less than an hour. As darkness fell, it became difficult to see the narrow road. Saint-Pol would be in total darkness by the time he arrived. John descended to five thousand feet. Swirling crosswinds shifted to head-on. That was bad luck. He couldn't afford its cost either in time or fuel. He had little choice. If he opted to go above, he'd be flying blind in the clouds.

Twenty minutes beyond Amiens, the road below disappeared in the darkness. John decided to change his flight plan. Looking at the map, he banked toward the northwest and headed for the coast. On his new heading, he'd cross the Lys River and reach the coast near Calais. From there, he could see the channel and follow the coast right to the field. Minutes later, he crossed a river he believed was the Lys.

John maintained his northwest heading. Approaching the

coast, a heavy mist totally obscured his view of the ground. His goggles fogged with moisture carried by the wind off the English Channel. He climbed to avoid it. At ten thousand feet, the mist grew thinner, but cold air blew in the cockpit and made his damp clothing become twice as cold. He saw nothing at all below the Spad. Clouds and misty haze blanketed everything below.

If the weather didn't improve, he could cross the coast. Then, the odds were only fifty-fifty that he'd turn in the right direction. At this altitude, he wouldn't be able see the coast. He had to descend to get a bearing. At eight thousand feet, rain soaked his flying suit. The cold air only made the chill worse.

He checked his watch and looked at his engine speed indicator. His was doing barely ninety miles per hour. Had he kept a straighter course to the new base, he might be near the field by now. He reasoned that his change in flight plan was sound. John brought the Spad down through the rain and fog, constantly wiping his goggles with the back of his leather glove. Depending solely on his altimeter, he kept descending lower and lower to break free from under the rain clouds. When he was able to see more clearly, the terrain below was totally unfamiliar.

Where's the damned coast? he thought.

The indicator fell to two thousand feet. Rain covered his goggles. No longer of any use, John took them off. A blast of air and rain stung his eyes. He squinted to give them relief. He cut the throttle back. At minimum speed, he risked stalling the Spad. He checked his watch. By dead reckoning, the coastline should be below the Spad. Why hadn't he seen it?

His only choice was to descend until he either saw land or sea. At five hundred feet, he finally he broke out of the heavy rain and caught glimpses of a large body of water on his left. He was over the channel. Belgium was in German hands north of the field. A forced landing in enemy territory was not in his plans. To be sure he hadn't strayed north in the rain and overflown Saint-Pol, he made a wide banking turn to the south.

The sun was well below the horizon. At two hundred feet, he saw the last glimmer of sunlight disappear. He leveled off. Any lower and he might strike trees. Visibility was poor. Ground fog was thick. He had to stay near the ground. His problems grew with the dark and his fuel. The fuel gauge barely moved when he rocked the wings. To his right, the faint line of a long low structure appeared.

"It must be a seawall," he said aloud, unaware that it existed. Landing from the channel side was unlikely with a wall blocking the way. He flew slightly inland to avoid any chance of hitting the wall or overflying the field in the dark. John cursed his useless goggles. The lenses were now wet on both sides. By the time cleaned them and put them back on, he could miss the field entirely.

Speaking aloud to vent his anger, he yelled, "Where are the goddamned field lights? The generator was gone when I left. They had to light the damned field! Where in hell is it?" Had he missed it? He had no idea whether he was in flying over France or Belgium. He dared not turn back a second time.

At that instant, John thought he saw a glimmer of light. Unsure, he turned toward the channel and dropped the Spad to fifty feet. He clearly saw light reflecting from the tops of waves. He leveled off and looked at his watch. He'd been flying for just over two hours. His fuel was nearly gone. If this wasn't the field, a decision had to be made—and soon.

He decided to ditch the Spad on the narrow shoreline. As the Spad swung back to the coast, the glimmer of light he saw earlier was stronger. Whatever it was, he might have time for one pass. Through the mist, he saw that the light was a beacon, a lighthouse on a point of land. Below the beacon, he saw a line of ships.

"That's got to be Dunkirk!" he exclaimed.

He turned south, hugging the coast, straining to see anything that looked like a landing field. Smaller orange lights caught his eye. He recognized them as coming from the doorways of open airplane hangars. John circled inland to land the Spad into the wind. Halfway into the turn, the Spad's engine sputtered and died. The propeller stopped turning. He had one chance to land. Unlike Nieuports, Spads were best flown to a landing. He had to make a dead-stick landing from one hundred feet. The Spad landed heavily in the mud and rolled until its undercarriage bumped into the seawall on the field at Saint-Pol-sur-Mer. The damage was minimal. Charles ran to meet him.

He later learned that Corporal James R. Doolittle wasn't as lucky. After only sixteen days with the escadrille, Doolittle's war was over. He was either dead or in German hands. He'd tried to land on a German airfield after getting lost in the rain and fog.

"Did he land on their field, Ted?"

"We don't know yet. They didn't send word. He had to come down in Belgium. He got separated from us and must have panicked. The Boche idiots should have let him land to capture him and his plane. An observer in the front lines said they fired at him when he veered off. He said he saw smoke, so he was hit."

"Is the field nearby?"

"It's close enough, John. Their field's near Courtrai. One of their best groups. Thénault said the base is being used by Jagdge-schwader 1. The British call them the 'Flying Circus.' Their commander is Manfred von Richthofen, the Red Baron. He's the best they've got if what they write about him is true."

At this announcement, John's lips disappeared against his teeth. Everyone had heard of Richthofen. In April, he'd been promoted to the command of a squadron with fifty-two kills already to his credit. It was already the July 18. John didn't know the Baron's latest count. He didn't want to know. He did know he didn't want to become another of Richthofen's statistics.

"It should be an exciting tour, John. Thénault said our job is to wipe out JG-1, including its commander!"

Passchendaele

AT SAINT-POL-SUR-MER, PILOTS TOOK OFF into the prevailing wind to give their airplanes added lift. The practice was common at bases they occupied. On the coast, the wind normally blew in from the channel. Water was everywhere in Flanders and never hard to find a few feet below the mud. The field soon became a quagmire of muddy, water-filled landing ruts. Shorter than most of the fields they'd used, the seawall at the end of the field was eager to catch a sluggish Spad that couldn't gain enough speed to lift itself out of the muck. Conditions were not ideal for taking off with a full load of fuel while carrying a load of live bombs.

The weather in Flanders was a sodden variety of mist, fog, or rain. During downpours, flying was impossible. The battlefields were worse. A marshy plain, Flanders was barren of live trees up to the Lys. No vegetation remained to soak up water. It wasn't uncommon for a British soldier to seek cover from a barrage by jumping into a watery shell hole and never be seen again. He'd slowly sink into the muck and disappear. A helmet, rifle, or raised hand marked his grave. If he didn't go completely under, he was fortunate if two of his buddies were able to pull him free. Walking was an effort. Legs disappeared in the ooze. When withdrawn, a leg often reappeared without a boot. John preferred Chaudun to Flanders. The fliers were grounded more often than not.

To stay busy, Charles pulled maintenance on the Spad's engine. John checked machine gun ammunition. Suspect bullets were replaced. The advice came from Lufbery—"A bad one can jam the gun." He'd shown John what to look for.

"Here's one. The brass is out of round. It could hang in the chamber, and the next would jam the gun. Look for bent rims. They don't seat well in the chamber. Missing primers are the worst."

His Vickers had only jammed once, but John adopted the habit. Once more might be fatal in a fight.

When they weren't taking care of their equipment, the talk centered on their opponents in Jagdgeschwader 1. Reports sifted up from Paris confirming an article found in a German newspaper that matched a rumor going around the field. In July, a British observer fired his machine gun at a red Albatros, wounding the leader of the *jasta*. The picture showed Richthofen wearing a bandage around his head. For now, his squadron flew without its commander. The news disappointed Lufbery. He'd hoped to meet the Baron in the sky over Belgium.

As they listened to Lufbery's records in the barrack during a squall, Luf told John, "The British damn near ran out of luck three months ago."

John hadn't followed the exploits of British pilots like Mannock, Bishop, and Collishaw. He'd heard the men talk about the new young menace to German aviation, Albert Ball.

"What do you mean by 'ran out of luck,' Luf?"

"They lost 150 airplanes last April. They call it Bloody April.

Most of them to Richthofen's squadron. They were flying D.IIIs out of Douai. And get this, John. They painted their planes every color of the rainbow. Richthofen flies a red triwing. The British call them the 'Flying Circus.' The paper said Richthofen's shot down five times as many planes as I have. That's what we're up against. He brings a lot of company with him on patrol. They haven't seen the bastard solo for months. We need to go high to keep a lookout for his patrol."

Lufbery's tone suppressed an anger he normally displayed when one of squadron's pilots was shot down. It caught John's attention.

"You don't like him much, do you, Luf?" John didn't expect his response.

"Let's just say that I don't like a man who collects souvenirs from the planes he shoots down. He's a cold-blooded son of a bitch. If I get that puffed-up Prussian bastard in my gun sights someday, he'll be redder than his goddamned triplane."

John had never seen Lufbery that upset at an enemy pilot. Raoul usually never referred to them by name. He usually called them "Boche bastards" or "sons of bitches." Obviously, his anger became more focused when speaking of Manfred von Richthofen. Usually, a loss in the squadron or bad weather was what made him angry. Those were eclipsed by a single enemy pilot.

"Are they still flying D.IIIs, Luf?"

"They could be flying kites, for all I know. Most of this comes straight from the British fliers in Saint-Omer, John. They say they got a model with a bigger engine. If they did, they won't be running away from us like they used to. Even so, that Prussian ass doesn't take chances, John. He's been going up with just about the whole goddamned group. Most of his hits are against two-seaters. He knows he can outmaneuver them."

"Sounds like you've seen him, Luf."

"I've seen him. Flying in V formation with four Albatroses. By the way, have you seen Thénault?"

"No. I've been in the hangar all morning."

"He told me to tell you to come to his office. He didn't say why."

"Okay, Luf. Anyway, I'm tired of sifting through these bullets. See you at lunch."

Thénault hadn't bothered to hold morning briefings. Rain had canceled patrols. The squadron was grounded until the weather cleared. John entered the office, soaked from his dash. When Thénault looked up, John couldn't read his expression.

"You wanted to see me, Captain?"

"*Oui*. Stand at attention!"

Thénault had never made the request of him before. John wondered if he'd done something wrong. Perhaps his dead-stick landing, when the carriage of the Spad hit the seawall, or maybe …

The door to the captain's office opened. Raoul Lufbery, Ted Parsons, William Thaw, and several other fliers of the escadrille came through the door. Thénault said nothing to them. John wondered what in hell was going on as they quietly lined up on either side of him.

"On behalf of Grand Quartier Général, I have the honor to inform you that my request for recognition of your exploit at Chaudun has been approved. Unfortunately, this award can only be given to an officer. Therefore, Lieutenant Morris, by authority of French High Command and in the name of France, it is my honor to award you the Médaille Militaire. Congratulations, Lieutenant. You have earned it."

The others applauded.

Having officially presented the medal, John returned Thénault's salute. The only words he heard himself say were "Thank you, sir!" Somewhat in shock, John was nearly knocked down by the crowd of cheerful buddies. They hadn't had a lot to cheer about since their arrival on the coast. As for himself, John was at a loss for words. Thénault's presentation was a total surprise. The celebration carried into the mess tent. They swept rain off their uniforms and ceremoniously opened several bottles of Vin Mouseaux.

"We didn't get the chance to drink to your first promotion, John."

"Hey, no promotion ever kept you from celebrating, Ted."

John noticed Lufbery standing off to one side. Lieutenant Lufbery seemed detached as he raised his glass to toast John. The celebration soon calmed down. John left the table and went to continue the conversation he and Lufbery were having before going to Thénault's office. Lufbery's comments on the Flying Circus called for a change in the tactics the squadron usually employed. Lufbery's concern over British losses had also registered concern in John.

"Maybe we can turn the tables on them, Luf. A thought came to me after what you said. Maybe we should go up in two teams, two separate fighter groups. Let's say Willis, Dud Hill, and Bill Thaw fly under the clouds. Ted, you, and me, we could fly in the clouds like top cover. If the Circus jumps them, we're bound to get a few before they see us come down."

Lufbery thought a moment. "It's the old *jasta* trick, John. They attack from the clouds. I don't think they'd fall for that old trap. I was thinking we run in two groups a mile or two apart. Then one group could help the other."

"But suppose one group lay back in full cloud cover. They'd never see us flying cover."

"You mean flying in formation inside clouds? I don't know. It would be damned near impossible to stay together. Maybe we should ask the guys. See what they think."

Lufbery and John returned to the table. The group was still drinking toasts. Lufbery sketched out John's idea. Ted wanted John to go into more detail.

"Luf said Richthofen doesn't like to take chances. He goes up with most of his *jasta*. The way I see it, the best way to break up their formation is to give them something to go after. I think we should go up in two groups. One group flies below the clouds, the other hidden inside."

Ted Parsons immediately saw the weak links in John's plan. "John, flying in heavy clouds isn't as easy as you make it sound. They couldn't stay together or on course with the group below."

"Hear me out. Bill leads the group below. He plots two or three courses by compass heading. He picks the best heading based on where the clouds are continuous. Wherever he goes, he flies about five hundred feet below the clouds. The high group goes into the clouds on the same heading. Bill knows we've got top cover. Richthofen's *jasta* can look for covering planes, but he can't see through clouds. He'll either have to take the bait and go after Bill's group or go home. Given his reputation, he'll go after Bill. That's when we spring the trap."

John paused for reaction and didn't have to wait long.

"You're talking about an ambush," Parsons said.

"That's exactly what I'm talking about! We get him before he knows what hit him."

"It's an interesting idea," Thaw said, "but it's still got a couple of holes in it. The men in the clouds must stay together. How do they know if they're getting ahead or falling behind?"

"Simple. We fly at the same air speed," Lufbery said.

"Okay," said Willis, "But how do the guys on top know when to come down? He can't see us, but we can't see him, either!"

Parsons nodded in agreement and added, "It's hard to stay together in clouds. If we don't come down together, it doesn't work, John."

"I agree, Ted. Any of you guys have suggestions?" John asked.

The group quieted down. John and Raoul looked at each other. The others stared at the table.

Dud Hill responded in an almost apologetic tone. "What if we used flares?"

After a short silence, Bill Thaw spoke. "That might work. But we don't have flare guns."

"The infantry does," Lufbery said. "We ought to use more than just one. Everyone flying below should have one. I'll ask Thénault to get the guns and flares. What color shows up best in clouds?"

"Red and green," Thaw said. "White can be mistaken for sunlight. Blue isn't bright enough."

"There's still one more thing," John said.

"What's that, John?" asked Lufbery.

"The group on top will have to practice staying together. We'll have to test different formations over the channel to see which one works."

"Flying alone in clouds is tricky enough," said Ted. "We'll need a lot of practice!"

After deciding who would fly in which group, the men broke up. In the space of thirty minutes, the mood among the men changed 180 degrees. Lufbery stayed behind. He directed a smile at John.

"You know, John, if this works, Richthofen will put you on his black list and try for another souvenir."

"Hey, Luf. He's probably already got you on his list. I'm just adding to his trouble."

"Just between you and me, this is the craziest idea I've heard. Trouble is, it makes sense. Anyway, I didn't hear any of them turn it down, and no one came up with a better one."

Within the hour, Captain Thénault drove to the nearest French infantry unit and had four flare guns in hand with enough flares to make the Fourth of July celebration two weeks before look like a kid playing with matches. For the next three days, six pilots practiced the ambush over the channel. After their first attempt,

Parsons suggested the lower group fire a green flare if they spotted enemy planes and a red flare to signal top cover to come down. His idea was accepted.

Lufbery suggested that the lower group fly abreast to make them a more tempting target. His idea was also adopted. The biggest problem was finding a cloud bank with a flat ceiling. Winds over the channel scattered clouds, preventing them from forming a neat layer. For his part, Thénault contacted forward infantry observers and asked them to call the base when they saw a heavy flat cloud layer resting over Courtrai. For the next few days, neither the weather over the channel nor Courtrai cooperated. Rain kept them grounded, not only interrupting their practice but preventing them from gathering aerial intelligence over enemy positions. Under these conditions, the battle known as Passchendaele to the British and ANZACs and the Third Battle of Ypres to the French began at the end of July 1917.

The Allied objective was the Gheluvelt Plateau, high ground between Ypres and the town of Klein Zillebeke. None of the terrain contested was higher than two hundred feet. But in Flanders, that was high enough for German spotters to observe the entire sector. It gave their artillery a commanding advantage and gave German reserves a place to hide behind the heights.

For several frustrating days, a downpour grounded SPA124, making air support for the British impossible. German counterattacks couldn't be observed or impeded by British fliers. The same rains bogged down the British attack. In the mud, the only headway made by the infantry was around Ypres. Scattered woods once seen in the landscape were no longer recognizable as stands of trees. Splintered stumps stood beside water-filled shell holes. The ground became a muddy, greenish slime filled with broken barbed wire—the battlefields of Flanders. British tanks employed in the attack weren't able to keep pace with the slogging, broken advance of the infantry. They broke down, easy targets for German guns firing from concrete pillboxes. Others simply stuck in the mud, deserted by their crews. At Clapman Junction, seventeen lay smashed in front of a pillbox on Menin Road. Several German pillboxes also became victims of the weather, sinking to the tops of their doors in the muck of Flanders. Weather was an enemy of the Allies and Germans alike.

The pilots at Saint-Pol-sur-Mer learned of the battle in snippets. John remembered the remarks Major Eddington had made to him on the bus to Chaudun. *We're going to get a crack at them soon.* A crack was about all the British made in the German lines. Even then, the crack often closed. The bulge in the British line at Ypres received constant shelling. The only victor was the squalid mud of Flanders. John wondered how any army could attack in such horrible conditions. As for fliers, they could only wait for better weather.

When the rain and fog cleared, the sky above the battlefields reopened to the fliers at Saint-Pol. Captain Thénault received a telephone call from a British forward observer. He listened as the soldier tried to explain the clouds Thénault had asked them to look for was over Ypres. Lufbery came into Thénault's office to ask for more flares. As it turned out, Thénault needed Lufbery's help. He was having trouble understanding the British caller. The problem was typical of low-level French-British communications as Sergeant Atkins's words attested.

"It's thumbs-up over Wipers and Pop, Capt'n. The Old Man told me to call you from the OP before we legged it from the coal boxes they're chucking about this boggy sod. Your fliers can chase the Alleymen to their hearts content over Wipers."

"A moment, Sergeant Atkins." The captain covered the telephone speaker with his hand and then said to Lufbery, "Speak with this lunatic! I have no idea what this man is saying."

Lufbery took the phone and introduced himself to the caller. Atkins repeated his words up to the same point and added a footnote.

"How come he put you on? I understood him well enough, I'm sure."

Thénault only heard Lufbery's side of the conversation.

"It's the other way around, Sergeant. Can you verify that Ypres and Poperinghe have solid cloud layers? ... Where's the artillery coming from? ... Have you seen any enemy aircraft in the area? ... How many?"

After answering Lufbery's questions, Atkins apologized and said the need to evacuate his observation post was urgent. Lufbery heard shells exploding over the phone.

"Fritz is starting to range our OP, sir. A bit of shrapnel just missed Johnny's napper. Me mate's and I got to get our arses out of here before we'll all gets a ticket to blighty. Good hunting, sir. We're leavin' before Fritz makes this hole our grave." The line went dead.

Thénault asked Lufbery to interpret the sergeant's trench language.

"He said the skies over Poperinghe and Ypres are what we've been looking for. He saw enemy patrols flying over both areas. As far as he could tell, one patrol flew over each town. He had to cut the call short. German artillery was getting too close to their observation post."

"Good. It is time we became fliers again. What was your reason for coming, Lieutenant? Is there something I can do for you?"

"Glad you reminded me, Captain. We're running low on flares, sir. Captain, with your permission, I'll tell the men we're ready to try the ambush."

"Of course. They must go now, before the weather returns. You have command of the high patrol. Thaw commands the low patrol. Tell Willis to take his camera. His photos will bring needed intelligence. Good hunting. Report to me as soon as you return."

"Yes, sir."

It took only fifteen minutes to muster the pilots and planes. Thaw's group took off first, followed by Lufbery, Ted Parsons, and John. Thaw decided it best to set their heading in the air. The general direction would be Ypres. Sixteen miles beyond the Belgian town lay the busy aerodrome commanded by Baron von Richthofen. The Lafayette Escadrille had bought front row tickets to his Flying Circus. They might even enjoy the show, provided they found the Circus willing to perform.

The Flying Circus

OVER THE CHANNEL, WILLIS AND Hill, on Thaw's flanks, banked to the left below scattered clouds. Directly above and behind, Lufbery led Ted Parsons and John in a similar turn. For the first time, two separate teams from SPA124 were flying a single combat mission. Thaw's group was the bait, Lufbery's was the bushwhackers. With a little luck, Thaw might lure Richthofen's *jasta* into an ambush. Getting to this point had been far from routine and very nearly never happened at all.

Thaw's team flew in the clear, offering themselves as targets. The high team had the more difficult task. Formation flying in heavy clouds was tougher than they'd thought. It was essential that Lufbery kept his planes together. But to stay close, they had to see each other. To surprise enemy planes in force, they had to dive together. Practice had shown mixed results. Flying abreast, the high group tended to lose contact or drift dangerously close to each other. Their first try experienced a near collision when John's wingtip brushed Ted's. John later told him, "I thought we couldn't hit what we couldn't see. We got to see each other up there! We've got to find a better formation."

"It goes beyond that, John," Thaw added. "If your group gets too busy trying to spot each other, you won't come down together, and the trap won't work. The first one down might surprise them, but one plane isn't enough to do break them up. You've got to come down together."

Lufbery's sole responsibility was to keep his group on course and speed. Clouds yielded a gray translucence, often totally masking the planes in his group. No horizon appeared in front of the cowling to tell him whether he was climbing, diving, or banking. No landmarks appeared below to set his position. In clouds, a gray gloom enveloped them. To stay on top of Thaw and on course, Lufbery depended entirely on his compass, altimeter, and tachometer. He watched the instruments constantly, lest the whole group stray off the course Thaw chose.

In practice, the formation had nearly ended in disaster twice, either flying in echelon or side by side. Visibility was close to zero. Normal formation made collision too risky. Unless a solution was found, they'd have to abandon the idea entirely. It boiled down to one last formation.

John suggested, "Let's try single file. Ted behind Lufbery, and me following Ted." They tried it over the channel. Most of the time, fewer than ten yards separated the tail of the Spad in front from the nose of the one behind. Even at that distance, the Spad ahead often appeared fuzzy. But flying single file eliminated the danger of touching wingtips, and fuzzy tails were more distinct than gray-green gloom. The tactic was adopted.

To reduce the problem, the time Lufbery's group spent flying in the clouds was cut. Until they approached enemy lines, both teams would fly under the cloud layer. The bushwhackers would fly directly above the bait until the time came for them to hide in clouds. Thaw would select a heading, hold course and speed, and signal Lufbery to climb into the clouds. The bushwhackers would slide into the cloud layer one at a time. Once they'd disappeared, Thaw's group would descend to a point four or five hundred feet below the ceiling, maintain heading and speed, and make themselves as conspicuous as possible. With any luck, a *jasta* would take the bait before the bushwhackers had flown in the clouds for ten minutes. Beyond that, they must come down.

A green flare signaled that the enemy was sighted. If followed by a red flare, the bushwhackers would spring the ambush. A third signal was also decided. If Thaw had to alter course, he'd fire a red flare first. The bushwhackers would descend to reestablish contact and follow Thaw's new heading. Fuel consumption limited the patrol to one hour and forty minutes. After that, they'd all have to return to base. Their last practice had gone without a major hitch. The day they'd all awaited had finally come.

Courtrai was less than forty-five miles from the base. To reduce their profile, Lufbery nosed his Spad just above Thaw's, far enough behind to see Thaw's hand signals. Following Lufbery's lead, Ted and John nosed above Willis and Dud Hill. At this point, Thaw was in charge of both groups. Evasive flying maneuvers were abandoned. At six thousand feet, Thaw proceeded straight and level for the town of Ypres. Approaching the front, they spotted two British fighter patrols, one north and one south. A third, a French patrol, crossed underneath, returning to its base.

The northern patrol had four Sopwith Camels followed a Sopwith Triplane, the first triplane John had ever seen. To the south, a second French patrol was heading for Armentières flying the new Spad XIIIs. John saw scattered clouds ahead. The view below was obstructed by Dud Hill's plane. To either side, a weak, milky haze emanating off the channel obscured the sky after a mile or two. These were not the conditions the pilots were told they'd find.

Thirty minutes into the flight, Thaw began a gentle bank to the right where the cloud layer looked longer and had a flat bottom. The change in heading was a few degrees. Thaw signaled them to climb. Both groups almost entered the clouds.

Not far ahead, John saw patches of woods, the first stands of trees he'd seen since flying to the coast. Near the tiny road below, piles of rubble were surrounded by hundreds of shell holes filled with water that mirrored the sky. The rubble formed what remained of the outskirts of a small Belgian town. Farther ahead, the broken shapes of larger buildings marked the town of Ypres.

All of the fliers saw Thaw's hand signal. Lufbery checked the heading on his compass and his engine speed indicator. He slowly gained altitude. Parsons lifted his plane behind Raoul's, and John drifted up to follow Parsons. Thaw glanced upward just in time to see John's Spad disappear into the cloud layer overhead. Thaw's gaze returned to his compass. His heading hadn't changed. His airspeed was steady at ninety-four miles per hour. Seconds later, they crossed directly over the mangled masonry that was once the town center in Ypres. John remembered seeing Roman ruins that looked more intact. Thaw and Lufbery checked their instruments. Nothing had changed.

Thaw could only assume Lufbery was overhead. He held his stick between his knees and raised both arms. His extended thumbs touched, and his index fingers pointed straight up. Willis began taking pictures with the camera Thénault gave him. Every twenty seconds, the shutter opened and closed, recording with incredible detail anything not covered by fog or smoke from spent artillery shells. In the clouds, all John could see through his goggles was the dark mass of Parsons's Spad directly ahead of him, surrounded by a sea of barely luminous, gray-green gloom never pierced by a single ray of sunlight. The effect was surrealistic.

John found himself checking his instruments, his only focal point in reality. Once, he lost sight of Parsons and gave the Spad a bit more throttle. In seconds, he dived to avoid dicing Parsons's rudder. His heartbeat doubled from the near miss. He eased the Spad behind Ted. Alertness returned very quickly as a rush of blood coursed through veins in his temples.

Below the clouds, Bill Thaw had run nearly half the length of the cloud bank. He began to look for a new heading when Dud Hill increased his speed to come abreast. Hill's hand slapped the side of his Spad. When Thaw looked, Hill pointed south, slightly below the group.

Thaw nodded when he saw a V formation. Five brightly colored airplanes had flown from under the mist two thousand feet below, a mile on their right. Thaw wasn't sure they'd been seen. He signaled Hill to dive and loop to draw their attention. It wasn't necessary. The German patrol had seen them and was coming up in pursuit. They'd taken the bait.

Thaw fired a green flare gun ahead of his flight path and watched it enter the clouds. In the clouds, the gray gloom turned a pearlescent green. John drew a breath of expectation and relief. They'd been in the clouds for almost four minutes. Up to then, no one was certain that the two groups had stayed together. Seeing the flares ended the mystery for Lufbery's group. The worst of the waiting was over. John's heartbeat increased, and with it, a dry-mouthed tension grew as the seconds passed, waiting for a red signal. Any moment now, Thaw might fire a red flare.

John was certain that Parsons had seen the green glow. His plane had momentarily dropped and then returned in front of his own. Obscured by clouds, Lufbery's plane was invisible to John. Since Lufbery led the group, John had to trust that Parsons was on his tail.

Thaw waited until the enemy squadron approached to within six hundred yards. The Circus was nearly level with Thaw's group. Staying in formation would not be prudent much longer. Raising a flare pistol, Thaw fired. Immediately, Willis and Hill broke formation, one peeling left and the other right. The enemy was closing quickly from starboard. Thaw's group was at full throttle before the red flare burst in the clouds.

John watched as the pale gray turned the color pink, reminiscent of strawberry ice cream. Without waiting for Parsons to react, he banked hard right and pushed the stick forward until his stomach felt like part of his chest. His count hadn't reached four when he broke through the cloud layer. Parsons was on his left, having started his dive without banking. Lufbery had made a turn to the right and was parallel to John.

Directly under them was a tangle of eight airplanes, and he recognized five immediately from Lufbery's description of Richthofen's *jasta*. No red triwing was among them, but the colors he saw offered enough to occupy his mind. Their dive ensured the advantage of surprise. A black-and-red Albatros had already fastened on Dud Hill's tail. John increased his dive, flying to intercept the Albatros. Within seconds, his Vickers was sending a thin stream of lead through the fuselage, just behind a very surprised German pilot. One of them cut a wire to his rudder, sending the plane into a wild spiral.

John banked to follow the plane when another Albatros painted bright yellow came at him from his port side, firing its twin Spandaus, tearing holes in John's upper-right wing. John turned directly toward his adversary to face the bright orange flashes winking at him from the muzzles of its machine guns. He dived slightly to evade and mislead his enemy, and then he quickly eased the stick back to put the enemy plane in his gun sights at close range.

At fifty yards, he fired the Vickers. Puffs of black smoke from the muzzles of his guns answered the flashes from the Albatros. Nosing down, John dived under the enemy plane, turning his head to see which way it banked to continue the fight. But the Albatros was heading away to the east, trailing a steady stream of white smoke from engine coolant. John thought about following the fleeing plane, but other targets were closer and not belching smoke. He assessed his position before making his next move.

The melee on his right was Lufbery trying to get behind a blue-and-red Albatros. Thaw had engaged a blue-and-yellow plane. He could no longer see Dud Hill's or Parsons's Spads. Willis was on his left, chased by two Albatroses—a white on blue followed by a newcomer with a green fuselage and red wings that followed the Circus into combat from somewhere below.

"Flying Circus, hell! This is like fighting a damn fruit salad," John said aloud, temporarily without an opponent. He steered straight for the green-and-red Albatros following Willis, but the alert German pilot saw him and sensed his disadvantage. Seeing only four of his comrades still in the air, the German climbed into the clouds and disappeared.

John looked to his right. Still engaged with his Albatros, neither Lufbery nor the German had gained an advantage. Hill had run from an Albatros on his tail, diving at full throttle, leaving the German behind, his speed too great for the slower plane. Once again, John looked toward Lufbery. Raoul was making a looping roll to gain a position above the Albatros.

Sensing his danger, the German pilot climbed into the clouds, and Lufbery lost him. The entire battle hadn't lasted five minutes, but the Circus had scattered. John rejoined Lufbery, who raised his right hand with its thumb pointed skyward. Thaw and Parsons eventually rejoined them and then Willis. Dud Hill's plane had vanished somewhere below.

John signaled Hill's last position, and without hesitating, Lufbery turned and began diving in the direction Hill had gone. The others were out of ammunition and signaled to John that they were flying back to the base at Saint-Pol-sur-Mer.

John waved them on and then followed Lufbery to look for Hill. Lufbery leveled off at five thousand feet, and John coasted alongside. Black smoke began to erupt around the Spads. Antiaircraft batteries had found their range. Both climbed to avoid a lucky hit.

Before leveling off, Raoul turned sharply to the north. John saw him fly toward an area where three airplanes were circling a fourth, trying to force it down. It was Dud Hill. The Circus was trying to capture him. The two Albatroses that had gone into the clouds had rejoined the flier they'd left behind. All three were picking on Dud's lone Spad. Hill was forced into a descending spiral. Dud was holding on, but three on one didn't offer very good odds against the Flying Circus.

Lufbery and John both dived into the trailing Albatroses, each taking one of the enemy planes that had run from them only minutes before. Following Hill's Spad, the Germans hadn't spotted either Lufbery or John. John focused on the green-and-red Albatros. He closed to within five hundred yards, nearly level with the banking Albatros. Its bank would cause it to slide directly in front of John's gun sights in seconds. Its undercarriage showing, John's approach was hidden by the green fuselage. If it continued on this path, he'd have an easy shot.

Lufbery went for the other Albatros circling Dud Hill. Its pilot spotted him and veered off, climbing to the left. Lufbery streaked by Hill, whose eyes were wide in amazement at seeing him. Raoul finally got the third Albatros in his sights and pulled the trigger on his Vickers. A dozen bullets later, Lufbery was out of ammunition.

As Lufbery emptied, John fired just ahead of the green and

red as it crossed in front of him. Several bullets slammed into the engine cowling on the left side of the Albatros. John touched the rudder to get behind the plane, still firing. His Vickers splintered a strut under its right wing, sending a shower of wood fragments into John's windscreen. John tilted the nose down, pulling the trigger again. His Vickers emptied as the gun sight came on target. His last burst wasn't needed.

The engine of the Albatros blew a cylinder and immediately erupted in flames. John felt its warmth on his face. He pulled up to avoid catching shards of wood and burning canvas. The right wing tore away from the German's fuselage. It spun toward the ground like an autumn leaf. The remaining wing soon followed, circling to earth. The engine fire blew its gasoline tank, exploding with such force that John felt the shock wave. He watched as the Albatros turned into a flaming projectile, dropping like a rock to a muddy grave below in the slimy muck of Flanders. It was time for Lufbery and John to fly back to base.

The plane that had eluded Lufbery before got away a second time. Raoul succeeded in bluffing two of the Albatros off Dud Hill's tail with an empty machine gun. The three Spads turned directly for the coast and the safety of western skies. In less than thirty minutes, the lighthouse on the point of Dunkirk came into sight. They landed into the prevailing winds blowing inland from the channel. At the seawall, they turned to taxi toward the hangars. Thaw's team was waiting for them on the field as they landed. Willis had given the camera to Thénault. Its photos would expose German positions on the Gheluvelt Plateau. Bill invited them to the mess tent to talk about the mission and some ideas he'd gotten on the patrol.

"I've got a better idea," said Lufbery. "Let's go to Saint-Omer and do some real celebrating."

The others smiled and overruled Thaw. They were always

willing to entertain Lufbery's idea. Before going, they bathed in the shallow waters of the channel and dressed in clean uniforms for the jaunt to Saint-Omer. Thaw borrowed Thénault's car for the trip. They'd have taken the lions along, as well, but there wasn't room. Thaw apologized to Whisky and Soda and promised he'd take them next time.

Parsons protested, "Let 'em come, Bill. They're full grown now. Maybe they'll get us free drinks. No barkeeper in Saint-Omer would refuse."

The others laughed.

Thaw answered on behalf of the lions. "Are you kidding? We'd have to buy them drinks too. They'd want to drink ours, as well!" The issue decided, they drove to Saint-Omer, crowded in Thénault's car, lionless. The mission wasn't mentioned. They needed a break from war. However, the subject wasn't completely dropped.

Sitting in his office in Courtrai, four pilots described the battle to Herr Rittmeister Manfred von Richthofen. The man known in Britain as the Red Baron was known in Germany as the Red Knight. Identity numbers from his victories filled the rear wall of his office, cut directly from the fallen hulks.

"*Wo ist Kleinbauer?*"

"*Tot.*"

After making their report, the *rittmeister* cursed their stupidity for having fallen for such a trick. They'd been taught a lesson they should have learned in flying school. The loss of two fighters did not please him in the least. Leutnant Frederick Otto Kleinbauer had led the *jasta* in Richthofen's absence to give the Baron's head wound time to heal. Now, a replacement had to be found. He demanded to know who was responsible for shooting down Kleinbauer. They described the markings on John's Spad. It was possible that he'd shot down another plane, as well, but they weren't sure. The attack came too quickly. They had to scatter. The Baron rarely exhibited rage. Richthofen put a price on John's head. On landing, the Baron would promote, on the spot, any pilot who shot him down, pay him six thousand marks, and give him five days in Hamburg with a certain fräulein who was known to entertain fliers horizontally. His squadron showed its approval by shouting, *"Jawohl, Rittmeister!"* As Lufbery predicted, John had made the Baron's blacklist.

Richthofen would have to wait. In mid-August, after less than a month at Saint-Pol-sur-Mer, Combat Group Thirteen was moved to Senard, below the Argonne Forest, twenty miles southwest of Verdun. The surrounding area had seen some of the heaviest fighting of the ground war. Even at eight thousand feet, the devastation was plain. Everywhere they looked, shell holes overlapped shell holes.

SPA124 had never flown in the sector. Moving to a new one always held unknowns. They'd have to get accustomed to its contours and landmarks. If the reason for past moves held true, the squadron knew that it wasn't sent to Senard for a rest. Something was brewing in Grand Quartier Général, and GQG selected Group Thirteen to do it.

Senard

The day they arrived at Senard, Général Guillaumat opened a weeklong barrage. Artillery shells flew in thundering cascades. Général Henri Pétain favored the tactic. Less judicious generals told their *poilu* to attack with élan, the sheer will to win. Élan, they said, terrorized the enemy. It didn't matter that such displays of courage had failed many times in the past. Yet even today, certain French officers believed a bayonet and élan was all the French soldiers needed to win.

Général Henri Pétain was more frugal with his men. His goal was to retake Le Mort Homme, the high ground east of Malancourt, ten miles below Dun-sur-Meuse, and west of the fortress town Verdun that was battered by German artillery in 1916. Pétain's artillerymen outnumbered his infantrymen. The air was thick with French shells when SPA124 flew into Senard. Many were fired near the aerodrome.

John's concern was landing in Senard. He could easily fly into the path of any of the thousands of French artillery shells. Having landed safely, he'd barely finished stashing his gear in the barrack when he received a telephone call from someone he'd forgotten since arriving in London. The noise of the barrage made hearing difficult. He covered his free ear with his free hand and told the caller to speak loudly.

"John! It's Eddie Rickenbacker."

"Rickenbacker? Is that you, Rick? Last I heard, the newspapers said you were driving for General Pershing. Is that true?"

"They got it wrong! I never drove for Pershing. I came in as an ambulance driver. I drove Billy Mitchell around for a while. He was looking for a spot for a training center for our pilots. That's how he found Issoudun."

"It's really noisy here, Rick. I'm having a lot of trouble hearing you. Where are you calling from?"

"Tours on the Loire. I—"

"Did you say Tours? I went through it a few weeks ago! What are you doing in Tours?"

"Let me explain, John! I'm at the French flying school. Twelve of us are about to become pilots. After that, I'll go to Issoudun for combat training. I called Saint-Pol. They told me the Lafayette had already moved to Senard. I was calling to see how you're doing."

"Senard's in the Verdun sector. How did you find out we were here?"

"I knew about it a week ago. I've got friends in high places, John. They come in handy."

"I guess so! We were told about it two days ago. Hey, Rick, I saw your escort in Liverpool while I was struggling to get through customs. It must be great to have friends in high places."

"Listen. That was no damned reception committee, John. I'll tell you about it sometime. Did you see any action in Flanders?"

John didn't hear the last part of the question clearly.

"We just flew in from Flanders a few minutes before you called. We haven't gone up yet. The only action here is artillery. Shells are thicker than the flies. We had a scrap with Richthofen's squadron near Passchendaele. Surprised them. They're good fliers. They go up in formations of at least five. When will I see you? Can you come to Senard?"

A short break in the barrage made it easier to hear Rick.

"I don't think so, John. Say, we need all the experienced fliers we can get. Have you thought about switching to an American squadron? We can use experienced combat pilots like you."

"I'll wait to see how it goes. It takes time for new pilots to get used to combat. We're all experienced, Rick. I can depend on them. Besides, the French give us a lot of freedom. I guess I'll transfer to an American outfit someday. Call me when you get assigned. I might need your high-placed friends to get me into your squadron."

"That'll be easy, John. We've only got a few fliers. When you get here, dinner is on me."

"Okay, Rick. I'll buy the drinks."

It was good to hear Rickenbacker's voice after all these months. John had answered Rick honestly. As far as John was concerned, the air arm of the United States was still wetting its diaper. John was surprised that Rick had mastered nausea to become a pilot.

In mid-June, two months before the British attack at Passchendaele, General Pershing had occasion to celebrate the arrival of the first contingent of the American army to debark on French soil. Nearly fifteen thousand members of the Sixteenth Infantry Battalion, First Division, arrived in Saint-Nazaire. A month later, he took the battalion to Paris to demonstrate America's entry into the war. Members of the Sixteenth marched with Pershing to Parisian cheers on the Fourth of July.

After the ceremony, Pershing gathered his staff to apprise

them of the enormous problems the American Expeditionary Force faced. If they were to succeed, he needed the cooperation and loyalty of his staff. He would tolerate nothing less.

"Gentlemen, what I've learned since coming here is what I'd suspected. Our allies have suffered losses much worse than first thought. Marshal Joffre was more than serious when he asked for American troops in Washington. You saw how Parisians cheered the men today—as if a single battalion could turn the tide of war. It's been made clear to me that both the French and British need to replace their losses. However, we did not come here to fill the holes in their respective armies. I've already dealt with their requests. I'm sure they will keep making them. Unfortunately, nearly all our tactical support comes from the French. In return, the Allies propose that we integrate our men into their armies. The president and I agree that must not happen. An American army must be formed.

"Until we can supply our own men, our independence will be in question. We need to equip and train tens of thousands, possibly millions, of our own men. We must get to work building the necessary lines of supply to support those men as quickly as possible. Otherwise, we will never have an effective army, much less an independent army. Set your men to the job immediately.

"The aeronautical service is even less prepared. At home, a handful of obsolete airplanes constitute our entire American air arm. Except for a few American pilots who fly for the French, ours are not practiced in combat tactics. In short, we've only begun to build an air service. Nevertheless, the development of the army must take priority. An army runs on more than its stomach, gentlemen. We need supply depots, transportation centers, maintenance shops, and training facilities. Time is not on our side. We need them now! We must do in months what the Allies took years to accomplish. Those who are unequal to this task will not remain on my staff."

His warning fresh in their minds, Pershing dismissed a sobered, more focused staff.

Unaware of Pershing's problems, the escadrille's task at Senard had priority. Captain Thénault called them into his office for instructions. Their primary mission was different from that at Saint-Pol-sur-Mer. Their mission was to prevent enemy observers from entering their sector and engage any German fighters defending the observers. Thénault also gave them insight into Pétain's plans for relieving the pressure around Verdun.

"Verdun has been a scene of battle since Attila the Hun. The Boche occupies Le Mort Homme. Last February, two million German shells smashed into the forts of Verdun. GQG estimates fifteen hundred shells were exploding every second. Douaumont was captured by a handful of Germans led by an officer carrying nothing more than a handgun.

"Pétain wants this artillery neutralized. When his barrage ends, this goal must be pursued with vigor. Never again must French soldiers bear such shelling! They are already replacing the supplies used in that barrage. You will destroy enemy depots and the main railheads used to supply those guns. The commander of Bomber Group One asked me to provide an escort for a bombing mission over Dun-sur-Meuse. You will provide escort to Dun."

"Covering them won't be easy, sir," Bill interrupted. "Those bombers have a maximum speed of a hundred miles per hour when they aren't loaded with bombs. They won't be able to keep up with us."

"Nevertheless, you will protect them. The bombers will attack the rail yard before our attack begins. German artillery and supplies must be smashed absolutely. General Pétain's offensive must succeed. If you must circle the bombers, then do so!"

Thénault called them closer to look at a map spread on a table. He pointed out the location of Dun, southeast of the Argonne.

"Dun is easy to find. As you see, it lies on the Meuse. The bombers will follow the Meuse north to Dun."

To end the meeting, Thénault relayed the part of his orders he knew they'd have preferred not to hear.

"This mission is to be commanded by the commandant of the bomber group. He wants the escort to fly in two groups on either side of his bombers. His orders are to engage enemy fighters that attack the bombers from the side. You will escort them to the target and back to Senard. That is all, gentlemen. Dismissed."

The order made no sense!

The protests of the fliers rang in Thénault's ears. The orders countered the most basic tactics of air defense and counterattack. Thénault could do nothing. The commander of the bomber group refused his arguments to fly top cover. The escort would fly as ordered. Rendezvous with the fighters was set over the Argonne Forest on the morning of August 18, two days before the ground offensive was to begin.

The skies were clear when the escort took off and headed to the assembly point. The bombers made an impressive sight as they left the field at Senard. They joined the escort over the Argonne Forest. The faster Spads flew at minimum throttle and moved in snakelike fashion to stay at the sides of the slower bombers. At any point, this inevitably forced half of the fighters to stray farther from the formation.

When John wasn't chosen for the escort, he asked Thénault to use him to replace any Spad that returned with engine trouble. He agreed. None did. The escort included Ted Parsons, Stephen Bigelow, Walter Lovell, Harold Willis, Henry Jones, and Andrew Campbell.

John waited in the barrack with Thaw and Lufbery. If needed, they were ready. The rest of the fliers went to the mess tent to pass the time waiting for the planes to return. After nearly two hours, the heard the sounds of the returning Spads. Two bombers and a Spad were not in the group.

On landing, Campbell broke a rule by turning straight into his hangar. He crossed in front of a landing bomber. In the collision, his plane flipped over, nearly killing him and the bomber crew. Livid with rage, Thénault's hands were tied. He could take no action against Campbell without the sanction of the war ministry. They'd forbidden him to punish any of the American volunteers. When Parsons landed, Lufbery approached to ask him the question that was on everyone's mind.

"Where's Willis?"

"He went down, Luf," Parsons said. "That's all I know. It's like they knew we were coming. Four and five Albatroses at a time attacked from both sides—and right after we crossed the lines! I think three hooked onto Willis. He was hit. Lost speed. I don't know if he landed or crashed. Coming back was worse than going out. I've never seen that many enemy planes up at one time. They must have sent every goddamned *jasta* in the area. If you don't mind, Luf, I could use a cup of coffee right now. Maybe one of the others saw Willis."

"Sure, Ted. Go ahead. Glad you made it back."

The story from the others was the same. Bigelow went to the hospital. Lovell chased several planes away from a stray bomber after shooting down an Albatros. They were in combat from the time they crossed the lines until they came back. They'd exhausted their fuel. Thaw's skepticism about the escort's defensive tactics was correct. They had been better off above the bombers.

French artillery resumed fire and continued to fire up to August 20. When it ended, Général Henri Pétain sent 150,000 French soldiers toward the hill held by Germans since 1916. To help the French retake the high ground, Thénault amended his pilots' mission.

"Hound the Boche lines until they are driven to ground like rabbits. If they stand and fight, strafe their positions. Destroy their guns. Cut their communications. Shoot down any fighter that challenges you. Deny observers the air over Verdun. They must not know our strength or position."

German artillery depended on its observers to find French targets. The escadrille's new mission supported the French attack by shooting down observation planes before they could report anything of value to their batteries. The escadrille went up to hunt German observation planes.

Alerted by the huge French barrage, German observation planes altered defensive tactics by going up in larger groups and forming into a circle, making it difficult to find a safe line of attack from above, behind, or the side. For added insurance, Albatroses covered the observers overhead, ready to pounce on an attacker. Approaching an observer from above or the side meant great risk to their Spads. Flying through the circle invited bullets from every rear gunner in the circle.

SPA124 had never seen the formation before. John spoke to Lufbery and Parsons, trying to find a way to break the circle. In the clear skies over Verdun, the idea of an ambush was dismissed. Something else had to be done. None of the pilots had an effective plan. Most said they'd have to take their chances when they came upon a large group of observers. Their mission gave them no choice but to attack. It was the only way to keep them over German-held territory.

On a more positive note, news filtered back that Willis was a captive. Since the Germans had not confirmed it, no one was certain. Thinking of Willis, John had an idea. On his first patrol, the day he thought Willis had gone mad and tried to shoot him down, he was mistaken. He'd also been surprised. To prevent German observers from forming a circle, they must attack with surprise. If the enemy didn't see the attack coming, they'd have no time to form into a circle.

The theory was sound, as long as surprise was on their side. It occurred to John that he hadn't flown a solo mission since Chaudun. His idea actually suited a single fighter. John didn't mention it to anyone. A single unobserved plane would certainly have the advantage of surprise.

German observers had to fly during daylight. They'd often form in early morning. John reasoned that if he took off alone, before sunrise, he'd fly over their field and wait for them to take off. The Nieuport was a better glider than the Spad, and a Nieuport 23 was still sitting in a hangar, not yet returned to the depot.

John told Charles Gallau, "Get the Nieuport ready to fly three hours before daylight, Charles. Don't forget to load the machine gun."

"*Oui*. The cables must be checked, as well. They loosen when she sits a long time. But why, *monsieur*? The Spad, she is much faster, much stronger."

"I want to try an idea, Charles. Get it ready. Double check the Lewis gun. Be sure it's loaded and the tank is full, understand?"

"*Oui*. I will check everything myself." Charles believed something was loose—and not necessarily the cables supporting the Nieuport's wings. Using an obsolete plane made no sense.

At four the next morning, John dressed in his fur-lined boots and heavy flight suit. He'd take the Nieuport to its ceiling, where the air was thin and freezing cold. Fitted with a Clerget 9B 130-horsepower engine, the ceiling of the Nieuport 23 was increased by several thousand feet. More importantly, its greater wing area would catch the thin air at nearly twenty thousand feet. John felt it prudent to stow two oxygen tanks in the cockpit. He had no idea how long the hover would last.

A large German airfield lay near Metz, fifty miles to the east.

John would bypass the closer fields and fly to the city, more easily seen in the early dawn light. Coffee was still brewing in the mess. He couldn't wait. In the darkness, on his way out of the mess tent, his eyes hadn't fully adjusted. Of all people, he ran into Raoul Lufbery again.

"Damn it, John, either you break this habit or I'll have to put a bell around your neck like a damned French cow so I know where the hell you are! Why are you up so early?"

"I'm taking the Nieuport to the aerodrome over Metz. I want to try something."

"Try what? I can think of a couple of fields closer than Metz!"

"I know. Sorry, Luf, I don't have time. Charles has the Nieuport ready. I've got to be over the field while it's still dark. Can't talk now." John didn't want to take time to explain. The sun never waited to rise.

"It might take an hour to get to Metz. You've only got fuel for a couple, John."

"I know. I'll be back after breakfast. Tell the cook to save a cup of coffee for me, Luf."

John didn't wait for an answer. He knew Lufbery would tell the cook the minute he walked in the tent. There'd be a whole pot waiting when he returned.

John ran to the hangar and stepped into the cockpit of the cream-colored airplane, the color that blended with the clouds, making good camouflage. Though he hadn't flown a Nieuport for many weeks, its familiar instrument pattern made him feel at ease.

Starting early meant that the Germans on the ground were still asleep. A lone engine shouldn't arouse much attention. He'd never flown a Nieuport fitted with the larger engine. Its sound was unfamiliar. John noticed the difference in the rhythm from the Spad's Hispano-Suiza. Accustomed to the Spad, John realized that sound was an integral part of flying. Over Metz, sound wouldn't be an issue. A gliding airplane made no sound.

The Nieuport left the field at fifteen minutes past four. John started to climb immediately. He needed as much altitude as possible before crossing the front lines. A headwind helped his climb but made the plane slower. If it died, it would no longer cover the droning of the engine. To reduce the chance of detection, John headed south of Saint-Mihiel, the tip of the long-held German salient southeast of Senard. Flying around Saint-Mihiel added fifteen miles to the flight but delayed his arrival over enemy territory. Fuel was a concern. Very little would be saved until he cut the engine over the German airfield. Crossing the lines at Pont-à-Mousson, he'd gained sixteen thousand feet and was still climbing over the Moselle, fifteen miles from Metz. He put on an oxygen mask and followed the reflection of the river north to Metz.

At this altitude, he saw the glimmers of dawn. Soon, the sun would appear. To the west, stars still shone under the canopy of darkness. Below, the reflections of the Moselle broke the dark void on the ground. An hour and ten minutes had passed when he saw Metz. At nearly twenty thousand feet, he cut the engine over the German airfield.

Floating on a wave of cold air, the silence was only broken by the hum the Nieuport's inter-wing cables and the frigid air wafting past an idle propeller. He hadn't slept well the night before. He'd never felt this tired or alone. If it weren't for the cold air, he could have gone to sleep with the wind whispering around the cockpit. It was difficult to imagine that war existed less than four miles below. For a moment, he tried to pretend that there was no war. His mind couldn't allow even that puny respite. He checked the altimeter. The Nieuport held altitude well. It had lost only five hundred feet.

Long shadows began to appear on the ground, growing shorter by the second. The boundaries of Metz loomed larger than he'd expected. He'd been gliding only a minute or two. John checked the altimeter in rising sunlight. He'd dropped three thousand feet, and the rate of fall was increasing. His lazy circles were reminiscent of a hawk searching for prey below. He cleaned his frosted goggles. Ground mist quickly evaporated in the morning sun. John saw a row of tiny tents and brightly colored toy airplanes on a grassy field below. It wasn't long before he saw activity.

A group of three toy German fighters took off heading west, looking like birds whose wings couldn't flap. He watched the flight until satisfied that they were not a threat. His attention turned back to the airfield. The observation planes on the field were idle. If he strafed them, he might put one or two out of action, but they'd only be replaced. John wanted the pilots. They were less easily replaced. His rate of fall increased. The altimeter read less than twelve thousand feet. He stowed his oxygen mask. Frigid air burned his nostrils and stung his cheeks.

"Damn. What if they aren't going up today?" He voiced the concern aloud to help him vent frustration. Seconds after he spoke, four tiny men walked to their toy airplanes. Soon, two DFW CV observation planes rolled down the little field to take off. They'd likely join others closer to the front. Like the fighters before, they hadn't seen him. At altitude, a CVs airspeed was under a hundred miles per hour. Catching them would be easy. John didn't wait for them to come up.

He began a steep silent dive at nine thousand feet. The propeller needed to spin rapidly to restart the engine. At the right revolutions, he turned the switch on. The engine coughed and came alive, sending a cloud of foul, oily smoke around the windscreen. John gave the Nieuport full throttle and quickly closed the gap between himself and the two Germans.

The observer in the lead plane wasn't aware that he was a target until the plane trailing was in flames a mile from its base. The time for escape had gone. Seconds later, the muzzle of John's Lewis gun came on target. Both the rear gunner and the pilot were dead before the first CV crashed south of Metz, well short of Verdun, its apparent objective.

The Nieuport had dropped below three thousand feet. John began to climb. His low altitude was a severe handicap if a fight arose over enemy territory. He looked toward his upper wing to see if anything was behind, completely forgetting that he was in the Nieuport. The mirror hung from the Spad's upper wing. Less than amused by the oversight, he muttered, "Idiot!" He rolled the Nieuport gently to the left, looked above, and then southeast. Satisfied, he rolled right and looked north.

The three Albatroses he'd seen earlier were diving straight for him. A mile out and three thousand feet above, they'd cut off a direct route to Senard. John glanced at his fuel gauge. An extended fight was out of the question. At full throttle, John slid the Nieuport in a sharp turn to the southeast, heading directly for Pont-à-Mousson. He needed more altitude to engage them should they succeed in closing the gap. The Nieuport gained altitude reluctantly. Its less powerful engine reminded John all too well why SPA124 preferred Spads.

In two minutes, the gap had closed. John had only reached seven thousand feet. To stay above him, the Albatroses also climbed. At eight thousand feet, they were still above and had closed to five hundred yards—too far for accurate gunfire. John saw Pont-à-Mousson in the distance, and against every rule of fighter combat, he put the Nieuport into a sharp dive to gain speed and elude his still-climbing pursuers. He could only hope that the Nieuport's wings would not peel away.

The tactic caught the three Germans off guard. Still pushing their Albatroses aloft, by the time they reacted, the gap had widened to over a thousand yards. They'd never catch him before he crossed the front lines. Fortunately for John, all three Albatroses broke off the pursuit. Had they known of his low fuel, they could easily have regained the advantage. His task accomplished, his only thought was to return to Senard.

Landing on the field, he realized how parched and cold he'd gotten in the air. In the mess tent, Raoul Lufbery handed John a fresh mug of hot coffee.

"Your shoulders are still shaking, John. A bit chilly up there before dawn, isn't it? You look like you could drink a whole pot. Mind if I have a mug with you?"

"I'd be offended if you didn't, Luf."

"How was it over Metz? Or did you just go to sample the morning sausage?"

John chuckled. "Not exactly, Luf. I prefer coffee and crepes. Chilly isn't the word! I should have brought a jug of this stuff along." John gulped a mouthful of the steamy brown brew. "Anyway, I was lucky. It worked okay."

"What worked?"

"My idea. It was like shooting ducks in a barrel. I caught two of them flat-footed. They never knew what hit them."

After another mouthful of coffee, John told Lufbery what happened over Metz. Raoul shook his head. He couldn't suppress a grin, suggesting bemused admiration.

"You've got a fine tactical mind, John. First a group ambush, now your own ambush. You know, you won't be confirmed for those two CVs. You were too far from the lines for anyone to verify the kills."

"I know. That's not why I went up. I wanted to try an idea. It worked. It's likely something that'll only work once, Luf, at least over Metz. They'll put spotters outside after this or tell those guys to look over their shoulders before they leave the field."

"Hell of an idea, John."

"Maybe so. If those three birds chasing me had caught up, they'd have had me cold. I got lucky."

"Well, they didn't, and it's not every day you get two in one pass. You did."

Lufbery grinned and raised his mug in silent toast to the younger man he'd learned to respect. Lufbery knew exactly what John had done and why he'd done it. He knew what John was up to the minute he saw John dressed to fly. He'd done the same thing over a German aerodrome in Flanders. He didn't tell John. It would only spoil the originality in John's idea.

Catherine in Paris—1918

CARRIED BY THE BREEZE, THE odor of salt water reminded Catherine that this was her first ocean voyage. For all its rolling turmoil, the sea was the mother of life. The thought calmed her. The air was very cool on the northern route. It offered relief from the summer heat of Baltimore. The first half of the voyage was uneventful. Without time to contact her mother or brothers, she felt wholly apart from her family for the first time. In her cabin, she wondered how best to phrase the news of her departure to her mother.

In Elizabeth's last letter, she complained of a soreness in her chest. A doctor came to the small cottage in Arizona to examine her. His answers to her questions revealed the truth of her condition. He'd written a prescription for pain and promised to send it to her the following day. Her letter said the doctor believed the new medicine would dull the soreness and allow her to sleep more comfortably. She needed sleep. That's all he'd recommended.

The letter was mailed after the doctor's second visit. Catherine was glad to have received it before taking the train to New York. She worried about her mother's condition. The news of this trip would only burden her, but it had to be done. She'd promised Michael that she would write, and Catherine kept her promises.

August 10, 1918

Dear Mother,

> I hardly know where to start. I must tell you that I am aboard a ship sailing to France. In my letter a month ago, I wrote that I might be asked to travel with members of the State Department. The request came suddenly. When my new assignment came, I admit I had misgivings. But I believe I made the right choice, though I had little time to consider it. It would have been wrong to refuse. I hope you are feeling better. I'll write when I arrive and have more to tell you.

Catherine didn't mention that she was traveling alone. She didn't want to add more stress to her mother. Learning that Catherine had left the country was enough for her to digest. Elizabeth's views had softened after John left. Catherine noticed this when she'd told her about her new position. She'd thought Elizabeth would oppose it out of hand. Elizabeth's original objection sprang from a natural impulse to protect her only female child, not a desire to steer her daughter's life.

> I believe you will support this decision. Since Father died, you've been more understanding and

have encouraged my work. Had the war not come, all of us might still be home. I truly miss that time, Mother. But since war has come, I believe we all must do something to end it. I will likely stay in Paris working at the American embassy, so I will be perfectly safe. You must not worry about me. I worry about your health. Your last letter was not encouraging. I hope this is only a temporary setback.

Michael asked me to tell you he was assigned. He is the assistant to the medical officer aboard his ship to Europe. He promised me he'd write to you as soon as he could. Surely, John and Michael have the same concern for you as I. We all miss you and want you to be well. Monroe has been wonderful taking care of the house. We are quite fortunate to have him look after things in your absence. If you can, please write to him. I'm sure he would enjoy getting a letter from you.

I promise to write again soon. My thoughts are with you.

I remain your loving daughter,
Catherine

Elizabeth never read Catherine's letter. She felt better with the new medicine but awoke with a severe cough one night. The doctor was called. Nothing could be done for her. She asked to be returned to Baltimore to be buried at her husband's side. Her last words expressed love for her children. She regretted not having had the chance to see them again. Elizabeth drew her last breath watching the sunrise over Arizona. She was returned to her husband's side before Catherine landed in France. Monroe was her closest mourner. Catherine wouldn't learn of her mother's death for weeks. The news would reach the embassy first. The ambassador would inform the staff at GHQ.

Catherine began to imagine herself married to Commander Fields. What was life like as the wife of a naval officer? She wished it would always be as wonderful as that day in Central Park. Would he continue to work in New York, or would his duties send him away? Would she follow and leave the State Department? Imagine becoming a mother! How many children would their marriage bring? The answers to these questions were both troubling and exciting. Babies were pure innocence. Wars might never come if everyone held on to a little innocence in their lives.

As the ship drew close to the war zone, her thoughts turned toward France. She thought of her brothers. They didn't know she was coming. Catherine wondered if she'd have the chance to see either of them. Questions like that brought other questions, not all of which were happy. The answers to her questions all lay in France.

On entering the port at Cherbourg, she discovered that the port was a mixture of military and commercial shipping. Gendarmes and military police directed hundreds of passengers and soldiers throughout the port. Ushered through customs, she found her escort, Madame Brousard, a very courteous and fashionable French-speaking woman in her early forties She gave Catherine the impression that she'd done this sort of thing many times. They boarded one of the busy trains to Paris. From a window in her compartment, Catherine watched in astonishment as French military police arrested a man in civilian clothes on the platform outside her coach. After a brief scuffle, the man was taken into custody and led away. He had the look of a captured animal. Madame Brousard seemed to shrug off the event.

In flawless English, she told Catherine, "I'm afraid that sort of thing happens quite often. Either he had no papers, or the papers he had were false."

"What will happen to him?"

"He'll be taken for questioning and either detained or deported."

As the train got under way, Madame Brousard related the latest maritime news.

"While you were at sea, they sank the *Carpathia*, the ship that rescued the *Titanic*'s survivors. It is beyond reason why such ships must perish at the hands of these terrible U-boats! They sank an English troopship off the Irish coast and an American ship sailing near Cape Cod! All in the last two weeks. It's terrible! The news is better here. General Mangrin recaptured Soissons. But I'm afraid your poet Joyce Kilmer was killed in action. A tragic loss. Was your voyage eventful?"

Catherine hadn't heard any of it aboard ship. "I wasn't aware of Kilmer's death. Our captain altered course twice and waited for darkness to come into port. Other than that, the voyage was uneventful."

Madame Brousard asked, "Have you been to France before?"

"No. This is the first time I've left the country. I've rarely been away from home. I'm excited to be here. I only hope I'll be able to find my brothers."

"Oh? I wasn't told you had brothers in France."

The mention of her brothers inspired Brousard to ask dozens of questions about Michael and John. Catherine hadn't been asked that many by the customs official! Nevertheless, she answered them all to please her escort. The conversation made the train trip shorter.

After a stop in Caen, the train passed several small towns before making a stop in Rouen. After an hour delay in Rouen to allow military transports to pass from Le Havre, the tracks meandered near the Seine all the way to Paris. Though tired, Catherine couldn't rest. Her excitement grew the closer they came to the City of Lights. Catherine began to ask questions of her escort.

"What is Paris like?"

"I'm afraid Paris is nothing like it was before the war. These days, it's the only topic of discussion. My knowledge comes from my husband. He works in the government."

"They must ask you to do this sort of thing often. I mean, escort new arrivals."

Catherine learned that her escort was the English wife of a French deputy and was often asked to be the escort of women entering into government service for France. On this occasion, the assistant to the American ambassador had asked her to act on his behalf.

Since Catherine's work at the State Department prevented her from keeping up with the war's shifting events, she listened to her escort's news with interest.

"The government nearly left the capital for a second time, like they did in 1914. Fortunately, your marines held Belleau Wood, so they decided to stay. I didn't like the idea of moving to Boulogne. In March, everyone worried about the explosion in the city. They thought it was a gas line. Then others came. One killed eighty people in a church. They said the Germans were bombing us from the air. The pope protested. Wilhelm ignored him! Our fliers finally found the source in a wood miles from Paris. So many young men are dead! It must end. No one knows how to end it!"

At noon on August 7, another train rolled to a stop at a station in Paris. Michael had arrived from Savenay only a few hours before, nearly crossing paths with his sister. He'd been given permission to stay at Savenay a short time and was grateful. On the train, Michael's thoughts were of James. Keeping track of his recovery had a high priority for Michael. He'd seen James take his first steps on an artificial leg. Now, he was on his way back to Chaumont to report for reassignment. The closer he came, the events in the Surmelin Valley returned to mind.

As a doctor, he'd expected to treat wounded men and to watch some of them die. Nothing had prepared him for those terrible hours of mangled flesh. Once, as he worked inside, those waiting to be treated outside began to sing. At first, the tunes were melancholy. Later, they sang a few bawdy barrack tunes. Michael's conscious mind was barely aware of the singing. On reflection, it had helped him stay calm and focused. Their selections revealed a desire to remember a better, happier time, when families sang together around the living room piano.

The thunder of guns drew stark contrast to their singing. It was as different as the odor of Carrel-Dakin solution burning bacteria from the odor of flowers around his home in Guilford. The pain it caused as it flowed into open wounds often brought cries that had no resemblance to the singing soldiers. Yet he'd done well and wanted to continue to work in an aid station.

Outside the station, Madame Brousard asked a porter to find a taxi. He said it was impossible. He hadn't seen a free taxi for hours. In her present mood, his response was far from adequate.

"*Imbécile. N'ayez pas peur essayer.*"

Catherine was as astonished by her heated criticism as to hearing her speak in French. It was true, the porter hadn't tried, but surely he wasn't afraid to try. Her reprimand had the desired effect. The porter sighed but relented. It was likely she'd dealt with him before.

"*Oui, Madame. Mais, je ne fais pas des promesses.*" The porter left to find a taxi, making no promises.

"Silly old man! Every time I come here, he says the same thing."

"You speak flawless French, Madame," said Catherine. They'd been speaking English for hours on the train. The sound of the tongue she'd studied for years took Catherine by surprise.

"Of course, my dear child. I'm may be English by birth, but France is my home. Few of these civil servants speak English. I prefer French. And you, my dear, do you speak French?"

Catherine recited a few lines of her favorite French poem.

"Ah! There's just a touch of the classical French in your accent. It's seldom heard in Paris. Do you speak other languages?"

"I studied Latin, of course, but never use it. My classes included two years in German and one in Spanish. I'm not as good with those. I couldn't have a serious conversation."

"Well! I can see why the embassy wants you. You've some talent, young lady. The embassy will appreciate you."

At being called a lady, Catherine was reminded of her father. She wondered what he'd have thought of her coming to France. She hoped he would have been proud.

"*Madame, le taxi.*" The porter's words startled them. He'd returned unnoticed.

Madame instantly turned and gave him a rather stern look. She was certain he'd surprised her on purpose.

"*Bon! Allez, monsieur!*" Madame said, acknowledging the news.

Madame Brousard accompanied Catherine all the way to the embassy and waited in the lobby for the meeting to end. With deference to Catherine's weariness, the ambassador kept the meeting brief. Introductions were exchanged. Ambassador Sharp made no connection with her last name to the name of the man who'd come to his office from England. More than a year had passed since John's visit. Catherine wasn't aware that the event had taken place. John never included it in his letters.

"I'll let headquarters know of your arrival. Pershing's staff is in a better position to describe your assignment. I can tell you that your service will be of invaluable assistance in securing our position." He ended the interview by thanking her and saying, "You've traveled far, Miss Morris, at no small risk to yourself. I suspect your willingness to help is more than matched by the importance of your task."

With that, the meeting ended.

Nothing about the meeting clarified her task. Her initial reaction was disappointment. Catherine hoped she might learn something more before going to headquarters. His comments only added to the mystery. The veil that surrounded her assignment became darker. She hadn't the faintest idea what he'd meant by his last statement and was too tired to ask for clarification. That would come in Chaumont. Time and distance remained before she'd have answers.

Madame Brousard took her to a small pension. The ambassador told Catherine to wait there until she was contacted. He expected that to happen shortly after speaking to headquarters. It was the only thing he'd said to her that was definite. It was the only thing he'd said that she was happy to hear. The voyage and train to Paris had drained her. Further delay would not make a short stay in Paris enjoyable.

A day later, after glimpses of Paris out her window, Catherine was told to board a train headed east to Pershing's headquarters. Perhaps then, she'd have answers to the questions that had nagged her since her conference with Frank Polk. She told herself that she would not be put off again. She'd either have answers, or they'd pay for her passage back home! Neither she nor Michael had any idea that they were on the same train to Chaumont.

Reassignment

AEF HEADQUARTERS WAS 136 MILES southeast of Paris. Michael had no idea that Catherine was in France. Pure coincidence brought them to Chaumont in late August of 1918. Though both boarded the same train in Paris, they didn't know the other was aboard. Several passenger cars separated them as they stepped off the platform near the Place de la Loge. Catherine noticed dozens of men in uniforms of every sort as the porter gathered her bags. He led her outside the station, where vehicles on two or more wheels were parked awaiting passengers or cargo. Michael became tangled in the crush of passengers trying to leave the platform. He didn't emerge from the crowd until reaching the street. Among a long line of taxis, trucks, carriages, and bicycles, he recognized the back of a staff car obviously from Chaumont. He called out to its driver, who was tying a piece of luggage to the rack on the rear.

"Sergeant! I'm to report to Colonel George C. Marshall at Chaumont. Are you going to headquarters?"

The driver turned to face him. Michael noticed an array of decorations crowding the marine's jacket. A stiffened leg caused the marine to walk with a decided limp. Michael couldn't tell if the leg was real or false.

"Yes, sir. You can share a seat with my passenger, sir, unless you'd rather ride in front. I was sent to fetch her to headquarters, sir."

"I'll ride in front." Michael walked toward the front of the car, opened the door, threw his small bag on the floor board, and got in. Without turning, he said, "I hope you don't mind sharing a ride, miss. I'm going to Chaumont too."

"Michael?"

At the sound of a familiar voice, he turned and saw Catherine.

"My God! Catherine? What are you doing in France? Why didn't you tell me? How long have you been here? Why are you going to headquarters?"

"Michael! This is amazing! I can't believe you're—"

"Cath, please! What in the world are you doing here?"

Michael scrambled out the door and rushed to the rear seat to sit next to her. After the sergeant finished securing Michael's duffel bag to the rack, he was surprised and puzzled to find his two passengers hugging and kissing each other in the rear seat.

Unsure how to address the situation, he said, "Sir? Ah ... I don't want to interrupt, but you're going to have to teach me your technique! That's one for the record books, sir."

Catherine blushed with embarrassment at the comment. Michael's explanation was brief.

"It's okay, Sergeant. She's my sister. We haven't seen each other in weeks."

"Wow! That's incredible, sir. I wish I had your luck."

The marine began the short trip to headquarters through the provincial capital of the department of Haute Marne. Here, the war was remote. Live trees lined the avenue. They could as easily have been driving through Guilford were it not for the soldiers crowding the avenues.

"Catherine! What's this about? Why are you going to Chaumont?"

She was overjoyed to see him; his questions could wait. Besides, she had no real answers and wouldn't know until she got there.

"It's a long story, Michael. I'm just happy you're here. I would have written, but there really wasn't time. I arrived only yesterday. I only hoped I might find you or John. You look wonderful—a bit tired. Are you all right? What brings you here?"

"I'm fine. I thought I'd see John before seeing you. Last I heard, his unit was in Senard. They move around a lot. Catherine, tell me why you are in France. Does Mother know about this?"

Catherine took his hands and explained as much as she knew.

"Mr. Polk said headquarters needed a liaison, and I'd be attached to the embassy in Paris. I couldn't refuse after promising to go wherever they needed me ... even if it meant coming to France. You aren't upset, are you?"

"No, Cath. But I am surprised. I never expected to find you here! It's great to see you." A bit shocked over their lucky meeting, Michael hugged her again. It occurred to him that she probably knew nothing about James.

"Catherine, Monroe's son is in France."

"I know, Michael. Monroe showed me your letter. Where is he? Is he still in the hospital?"

"Yes. Savenay. I went to see him and stayed for a while. I'm just now coming back."

Michael finished telling her about James and his stay at the hospital as the staff car pulled up to the building that held the office of George Marshall. Catherine's appointment was in another building not far away.

"If I'd only known you were on the train, we'd have had more time together," she complained, close to tears at having to separate after only a few minutes. Michael didn't want to go, either, but his appointment couldn't wait. The driver sympathized with the problem and offered a solution.

"I could tell Colonel Conner you'll be a while, Miss Morris. Would that do?"

"No, Sergeant. But thank you. The ambassador said I must see the colonel as soon as I arrive. Michael, it must have been awful for him. He'll be all right, won't he?"

"I think so. He had a bad time at first. He's okay now. I'll keep informed through Dr. Burns at Savenay. I wrote to Monroe about his progress. I don't know why they never told us he was here. I didn't ask James about it. Well, I've got to go too, Cath. I hate leaving you like this. Will you be in Chaumont for a while?"

"I don't know. I wasn't told very much. They may keep me here for a while, but I don't know. They could send me back to the embassy. I'll let you know as soon as I do."

Michael thought a moment and then proposed the only option open to him.

"Okay. If we don't see each other again, I'll address my letters to the embassy in Paris. Send yours here in care of George Marshall. He'll know where I am. I'll come to you if I can get away, Cath. We need more time to talk."

"I wish we had time. I'll write as soon as I can. I want to see you again—and John too. Let me know when you find him, won't you?"

"Of course, Cath. If I'm not assigned right away, Colonel Conner will know where you are. I'll write to let you know."

He gave her one last hug. Good-byes were not exchanged. They didn't want to say good-bye. Michael waved as the car pulled away, watching until it turned the corner of the building. He went straight to Marshall's office.

Marshall was expecting him. Recently promoted to full colonel, Marshall handed Michael his orders personally.

"You mentioned you wanted to stay assigned to an aid station, Michael."

The assignment took immediate effect. Michael was to report to the field headquarters of Major General Joseph T. Dickman, commander of the US Fourth Corps. He was responsible for preparing and coordinating advanced medical collaboration for three divisions.

"We touched on this before. It's time we tried to get our boys the care they need when they need it. Your job is to find the best way to get it done. Dickman will take part in the first entirely American operation in the Champagne sector, near Saint-Mihiel."

Before dismissing Michael, the colonel had another order that concerned him directly.

"Lieutenant, Captain McKay's report on your work in the valley drew the attention of the General Pershing. His recommendation was approved several days ago. Your promotion to lieutenant commander became effective as of August 28."

Marshall shook Michael's hand. He gave the newly promoted medical officer two brass oak leaves and new epaulets. "Congratulations, Lieutenant Commander. You've earned them. A staff car should be waiting outside to take you to your new sector."

For a second time that day, Michael was caught by surprise. He already had something to tell Catherine. Sadly, he would not have a chance to tell her in person. Setting up medical facilities for three divisions would occupy his time for the foreseeable future.

General Pershing was with Marshal Foch at French Army headquarters in Ligny-en-Barrois. Catherine was directed to Major General James W. McAndrew's office. McAndrew, Pershing's chief of staff, welcomed Catherine on his behalf.

"Your qualifications seem to fit the job, Miss Morris."

He wished her well on the assignment without saying what it was. Since she still didn't know anything about her assignment, his welcome prompted a modest "Thank you."

Catherine wasn't concerned about her qualifications. She'd crossed an ocean to be closer to the war and her brothers and to learn the details of her assignment. The general didn't say anything about the subject.

"General, when will I learn exactly why I'm here?" She couldn't put the question any more clearly than that, and the general was aware of the reason she asked.

"The details will be given to you by Colonel Fox Conner, Miss Morris. I can only say that General Pershing himself requested that the State Department send an appointee. I'm sure you will serve in the same spirit as others. Our country is fully committed to winning this war. The sergeant outside will escort you to Colonel Conner's office. Good luck, Miss Morris. I hope to see you again before your return to America."

"Thank you, sir." Glad the welcome was over, she finally knew that Colonel Connor was indeed the man to see. His office was in the same building. Each step toward it increased her excitement. An uninvited anxiety kept equal pace.

Classified G-3 at Chaumont, Colonel Fox Conner's door was marked with his name, rank, and the title "Commanding Officer, SA." He had hoped that Washington would send someone less attractive—and therefore less conspicuous—for the task he had in mind. His first impression led him to believe her good looks might work against her. He had no doubt that she commanded the French language. His immediate problem was to explain why she was here without fully exposing the sensitive nature of the assignment. Until he was certain that she'd accept the assignment, he had to be cautious not to reveal everything at once. She could still refuse to accept.

"Miss Morris, the president set a task for General Pershing. That task was to command a wholly American sector under the American flag. Up to now, that idea has not been well received either by the British or French. Should he succeed in convincing Marshal Foch to give our army its own sector, we must make every effort to assure the success of any operation the general is given to complete."

Conner's pause suggested that he was awaiting a response. Thus far, he hadn't said anything she needed to know. Catherine had come too far and waited too long to continually be put off. She deserved to know why she was here. She'd never found anger a useful tool in situations like this, but she was definitely losing patience.

"Colonel Conner, I know General Pershing asked for a person with my qualifications. Mr. Polk asked me to accept this assignment. I agreed. It took weeks for me to arrive here. I assure you I didn't come to France over a submarine-infested ocean as lightly as I'd make the trip to downtown Baltimore! Major General McAndrew told me you'd give me the details of my assignment. Now that I'm here, at his request and authority, I believe I deserve to be trusted with the reason for my presence."

Conner heard words laced with impatience. She wanted the truth, and she wanted it now. Her attitude convinced Conner of her commitment. His doubt over her looks disappeared. Catherine had spunk, the one trait that had the most value to him and to her assignment. Her commitment known, one concern remained.

"Thank you, Miss Morris! I admire a woman who speaks her mind. I can see why the State Department selected you for the job."

"Thank you, sir." Her tone was professional. It showed no shyness at his compliment. Her continued stare let him know that he still hadn't addressed her question.

Conner watched her eyes longer than seemed necessary. His

position and her assignment demanded that he was absolutely certain she was the right person for the job. His face grew very serious. His next words were carefully chosen.

"Miss Morris, you were picked for this assignment only partly for your knowledge of French. Unfortunately, I can't give you all the details just yet, but I can tell you this. If you accept, you will be sent to a town close the current line of battle. Your job there will entail total secrecy. The *SA* on my door stands for 'Surreptitious Activities.' Do you understand?"

"I believe I do, Colonel."

"Given that, are you willing to take this assignment?"

Catherine hadn't come thousands of miles to turn around and go home. "I am."

"Good. Then I can tell you that will pose as the daughter of the manager of a hotel. You have just arrived home from the university in Paris. You have plans to become an instructor in English. You've been away so long that no one but your father will recognize you. I'll proceed once you take some time to think that much over." Conner waited.

There it was! Conner's eyes never left Catherine's. He watched for her reaction. He wasn't disappointed. Catherine was wide-eyed. His description, though brief, was powerful.

After a few seconds that seemed like minutes, he said, "I hope I'm not going too fast for you, Miss Morris."

"I understood what you said, Colonel Conner. You've drawn quite a picture. As I knew nothing about it before now, I'm naturally surprised."

"Good. For a moment, I thought I'd scared you off. Before I continue, you should know that you may still withdraw at this point with no ill feeling. Shall I continue?"

The choice was hers. Without the chance to consult anyone, Catherine, for the first time in her life, was given total control over her own destiny. She inhaled deeply.

"Colonel, I don't see how posing as someone's daughter changes anything. Please go on."

Conner smiled, confident that she was the woman they'd hoped to find. To be sure, he tested her French and suggested that she loosen up.

"Please sit down, miss. I'll begin at the beginning. Belfort is a small town near the Swiss border. Consequently, both sides use Belfort to gather information. It's not the same town it used to be. G-3 believes German operatives find their way into town from Switzerland. As a neutral, the Swiss don't really care who enters or leaves the country. It's become a prime locale for intelligence agents. Some are certainly German spies. We need to know who those German spies are.

"What we want from you is to keep your eyes and ears open. Notice anyone overly curious about what's happening in the sector we occupy. I mean *anyone*, Miss Morris! If possible, learn their names. We'll need complete physical descriptions, so pay attention to their ages, color of hair and eyes, heights, weights, and any distinguishing features like scars, accents, even mannerisms— things an average person doesn't notice that will point them out to us."

"I can handle that, Colonel. Do you think my French is convincing?"

"Yes, but be very cautious of what you say and how you say it. You have two ears, Miss Morris, and one mouth. Listen twice as much as you speak. Any German agents you may chance to meet will be passing themselves off as anything but German. French intelligence informs us that they know of no double agents in Belfort. I assume you heard what happened to Miss Mata Hari. From the minute you leave this office, you must think and be French! Less may mean failure or worse. You are a graduate and the daughter of a hotel manager from the time you leave this office.

Don't fish for information that isn't volunteered. Enemy agents, male or female, are trained and suspicious of anyone who asks too many questions. Should they suspect that you are not what you claim to be, they will certainly ask themselves who or what you really are. Neither your words nor your deeds must arouse any suspicion."

Her original question answered in full, her assignment inspired many others.

"When do I leave? Where do I go when I arrive? Should I contact you, or will you contact me?"

Conner raised a palm to arrest her inquiries. "Let's take it one at a time, Miss Morris. I will either come to Belfort or send someone to contact you. Stay as close to the hotel as possible. The manager is one of our French operatives and can be trusted. He's been told that you will be posing as his daughter, and that's all he needs to know. The fewer people who know of your assignment, the better. No one outside this circle must know where you're going, what you're doing, and especially why you're doing it! Do we understand each other, Miss Morris?"

"Yes, Colonel. I should tell you that my brother Michael knows I'm in Chaumont. He's expecting me to tell him where I am. I met him quite accidentally at the railway station. He's a naval medical officer and is here for reassignment."

"I see. Well, that was lucky for you but unfortunate for your purposes. You couldn't have told much to him, as you knew nothing up to now." Conner arose from his desk with chin in hand, thinking through the new predicament.

"Before you leave, I want you to write a letter to your brother without dating it. Do not tell him you're going to Belfort. He mustn't know about that. Say nothing about your job. Will he try to contact you here or through the embassy?"

"He said he'd write to the embassy."

"Good! Tell him you're assigned to embassy. There's some truth to that. He'll believe it. Once I've got the letter, I'll send it to the embassy with instructions to mail it a day or two after they receive a letter from him. Tell him they'll return you to Washington once your work with the ambassador is complete. If he tries to see you, the ambassador will say he sent you off somewhere on an errand outside Paris. Is there anything else I should know about?"

"Yes, Colonel. I'd like to know something about my brother John. He's been with the Lafayette Escadrille for over a year, and I haven't received a letter from him in months."

Conner seemed more amused than concerned. "Good God! Is the entire Morris family over here fighting the kaiser? I'll look into it for you. I should have something to pass on in perhaps a week or so. Now that you're fully informed, Miss Morris, are you certain you want to go through with it?"

She answered the question immediately. "When do I leave for Belfort, Colonel?"

Conner smiled. "A train leaves tomorrow afternoon. The driver who brought you here will take you to a room in town for tonight. Come back here tomorrow morning by 7:00 sharp. Use a French taxi. We'll go over everything, and I'll give you any new instructions. Do you have any questions?"

"No, sir."

"Good. We'll meet again tomorrow."

The meeting over, Catherine was driven to a small pension in the center of town.

The following morning, Fox Conner had a long meeting with Catherine that reviewed all pertinent points in detail, including her new name. He reminded her that Belfort was an old town near the southern tip of Alsace province in the Vosges Mountains, some thirty-five miles from the Swiss border. He gave her a student identity card with her new name, French francs and coins, the name and description of her French father, and the location of his hotel in Belfort.

"I can show you better on the map, Miss Morris. Belfort is there. Basel is across the Rhine. The nearest large French town is Mulhouse to the northeast. The old town of Besançon is about ten miles southwest. Right there. The hotel in Belfort is called l'Hôtel du Sud Vosges. Any taxi or horse carriage can take you there." Once again, Conner asked whether she had any questions.

His mention of Besançon distracted her. Her father had walked the fortress walls in Besançon before she was born. She couldn't remember if he'd spoken of Belfort, but he'd certainly told them about his adventures in Besançon. Thinking of it now nearly brought tears. She wondered what he would have said about her assignment to Belfort.

"No, Colonel. I think we've covered it very thoroughly."

"Fine. Miss Morris, stay alert and good luck. I'll be in touch in a week or so."

Return to Chaudun

LUCK PLAYED A ROLE IN the exploits of SPA124. Near the end of their stay at Saint-Pol-sur-Mer, a German bomber raided the field, setting a hangar on fire. Several of Group Thirteen's planes were burned. Though scorched, John's Spad escaped the flames.

Flying cover for a photo patrol, Lufbery, Parsons, and Walter Lovell watched as the Flying Circus put on an aerial show, challenging them to fight. They accepted. The dogfight lasted less than half an hour. No side prevailed. A single bullet found Lovell's upper wing.

Like a coin, luck has two sides. Two days before SPA124 returned to Chaudun, authorities identified the burned, shattered body of the famous French ace Georges Guynemer. A tidal wave of remorse rippled through France. A member of the Storks, Guynemer's untimely death became a portent of bad luck for the squadron. Several members in the squadron were shot down. A few transferred to other squadrons. The escadrille was not up to full strength.

In late September of 1917, SPA124 returned to Chaudun on the Aisne. New aircraft came, replacing those that had burned. Lufbery added victories to his record with uncanny flying skill. Once again, SPA124 supported the French army on the ground. In late October, the French attacked German positions along the eighteen miles of the Chemin des Dames ridge, from Allemant above Soissons, to the town of Craonne. By the end of the first week of November, the French had captured 7,500 Germans. Some of the prisoners still recalled the day a mad pilot strafed their position along the ridge, killing many of their comrades. John's attack was more memorable to the Germans than his squadron. Three weeks later, Canadians won Passchendaele Ridge. Growing short of men in 1917, Germany was losing the high ground on the western front.

In Chaudun, the mission of SPA124 was extended. Enemy observation planes remained their primary targets, but German observation balloons were added to the list. Tethered to the ground, observation balloons were large stationary targets. Protected by fighters above, preranged antiaircraft guns defended the balloons from the ground. The balloonists' view of Chaudun bore no likeness to what was once a pastoral countryside. Ravaged by three years of war, the landscape of northern France was scarred by trenches, devoid of living trees, poisoned by gas, buried under tons of rusted barbed wire, and riddled by thousands of shell holes filled with stagnant water and corpses. Soldiers risked life and limb trying to recover the dead and wounded from the fields.

Burned-out tanks and twisted trucks competed for pieces of mangled earth among splintered supply wagons and the bloated bodies of dead horses. The corpses of both armies lay joined in death among the rest, littering every battlefield. The odor of decaying flesh was so strong that it could be tasted. From above, the dead looked like carrion thrown from the table of a carnivorous giant.

On the ground, the sickly sweet odor of decay was sharpened by acrid wisps of artillery smoke and waves of human sweat emanating from the trenches.

Balloonists hung above the wasteland, binoculars fixed to their eyes, spotting for artillery, looking for movement on a road, a sniper in a broken steeple, a head peering over a trench or behind a stump, wherever an enemy might be seen to move. They marked the smoke of a firing cannon, dust rising from a supply road, a glint of light where darkness should be, an enemy helmet. Spotting any exposed enemy movement, he would target it for destruction. A simple telephone message sent new artillery shells, adding to the heaps of earlier destruction.

Before they made another call, Thénault wanted all enemy balloons shot from the sky. Ordinary bullets didn't ignite the hydrogen gas that filled them. Several Spads, including John's, were fitted with a new weapon that improved the odds for success. Between their wings, brackets were fixed to the outer struts on each Spad. Eight electrically fired Le Prieur rockets were slipped into the brackets. To account for the effect of gravity, the rockets pointed slightly upward, not parallel to the fuselage. The pilots practiced to become familiar with their flight characteristics. John's first dive wasn't steep enough for his altitude. He overshot the large target laid out on the ground by eighty yards. On his second run, he waited longer before firing and dived at the target more sharply. Two rockets struck the circle, arching neatly toward its center. He couldn't resist showing his joy by doing a looping barrel roll that severely tested the strength of wings made heavy by the six unfired rockets. The wings groaned but didn't break. A Nieuport would have lost a wing.

Two sets of three trenches formed the line of battle—three for each opposing side. The killing ground that separated the forward trenches earned the name "No-Man's-Land." In Flanders, John had often seen the zone narrowed to a few yards. More often, several hundred yards separated the lines. To penetrate the enemy's rear area, the fliers crossed six jagged scars in the landscape. All six trenches could be plainly seen from the air, since stands of trees had become mere stumps.

Two groups of enemy balloons floated behind the lines not far from Chaudun. Thénault wanted all four shot down at the same time. The task was split between two fighter groups. Thaw's patrol was to hit the closest pair. John's group was to destroy the two a half mile beyond Thaw's. A third squadron was to fly loose cover for the planes in both groups. As the balloons were strung up at odd distances, coordinating the attack was difficult at best. When attacked, balloons could be quickly winched down. Thaw's squadron was successful and flamed the first two. German ground crews lowered the two remaining balloons, escaping the attack of John's squadron. They hadn't fired a single rocket.

Frustrated, John signaled his planes to link up with Thaw and return to the field. John remained anxious to try the new weapons. He looked for any excuse to fire them on the way back to the field. He noticed a column of German trucks moving slowly toward their lines. In seconds, he'd be past the column and lose the chance to attack with surprise. He signaled Thaw that he was going down to attack. Thaw didn't see his signal. John descended without a single fighter flying cover. He dived straight for the rear of the supply train, raising dust on a narrow French road. In leaving the formation, John's Spad caught Thaw's attention. Bill signaled the others to return to the field and turned to join John. Three thousand feet behind John's fast-diving Spad, he watched in fascination. His instinct and training forced Thaw to look for enemy aircraft.

Seconds later, John saw the conical noses of artillery shells being towed on carriages hooked to trucks moving slowly toward the German cannons behind the Chemin des Dames ridge. Behind them, two lines of replacements marched along several teams of horses pulling caisson-filled wooden crates, obviously intended to support the German forces remaining on the part of the ridge not within French control.

John pushed the joystick forward and gave the Spad full throttle. The engine responded, pulling a hurricane of air through the propeller. At 130 miles an hour, he began to level the Spad at five hundred feet, eight hundred feet behind the column. The men on foot began running off the road, looking for the cover of a ditch, a tree stump, a dead horse, or a shell hole. The entire column halted. Those who were riding ran for cover. John pulled the charging handles on his machine guns and started firing at three hundred feet. Fifty feet lower, he loosed four of his rockets at the carriages filled with artillery shells. The six carriages beyond those carried boxes of high explosives. John launched his remaining rockets at these. The first explosions were his rockets, immediately followed by a single larger explosion. Then Armageddon visited the roadway. Explosions overlapped in a crescendo of sound and crush of pressure that hurt John's ears and shook the Spad nearly half a mile past what remained of the burning supply line. John turned his head to see the destruction. There was little to see but fire and a column of smoke that had already risen higher than the Spad.

Fragments from exploded shells whizzed past the Spad, tearing fist-sized holes in its wings. At 250 feet, John dived to avoid the hot shards chasing the Spad. He leveled off just before missing a leafless tree. A wave of air pressure heaved past the fuselage, causing a temporary loss of control. The shock wave tossed the Spad like a toy. It took all his talent to prevent the plane from nosing into the ground at 125 miles an hour. John regained control just as the Spad's right wheel struck the top of a rotten tree, splitting it in half. The jolt caught John's attention. The Spad seemed to handle differently. Something wasn't right.

The plane listed ever so slightly to the left. Looking over the right side, John saw that his right wheel was missing. The wheel carriage was loose and bent backward. He watched the wheel as it fell to the ground, hitting some luckless German's helmet, breaking his neck just as he squeezed the trigger of his machine gun. The German had John in his sights. The wheel bounced nearly half the height it had fallen. In death, the German's finger froze on the trigger. The mindless gun put four neat holes in John's wing. The dead man fell, still firing. The gun swiveled, killing two of his comrades before running out of ammunition. John's gaze returned to the front. He turned the Spad toward the field, bullets flying past his ears, ripping holes in the Spad.

Concerned about his missing landing gear, John climbed along the hornet's nest near the Ailette River, drawing fire from every German rifle and machine gun within range. He banked the Spad south to fly across the ridge with barely enough altitude to clear its crest. Bullets continued to rip through his plane's wings. One smashed his mirror. Shards of glass flew into his face, cracking the lenses in his goggles. One punched a hole through his cockpit, striking the altimeter, breaking its glass, and sending more shards flying. John groaned as the ricochet struck his left arm, numbing it from his elbow to his fingertips. Luckily, he'd raised his hand toward his bleeding face. If he hadn't, the bullet would have taken his eye. Spent, it struck his temple like a hammer, knocking him dizzy for several seconds and bringing on the world's worst headache.

As fast as the hailstorm of lead had come, it stopped. He was clear of the ridge. John felt warm blood trickling from his forehead. Propeller wash streamed blood on his goggles. He ripped them off his bleeding forehead. With one arm useless, using sound more than sight, John reset the throttle with his right hand to lower his airspeed. He had no feeling in his left arm. His face bloody, his eyes nearly closed, John used his good hand to place his left on the control stick, checking to be sure it was there. He rested his left leg gently against the joystick to sense unwanted movement. Adrenaline pumped through his veins. He bit the middle finger of the glove on his trembling right hand and slowly pulled it off. Carefully, he felt for glass fragments, picking the larger ones out of his face between unsteady fingers. In the cold wind, his cheeks and chin began to sting when the glass was withdrawn. The pain was welcome. It helped keep him conscious.

In its current condition, landing the Spad was not something he looked forward to. The memory of what had happened to Outlaw at Pau was not as welcome as the pain. Retaking the stick with his good hand, he focused on flying the crippled airplane. An airplane edged by on his right. John's heartbeat soared as his right hand reached for the Vickers's trigger. It returned to his joystick. Bill Thaw waved to him, signaling him to follow him back to the field. Thaw pointed to his landing gear. John nodded, remembering the missing wheel. His good hand trembled from the surge of adrenaline caused by Thaw's sudden arrival. He followed Thaw, guiding the crippled Spad as best he could. Seeing was becoming a problem. His cheeks began to swell. Blood continued to make it difficult to see. His left arm began to throb as feeling started to return. He hadn't looked for bleeding from the arm. It felt more like a dead weight than a living thing. It didn't matter. His concern was his eyes. He needed them more than the arm. He pushed the throttle in to lower his speed to less than ninety miles per hour. Thaw slowed his plane likewise to stay alongside and slightly above.

As the field came in range, Thaw signaled John. They made a slow, arcing descent. John knew that he'd have to keep the Spad on its left wheel as long as possible. The stronger Spad didn't float like the lighter Nieuport. He'd have to fly the plane all the way to landing. Seconds before touching down, John lowered the aileron on the right wing, canting the Spad as though making a slow banking turn to the left. He swung the rudder in the opposite direction to keep the Spad straight. It landed heavily on its left wheel. The left wing scraped the grass on the field as it landed. Thanks to Outlaw, John remembered to cut the engine. The memory of what had happened saved John from flipping or burning.

On one wheel, the Spad seemed to circle forever, crossing landing ruts that threatened to flip the plane. John gave the right wing all the lift it would take to keep the Spad off the wheelless right carriage. If the axle dug into the dirt, the Spad would surely flip and might still catch fire if fuel found a hot exhaust manifold. Listing badly, the Spad's lower-left wing skipped over the field, cutting a groove as it went. John fought the Spad with all the strength he had in his good arm.

The Spad slowed, lost lift, and began to roll to the right. The axle scraped the field, turning the Spad in an ever-sharper clockwise circle. The Spad came to a spinning stop. Momentum brought the tail sharply upward, snapping the right wing. The propeller hit the field, cracking like a whip. It prevented the Spad from flipping completely. What was left of the Spad fell inelegantly on its tail, cracking the fuselage, releasing a taut rudder cable. The cable whipped through the canvas of the right wing, adding insult to injury. John had made better landings, but none as eventful. He checked the switch to be sure it was off. He knew that he should leave the plane immediately. Totally spent, he rested his head on the cockpit's padded leather roll and whispered a short prayer of thanks.

Charles Gallau watched John come in and was one of the first to run to the wreck to help John from the cockpit. Others ran past Gallau, his shorter legs losing to their longer ones. Among them was Thaw, who had stopped before John and had seen the entire event.

"Are you okay?" Thaw asked. "I didn't think you'd come out of that in one piece!"

Barely conscious, John managed, "I wasn't sure myself, Bill. I'm a little roughed up. I think I'll be okay."

Thaw grabbed his partially numbed arm to help him out.

"Ow! That one's pretty sore, Bill. Ricochet."

Thaw helped John ease himself slowly from the cockpit. Charles arrived out of breath and surveyed the twisted pile of junk that was his Spad.

"*Mon Dieu, monsieur!* You look worse than the Spad, and she is one big mess. You must go to hospital, *monsieur*. Your face."

"He's right, John. You're going to need some stitching up. Can you walk?"

John nodded.

"Good. I'll borrow Thénault's car. The hospital's on the Rue de Saint-Lazare in Soissons. Can you walk on your own?"

John's unsteady legs prompted Thaw's concern.

"I'm still a little weak in the knees. Give me a minute. Sorry about the Spad, Charles. It got pretty nasty over the ridge."

"Don't worry, *monsieur*. I will ask for a new Spad from the depot. We may get the new model!"

Bill escorted John to Thénault's office. Halfway there, Ted Parsons came running from the wreck of John's plane to catch up to them.

"You taking him to Soissons, Bill?"

"Yeah."

Ted decided to go along. He looked concerned. John's injuries were difficult to assess. His face was covered in blood. The wash from his propeller had streaked blood around his ears and behind his neck. His cheeks and chin bled, he was holding his arm, and his legs were unsteady as he walked. Nothing about John was recognizable, the same as his Spad.

John's cuts began to throb. When his mouth moved, the pain was intense. John remained as quiet as possible. Ted was curious. "What in hell happened, John? One minute you were headed home, and then you peeled off to go after something."

Relieving John of the effort to talk, Thaw told Parsons everything he'd seen.

Thaw drove Thénault's car, trying to avoid bumps so as not to jolt John too much while going as fast as he dared. Soissons was five miles northeast of the field.

"We should inaugurate him into the should-be-dead club, Bill. What about the supply train? Did you get a look at it?"

"Oh, yeah! I was well behind and stayed above. I didn't want to be around when John fired those rockets. After the fireworks, I counted at least four craters over a stretch of several hundred yards. At least a hundred feet of road was blown all to hell. I didn't see much moving. Nothing was standing. Those still alive were on their knees. The whole damned area was leveled like some giant had stepped on it and mashed it flat. I've never seen so much destruction by a single Spad!"

Parsons added an epilogue. "I looked over your Spad, John. It's a total write-off. You're lucky nothing hit the tank. It's hard to believe you landed that wreck. Answer one question for me, will you?"

John nodded to keep his mouth closed.

"Why? You could have blown up yourself in that escapade!"

The question amused John, but he didn't smile. He had no single compelling reason. The sights, sounds, and smell of war were commonplace. They overrode reasons. It occurred to him that he'd rationalized death, even his own. The training, the trip from Saint-Nazaire to Le Mans, Paris, the death and destruction he'd seen from the air, the deaths of his fellow fliers and enemy fliers alike had dulled his instinct to survive. The indiscriminate killing and destruction of treasured, irreplaceable things replaced his viewpoint on what he valued. They cheapened everything. They devalued life, human or animal. He was locked in a ruthless world that made no sense, a world that had only one truth. Some would live; others would die. No justification could be made for either case. John didn't know which group he'd finally belong to. In war, the judge was time, the winner was death. As time passed, he cared less about time and death than he had the day before. A day was like the last and the next to follow. Life and death were two sides of the same coin. If his came up life, he'd survive. What sort of man would he be if he survived?

Parsons repeated the question. "Why'd you do it, John?"

Parsons knew that John's target was opportune. What John had done had little to do with why he'd done it. The economy in John's response waived further explanation and answered Parsons's question. Though brief, it explained why.

"They were there. So was I."

Parsons understood the simple and profound truth his words expressed. That was war.

A Change of Venue

THE DOCTOR TOLD JOHN THAT his wounds were mostly superficial. "The scars add character to your face."

John didn't mind scars, but the pain reminded him of his brush with death.

Thénault ordered him to rest. "Until the swelling recedes, flying is out of the question. What is more, you have no airplane. Perhaps in a week or two. For now, take the time to regain your spirit and the full use of your arm."

John had little choice in the matter, and he would have agreed with Thénault even if he did. It would take a week or two for his new Spad to arrive and for Charles to assemble it and thoroughly check it out.

His stitches precluded facial movement, and his swollen cheeks forced him to open his eyes wider to see. Even then, his bandages restricted peripheral vision. The huge bruise on his arm reminded him of the rainbow of colors a drop of oil makes on the surface of a pond. During the first few days, he kept himself busy by writing letters to Michelle and Catherine. After that, he began to pester Thénault to discover when his new Spad would arrive. At first, this pleased Thénault. His eagerness meant that John's wounds hadn't tainted the spirit of the fighter who'd strafed an enemy column. But after days of answering the same question, his response boiled down to "Be patient. It comes when it comes!"

It took several days for the swelling in John's cheeks to subside. His bandages were removed. The stitches remained, but they didn't interfere with his vision. That same day, John entered Thénault's office to ask a favor. Before he could speak, Thénault yelled, "*Mon Dieu!* It is coming today! Go away! Do not bother me anymore!" Thénault's irritation made him more than happy to lend his car to John, if only to get rid of a nuisance.

John drove to Senlis to look for another mirror for the Spad. The owner of the junk shop reminded him he'd gotten the only one he had the last time he'd come. He didn't know where he'd find another. Paul, the owner's eleven-year-old son, overheard John's broken French and knew exactly where to find one. Paul didn't approach John until he went outside to get to Thénault's car.

"*Monsieur,* I get you a mirror. A very good mirror!"

Before John could respond, Paul was in the car giving him directions. He took John a half mile or so to the head of an alley off the main street.

"Here, *monsieur!* Stop here!"

"Okay. What now, Paul?" John began to get out.

"Oh, no, *monsieur.* You stay. I go alone."

John waited, somewhat puzzled, because the boy hadn't asked for money to buy a mirror. Five minutes later, the boy hurriedly returned carrying a shiny mirror very similar to the one John had lost.

Only then did John notice the end of a small wrench sticking from his pocket. He was about to ask Paul where he'd gotten the mirror, but the boy was anxious to return to his father's shop—and with good reason. A robust, middle-aged man wearing a large scowl came running toward the car from the alley. Realizing the boy's theft, John could have waited for the man had his French been more fluent. As the man was angry and yelling in his native tongue, John believed there was little chance for intelligent conversation. Moreover, he didn't want the boy to get into trouble. To the vast relief of the boy, John shifted into first gear and sped away. Briefly stopping, John reached into his pocket. He had no idea how many francs he'd thrown on the pavement. But as he looked in Thénault's rearview mirror, he noticed that the Frenchman had stopped to pick them up and also stopped yelling. John thought he saw the man smile, but he couldn't be sure.

He looked at Paul and grunted. In spite of his painful stitches, he grinned. Paul laughed, asking for nothing in return for the poached mirror. This was justice. John didn't want to reward the theft beyond the satisfaction the boy got from stealing. Though he'd probably overpaid, John was glad to have the mirror. His Spad had arrived.

Two days later, Charles had the Spad assembled. He tuned the engine until he was satisfied that it ran better than the last. He mounted the purloined mirror. John didn't tell him how he'd gotten it. With nothing more to do, John wanted to take it up. Thénault happily gave his permission but advised him not to strafe any supply trains at close range. Thénault also had something pointed to say that involved the loss of a Spad and cost of a new one. John accepted his advice politely and promised to be more careful in selecting targets.

The lecture given and received, John went to the hangar. Lufbery was there and asked him to fly as his wingman on an unscheduled patrol, an odd request from the man who usually did his off-duty hunting alone. Luf wanted to take off as soon as the Spads were fueled and their guns loaded and checked. He told John to bring an oxygen tank.

At 3:00 p.m., they left the field at Chaudun in the direction of La Fère, almost due north. Lufbery chose the route. Richthofen's Circus had moved to a field within range near Saint-Quentin. Not having seen the Baron in the dogfight over Ypres, Raoul was primed to hunt for him and his bloodred Fokker on his own terms by stalking his field from above. He led John in a circling climb that edged closer to La Fère.

Abreast and at high altitude, John saw Saint-Quentin long before they were close to it. Where his scars were still fresh, wind began to burn his face. The pain was worse than he'd experienced when he was first cut. He shifted his scarf to cover his throbbing cheeks. Warm breath exhaled from his nose and open mouth gave rhythmic relief. Raoul steadily climbed. Oxygen masks became necessary. John didn't mind. The mask kept the wind from his cheeks.

Curious about their altitude, John rubbed a layer of frost from the altimeter to check the dial. He'd seen the needle at nearly four miles only once before. To convince himself the reading was true, he tapped the lens. The needle wiggled slightly and came to rest where it was before. His fingers grew numb and then his toes. Worse, the inside of his goggles kept fogging in the cold damp air. Feeling light-headed, he consciously pumped his lungs to get more oxygen into them. *Lufbery hunts awfully high*, John thought. Had he known, he'd have asked Charles to warm the oxygen tank before leaving. Even so, both men couldn't stay that high very long.

The Spad ran well enough, but John worried that the cold might stiffen the oil in the Vickers, causing it to jam. He fired three rounds to test them and warm them up. Lufbery looked when he heard John's guns. He nodded to John and then tested his own. The guns on both planes worked. To his own patient routine of checking ammo, John had told Charles to oil the acting metal surfaces of the Vickers. The time was well spent. Months had passed since it had last failed. Raoul finally leveled off just under twenty-one thousand feet.

Clouds were wispy at that height. Below, heavier broken clouds hovered over the ground, partially obscuring Saint-Quentin. The sky looked empty of planes. Minutes later, over the town, Raoul edged ahead of John's Spad and pointed nearly straight down. John quarter rolled his Spad for a better view and immediately saw five brightly colored airplanes about five thousand feet below, literally appearing out of thin air. All five were fighters.

The lead machine was bright scarlet. Richthofen was fond of advertising his Fokker Dr.I triplane. Once again, he was flying with his *jasta*. John's heartbeat quickened. The sight of the staggered V formation troubled him. Five against two were not the best odds against Richthofen's *jasta*. He couldn't help feeling a little rusty. It seemed like he hadn't fought for months, instead of weeks. John looked toward Lufbery. He'd begun to circle. John followed.

Below, the sight of Richthofen leading his entourage gave the impression of the kaiser's imperial guard following the royal procession. They were the most successful *jasta* the war had produced. John completely forgot about the cold, thin air. That no longer mattered, not here and not now. His thoughts focused on the menace below and on what Lufbery had planned for it. Instinctively, he scanned the area and noticed a second flight.

Pulling ahead of Raoul, he pointed ahead of the Baron's patrol. Below the Baron, four planes flew ahead. Two were fighters flying above two observers. Richthofen was flying cover for all four planes. The two fighters immediately covering the observers were not enough to discourage a small group of Allied fighters. To John, it looked like a trap. The observation planes were meant to lure

Allied planes into attack. Planes that attacked might only see the two covering planes and give the Baron a chance to spring the trap from above. Lufbery had seen the Baron do it before, and it was why he'd led John to maximum altitude. He signaled John to follow him. John drifted behind Lufbery's Spad. They'd discussed Raoul's plan of attack briefly before takeoff. Lufbery had stressed the element of surprise.

If the Circus was flying, Lufbery said it was likely they'd encounter the Baron flying high, covering a patrol flying low. As the Spad leading the attack, Lufbery would scatter the Baron's fighters by surprise. If successful, single combat was likely for a short time. If the formation didn't break up, they'd pass through Richthofen's JG-1, the Flying Circus, and attack whatever was below, whether fighters or observers. Surprise must be total, made with speed and as much aggression as their Spads brought to the battle.

Regardless of what they found, Raoul's intention was to punish JG-1. The low group was not his concern. Whatever happened, John felt the action must be brief. Combat normally forced planes to lower altitudes. The two fighters below Richthofen would have time to climb and join the fight. Extended contact meant risking a hail of crossfire from every German plane as they lost altitude. Their only advantage was surprise. Until the Circus realized that they were only being attacked by two fighters, Lufbery and John would have the advantage.

Banking left, Lufbery came behind the Baron's squadron headed southwest toward a British sector over Montdidier. His throttle wide open, Lufbery raced to put the sun behind him for his final approach. John's heart pounded. Each beat expanded veins in his forehead and neck. His cheeks throbbed at each beat, and his stomach knotted and nearly heaved. John copied Lufbery's wide, banking turn. He needed to become a falcon, about to grapple with its prey. The last time his stomach felt this way, he'd just shot down his first enemy plane. The return of the old feeling came as an unpleasant surprise. *Am I ready to fight?*

Perhaps it was just nerves, as it had been then. But no, he wasn't nervous. The nausea came from the anticipation of his first fight in weeks. That mattered little now. Every Allied pilot knew the record of JG-1. Fighters often avoided engagement with the Baron's squadron. The odds John and Lufbery risked were evident to them even before they took off. John knew that death came more often to green, unwary pilots, pilots who allowed themselves to be surprised. Those who attacked with surprise always had the initial advantage. Today, it was their turn. The trap set by the Baron might trap him.

At that thought, John's stomach grew calm, and the cool concentration of a falcon eyeing a flock of luckless pigeons masked any concern over the odds. It was how he'd felt when he'd surprised the pilots over Metz. They'd discovered their peril an instant before they died. It occurred to him that Richthofen had probably known the feeling too, maybe more often than either he or Lufbery. Surprise was his favorite tactic. His victims often never saw their executioner. Lufbery's plan became crystal clear. He was using Richthofen's own tactics against him.

For nearly four minutes, Lufbery edged ahead of Richthofen. The pale clouds above Lufbery and John matched the color of the Spad's underwings. They hadn't been seen. Only sharp eyes looking above could spot them. The Baron and his men were paying attention to the planes below. None expected attack from above. At this point, Lufbery's plan was working well.

Soon the Spads arrived at the ideal spot for attack out of the sun. Lufbery raised his left hand in a fist and began a gentle, gliding dive that slowly increased in pitch as he descended. The sun was directly behind him. John flew directly behind Lufbery, following his every move. One airplane was harder to see than two. They removed their oxygen masks at sixteen thousand feet.

Lufbery covered the distance in less than a minute, though it seemed like hours to John. His dive was aimed directly for the enemy leader. At a hundred yards, Lufbery opened fired on Baron von Richthofen. Instantly, the red triplane lifted out of the line of fire, quicker than John had ever seen an airplane move. Although the Baron eluded the attack, Raoul did succeed in scattering the Fokkers. John had a perfect line on one at the rear of the scattering V. He watched his bullets punch holes in its right wing before it too veered away, rising out of the Vickers's gun sights. John saw Lufbery rising on a lone Fokker.

Looking in his mirror, a red Fokker had spun around to get on John's tail. John knew the Baron was at its controls. John's greater speed gave him the only action he could take to avoid the diving plane. He pulled the stick back as far as it would go, and the Spad shuddered in a climb that caused John's eyesight to tunnel as the blood rushed from his head. Dizzy, he kicked the rudder and stick to the right, rolling out of the climb like a boomerang coming back to its owner. The Baron flew past him not thirty feet away, close enough for John to clearly see the expression on the man's face. The Baron began to climb once more.

John's maneuver had not only saved him but put him in position to attack another Fokker less than a hundred yards below, still recovering from Lufbery's charge. The Fokker's climb would bring it into his sights for a few seconds. John banked to the left to follow its path. At forty yards, he pulled the trigger on the Vickers. Again, he watched bits of fabric tear away from a wing and a tail. The Fokker rolled, and John had to veer to the right to avoid flying beyond, exposing his Spad's tail to its machine guns.

"Damn! These bastards are good!" he said aloud.

The words no sooner left his mouth when holes began to appear in his left wing. Without turning to see his adversary, he snapped the stick back and to the right, putting the Spad in a half roll.

Once again, the Baron flew by, closer than before. John completed the roll. When he leveled out, nothing was in view. He looked for Raoul above and below and saw two German fighters below break away from their observers and climb into the combat. They joined the fight in minutes. The odds began to favor the Germans.

Noticing a melee of planes to his left, he spotted Raoul's Spad at the top of a loop that formed a circle of three with Raoul's Spad between two Fokkers. Without hesitation, John headed for the Fokker behind Lufbery. The Baron was nowhere in sight. As his Spad gained speed in a shallow dive, John approached to meet the Fokker as it reached the bottom of the loop. At sixty yards, the pilot hadn't seen him. He opened fire. The Fokker flew in front of the spitting Vickers. Bullets ripped into the cowling and along the fuselage as the plane flew through the stream of lead. John saw its pilot jerk to the side. The Fokker peeled out of the circle in a steep dive into a cloud trailing black smoke.

Once again, John searched the skies. The Fokkers were widely scattered. Three headed northeast toward their field, but something told John to climb. He pulled the stick back, holding it there as the Spad entered a loop to the left. At the top of the loop, John saw the Baron turning to his right just below. His instinct and training had saved him. He rolled the Spad, putting it in a shallow dive. The engine raced with the throttle of the Spad opened wide. John steadily gained on the red Fokker. Banking left, the maneuver put the Spad on the Baron's tail for the first time.

From the corner of his eye, John saw Lufbery swing around on his right. Luf pointed at his Vickers and drew his fingers across his throat. Raoul was out of ammunition. John hadn't even considered his own. The combat had lasted longer than he'd thought possible. Below, three Fokkers joined the Baron going northeast toward their field. A fourth trailed a thin stream of black smoke. Only then did John notice a large group of British SE5s bearing down on the fleeing Flying Circus. The British entered the chase and wanted a share of the fight. Richthofen led the remainder of his group home with all the speed their new Fokkers could muster. At once relieved, John almost felt disappointed. By John's count, twelve SE5s composed the British squadron. Had they joined the fight earlier, the Flying Circus might never have performed again. At their distance, they had only even odds of catching Richthofen. John throttled back to rejoin Lufbery. Together, they returned to Chaudun. After landing, Lufbery sauntered toward John, wearing a grin. John unbuttoned his flying suit, shivering from the cold and the excitement of the dogfight.

"John, after today, the Baron is going to have to scratch you off his list. You're just too tough to bring down. I don't think he liked seeing you on his tail. By the way, thanks for taking that Fokker off mine. He was beginning to become a real pest."

"My pleasure, Luf. We found a big hole in his trap, didn't we? He may have to rethink his tactics. I think those British fliers would have to get lucky to catch up to him. If they do, he'll wish he hadn't returned to combat so soon."

"I agree. But I don't think they'll get him. They were nearly a mile out when I saw them. The Circus was leaving town in a hurry! Can I buy you a cup of coffee?"

Lufbery flashed his rare smile, and John laughed at the parody. It was as close as Lufbery came to telling a joke. John appreciated Raoul's pleasure at bettering the Baron in a dogfight. They'd downed two of his fighters and scared the others away.

"Anytime, Luf. You know, for a while there, he almost had my initials on his wall. They're the best I've even seen. Next time, we should try with the whole squadron. They scattered, but they outnumbered us when they recovered."

"Maybe so, John. It'd take their edge away. This much I know. If those pilots weren't that good, they'd have been so many targets for us to hit. We'd have knocked down two or three more before they ran off. The V formation gives them a punch, but it didn't help them today. Surprise had them beat. We proved that when you smoked that bastard on my tail."

It was an interesting point. By design, fighters could only fire straight ahead. In a fight, a pilot could only deal with one opponent at a time even when many planes were fighting. Logically, airplanes would have to evolve into even faster machines with weapons that fired at targets without having to aim the airplane at them. Fighters with fixed guns were limited to what came into their gun sights. Advances in aeronautics had only had a dozen years to progress, and most had advanced because the air war demanded it.

"I was thinking, Luf. Future fighters will make a Spad look like a child's toy."

Lufbery wasn't thinking in those terms. "Maybe so. First, we've got to win this one. If it ends now, there won't be a country in Europe that'll want any part of another war. This one's been too costly, the worst ever. The next? I hope I'm not around to see it."

"Let's get some coffee, Luf. I haven't shaken off the cold, and my face hurts like hell. You sure like flying high! For a while there, I thought I was going to empty my oxygen tank."

Lufbery was right. The war still needed to be won. Maybe then, when the world had time to reflect, men might realize that war was so wasteful, so abhorrent, that they'd pause before starting another war. John's educational background embodied too much history to believe the world was likely to abandon war. Millennia of war had never deterred man from inviting its consequences. No war in history had constrained men from engaging in war. War, and those who waged it, had become more mobile, more destructive, and deadlier. History had proven that man's ambition could turn toward war as easily as war made him turn toward peace.

The Lafayette Escadrille spent its last Christmas near La Cheppe. By the middle of February 1918, it had dissolved into the new American units. Rickenbacker was right. They needed pilots who'd flown in combat with the French. The American school for pilots at Issoudun was a muddy field with a few buildings planted on it. Their training required only slightly more solo time than the British schools. Most trainees averaged two dozen hours before going to gunnery school at Cazaux in southern France. The time spent to train American pilots was a third of what John received at Pau, and training in combat flying tactics lacked in both quantity and quality.

American pilots learned combat flying techniques largely on patrol. Those who survived long enough became leaders. Both Major Raoul Lufbery and Captain John Morris preceded Lieutenant Eddie Rickenbacker into the US Ninety-Fourth Pursuit Squadron by two months.

Thirteen miles west of Châlons-sur-Marne, the aerodrome at Villeneuve served as base for the newly formed Ninety-Fourth and Ninety-Fifth Squadrons. Major John Huffer commanded the Ninety-Fourth. He'd lived in France for many years and was a pilot in the Lafayette Flying Corps, a large group of American fliers, many collected by Dr. Gros.

The squadron's secondhand Nieuport 28s arrived unarmed from the French and were still unarmed when flight leader Raoul Lufbery led the first American fighter patrol over the German lines. Lieutenants Eddie Rickenbacker and Douglas Campbell were the fliers he selected for a routine training patrol to take off in the clear skies of early March 1918.

Lufbery knew that his protégés were without machine guns. Their first flight exposed them to no danger that Lufbery hadn't planned for them. He flew his wingmen straight over the antiaircraft batteries guarding Suippes. Lufbery made similar flights with many of the pilots who joined the group. John knew what Lufbery was up to and simply shook his head.

"Think of it as a baptism, John. They've got to learn there's a hell of a lot more to worry about from enemy fighters up there than the damned antiaircraft fire. If they panic flying over a few puffs of smoke, they shouldn't be up there in the first place."

"I know, Luf. But it's a hell of a way to break them into patrol. They're probably spooked already. They haven't got guns."

Lufbery grinned. "I don't. Don't worry about it, John. I'll take care of them."

Again, Lufbery took off with his fledglings. Rickenbacker suffered an acute attack of nausea trying to copy Lufbery's corkscrew flying pattern and maneuvers he hadn't even experienced on a roller coaster. Until his plane shook from antiaircraft shells over Suippes, Rick had to fight the urge to evacuate his stomach in his Nieuport. For all his prior training, he hadn't entirely won the battle of the breadbasket.

On returning to the field, Lufbery quizzed the visual acuity in his wingman.

"What did you see up there, Rickenbacker?"

"Nothing much, Major. Except for the archie, the sky was clear, sir."

Raoul had a different story, culled from experience and a more observant perspective.

"Well, aside from the five Spads I saw after we took off, five more flew by fifteen hundred feet below us. Not long after we passed the antiaircraft, four Albatroses crossed in front of us, and an enemy two-seater flew by closer than those."

Rickenbacker was skeptical of the revelations. "I didn't see anything like that, sir."

To prove his point, Lufbery took Rickenbacker and the others to Rick's Nieuport and began poking his finger through the holes in its tail and wings. One bullet had gone through both wings very near Rick's cockpit, inches from where he sat.

"That one damned near shot you a new asshole, Lieutenant. I advise all of you to stop concentrating so hard on flying and to start looking beyond the formation. Otherwise, the Germans will see to it that your careers aren't long enough for you to brag about! Understood?"

"Yes, sir!" the men chorused, duly chastised.

Later, Lufbery mentioned the problem to John. John attempted to defend their inexperience.

"Luf, you know as well as I do that those guys have barely been in the air before today. They're still worried about staying in formation. Maybe you did them a favor. They know those holes weren't put there by termites. You can bet they'll start concentrating on what's going on around them the next time they go up."

Rickenbacker had respect for Lufbery's flying skill and went up with him whenever he could. He practiced the corkscrew and eventually overcame his air sickness. Until their guns arrived, they couldn't fly aggressive patrols, so time was spent gaining flying experience. For Rickenbacker, the dividends would accrue very soon.

In the foggy predawn of March 21, *Der Tag*, "the Day," was announced with the thundering of thousands of German artillery pieces firing for five hours, many brought from the Russian front after the Russians signed the Treaty of Brest-Litovsk. General Ludendorff had thousands of fresh troops to deploy from the eastern front to launch Operation Michael. The German spring offensive of 1918 produced a fury that decimated British and French lines. The war's tide had turned. The attack bore very heavily on a fifty-mile front from Arras to La Fère, the sector opposed by the British Fifth Army. The object was to split the French and British lines, isolating one from the other. Accompanied by fog and poison gas, the shelling blinded the British. Those without masks died. Those who wore them saw little through their lenses. Fog, smoke, gas, and the sweat of English brows obscured their field of fire.

Positions from which General Haig had intended to provide flanking fire were useless against attackers who couldn't be seen. Before the Tommies could take aim, the enemy was upon them. Haig had not invited use of the new French defensive tactics. As a result, the British line was not designed to yield and quickly became indefensible. His army was overrun.

Belfort

For the third time since entering France, Catherine was on a train. She was alone. Her thoughts drifted between her mission and her brothers. Running into Michael had been pure luck. Running into John was unlikely. Colonel Conner hadn't said how long she'd be impersonating the hotel manager's daughter. She might be in Belfort for weeks. Before leaving Chaumont, Conner briefed her once again on the town, the hotel, her French father, and her presumed background.

"From now on, you are Claudie Giraud. Your father, Arnaud, owns and operates the hotel. For nearly a year, without the knowledge of its residents, he's worked for the French in the l'Hôtel du Sud Vosges. He is a widower. For months, he's been bragging about his daughter studying English at the Sorbonne in Paris. He's been complaining that she hasn't sent pictures, her letters arrive late, and the war has prevented her from visiting. After four years, he barely remembers what she looks like. Now that she's graduated, he expects her to come home."

Just before she left, a deadly serious Fox Connor advised, "Listen closely, but don't show undue interest in anything you hear, Miss Giraud. Stay alert. Avoid conversation about yourself or the war. A young girl in your position is more interested in meeting young men."

The colonel's last piece of advice came a bit more awkwardly.

"One more point. Your appearance. You are quite attractive. Avoid using makeup. Wear glasses if you have them. Style your hair like a girl from a small French town. Make yourself inconspicuous. You're hardly a woman who ... well ... who doesn't do that. I don't want you to draw undue attention, or you may come into contact with men who have less than honorable intentions. For your own safety, the less attention you draw, the better!"

Catherine managed a smile. "I understand, Colonel. Thank you for the compliment." Catherine took a pair of reading glasses from her purse.

"I normally use these to read. I'll wear them if you wish."

"Good. That's much better. Perhaps a change of clothes. Something less revealing. Use your own judgment. Good luck, Miss Giraud!"

As advised, Catherine changed clothes and hired a small buggy to take her to the station, bought a ticket, and carried her smaller bag to the platform. The buggy driver brought two others. Conner advised her not to get a separate berth but to blend in with the passengers. In spite of her new confidence, the fact that she might come in contact with German intelligence agents prompted wariness on her part. She'd never dreamed that she'd become a counterspy on General Pershing's staff. Male passengers who so much as glanced at her caused her discomfort. Nothing supported a feeling that she was being watched, but she simply couldn't get the idea out of her mind. The blame, she knew, lay in the nature of her assignment. She was not a practiced actor, and the part she was to play wasn't on a stage. That thought, and the fact that she was on her way, sent a nervous shiver up her spine. Catherine straightened her back, cleared her throat, and boarded the train. For the first time, her fate lay solely in her hands.

The train followed the Marne southeast toward the Vosges. After a stop in Langres, it entered the foothills of the mountains she'd seen approaching from a distance. She lost herself in the passing scenery as the train slowly made its way toward the mountains. The scenery was lush, beautiful, and showed little sign of war. The regular pace of the train nearly put her to sleep by the time it crossed the Saône.

In Lure, she took time to detrain. On her way to a small refreshment stand near the platform, she noticed a schedule for northbound trains. One of the stops was Luxeuil. In a rare letter, John had told her that the Lafayette Escadrille had gotten started there before he'd joined. Sipping a tepid, lemon-flavored tea she'd bought at the refreshment stand, Catherine wondered where he might be now. She hadn't received a letter for some time.

The train's bell interrupted her thoughts. The time to board the train had come.

A middle-aged man sat next to her before the train reached Ronchamp. He began a conversation by giving his name as Gauthier Robleur, a French name. He told her he lived in the Vosges and compared their beauty to the bolder majesty of the Swiss Alps. When he asked for her name, she had to think for an uncomfortable instant.

"Claudie Giraud," she replied, speaking fluent French.

Robleur said he liked her name and continued to carry on a rather one-sided conversation. "I had a farm near Ypres until the Germans forced my family from the farm and used it as their headquarters."

Catherine continued to speak in French, saying, "I'm sorry to hear that," and continued to listen. He spoke without emotion. She asked no questions. His monologue made questions unnecessary. She assumed he'd either reconciled his loss or had made a better life in the mountains. Her thoughts wandered between listening politely to the man and concern for her two brothers.

She became aware of his curious accent. His occasional transposition of time and place was unlike the French she'd learned or heard in Paris. Perhaps his manner of speech was common to his former home. She simply didn't know. She'd learned formal, less colloquial French. His conversation continued, interspersed with an occasional acknowledgment from her. He asked from where she came.

"I've been in Paris at the university, studying English."

Gauthier suddenly switched from French to English. "And your destination, Claudie?"

Catherine felt obligated to reply in English. "Belfort, sir. I'm going home from to see my father."

She again noticed his eyes jumping from her bosom to her eyes.

"Perhaps I will see you there. My home is south of Belfort, below the river Doubs in Montbéliard. Often I go to Belfort to shop, but I prefer a smaller town where people know you."

Catherine took the colonel's advice and did not respond. She was becoming annoyed by his more obvious attention. She turned her head toward the window and made a comment on the scenery, completely changing the subject of conversation.

Sensing the conversation had ended, Gauthier, excused himself and returned to his seat as the train entered Belfort. The Rue Thiers was only a block from the station. Catherine tipped an enterprising French boy to carry her larger bags. She took the smaller one herself.

Conner had called Arnaud to alert him of her arrival. He described her without giving her real name. His description wasn't necessary since Arnaud rarely saw young ladies enter the hotel alone, certainly not with three bags. He greeted Claudie as he would a daughter after a long absence, especially an only child. Arnaud took his new daughter to her room. Though curious about her origin, he was told not to ask her anything about her true identity. He spoke to her in somewhat broken English, briefly explaining that after his wife was killed, he wanted to join the French army. Because of his age and health, the army turned him down.

"Your wife was killed?" she asked. Arnaud became gloomy. His voice trembled.

"It's not a story I want to tell. Our little inn was in Revigny," he said, staring blankly at the floor. "When the Germans came, they burned the houses except those used by the officers. Our inn was spared. Their dislike for the French was obvious. They tied my hands and feet and forced me to watch them rape my wife. It was horrible! I could do nothing! When they finished with her, they murdered her." His voice cracked. "They forced me to dig her grave behind the inn." He paused and stared at the floor. What he saw wasn't on the floor. He wiped away tears with the back his hand.

The story shocked Catherine. A combination of pity, horror, anger, and a feeling of utter disbelief came to her at the inhumanity of the deed. Speechless, she waited for him to speak. He hadn't described how they'd killed her. Catherine didn't ask. Arnaud had never described the event in full, not even to French authorities. How does one maintain composure to describe the path the bayonet took though her chest, or if she was dead before the second thrust came?

"I worked like a slave for them. They never let me leave their sight—not even to relieve myself. Their leader said they'd let me go when they left. But the officer guarding me said they'd shoot me if they were forced to leave the town. They shot me when the town was taken by the French Fifteenth Corps. In the haste to leave, he fired only once. He thought I was dead or going to die."

After his wound healed, Arnaud demanded that the French army let him fight. Once again, they said no. His wound wouldn't allow him to keep up with the younger men. When the Americans came, he begged them to let fight with their army.

"They told me about the hotel in Belfort. They gave me money to buy the hotel. I was told to operate the hotel and wait for instructions. I was to keep my eyes and ears open. I left Revigny and the little inn we had run since our marriage. One day I will return and lay a wreath on her grave. Here, I may chance to avenge her murder. I am sorry if this upset you, Claudie. Perhaps I should not tell you my story."

She'd read of German atrocities in Belgium. The German government denied everything, saying it was war propaganda designed to stir anger against Germany and bring America into the war on the Allied side. The doubt the denial created mitigated the validity of the reports in the eyes its readers. Americans reacted with condemnation, but America maintained neutrality. Arnaud's tale ended all doubt.

Catherine began to cry. Arnaud comforted her as he would a true daughter, sorry that he had shown the anguish in his loss. He stayed with her until she was calm. Catherine abhorred war. After hearing his story, she hated it even more. She couldn't believe the kaiser would condone such behavior. For the first time, she couldn't suppress the idea that America should have entered the war sooner. Perhaps an earlier entry might have prevented crimes like those against Arnaud.

Later, he took her on a tour of the hotel that included the lounge where she'd act as hostess.

"Make our customers happy. Smile. Be friendly."

Under Arnaud, the hotel lounge became a fashionable place to go. Travelers from Switzerland on their way to Paris came often. For days, Arnaud introduced his regular guests to his daughter and made her aware of those who were strangers to him.

His success allowed Arnaud to hire a small group of local musicians who played popular songs in the evening. They even played German tunes that became popular on both sides of the front. "La Marseillaise" always closed the lounge to a cheering crowd. When she entered the lounge that night, they were playing "The Japanese Sandman," and many of the regulars were dancing.

Catherine began to enjoy her new role in spite of its latent danger. Several French and American military officers had already made playful advances. To discourage them, she invented a boyfriend in Paris. One evening, to her surprise, Mr. Gauthier Robleur walked into the lounge looking for his train companion. He complained of loneliness and told her he'd come to Belfort for a few days.

"I needed a change," he said in English. "It is good to see you again."

Catherine brought him a drink and was about to leave when he grabbed her arm, insisting she stay and talk.

"But I have other guests."

"They will wait, Claudie. Tell me about your study at the university."

"I studied to become a teacher of English. It was what I wanted to do."

"Ah, yes. A teacher," Robleur said. "I must speak English in the market near Calais. I once sold ham from my farm. Before the war, the tourists came to the market from England. I know the English from many years selling to them. I speak not well in English, but the tourists like my ham. I sold a dark beer also. Now, I make no beer."

He spoke with the same atypical syntax as his French. She thought the syntax odd. He seemed to struggle with the both languages. She humored him, staying alert to guard against revealing ownership of an American accent.

"You speak English well enough, considering how you learned, Mr. Robleur. Did you live in Calais long?"

"No, Claudie. Saint-Omer. Weekends, I go to Calais to sell in the market," he explained, immediately dropping the subject. Abruptly, he returned to speaking in French.

"When the war starts, my family was gone. I came alone to the Vosges."

"Well, it was nice to see you again, but please excuse me. I must attend to the other customers."

"I wait for you. When you come, you will bring another drink."

His interest seemed as unnatural to her as his speech. The juxtaposition of time before action or action before place was more common to the German language. She might have noticed it sooner were she from France. Catherine had taken a short course in German at high school. Robleur's syntax was closer to German syntax. Still, the fact that he said he'd originally come from the coast near Belgium might explain it. Belgians were known for being multilingual. Many Belgians were fluent in Flemish, French, English, and German.

Catherine noticed his hands as he sipped his Moselle. They weren't the hardened hands of a farmer. His fingers were long and slender, more like her father's. Wearing glasses with round lenses, he reminded her more of a mathematics teacher than a farmer. His choice of clothing suggested nothing of the farmer but closer to an overworked bank clerk. Was his attention toward her the interest of a lonely widower? If so, he was a harmless, lonely man who simply needed to become socially integrated into his new home.

Seeing that she was free, Arnaud called her to a side of the lounge away from the crowd. A message had arrived for her from Chaumont.

"I do not understand it." Certain they were away from unwanted ears, he quietly relayed the message exactly as he'd heard over the telephone.

"A man said the general was successful. Colonel C. is not coming, but Colonel A. C. will arrive soon."

"Was that all?"

"Yes. That was all he said."

"When did the message arrive?"

"Less than an hour ago."

As Catherine understood it, Pershing had succeeded in convincing Foch to let him command his army and assigned him a sector. Fox Conner would not be coming but was sending someone called A. C. to Belfort. She supposed Pershing wanted Conner to stay in Chaumont, and he was sending someone to contact her in his place.

When she returned to the lounge, she saw no sign of Robleur. His glass was empty. He hadn't stayed for another. Catherine was relieved. She had time to mingle with other guests. Most of them were in French uniforms, but several wore American uniforms. Their discussions centered on the latest war news and local activities rumored to be related to the war. She heard one say that four American officers were seen walking toward the Belfort Gap. Others had seen them, as well.

Speculation was growing that they were sent to map the area in preparation for an Allied attack toward the Rhine. Their conversations usually ended when she approached. The snippets she'd overheard indicated that American officers were nosing around the countryside. The Belfort Gap wasn't exactly nearby, so it was unlikely that they would walk for hours simply to enjoy the scenery.

The next day, Colonel A. C. Conger arrived from Chaumont. He told Arnaud that he'd taken a few days' leave to relax at the hotel. He asked that a bottle of whiskey be brought to his room and specifically requested that it be brought to him by the young hostess he'd seen in the lounge. Conger's room was on the second floor, two doors from Catherine's across the hall. Catherine brought a bottle and small glass on a serving tray.

She found it difficult to control her excitement. Was Colonel Conger the man Conner sent in his place? If so, she hoped he'd brought news of John as Conner had promised. Her knock broke the silence inside his room.

Conger cracked the door open just enough to see his visitor. Without saying a word, he looked down both ends of the hallway. Satisfied that no one else was about, he said, "Come in, miss." Before closing it behind, he again he looked down each end of the hall. Conger was a cautious man.

Catherine's question wouldn't wait. "Did Colonel Conner send you?" Before he could answer, she added, "I hope you came with news of my brother John."

Conger immediately disappointed her by placing a finger across his lips. "Quietly. The colonel is awaiting a communiqué confirming his location from the French air service. Security prevents them from divulging the location of a squadron over a phone line. The colonel won't know until he receives word. They'd only say his name wasn't on the last casualty list. Conner said your other brother wrote to the embassy in Paris."

Conger handed her a copy of the letter from his jacket pocket and waited as she read it. Michael mentioned his appointment to an aid station. Censorship prevented him from specifying its location. Finding John, he said, would be difficult. The staff at Chaumont wasn't currently on the best of terms with French military authorities. He suggested that she might have better luck finding him through the Red Cross. Catherine's disappointment showed.

"Let me know when the colonel receives word."

"Of course. You can rest your mind on that. If I know Conner, miss, he'll keep pestering them until he gets an answer."

The colonel shifted the discussion to the purpose of his trip. He was told to use her French name.

"Miss Giraud, have you noticed anyone exhibiting unusual interest in the movements of American military personnel in the area, anyone speculating on our war plans?"

The change in topic refocused her attention. She tried to remember what she'd observed in the brief time she'd been here.

"I overheard several French and American officers talking about American officers they'd seen walking toward the Belfort Gap. They seemed to believe the officers were gathering information, possibly for an attack through the gap."

Awaiting his reaction, she'd omitted the description of the officers. She didn't wish to cause them unnecessary trouble. Conger didn't ask for their names, ranks, or descriptions.

"Is that all? Nothing else?"

"I can't be sure. I suppose I ought to mention the old gentleman I met on the train. I saw him again yesterday. He said he lived near Ypres and then moved to Montbéliard."

"He certainly didn't walk to Belfort. Montbéliard is about fifty kilometers north of here. Did he approach you, or did you approach him?"

"I certainly did not! He sat next to me on the train to Belfort. I was looking out a window. He opened the conversation. I didn't like him or his attention."

"Other than the train, had you ever seen him before?"

"No. He insisted we speak last night. I finally had to excuse myself to serve other guests. He asked me to bring him a drink when I returned, but he'd gone without saying another word."

"I see. French intelligence advised us a week or so ago that some civilians in or around Ypres reported that a stranger, a middle-aged man, was asking questions about the movements of Allied troops in the area. They investigated, but he didn't turn up. Unfortunately, reports like that are common these days. Most are either false or meant to cause trouble for personal reasons. Nevertheless, we look into them. Tell me what he spoke to you about from the beginning."

"Well, I remember getting off the train to get a lemonade. He sat next to me after I boarded the train. The train left Langres before he spoke to me. His conversation was quite ordinary."

"Tell me about his ordinary conversation."

"It was quite innocent, really. He asked my name, of course. I told him Claudie Giraud. He said he'd lost his wife and his farm and came to live in Montbéliard. He said he preferred small towns to large towns."

"Did he give you his name?"

"Yes, Walter Robleur."

"Walter Robleur?"

"Sorry. I'm so used to translating. His name is Gauthier, French for 'Walter.'" She was becoming unsettled by the interrogation. She thought Robleur was a curious, lonely old man but quite harmless.

Conger noticed her discomfort.

"You're doing fine, miss," Conger said with a reassuring grin. "I want you to be sure about this. Exactly when was the first time you remember seeing him?"

Surprised by the question, she tried to remember. "I really wasn't paying any attention to him, Colonel." She paused. "I believe it was near Lure." Glimmers of her trip grudgingly returned. "No, wait. I remember passing him in the aisle when I boarded the train in Chaumont."

"That's important." Conger paused again and thought.

Catherine noted Conner's highly detailed interest in the man.

"Did you tell him you'd come from Paris?"

"Why, yes. I'm quite sure I told him that I'd come from the university and was going to Belfort. He spoke French in an unfamiliar way, somewhat strange to me."

"You say he initiated the conversation. He probably told you exactly where he once lived. Did he say where he came from originally?"

"I can't remember. He mentioned Saint-Omer. He said he sold ham and beer to the soldiers in a market in Calais."

Bits of the puzzle were starting to come together. Conger's suspicion was growing.

"What of his family?"

"He said they were gone."

"Did he say how he lost his family?"

"No. He said the Germans evicted them from his farm."

"I don't suppose he told you any more about his family."

"No, he didn't. How did you know?"

"We're able to verify most civilian deaths by asking neighbors or coworkers. You've done very well, miss. Your work is just beginning. The colonel told me to take you to the next step if you'd met anyone suspicious. To be what he claims to be, Mr. Robleur would be the luckiest refugee I've ever heard about. If he was forced to evacuate his farm, he'd have very little money in his pockets to buy a home clear across France, even without a family. I'm unaware of any refugee who's that fortunate! What's more, he didn't have to come all this way to find a small town. I count him as very suspicious."

Conger's deductions made sense. The idea that Robleur may not be who he claimed sent a shiver up her spine. If he was an enemy spy, she'd been exposed to a German agent before she'd even arrived in Belfort! The thought had unsettling implications.

Conger partially revealed American intentions and hinted at a plan to discover who Robleur actually was. "As Colonel Conner probably made you aware, Pershing wants to lead his army into battle as its sole commander. If Robleur is what I suspect he is, it's up to us to see that he is either uninformed or misinformed. If he's a German agent, he will almost certainly have contacts in Switzerland and probably one or more here in Belfort.

"The officers you mentioned earlier are doing what they were told to do. The French are not aware. I remind you that what I'm telling you is strictly secret. We are trying to convince French soldiers and any German spies in Belfort that an attack will come through the Belfort Gap toward the Rhine. That's what we want them to believe. I can't say any more. Now, Miss Giraud, I understand you can type."

"Yes. Is there something you want me to type for you?"

"No. Not now. You can expect another visit from this man. When that happens, my behavior may seem a bit strange to you. It aids our deception. I want you to treat me exactly as you would any man exhibiting that behavior. However, if I ask you to type a letter for me, you must agree to do so. Do you understand?"

"Not exactly, Colonel. But I will do as you say."

"Good. I don't want to scare you, miss, but I must warn you that Robleur may suspect you are not who you seem to be. You said you came from the university in Paris. He may have seen where you boarded the train in Chaumont. That could complicate our mission. He'll wonder why you boarded in Chaumont. Everyone knows Chaumont is headquarters of the AEF. He'll need to verify who you are and probably ask questions designed to find flaws in your response.

"We must assume he's been sent here to learn our plans. His estimation of you will be crucial to believing anything he learns from you either directly or indirectly. To put it simply, if he's what I think he is, he must be convinced that you are who and what you say you are. If he's not convinced, you could be in danger."

At that, she felt her heart beat faster. Tiny beads of sweat formed on her brow, and her stomach began to quarrel with her. Catherine had never seriously imagined she'd ever be in real danger. Conger noticed a reddish glow on her cheeks and neck.

"I'm sorry to be so blunt about this, miss, but spies are not nice people. What they do to women they claim to be spies was demonstrated when they executed Edith Cavell. They deal very harshly with those who get in their way. If I'm wrong, you have nothing to worry about. If I'm right, he must be convinced. I don't want German intelligence to decide your future!"

Spoken plainly, the colonel's warning struck her like a slap in the face. Catherine now realized the import of her assignment and its real danger. Thoughts of her older brother helped calm her. Any risk to her was less than what John experienced for the last two years. Gathering herself, she was resigned to see the thing through to the end. Hesitation changed into a feeling of purpose. Pleased by the change, she realized she had control of her fear. She felt closer to her brothers than she'd ever felt in Guilford.

"I understand, Colonel. You can depend on me."

"Good."

"Colonel, why wouldn't he be asking questions of the soldiers that come here? Why me?"

"He knows every soldier has been ordered not to speak to civilians about the war. If they did, they'd face a court-martial. Besides, he'd expose himself by asking questions of them. As their hostess, you have contact with them every day. You're in the best position to overhear them speaking to each other. He'd want to know whether you heard anything of value to him. It's up to us to see to it that he learns what we want him to learn. That's why he must know whether he can trust that you are who you say you are."

"I see. You've made it all very clear, Colonel. Thank you."

"You needn't thank me, miss. It's I who must thank you."

Preparation

COLONEL CONGER'S WARNING WAS ON Catherine's mind when she awoke the following morning. The night before, when Gauthier Robleur had left his table, she'd scanned the lounge looking for him. She was puzzled by his disappearance. Gauthier had said that he wanted to speak to her once she'd finished serving the others. No one said that they had seen him leave.

Unsure who'd be knocking at her door so early, she asked, "Who is it?"

"Your father. Claudie, I must ask you to take the bicycle into town. The kitchen needs fresh fruit. The shipment from the valley of the Doubs should have arrived yesterday. Sometimes it comes late. This time of the year, fresh fruit can be impossible to find."

Winter was only a month away in the Vosges. The last was awful.

Since the colonel was here, Catherine saw no reason to refuse his request. She hadn't much to do until evening when the lounge would be filled. She asked Arnaud for directions to the market.

"It's on the quay. Go east on the Rue Thiers, cross the canal, and follow the road north."

Using Arnaud's bicycle, Catherine took his directions to the small outdoor market that opened on the weekend. She put the bicycle among others parked by a row of trees.

Her first visit to an open-air market since the trip to New York, she wished Monroe was with her to help choose fruit. None of the melons looked very good. Only seasonal fruit seemed worth buying. Apples and peaches were plentiful. Down one aisle, she found blackberries. Vendors put the fruit in small paper bags after either weighing it on spring scales or counting fruit she'd handpicked. Catherine employed the French habit of bartering for lower prices. She recalled Conger's warning of the possible presence of other spies and employed the practice to authenticate her role to those nearby. Finished, she carried the bags to the bicycle and put them in the wicker baskets straddling the rear tire. As she was about to mount, an all-too-familiar voice from behind caused her heart to sink.

"Hello, Claudie. I am glad to see you."

Catherine turned to face Gauthier, doing her best to hide her fright behind an invisible wall of defense that immediately surrounded her. "Mr. Robleur! You startled me."

He carried a small bag of fruit that he'd bought in the market. She took that fact and Robleur's apologetic response to mean that he hadn't followed her but had preceded her to the market.

"I apologize for not waiting last night. A message came. I had to leave. Do you buy fruit for the hotel or for yourself?"

Her heartbeat returned to an uneasy calm. "The hotel. Father sent me to buy fruit." Attempting to make Robleur the topic of conversation, she continued, "I looked for you last night. Is everything all right?"

Gauthier came closer before answering. "Not yet. Time will

make it so. You saw the apples? On the weekend, I buy apples. Now is the best time. They are ripe. What did you buy in Chaumont? You brought only a small bag on the train."

His question instantly revived her fright. He was testing her. His body language revealed no threat, but his eyes were locked on hers. His smile grew narrow, forced, almost a smirk. Colonel Conger's conclusion was correct! Robleur had been suspicious of her from the time she'd entered the train and said she was on her way home from Paris.

Catherine showed no anxiety. Robleur's question had the opposite effect. Conger's warning had given her time to consider responding to questions concerning where she'd boarded the train. The memory of her Victorian father's advice about responding to inquisitive men suggested the tone of her response. Gentlemen didn't pry into a lady's personal affairs! She grew visibly annoyed by his challenge, and her tone displayed annoyance.

"I didn't know you thought I'd bought anything in Chaumont, Mr. Robleur! If you must know, I was looking for a sweater. I've been away from home for years. My old sweater is worn and no longer of any use!"

Whether or not the story satisfied his curiosity remained to be seen. In taking offense at his inquiry, she succeeded in putting Robleur on the defensive. She'd made their conversation a war of words.

To defend the logic of his question, Robleur tried to explain. "But, Claudie, Paris has many shops to sell sweaters. You did not find a sweater in Paris?"

She hadn't anticipated that question. This time, her father's frugality supplied the answer.

"Mr. Robleur, you must know how expensive sweaters are in Paris! My father would punish me if I bought it in Paris. He's warned me more than once that their prices are too high, especially now with the war going on!" A true Frenchman would know.

Gauthier's smirk vanished. He reached into his bag and withdrew an apple. His glance shifted from her eyes to her bosom. He needed time to think. After a bite, he didn't speak until he'd chewed and swallowed. No further questions about Chaumont or Paris arose. His face took on an apologetic look.

"Of course, Claudie. You are quite right. Again, I apologize for last night. I should have left a note, but my business could not wait. I am sorry. I ask too many questions. It is my nature to be curious. A habit of my youth."

"You needn't apologize, Mr. Robleur. Perhaps you will come to the lounge tonight. I've never been to Calais. You could tell me how the market there compares to this one. I must go. Father is waiting."

Her invitation seemed to satisfy any remaining doubt about her. "Thank you, Claudie. Of Calais, I am happy to tell you."

Robleur wiped his hands on a handkerchief and began to walk back to the market. After a taking a few steps, he stopped and turned. He waved. "*Au 'voir*, Claudie." His smile revealed a row of irregular, stained teeth.

Catherine's heart began to beat more normally as she watched him walk away. She mounted the bicycle. She believed that he'd accepted her tale about the sweater. Relieved, she went back to the hotel with mixed feelings about seeing him that evening.

Arnaud helped her carry the fruit into the kitchen. She asked if the colonel was still in his room. Arnaud said that he'd come to breakfast and asked the same question about her. When he told the colonel she'd gone to the market, he'd looked concerned. He wanted to know the minute she returned. Arnaud gave her an apple and told her to take it to the colonel's room.

Guests began to enter the lounge. The morning newspaper had arrived. Catherine took one of the papers and walked toward the stairs. The headline announced that Marshal Foch had given General Pershing sole command of the American First Army.

The article described the ceremony. Generals representing each Allied army attended. Afterward, Pershing returned to French army headquarters at Ligny-en-Barrois. The article didn't speculate on the place or time he might choose to attack. It claimed that he might coordinate his attack with the next French assault.

Catherine remembered seeing a newspaper rolled under Robleur's arm at the market. He was aware of the news. Conger said Robleur needed to trust her. That accounted for his questions.

She knocked at Conger's door.

"Just a moment."

The door opened. At seeing Catherine, Conger quickly inspected the hallway as he'd done before.

"I'm glad you're back. I was worried. It's best you stay in the hotel with Robleur wandering about."

She handed him the apple and the newspaper and told him she'd met Gauthier Robleur at the marketplace by the quay. Conger was visibly distressed by the news.

"Do you think he followed you to the market?"

"No. I believe he'd already bought a bag of apples." Catherine told him about their conversation.

"Are you sure he believed you? It's important that he believe you. I can't explain now, but a lot depends on it."

"I can't be absolutely sure, but I believe he did. He dropped the subject once I'd explained. I suggested he might return to the hotel to tell me about the market in Calais. Was that all right? I hope I haven't overstepped your plans. Oh! And he had a newspaper tucked under his arm."

"Not at all! That's perfect! His knowing about Pershing fits into our plan. Tonight may be our night. If he shows up, we'll know he's interested to learn more. The hotel is the only place in town where he can get information. If he is who I think he is, this will bring him here tonight. Will you be all right? I'm depending on you."

"Yes. I'll be fine."

"Good. Treat him normally. Don't try to get any more information from him than he volunteers. His suspicion would return and give you away. It isn't wise for us to be seen together before tonight. If he comes, you can expect me to show up and ask you about typing. Do you have any questions?"

"No."

The colonel opened the door to check the hallway before Catherine left. Telling Arnaud she was tired, she went to her room. She spent most of the day in the quiet of her room. To occupy time, she began writing a letter to Michael. The prospect of seeing Robleur again worried her. Unable to shake the idea of Robleur's sudden appearances, she locked her door. She never wanted him to surprise her again. If he discovered her letter, it would ruin everything. The consequences for her were best forgotten.

Around noon, she thought she heard someone outside her door. The knock on the door instantly frightened her. Arnaud's voice quashed her fear. He'd brought her a peach and sandwich and asked if she'd eaten. After meeting Robleur earlier, she hadn't thought about eating. She thanked Arnaud for thinking about her. Catherine ate while finishing her letter to Michael. Tired, she lay down. Soon, she was asleep.

Arnaud woke her at six. By seven, she went to the lounge to resume her role as hostess. By ten, Catherine's nerves were on edge. The evening was mostly gone. Gauthier Robleur had not come to the lounge. She couldn't remove the image of his thin, sneering smile from her mind and couldn't help looking at every new arrival. She wondered why he hadn't come. Waiting only made her imagination run wild. Had he believed her? Was he devising some new plan to entrap her? The colonel arrived in the lounge and was engaged in animated conversation with a young French officer at the bar. He didn't seem to notice her.

On weekends, the lounge stayed open until one. The bar stayed open until midnight. Colonel Conger had already sipped three or four drinks to kill time and had ordered another. Many of the customers had left the bar and returned to their tables. In a few hours, the lounge would close. To distract herself, Catherine invited herself to the table of the wife of a local businessman. Their conversation served to distract her as she waited for the man Conger said would certainly come to the lounge. Ten minutes into a discussion on having so many soldiers in town, someone's fingertips touched her shoulder.

"Good evening, Claudie. As promised, we can talk. Please join me at my table."

The combination of his touch and the realization that Robleur had once again arrived unseen from behind sent her heart beating. Sheer will kept her from jumping from her seat.

Annoyed by his stealthy approaches, she immediately said, "Monsieur Robleur. You must stop surprising me from behind!"

He apologized and reminded her of what she'd said on the quay about Calais. She excused herself from the table and accepted his invitation. He led her to a small table near the center of the lounge. To assure her that he was a gentleman, he held her chair as she sat. Robleur sat opposite her. He asked whether she preferred French or English for their conversation and if she wanted a drink.

"Father doesn't like me to drink on duty. If you don't mind, I prefer English. It will give me a chance to refresh my studies. The Americans are the only guests who speak English."

"Ah, yes. Your subject at the university. For coming so late, I am sorry. I had to make several telephone calls. The connections are terrible these days. Have you eaten dinner, Claudie? May I order anything for you?"

"Yes, I have. Please order if you are hungry."

He placed an order for a chicken dinner with potatoes and chard. He asked if she'd like a cup of tea.

"No, thank you, Mr. Robleur. I'm fine."

"You must drink with me, Claudie. Let me order you a small glass of wine. Your father is French! He must allow his daughter to drink wine!"

Catherine relented. He ordered two glasses of a local red wine. After a discussion on the virtues of fruit and the tradition of drinking wine for medicinal purposes, Robleur finally arrived at the subject of Calais.

"In Calais, the soldiers carry rifles. On a clear day, you can see the cliffs of England across the channel. Warships fill the channel. The sea is dangerous."

"War is terrible, Mr. Robleur. I'm glad we live so far from the fighting. When do you think the war will end?"

"The Americans have many soldiers in France. The newspaper said Foch gave General Pershing his wish. His headquarters are in Chaumont, you know. Where you came to the train. Soon, he will take his army against the Germans. Maybe Saint-Mihiel. Maybe here. American officers were seen walking …"

At that moment, an American colonel approached the table and rudely interrupted. It was Colonel Conger. He appeared to be thoroughly drunk.

"Pardon me, folks. My name is Conger. I couldn't help hearing you mention Chaumont, sir. That's my outfit. Anyway, I've been lookin' for Miss Arnaud here. Her father steered me over here. If you're her, miss, I need to borrow you for a short while."

"I beg your pardon! I'm with a gentleman, as you can see." Her response was genuine, the inborn nature of a Victorian upbringing. Conger had told her to respond naturally to any unusual behavior he displayed, and she had done just that.

Gauthier examined the intruder with a mixture of curiosity

and distaste. Catherine's reply saved him the trouble of telling Conger to go away.

"You are Miss Claudie, aren't you?"

"Yes, I am! However, I'm—"

"Good. I'm glad I found you. Your father said you type, miss. Is that true, or was he just bragging? I need somethin' typed up." Conger wobbled as he spoke, looking very drunk.

At this point, Gauthier felt obligated to enter the dialogue to demonstrate a measure of displeasure. "Colonel Conger, I—"

Conger interrupted. "You won't mind if I insis', sir. I been looking for a typis' all day. Miss Claudie, your father said you'd help. I got to get a letter off to Chaumont tonight, or I'll be in lots of trouble. I'm sorry to interrup' your dinner, but this won't take long. How about it, miss? Will you help?"

"I'm sorry, Colonel. I promised Mr. Robleur we would talk." Conger nearly fell over backward. She was supposed to accept his request!

At the mention of Chaumont, Robleur's interest piqued. Since Claudie was doing her best to discourage the colonel, he was forced to change her mind.

"Claudie, perhaps you should help this officer. We must do what we can to win the war. He said it would not take long. We will have much time to talk."

"But it would be rude to leave after you promised to—"

"Please, don't worry. I will finish my dinner and wait here. Go now, Claudie. This may be important."

"Well, if it's all right with you, Mr. Robleur."

"The officer needs your help. We must do what we can to help our soldiers. I will be here when you return."

"Thanks, Mr. Robbler. You're a real patriot. I'll bring her back soon as we're done. Let's go, miss. I'd do it myself, but right now, my vision is a little fuzzy."

The colonel took Catherine's arm and led her away without looking back. When they turned the corner of the stairway, out of Robleur's sight, Conger stopped to peer around the corner. He saw Robleur leave his table and talk briefly to two men sitting at the bar.

In Conger's room, he turned and hugged her, a spontaneous reaction Catherine didn't expect. For her part, the time to breathe normally had come. Her nerves were unsettled even before Robleur arrived in the lounge. After he came, she'd had to consciously suppress them.

"You did say to act normally, Colonel. I hope I did the right thing."

"Miss Giraud, you were perfect! How did you get the idea of putting me off? It was brilliant! He took the bait like a hooked salmon!"

"I didn't plan it that way. I just acted naturally. The way you said."

"It was natural, okay! For a minute, I thought you meant it. I think it convinced him. He must trust you. I heard him mention Saint-Mihiel. What was that all about?"

"He said General Pershing might attack in Belfort or Saint-Mihiel."

"He means the Belfort Gap. Which one was his first choice?"

"Saint-Mihiel."

"Chaumont expected that. Every taxi driver in town says the same. Unfortunately, he's right. Pershing plans to attack Saint-Mihiel. The only thing they don't know is when. Our deception may be the only chance we have to ensure the success of the attack. If we can get them to move just one division, that's a division that we won't have to fight in Saint-Mihiel. We'll wait here awhile, then go back down."

"What about the typing, Colonel?"

"I've already done that, miss. I'll take you downstairs. After tonight, you'll have to stay in Belfort for a while. They may be watching. If you were to leave prematurely, they'd get suspicious. If this works, they won't be very happy with Robleur's information when the fighting starts. Stay on your toes. As long as they think you're okay, you'll be okay. He'll blame me for giving them bad information. If things do go wrong, we'll have to deal with that possibility when it arises."

She was a bit puzzled by his comments.

"Colonel, you said *they* would be watching. Are other German agents working with Mr. Robleur?"

"I'm depending on it! A couple of new guys came into the bar after Robleur arrived. They kept looking toward his table. I saw him talk to them when we left the table. When we go back, don't look at them. We don't want to arouse any suspicion in these men. If Robleur asks, tell him nothing about typing. I'll help you with that. He's bound to ask you about it when I leave. Tell him I made you swear not to talk about it."

Catherine saw Conger remove a carbon from between two sheets of typewritten paper. He balled it up and threw it into the wastepaper basket beside his desk. He folded the two sheets and put them inside an envelope in his jacket pocket.

"Okay. Are you ready?"

"Yes."

As they descended the stairs, he began to thank her for helping him, advertising his gratitude all the way into to the lounge. As promised, Robleur was waiting for her at the table. He stood as she arrived.

"Great job, Miss Claudie. I'm sorry I can't take you with me. Thanks for loaning her out, Mr. Robbler. She saved my neck. Just remember your promise, miss. Don't say anything to anyone, all right? I might need you to type something some other day."

Conger turned and went back to the bar to order another

drink. Robleur sat down. She looked at him, casting her eyes briefly upward as if to say that she was glad to be free of the drunken man. Gauthier grinned, wondering how best to start prying.

"Such an interesting man! He seemed grateful to you, Claudie. Was there much to type?" He asked the question casually, trying to conceal his curiosity. He avoided looking at her, choosing to play with his spoon.

"No. But he made me promise not to say anything about it to anyone. Anyway, it was all in military talk. I didn't understand any of it. I see you finished your dinner."

Robleur smiled, looked toward the bar, and nodded. Catherine didn't turn to look.

"An old friend. He always asks me for money."

"You were talking about Calais before the officer interrupted."

"Yes, Calais. A busy place, very busy."

The conversation renewed, Robleur told her more about Calais and his farm. He said nothing of his supposed family. In fact, none of the details revealed any importance at all.

"It's getting late, Claudie. I must go. In the morning, I will return to Montbéliard. Next weekend, I will see you when I come to Belfort."

With nothing interesting to tell the colonel, she was disappointed. Conger had wanted to try some sort of deception. He hadn't told her what it was or what her part might be. If Robleur was going back to Montbéliard, he'd have no chance to carry out a deception. She could not ask Robleur to stay. That would be out of character and might cause him to revive his suspicion.

"That would be nice, Mr. Robleur." They said good night. Robleur left without so much as offering his hand.

Catherine went to her room. Unable to sleep, she heard footsteps in the hall. A faint knock came at her door. The lounge had closed. She couldn't remember if she'd locked her door. She put on a dressing gown. The knock came again. Her heart began to pound as she wondered who'd be calling at such a late hour.

"Who is it?"

"Conger." Catherine breathed a deep sigh of relief at his familiar voice.

She opened the door. Colonel Conger entered, closing the door behind. His appearance at this hour either meant something was wrong or he wanted to know what Robleur said once he left the table. Before he said another word, he gave her a bear hug that surprised her more than any of Robleur's surprises from behind.

"What's happened? Is everything all right, Colonel?"

"It's gone. They took it!"

"Took what? Who?"

"Them, miss. The carbon copy is gone. They took it from my wastebasket!"

"I don't understand. Is there something we should do?" Her question brought a smile to Conger.

"No, miss. It's done. They fell for it! They took the bait!"

Then she understood. The entire ruse became clear.

"Of course! You wanted them to take it! I thought it careless of you to throw that away! A maid could have taken it! I'm glad, Colonel. I had no idea you'd done it intentionally. I should tell you that Mr. Robleur said he was going home tomorrow. I thought our chance to deceive him had disappeared."

Feeling tremendous release from the tension building since her arrival, Catherine returned his hug. Now that it was done, she'd be able return to Chaumont and direct her energy to seeing Michael and finding John.

"That's the clincher, miss. He wouldn't be going home if there were reason for him to stay. I don't think you realize how big a part you played in this. You must be wrung out after all that's happened over the last few days. Get some sleep. You've earned it. I'll be in touch with Colonel Conner tomorrow. He may ask you to stay here for a while."

Conger didn't have to suggest sleep a second time.

"Thank you, Colonel. I'll think I'll sleep better now than I have in weeks. You'll let me know what Colonel Conner says?"

"You bet. We'll talk again tomorrow, miss."

Transfers

When General Pershing landed in Boulogne on June 13, 1917, Wilson's orders defined his policy on the deployment of the AEF. The *A* in AEF stood for "American," not Allied. Wilson wanted his men to fight under the American flag. Pershing could cooperate with the Allies, but the American Expeditionary Forces were to remain intact. Pershing parried requests of French and British commanders to fill the vacancies in their armies. Many of the debates were heated. Pershing got his wish—a wholly American sector that included German-held Saint-Mihiel.

During the ceremony, the sector's French commander handed Pershing his plans for an attack on the Saint-Mihiel salient. The volume was easier to weigh than read. Pershing accepted it in view of the occasion but was capable of generating his own plans. No commander could predict what might occur in battle. That was a problem his allies had experienced. Their plans depended on estimates of enemy strength and deployment. They drew lines on maps. They had expectations for attacks. It made no difference that these methods had never worked. They'd learned nothing from constant failure and less from the enemy's use of successful tactics. Allied soldiers had died futilely time and again for temporary gain. In spite of their bravery, retreats followed advances. The only thing won were headlines in Parisian gazettes and the *London Times*. Pershing wanted no part of it. He'd lent some Americans to fight with the British in Flanders, with the French on the Marne, along the Paris road, near Soissons, in Bazoches, at Sergy, from the Ourcq to the Aisne, and east to the Vosges. They'd done well, when allowed to do so.

Colonel George C. Marshall, chief of operations on the First Army's staff, assisted Pershing in drawing an outline for the attack. In comparison, Pershing's plan was brevity itself. Six pages were all Pershing needed to write the destiny of the German salient. His plan showed Pershing's absolute faith in the ability of his officers and men. It established objectives but stressed individual initiative. It gave wide latitude to the officers who'd lead the men in assault.

George Marshall also made a phone call for Lieutenant Commander Michael Morris before he left Chaumont to begin arranging medical facilities below the southern face of the salient. Michael asked Marshall to verify the regiment's location. The route to General Dickman's headquarters would take him through Vitry-le-François, near the sector occupied by the 369th Regiment. Michael told Marshall that he wanted to look up an old friend, Staff Sergeant Josiah P. Williams. He was given two days to report to General Dickman's headquarters.

"According to General LeBouc's headquarters, the regiment's been moving around. Right now, they're camped at Saint-Ouen for training." Marshall looked at a huge map on the wall of his office. "It's below Dompret, about twenty-five kilometers south of Vitry-le-François." Marshall pointed to its location with a riding crop.

"Thank you, sir." Michael saluted.

Marshall preferred to shake his hand. He admired the surgeon who chose to be close to the lines.

"Good luck, Michael. I hope they won't need your skills as much as they did on the Marne. The force of that attack was unexpected and barely contained."

"Yes, sir. Bad timing but a great learning experience, sir."

Marshall called for a car to take Michael to General Dickman's headquarters. It pleased Michael to see the same marine sergeant who'd driven Catherine and him to Chaumont waiting in the courtyard.

"Good afternoon, Sergeant. Looks like I'll have a chance to give you some tips on women, after all."

"Sir?"

"Wasn't that what you asked the last time we met?"

"Oh, that! Yes, sir. Gosh, I didn't know she was your sister, sir. I hope you don't think—"

"Just kidding, Sergeant. Do you know where we're going?"

"Yes, sir. They said to take you to Ligny-en-Barrois. I've never been there before, sir. It's a new headquarters."

"I'd like to stop at Saint-Ouen first."

The sergeant got behind the wheel of the olive-colored Model T Ford used by lesser staff. Michael sat in front. The sergeant began driving north along the Marne toward Saint-Dizier.

"Lieutenant Commander Michael Morris, Sergeant. I didn't get yours."

"Marine Sergeant Joseph Marcello, sir, Second Division, from Ohio. I got hit. They were going to send me home. I asked if I could stay. They made me a driver. I didn't think I should be sent home for a leg wound, sir. A lot of other guys got hit worse than that."

"You had a chance to go back to the States?" It surprised Michael that he'd asked to stay when he could have returned home.

"Yes, sir. I mean, I guess it would've been okay, but I felt funny about goin' home while my buddies are still over here. You know, sir? I guess a driver isn't the same, but it's better than going home. They won't let me fight, but I'm still helping out."

"I understand, Sergeant. I admire your dedication. The man I'm going to see in Saint-Ouen carried his buddy to my aid station. He lost a leg near this river."

"That's too bad, sir, about his leg. They saved mine. The bullet messed up my knee. The doc said it's always going to be stiff. He said it'd give me something to tell my grandchildren. I saw some other guys getting carried out of the woods. Believe me, sir, I was lucky. A lot of them died."

"You mean Belleau Wood?"

"Yes, sir. They had machine guns set up to cover all open lanes in the woods. We had to take them one at a time. Our brigade got shot up pretty bad. Some were killed in the gullies ... potato mashers. I got hit when they told us to get the hell out of there. They wanted to hit it with artillery. HE. High explosives. They told us to get out fast. We were pinned down pretty good but had no choice. We either got out or we'd be duckin' our own shells. They blew the woods to splinters, sir."

"Were you shot trying to get out?"

"Yes, sir. Ricochet. A lucky shot. Thought I picked off the machine gunner. I dived between some rocks. Turned out to be his feeder, not the gunner. The gunner went a little crazy. He started yelling something in German and kept firing at our position. He had the whole squad pinned down. Bullets were bouncing off rocks thicker than hornets from a busted hive. I got hit by some rock shards, nothing bad. Then the ricochet broke my knee. It was still hot. Most pain I ever felt."

Michael's attention was drawn to the ribbons on the marine's uniform.

"Is that where you got the DSC?"

"Yes, sir."

"You don't have to tell me about it if you don't want to, Sergeant."

"Oh, I don't mind, sir. I just don't know why they made such a fuss about it. One of us had to stop him, sir. He was trying to issue a harp to all of us. The squad kept his head down long enough for me to crawl closer. Two of my buddies went down. Without his feeder, I waited for him to change belts. That's when I got him. He had the strangest look on his face when he saw me get up on my good knee. Must have thought I was dead. He looked at me like I was some kind of ghost. Eyes big as golf balls."

Michael heard of heroism on the Marne. It would've been no less honorable for the sergeant to crawl to the rear and get care for his wound. The difference between what was honorable and what was courageous lay inside each man. The men Michael had treated on the Marne were all honorable men. Some had risen above honor and shown valor, careless of danger, unmindful of wounds, concern for a comrade. It was often a simple question of circumstance.

Traffic grew heavier near Saint-Dizier. Only one bridge was passable across the Marne, and vehicles of every type were waiting in line to use it. Most were going east toward Toul and Nancy. Many were headed north toward Verdun.

The route to Vitry-le-François led west. Once they crossed the fork in the Marne, traffic was lighter. Most of the road was occupied by French and American soldiers marching through the junction in the center of town, following their supply trucks to the front.

"Would you like to stop for something to eat, sir? We're still about fifteen miles from Saint-Ouen."

"It's okay with me. I haven't eaten since I got on the train to Chaumont. We can't waste too much time. It'll be dusk when we get to the camp."

Instead of a tavern, they stopped at a bakery and bought fresh bread made that afternoon. On advice of the baker, another stop was made for cheese and wine. After eating their simple meal, they went southwest to the camp where Josiah was billeted. Michael eventually found the tent where Josiah bunked and waited for him to return. It was the least he could do after all Josiah had done for James. When he arrived, Josiah was stunned to see Michael waiting for him. Josiah must have repeated a dozen times how happy he was that Michael had gone out of his way to see him. Michael had to cut the visit short. When they left, dusk was falling among the smoke-filled paths of the camp. Near Vitry, traffic flowed slowly in both directions. Though the town was mostly intact, refugees and scattered ambulances moved south. Many of its citizens had already left on the advice of military police. Those leaving later caused delays on the main road.

They hadn't thought they'd taken the wrong fork out of Vitry, though they crossed the Marne shortly after leaving town. They stopped a farmer on a wagon headed back toward town and asked if he knew the way to Ligny-en-Barrois. Neither Michael nor the sergeant spoke French. The Frenchman resorted to hand signals. They gathered from the farmer's gestures that they didn't have to return to Vitry. They could continue to Bar-le-Duc and get directions there to Ligny.

"Okay, Sergeant, let's try it. Did you bring a map?"

"Sorry, sir. It's in the staff car. I should have remembered it. Are you sure we shouldn't head back to Vitry?"

"Yes. It's getting late. The farmer seemed to think this was the best way. Bar-le-Duc can't be very far."

"Okay, sir."

They continued on the road, passing through the broken town of Sermaize. The farmer had indicated that they should go through the town and follow the road to the next where they'd pick up the road to Bar-le-Duc. They'd have to depend on signs pointing the way.

Rivgny was almost totally destroyed. They stopped to ask directions from an American infantryman and were told to take the road southeast out of the town. He pointed it out to be certain they saw it. Darkness made it difficult to see. Many of the roads were no longer marked. Sergeant Marcello turned on the hooded headlights.

"They took the signs down to confuse the enemy, sir."

"Okay, Sergeant. Are you sure this is the road?"

"Yes, sir. He said it goes straight to Bar-le-Duc."

Bar-le-Duc was exactly where the soldier said it was. The town was less damaged than Rivgny. Even in darkness, its former beauty was evident. For a third time, they stopped to ask directions. The MP directing traffic with a flashlight said the road ahead was blocked by debris.

"Go across that bridge and turn right, sir. You'll pass four villages between here and Ligny. The supply trucks make it in fifteen or twenty minutes."

In the darkness they crossed two bridges, one nearly right after the other. The first was the river. The second crossed a canal. They missed their turn by one bridge. The fork they took after the second bridge led northeast. Past the second village, not a single vehicle of any type appeared on the road. Michael thought it strange, but since no one was around to ask, they continued. In fifteen minutes, four villages lay behind—the wrong four. Without knowing, the road led them straight to the German-held salient at Saint-Mihiel. After driving over twenty minutes, Michael worried that something wasn't right.

"Did the MP say how many miles to Ligny?"

"No, sir. It can't be far. He said we'd pass four villages. We went through the last one about five minutes ago. The road's pretty clear, sir. We should be getting close."

"I haven't seen anything on the road since we passed that second town, not even a cart. I thought we'd be there by now. If we don't see Ligny soon, we'll have to turn back. It doesn't seem right that no one's using the road so close to headquarters."

"I hadn't thought about it that way, sir, but you're right. I—"

No sooner had the words left his mouth then the sergeant stopped the car and immediately turned off the headlights. Michael didn't have to ask. The whistling arch of an incoming artillery shell was unmistakable. It hit the road thirty yards ahead—exactly where the car would have been if they hadn't stopped. Seconds later, it was followed by another that landed on the road just behind.

"Who the hell's firing at us?"

"Shit! That's German artillery, sir. We've got to get the hell out of here, sir. They've got this goddamned road zeroed in. They won't stop until they hit us."

"Make it fast, Sergeant!"

The sergeant yanked the wheel. The Ford spun around quickly and began speeding back toward Bar-le-Duc.

There was no escaping the hole that appeared in the center of the road as the third shell hit. The sergeant veered to avoid it, but the wheel on the driver's side went down, hitting the opposite side with terrific impact, throwing the rear of the car skyward.

Its canvas roof not in place, Michael was thrown headlong from his seat. His knees struck the top of the windshield, flipping him like a coin. Time began moving slowly for Michael. Trees beside road passed by his head as shadowy scenery. Everything was upside down and backward. The road disappeared, and strands of grass knocked his hat from his head. A tree limb broke on his arm just before the world went totally black. Michael struggled to regain consciousness.

Time moved backward. He found himself with Catherine and Monroe on the Philadelphia Road. Monroe had tried to prevent the

Stutz from hitting a big oak tree. Not satisfied that it still stood, Monroe kept hitting the tree over and over again. He and Catherine were both laughing at Monroe trying to knock a tree down. Why did his head hurt? Nothing made sense.

Monroe said that they'd be getting to the hotel late, because every time the Stutz hit the tree, another tire went flat. Finally, he stopped trying to knock the tree down. Michael was confused. He'd never seen Monroe behave like that. He had to be dreaming.

He felt someone grab his shoulder, but his eyes wouldn't open. His legs wouldn't move. Legs without bodies and boots began marching up Philadelphia Road.

"Sir! Sir! Are you all right? Wake up, sir! Can you hear me?"

Monroe's words were clear. His voice was strange. It called to him from outside the Stutz. It wasn't Monroe. Catherine was sleeping on the seat next to him. Michael didn't understand what was happening. Was a soldier standing outside asking him to wake up? Who could that be? His legs wouldn't move. Why was Catherine asleep?

"Sir! Wake up, sir! We've got to get you to a hospital. Can you hear me?"

The voice became clearer. Was it the gate guard in New York? No. It couldn't be the guard's. He remembered reporting to the hospital. His chest felt heavy. His ribs were sore. Someone was pulling him up by the shoulders.

"Please wake up, sir! Don't die on me out here. Wake up!"

Michael regained consciousness. He wanted to breathe deeply, but his chest hurt. He began to cough. Cool, moist air entered his lungs. His mind began to clear. Coughing caused pain. The pain awakened him. He opened his eyes. He coughed. The pain made him wish he were still asleep. Through half-opened eyes, the darkness made him remember. He was lying on a road in France in enemy territory, and he was in great pain.

"Are you okay, sir? Can you hear me? It's Joe! Joe Marcello, sir."

"Joe. My chest." Michael's voice was weak. Speaking renewed the coughing and the pain. "I'm sorry, sir. We hit a shell hole."

"Shell hole?" Michael asked, his head spinning.

"Yes, sir. You were thrown out. You hit a tree. You've been out since they stopped shelling. I'm worried they're sending a patrol, sir. We got to get out of here."

Michael remembered it all now. With the exception of his legs, everything he moved seemed to hurt. The pain in his chest was strong. It was hard to breathe. As a doctor, Michael realized that his injury was serious.

"How long have I been out?"

"Maybe two or three minutes, sir. I was out a few seconds myself. My arm's broken, but it's mostly scrapes and bruises. I'm okay. Your head's bleeding, sir. You're gonna need help."

Michael had trouble keeping his eyes open. As a doctor, he knew he shouldn't let them close. The places that gave him pain didn't worry him. Broken bones could heal. It was the cough and the discomfort it brought that told him that something wasn't right. He had to get to a hospital.

"There's blood coming from your mouth, sir, and one ear. I've got to get you to a hospital. The car's on its side, but I think it'll still run."

"Can you turn it over?" Michael's cough returned.

"I think so. It's on two wheels already. I'm worried about you, sir."

Michael's eyes wanted to close, but he knew he might go unconscious if they did. He fought to keep them open.

"We must have taken the wrong road, sir."

Breathing was difficult. Michael was too dizzy to stand. He turned his head slowly from side to side, checking himself for neck injury. His neck hurt but wasn't broken. Moving his arms and shoulders caused pain, but his legs started to move without much trouble. He'd hit the tree squarely with his back. A limb must have flipped him upright as he fell back to earth.

His cough returned, and he felt a sharp pain in his chest. "I must've punctured a lung. Can I help you get the car upright?"

"Let me try, sir. It's not heavy. You should take it easy, sir."

"Okay. But if you hear anyone, get out of here. That's an order." It was hard for Michael to speak but easy to remove the driver's choice. He knew the sergeant wouldn't leave him. Without orders to leave, he'd become a prisoner. A German patrol was bound to come and investigate.

"Don't worry, sir. I'll get us both out of here."

The sergeant walked toward the half-overturned car. He put a shoulder under the door. Using all his strength, he righted the car by rocking it a little more upright each time his legs pumped. He paid no attention to the pain in his broken arm. His only thought was to get Michael to a hospital as soon as possible. He wasn't going to leave Michael to bleed to death under a tree. Michael's order didn't make any more difference to him than the pain in his broken arm. One more push righted the Ford. With its lights back on, the guns would start to shell the road again.

Pershing Versus Foch

For years, Pershing dreamed of leading an American army into battle, a dream he'd held before graduating from West Point in 1886. The sweaty, fruitless march through northern Mexico to capture or kill Pancho Villa had proved disappointing. In France, the West Pointer had tried for months to get Foch to give him a sector. Pershing wanted to show the world what an American army could do under an American commander. The word "stalemate" didn't appear in the general's vocabulary, and the thought of retreat never entered his mind. To end the war, he'd drive the enemy from France back to Berlin. He believed Allied victory had to be decisive. The Central Powers had to admit defeat. The Austrian emperor was dead. Germany must depose the kaiser.

Marshal Foch, chief of the general staff, agreed to Pershing's constant demand. His approval to commission the First Army came on July 24. In a quiet sector, the town of Saint-Mihiel lent its name to a salient that the Germans had held for four years. The

Côtes de Meuse formed the western leg of the salient, a high plateau broken by deep gorges. The eastern slope of the Meuse River ran roughly along the heights east of Verdun and south to Saint-Mihiel. Its southeast leg lay from Saint-Mihiel to Pont-à-Mousson on the Moselle, the town John had flown over on his way to the German air base near Metz. The leg continued across the Woëvre Plain, a marshland spread between the Meuse Heights and the rises along the Moselle. Pershing got the sector and command of his army.

On August 10, after further debate, Foch assigned the reduction of the salient to Pershing. The same day, Foch and Major General Maxime Weygand met with Pershing and proposed plans in direct conflict to what Foch had just granted Pershing. They amounted to the dispersal of Pershing's whole army—a million American soldiers. Pershing had reached the end of patience and the limit of his tolerance. He'd waited and debated too long for his wish to be overturned at the last minute. Foch was commander of all Allied forces, and his plans had changed.

Pershing had counted on leading his men in an attack to destroy the Saint-Mihiel salient held by Germany. Now, on the very day he'd given his permission, he'd turned the situation completely around. Pershing was disappointed and chagrined by the change. He could not tolerate any change in plans that Foch had agreed to without a fight. It would practically disband Pershing's army, and leave him to face the condemnation of his president.

Foch's reply implied that if Pershing had a solution, he'd give it consideration. Pershing felt that consideration was all any solution he offered would ever get from Foch. Foch suggested Général Degoutte as advisor for the Aisne offensive. Pershing strongly objected. Degoutte had already wasted too many American lives. In response, Foch became patronizing, almost insulting, by asking whether Pershing wished to take part in the battle.

Pershing's reply assured that Foch that he did. But, demanded the American army remain intact. He would accept any sector Foch handed to him.

At being reminded that France was supplying all of his artillery and auxiliary support, Pershing reminded Foch that French authorities, including Foch himself, had insisted that American infantry and machine gunners fill gaps in the French lines. Thus, their transport had been given priority over American weapons, supplies, and services. Pershing insisted that Foch keep his promise to form the American First Army and assign it a rightful share of the front. In spite of his promise, Foch begged the question. Now August 30th, the Meuse-Argonne attack would begin on September 15th. It was a question of time. Pershing would have only two weeks to complete the original task.

Foch knew that if he delayed handing over French artillery, Pershing couldn't attack the salient until the twelfth. He did not accept Pershing's request to assign a front to American forces. He refused even after Pershing offered to extend the American front, a move that would have freed every French unit from Belfort to the Argonne Forest. Foch seemed immovable.

For Pershing, this was too much. He'd already given Foch the equivalent of twenty French divisions, more men than he could justify losing and still maintain an effective army. To disperse what remained of his men just as they were preparing to go into battle was unthinkable. America wanted its army to do battle under its own flag and under its own leader.

Pershing told Marshal Foch he had no authority as Allied commander in chief to call upon him to yield command of the American army and have it scattered among the Allied forces where it will no longer be an army at all.

Foch insisted upon his plan.

Pershing told Foch he may insist all he pleased. Pershing declined absolutely to agree to his superior's plan. The American army would fight wherever he decided, but it would fight as an American army or not at all.

His statement boarded on insubordination. Nevertheless, Pershing stated his country's position in terms that even Foch could understand. The meeting came to an end. Foch laid his disputed memorandum on the table, leaving the question unresolved. Pershing returned to his office, disappointed, frustrated, but hardened to his president's, and his country's, military posture. Foch's position of command was strong. The agreement made by the Allied commanders on March 29, 1918, placed Marshal Ferdinand Foch in charge, responsible for determining war strategy with total authority to deploy all Allied armies.

The following day, the debate continued. Pershing had to honor the fact that France supplied the American army with all of its artillery pieces, all of its shells, all of its tanks, and—together with the English—all of its airplanes. How did these weigh in Pershing's opposition to Marshal Foch's plans? The facts in mind, Pershing would not budge an iota from his objective.

Though Pershing appreciated the awkwardness of his position, he again told Foch that although operational strategy was Foch's responsibility, the American army must not be dispersed.

Foch told him the French Army was exhausted, and the English had suffered heavy losses in the spring offensive.

Pershing reminded him that America wanted to know what their army was doing to win the war. Dispersing the army would destroy its identity as an American fighting force.

The Aisne attack would go forward. Foch said his plan took precedence over a purely political goal.

Pershing explained that by the summer of 1919, America would have an army of 3.5 million trained soldiers with the goal of liberating France. Even without his British allies, that force alone would be large enough to defeat Germany. Surely, he must agree that their presence as a unified force is essential to winning the war. Every battle American soldiers had fought proved their ability and courage under British or French command. At Château-Thierry, American marines had turned the tide of war in favor of the Allies. Once the Saint-Mihiel salient was reduced, the pathway to Metz would open. When Metz was taken, Allied victory was assured.

Foch continued to debate. Pershing continued to insist. After several more meetings, Foch was finally ready to compromise. He reset the date of the Aisne offensive by two weeks, but with one condition.

The First Army could take the salient. But immediately thereafter, Pershing must move his army between the Meuse River and the Argonne Forest to begin an offensive in concert with the French attack on the Aisne.

The task was daunting, but it was the only way Pershing would finally be able to show what an American army could do under an American flag and commander. Pershing agreed.

Finally, Pershing had won his most exasperating battle—the battle with his allies—a long, drawn-out battle to form an army from practically nothing, train it, lead it, and put it on the battlefield under its own flag. That battle meant the war would end. In seventeen months, Pershing had done what Congress had avoided doing for years. A commander to his core, Foch couldn't resist commenting on the impossible task Pershing had accepted.

By consenting, Pershing had not only agreed to take the salient but had accepted the incredible task of moving a 550,000-man army and all of its equipment sixty miles over narrow, crowded, muddy byroads in time to begin the American Meuse-Argonne offensive. It meant winning the salient and immediately transporting a battle-weary army, within range of enemy artillery, to fight on a strange front without pausing for rest. He had less than two weeks. The task was massive, perhaps impossible, but his army stayed intact.

Foch expressed his concerns to Pershing before the battle. The German positions around Saint-Mihiel are very powerful. Prior attempts to take it made that all too clear. They had been building their defenses into the hills for more than three years. Did Pershing truly believe his untried army could succeed in taking the objective?

Pershing's answer was based on the recent performance of his men. Neither Foch nor he could doubt the ability of the American soldiers to achieve their objective. Of the two, only Pershing believed that after the attacks succeeded, the war would end before the end of the year.

The marshy Woëvre Plain was to be the point of Pershing's initial attack in the reduction of the Saint-Mihiel salient, the first combat assignment of an American army on the western front. Foch committed units of the French army to simultaneously attack the northwestern corner of the salient, completing a pincers maneuver. Pershing accepted this plan. All that remained was to win the fight.

Prior to the attack on Saint-Mihiel, German intelligence received reports that an Allied attack was imminent through the Vosges toward the Rhine. It would come through the Belfort Gap. A German agent in Belfort had obtained pieces of carbon paper detailing the problems of supplying the American forces for the upcoming attack.

Such an attack was considered improbable by the German high command, but the Allies had attempted foolish assaults on other fronts during the war. It was known that American officers had patrolled the gap. Their fliers had taken photographs to fix German positions. Other agents had detected increased American radio traffic in the area. Lately, American corps commanders had established a headquarters near Belfort. Taken together, the activity was enough to convince the German field commander to take immediate precautions.

The commander of the German army thought it insane for Americans to attack through the Belfort Gap, but he made preparations. The German-occupied towns of Altkirch, Ferrette, and others east of Belfort were evacuated. German hospitals were moved to safer locations. Appeals for public calm sprang from burgomasters even farther east. German artillery was moved to guard the Rhine. Ammunition dumps were moved farther to the rear. Three divisions were moved behind the Rhine as reserves. The deception in Belfort had worked beyond the expectations of Chaumont. When the shift in German forces was confirmed, its effectiveness brought smiles to the faces of Colonels Fox Conner and A. C. Conger at First Army headquarters. General Pershing was made aware. The latest intelligence suited his plan for Saint-Mihiel.

In Belfort, Catherine could only wait. Gauthier Robleur postponed a trip home. He came to the hotel more often, constantly talking about new war rumors. He asked Claudie if she'd heard from the American colonel who'd borrowed her the night they'd had dinner. His questions were incessant.

She denied knowing anything about the rumors. "The last thing he said to me was that he must go back to see everything was properly done. He was quite concerned about it."

"Surely his plan must be right! The people still talk about the soldiers in the mountains and the airplanes flying over the gap. Why would he be concerned?"

"I don't know any more than you, Mr. Robleur."

Gauthier had orders to determine the strength of the Americans, identify the units assigned to the attack, determine the specific point of attack, and most of all, discover the probable time of the attack. Some of this he knew already. He was familiar with American military insignia. Armies needed to stockpile supplies, and the local paper had mentioned an increase in military traffic near Belfort. Weather always bore on the timing of an attack. But his superiors wanted hard evidence in order to prepare defenses and locate strategic reserves. This posed a challenging problem for Robleur. Neither he nor his associates had been able to discover the point of attack, its time, or the number units that would compose the attacking force. Up to now, fewer supplies than expected had been stockpiled in the areas of probable attack.

"Why he is worried, I don't understand, Claudie."

"I wouldn't know about that, Monsieur Robleur. That was all he said before leaving the hotel. He didn't even say good-bye."

"Surely he must have said something the night he asked for you. You typed his paper."

"I've already told you that it was in military language. He made me promise—"

"It's very strange he said nothing of concern."

"Nothing at all," she said.

Catherine didn't know why she couldn't convince him. She decided to agree with Gauthier that nothing could possibly be wrong. The comment had the desired effect. Gauthier backpedaled, realizing he was pressing too hard. Not quite satisfied, he could think of nothing more to say that might prod a useful response.

"I suppose he knows what he is doing. I will see you again, Claudie? I enjoyed our dinner and enjoy talking with you. Perhaps we can do it again?"

"Possibly, Monsieur Robleur. I must return to Paris soon to find work in a school. Those who teach English are in demand in Paris. Perhaps you should consider offering your services, as well. You speak English well enough."

"An interesting idea! English is a second language in Paris. I will consider the suggestion. Thank you."

"I must wish you good day, *monsieur*. There are many things to do."

"Of course, Claudie."

Although Fox Conner wanted Catherine out of Belfort for her safety, it was impossible to remove her before the battle actually began without raising suspicion. For that reason, he decided to withhold news of John's current location, though the information had been in his hands since he'd gone to Belfort. John was transferred to the American Ninety-Fourth Pursuit Squadron. Their insignia—"A Hat in the Ring"—served as a challenge for German fliers to fight.

The Ninety-Fourth formed a large part of the attack on Saint-Mihiel. Colonel William ("Billy") Mitchell would command 1,480 fighter and bomber pilots in the strongest concentration of airpower ever assembled. Their objective was to destroy as many German airplanes, supply bases, and German positions as possible and to assume total control of the skies over the Woëvre Plain. Nothing close to that had ever been attempted on either side.

Much had changed since John joined the squadron. Manfred von Richthofen was dead, shot down over Allied lines. In honor of his demise, British and Australian soldiers carried out an elaborate military funeral. After a long procession, they marched into position near the grave. A chaplain offered the service. The Australian contingent fired rifles in salute, turned their rifle barrels bore down, solemnly folded their hands on the upturned butt plates, and rested their foreheads on their hands. A film of the ceremony was dropped by an Allied airplane over German lines. The Flying Circus named a new commander, a lesser ace called Hermann Goering.

Weeks later, on May 19, Squadron Commander Raoul Lufbery took off from Toul in another pilot's Nieuport to engage a two-seater flying near the aerodrome. His own plane was being overhauled. The dogfight carried east of the airfield. His approach was so close that those watching on the ground thought a collision was imminent. The Nieuport's guns jammed almost immediately.

Lufbery circled to clear the breeches. Rickenbacker told John the rest.

"The enemy plane was armored. Luf got too close. The rear gunner couldn't miss. His plane caught fire. Flames forced him from the cockpit. Guys below said he climbed onto the tail to avoid them. Either the plane rolled, or he jumped from a mile up. He landed on a fence in somebody's garden below Nancy. His face was seared. A bullet wound in a hand. He was a great pilot, John. If he'd been in his own plane, it would have come out differently. You know how he always checked his ammunition. Knowing Lufbery, burning to death was not how he wanted to die."

Lufbery's death angered John. Some pilots didn't give the same attention to their guns as Luf. What bothered John most had been bothering him since June. Two German pilots, one of them Ernst Udet of the Flying Circus, had jumped from their stricken planes and coasted safely to the ground wearing parachutes. He let Rickenbacker know what he thought.

"Remember Walter Smyth and Alexander Bruce? They brushed wings. Both planes went down. You'd think those brass-hatted idiots would give us parachutes! The damned kaiser seems to have a higher regard for his pilots! What in hell's the matter with command, Rick? Why don't they issue parachutes? They'd all be alive if they'd had parachutes! Luf was a damned good pilot. So were Walt and Alex! Don't they give a damn? It's unbelievable! For God's sake, Rick, the Germans even give their balloonists parachutes!"

John had to vent his anger. Lufbery was at the top of his career, a double ace. John couldn't accept his death for the lack of a parachute. Rickenbacker more than sympathized.

"You're right, John. The balloonists have them. If the Germans have them, there's no reason why our pilots shouldn't. That's why I do my best to kill the pilot. It's the only way to keep him out of the air for good. If he parachutes out, I'm okay with that. I'll get him next time. If he stays with his plane, I'll get him. He won't come up if he's dead."

"What's their real reason, Rick? Why aren't we getting chutes? Don't they understand? They're losing good pilots! We can replace planes. We can't replace experienced pilots."

"It sounds crazy, I know. I asked a major about it once. You'll never believe what he told me. He said they don't give us parachutes because we'd jump whenever we got in a tight spot. He said they'd lose a lot of airplanes. I swear, John. That's what he said."

John's anger soared at the ignorance in this thinking. "Jesus! Airplanes? Hell, they're losing trained pilots! It takes months to train a good pilot. It probably costs them more to train a good pilot than to build a goddamned airplane! They can build a dozen planes a day. What the hell good are they without trained pilots to fly them? I've never heard anything so goddamned stupid, Rick! It's worse than stupid. It's contempt! It's an insult to every flier!"

"Hey, John, I know. I got so damned mad at him that a couple of officers had to step in to keep me from knocking him down. A good thing they did, or he'd have court-martialed me."

"Luf would never have bailed out just because an Albatros got on his tail! If you ask me, those brass hats should be sitting on their asses, not their heads. They'd change their minds damned quick if they went up."

"I won't argue, John! I said as much to the major and then some! It's bad military thinking. More like a political than an economic thing. The French supply the planes. We supply the pilots."

John couldn't suppress a scornful smile at the idea that politics might be involved. It added to his deep contempt for politics and politicians. Some things never changed. That's why he changed the subject. He needed to break the tension.

"Let's get something to drink. I want to talk to you about the mission we're flying over Saint-Mihiel. What's your opinion of Billy Mitchell? By the way, is there any truth to the rumor that you're going to become CO of the Ninety-Fourth?"

Avoiding the questions, Rick replied, "John, for a guy who was mad as a wet cat a minute ago, you dried off awfully fast!"

"It's the damned war. I've watched our guys die needlessly one at a time for too long. I'm worried about my brother. I should have heard from him by now. Catherine wrote a while back. She said he was working in an aid station on the Marne. That's all I've heard. I thought they'd put him in a hospital, away from the lines."

"Don't worry, John. They're probably just breaking him in. They need good surgeons. For all you know, he's working in a hospital right now."

What John didn't know was that Michael was only twenty miles away in a staff car with Joe Marcello. He was just leaving the town of Bar-le-Duc and about to take the wrong road to Ligny-en-Barrois. He was minutes away from the binoculars of a German artillery observer's curious eyes.

In trying to start the Ford, the backfire through a flooded carburetor renewed the shelling on the road below Saint-Mihiel. But the engine started! Sergeant Marcello wasted no time taking Michael to Bar-le-Duc. Minutes passed like hours before they crossed the canal. Seconds later, he crossed the river, and Marcello realized their earlier mistake. He immediately felt personally responsible for what had happened. The trip would have gone differently if he'd remembered the map.

There was no time to think about that now. The MP directing military traffic through town told him that no one in Bar-le-Duc could perform surgery. The nearest hospital was in Saint-Dizier, twelve miles to the east. The road was direct and passed through three villages. Sliding in and out of consciousness, Michael told him to drive to the hospital. He needed surgery as soon as possible. On the vehicle-choked road, half an hour passed before Michael arrived in Saint-Dizier.

Saint-Mihiel

On the morning of September 12, 1918, rain grounded the Ninety-Fourth Pursuit Squadron. Clouds covered Saint-Mihiel as the Americans began to attack its flank. For four hours, the most concentrated artillery barrage of the war fell on German positions. In the downpour, the assault fell on the town of Vigneulles, the center of the salient. Rain and fog concealed the infantry's advance. It also hid the enemy's positions. The Flying Circus was also grounded. The weather wasn't any better over Metz or Mars-la-Tour.

John didn't want to miss the first wholly American battle. He'd caught only glimpses of British and French attacks. Rickenbacker felt the same way. Rick invited John and Reed Chambers on a sortie over the salient below the clouds. They'd have to return if the weather got too bad.

"We'll likely be the only fliers up there."

John agreed. "You're probably right, Rick. Just in case, I'm going up fully loaded. The barrage alerted the Germans to the attack. They might try to bring up reserves. From what I saw on our last patrol, they were pulling back their artillery."

"We've flown in better weather," said Reed, "but never on a better day in this damn war. Let's get going before it gets any worse."

Chambers's comment ended the exchange. In ten minutes, their mechanics had three Spads on the field, motors running.

Storm clouds hovered at three thousand feet. At one thousand feet, it was impossible to see the ground with clarity. They dropped to six hundred feet. Smoke partly obscured the southern face of the salient. The German lines were broken by the barrage. Some units had blown barbed wire with explosive charges. Others sections were bridged with chicken wire. John saw a solid wave of Americans moving forward. They carried the fight into the Germans lines in a furious assault, cutting down everything and everyone that stood in their way. They attacked with machine guns, grenades, bayonets, and rifle butts. The salient became a killing ground.

John had never seen the likes of it. Men fell by the hundreds on both sides. Even at five hundred feet, it was clear which side was the more determined. Nothing withstood the American attack. Flushed onto open ground, the enemy fought bravely. They were no match for the Americans. Many German units had already begun to retreat. They burned their equipment, blew up stores of ammunition, set fire to buildings, turned briefly to fight, and then retreated.

The three Spads flew beyond the main assault and came upon a scene they seldom saw in daylight. To avoid capture, a column of horse-drawn wagons was slowly moving to the rear, hauling heavy artillery pieces on a narrow road choked with vehicles. Rickenbacker flew straight at them, followed by Reed and John.

One pass was all they needed. Horses stampeded. Wagons spilled over, artillery pieces were strewn along the road. Men in field-gray uniforms ran from the road as bullets ripped through the panicked column. Many were killed and wounded, ending their war on a narrow French road far from their homes in Germany. The column stopped. The mud, overturned wagons, and twisted bodies made the road impassable. Artillery pieces looked like felled trees.

Rickenbacker signaled that he was flying toward the field at Toul. He'd tell the artillerymen about the road filled with Germans trying to retreat. Chambers followed to be sure arrived. John remained, fascinated by the events below. He flew back toward the line of battle. Compared to what he'd seen days before, the ground was no longer recognizable. The barrage had reduced every tree to splinters, every landmark to rubble. The lines were a tangle of torn wire, upturned earth, fire, and acrid smoke. Everywhere he looked, the dead and dying lay in grotesque, twisted poses resembling nothing like men at rest.

The first assault wave was already past the initial lines of battle. A curious calm had settled over the area, as though the rain had dampened its fury. Rain had removed the smoke of the conflict. If it were not for the shell holes and bodies, one couldn't tell a battle had been fought. Above it all, John felt detached from war. Looking at the carnage below, he was a spectator, an observer, suspended in time and place, viewing the scene through impartial eyes. Months before, he'd lamented the loss of historic buildings and the death of men he'd flown with in the escadrille. The violent posture of the bodies below verified the cost of war. Buildings could be rebuilt, not lives, whether Allied or German. A simple truth followed. In death, the men below were at peace. Until the war ended, the only peace any man found in war was the peace of the dead.

He thought of Michael. The dead men below were someone's brother, someone's son, someone's husband, or someone's father. In the Cathedral of Saint Paul, he'd prayed for the dead Allied soldiers. The impact of what he saw below stirred sympathy toward all the dead. He didn't understand why the feeling commingled with a sense of relief. Was victory near? The war might end soon. Was it a sense of value for a human life? He valued his own. How had he survived so long? Was it guilt for having survived beyond those below? John saw no winners in war, only losers. Why did sensible men go to war? Both sides lose.

"The goddamn politicians! If they could see what I see now!"

No politician and no field commander had ever experienced the view from his airplane. The scale of death and destruction went on for miles. For over a year, he'd witnessed the most costly conflict in human history. Like himself, the call to arms had come to each of those men. Ordinary men on both sides were persuaded to join in a righteous cause, swayed by speeches, impassioned pleas, stimulated by the prospect of noble deeds for God and country. Was it noble to fight for noble words? How could noble words engender such ignoble deeds? The living called the dead glorious. Were the men below glorious, or were they simply dead, food for the hordes of rats and lesser vermin? He'd never considered war in those terms. His eyes closed in respect for those below. He opened them in dread for the cause of their death.

John realized that the dead below were the bequest of his generation to the next. They'd died believing that future sons would live in peace. Perhaps they would. After this, How could anyone would want another war like this? This was a war fought to end all war. Nothing else about the war could be called noble. Raoul was right. If the sacrifice was great enough, the world would be less willing to go to war. The sooner it ended, the sooner men would accustom themselves to peace.

Guiding the Spad toward the field, he looked away from the carnage on the marshlands. Soon, the only combatants would be the rats fighting over pieces of flesh and broken bodies. A strong urge to see Catherine and Michael suddenly possessed him. He attributed his survival to the fact that he hadn't expected to survive. Now, he hoped to see them before he too lay in a grave in France.

Belfort

In Belfort, Catherine counted the minutes before Pershing's attack started. Then she could return to Chaumont. Gauthier was true to his word. Her tormentor came almost every night, inserting questions into the conversation that appeared to come from his curiosity. Had she heard from the colonel? What were the latest rumors around the dining room? Did she know any of the new soldiers in the lounge? Catherine tried to discourage Gauthier by claiming not to know. It stopped his questions about her customers. His new questions took interest in her family life. When did her father buy the hotel? How had her mother died? When was she leaving for Paris? Interspersed in the conversation, they seemed harmless enough. But, she became concerned.

She told Arnaud of Gauthier's prying interest. Like a real father, he was troubled. Becoming more alarmed as she continued to relate her experience, Arnaud called Fox Conner in spite of his warning that the phone might be tapped.

"What can I do, Colonel? She may be in danger."

"The attack has begun. Her job is finished. I want her to avoid any further contact with Gauthier Robleur. Put Catherine on the next train out of Belfort, Arnaud."

"Yes, Colonel. I agree."

Arnaud told Catherine to stay in her room, pack her things, and be ready to leave as soon as arrangements were made. For the first time since she'd come to France, Catherine felt something like relief. The time had finally come. A train was scheduled to leave Belfort for the east that same evening.

"Will you accompany me to the station?"

"Of course, Claudie! You need not worry; I will take you myself. In case Robleur or anyone else interferes, I will bring my revolver."

"That shouldn't be necessary, Arnaud. We've managed well enough this far. I expect Monsieur Robleur is more concerned about how he will explain his failure. He didn't come to the hotel today. He said he was returning to Montbéliard."

"I don't trust that Boche! He asks too many questions!"

"Perhaps you're right, Arnaud. I don't trust him. I'll be safe in my room for now."

The train was scheduled to depart in four hours. Time passed slowly. Catherine spent it packing clothes, writing to Michael, and thinking of John. She'd lost track of time when a soft knock at her door startled her.

"Who's there?"

The knock came again. Catherine grew afraid.

"Who is it?"

"It's Arnaud. Time to go, Claudie. It's raining. Wear a coat."

Arnaud loaded her luggage into his one-horse carriage. He'd raised its top. Clouds and rain darkened the twilight. Arnaud jogged the reins. A huge weight lifted from her as she realized that her stay in Belfort was at an end. The sound of hooves reminded

Catherine of Commander Fields and their ride through Central Park. She relaxed until Arnaud adjusted the butt of the revolver protruding from his belt.

"It's only a precaution, Claudie."

At the station, he helped her with her luggage and said good-bye. He'd been like a real father to her. Arnaud noticed Catherine's tears. He hugged her and whispered good-bye. For a moment, she found it difficult to leave. Arnaud had been her father for weeks. His concern for her was the same as her real father would have shown. She'd miss Belfort. It was a lovely town, far enough from the fighting that the sound of guns seldom carried over the hills. Someday she'd return to visit Belfort and perhaps go to Besançon on the river Doubs, where her father had gone as a young man. Arnaud stood on the platform until the train was gone.

The train stopped in Lure to board and detrain passengers. It began rolling again toward Chaumont. Though dark, she could see the silhouettes of the mountains from her compartment window. Arnaud had paid for her ticket, insisting that she travel in a private berth. He said it would give her time to rest away from the passengers.

"*Billet, billet, s'il vous plaît!*" the conductor called, walking down the narrow aisle, asking for tickets. He'd checked hers shortly after leaving Belfort. She'd forgotten to ask him for the location of the dining car. She opened her door. As he approached from the front of the train, she asked, "*Monsieur. Où est le wagon-restaurant?*"

"It is three cars behind this one, Claudie."

Catherine had to suppress the urge to scream. The voice behind was unmistakable. Gauthier Robleur was on the train. She spun around to face him.

"Monsieur Robleur! Once again, you startled me! I thought you said you were going home!"

"I'm sorry to frighten you. You could not know I was on the

train. I have always wanted to go to Paris. A friend suggested the trip. So I am here. I am happy to see you. You have the same destination, of course. You go to find a teaching position. You must be excited, yes? You must tell me all about it."

Gauthier's questions seemed sincere. Nothing of suspicion was apparent in either his tone or his body language. He couldn't possibly have known she'd be on the train. She'd done nothing to suggest that she was anything more than Arnaud's daughter. Perhaps Arnaud's concern was overstated. In her judgment, Gauthier had no reason to suspect that she'd had a role in Pershing's deception. Besides, the coach was filled with passengers. Many were American officers. Three were sitting in the compartment directly across from hers. She was perfectly safe.

"Please come to the dining car with me. We will have dinner and talk about Paris."

"No, thank you, Mr. Robleur. I don't want to eat just yet. Perhaps later."

Her refusal to join him either disappointed or simply annoyed him. She couldn't tell.

"Then come to my compartment. It is only one coach away. I have a bottle of wine."

"Really, Mr. Robleur! That would be quite improper. Father would object. Besides, I was just about to write a letter. Afterward, I may go to sleep. I feel very tired."

Gauthier seemed agitated. "I won't keep you long. A minute or two?"

"All right, then, but only a minute or two. ."

The soldiers across the aisle made her feel safe. Catherine and Gauthier stood near her open door in plain view of the soldiers in the opposite compartment. Now and then, their laughter came into the aisle. They were telling jokes and exaggerated war stories. Their mere presence reassured her. Gauthier began the conversation.

"I thought I might never see you again, Claudie. I wanted you to know what has happened. Seeing you is very fortunate. But you, Claudie … you said you are going to Paris to find a teaching position?"

"Yes. I want to teach in Paris, of course, but I will go wherever my work sends me. And you, Mr. Robleur? What will you do in Paris?"

"I have no special plans. I have never been to Paris. I may stop at the Ministry of Transportation and Tourism. They must have need of people who traveled in northern France."

"Perhaps they do. You could make use of your ability to speak English."

"Quite so, Claudie! I had not thought of it. No doubt American soldiers could use my help with directions to the hotels and bars. Few speak French. They are very clever, these Americans. An unexpected attack … unexpected. What a surprise! Very clever."

Robleur's comments would not have been so stunning if he hadn't been staring directly into her eyes when he uttered them. Her heart began to race. He suspected something. Catherine looked at the floor and brought a hand to her mouth.

"Oh. You are tired. I have stayed too long. It is late. I don't want to keep you from your letter writing. Write to your father, Claudie. You know how fathers worry when their daughters travel alone. Perhaps we can take breakfast in the morning?"

Catherine responded to the suggestion by repeating the word. "Perhaps."

Surprised that he'd decided to leave on his own, she offered him no incentive to stay.

"Good night, Monsieur Robleur."

"*Adieu*, Claudie. *Adieu*. Later, we will have more time." Gauthier's smirk was even thinner than usual. He glanced briefly into the compartment where the soldiers sat, turned, and walked briskly toward the rear of the train.

As he left, an officer in the opposite compartment came to its door. He looked down the aisle both ways.

"Sorry about the noise, miss. Are you going to sleep now?"

"Yes, I think I will."

"I'll tell these guys to keep the noise down. Good night, miss." He partly closed his door.

Catherine began to breathe easily the moment Robleur left, though his compartment was uncomfortably close. She couldn't help wondering why he'd decided to go to Paris or how he'd managed to be on the same train. Was it a coincidence? If so, it was a very unfortunate coincidence. She had no reason to believe—and she didn't *want* to believe—it was anything but a coincidence! The alternative was too frightening to contemplate. Her hands shook just thinking about it. Nothing she could do would change the fact that he was on the train. She closed her door and sat on the edge of her bed.

The sound of steel wheels skipping over steel rails helped to relax her. Each rail meant that the train was closer to Chaumont. The pace of the train had seemed faster when it left Belfort, but now it seemed slower. The closer it got, the slower it seemed to go.

Another stop was made in Vesoul before resuming speed to Chaumont. Catherine checked the lock on the door of her compartment. She decided to keep it locked until she reached Chaumont. Her talk with Gauthier had gone well enough, but knowing that he was so near destroyed any desire to write a letter. She tried to forget her tormenter. He'd frightened her too many times! Her job was done, and nothing Robleur did or said would change that.

Chaumont grew nearer by the minute. Perhaps Conner would send her to the embassy in Paris. From there, she'd find Michael. Germany had been on the defensive since late July. She'd heard the soldiers across the aisle say that the battle for the salient was a certain victory for the Americans. Victory might help her gain the cooperation of French authorities in finding John. Her own work had been valuable to the Allies. They couldn't refuse to help her. Tired and self-assured, Catherine was ready for bed.

As she lay down, her thoughts wandered back to Kew Gardens. She felt a strong desire to leave France and return to William. As much as she loved her brothers, Catherine wanted to be with him. She felt secure with William. Each night she lay in bed, the memory of their last night together returned in detail. Even now, her love brought on a strong physical and emotional response. She knew she'd been vulnerable, anxious about her voyage and her assignment in France, and it had contributed to her impulsiveness that night. What had happened that night still surprised her. Her love for William made that night completely lacking in guilt in spite of her Victorian upbringing.

The more she thought of him, the more she relaxed. Twice he'd asked her if she were certain that she wanted to sleep with him. His concern only endeared him to her more. He'd asked her to marry him. She'd said yes. With these comforting thoughts, Catherine closed her eyes. She was put asleep by the steady rhythm of steel wheels hitting joints in the tracks.

A metallic scratching coming from her door partly roused her. The low light of the aisle dimly backlit her doorway. How had her door come open? A silhouette appeared. Eyes wide, she recognized the silhouette of Gauthier Robleur. Were she still asleep, he could have stood close enough to touch her. Terrified, she didn't scream. He took a step toward her bed. Something metallic glinted in his hand.

A pistol shot rang out so loudly that her ears rang. Temporarily deaf, Catherine shrieked. A second, even louder shot rang out, so near that its flash lit up the room. She felt its shock. Robleur stumbled toward her. She screamed.

For a moment, he stood motionless. A low moan escaped his lips. Paralyzed with fear, she watched him stoop toward her. Something clattered on the floor next to her bed. She jerked backward at the noise. She grabbed her knees to protect herself.

Robleur lunged toward the edge of her bed. Again, Catherine screamed. She pressed herself hard against the wall, getting as far away as possible. If he'd shot her, she felt no pain. Was shock preventing her from feeling pain? Unable to retreat any farther, she cowered, wide-eyed, staring at Robleur. He said nothing. He sank to his knees at the edge of her bed. Sound slowly returned to her ears. She heard another moan and a long sigh. He fell to the floor like a bag of dirty laundry. Her heartbeat was in perfect rhythm with the clatter of the train's steel wheels. The train was moving much faster.

After, reassuring startled passengers that everything was under control, the soldiers in the opposite compartment were told to escort them back to their compartments.

"It's over, miss. He won't bother you again."

She hadn't noticed the man in her doorway. His voice startled Catherine, but it was an American voice. The man entered, holding a revolver. He switched on her light. Catherine didn't move. She was shivering with fright, trying to make sense of what had happened. The scene played over and over in her mind. What seemed like hours to her had lasted only seconds.

"Miss Morris, I'm Captain Winters, military intelligence. I apologize for upsetting you. Are you okay, miss? You look pretty shaken. I can't blame you a bit! It's not every day something like this happens in front of you. We were aware of this man's description. We didn't know he was on the train."

Catherine hadn't moved. Her eyes were locked on the man lying on the floor next to her bed. Blood spatter covered the end of her blanket.

The captain took another blanket from the closet. He covered the corpse with the splattered blanket and covered her with the clean one. He called to the men across the aisle, handing one of them a stiletto he picked from the cabin floor. Winters barked his instructions.

"Get this piece of garbage out of here. Put him in the baggage car. Find the conductor. Tell him what's happened. Tell him I'll explain later."

Catherine's face fell into the blanket. She began to cry. She was shivering badly and sobbing uncontrollably. She'd never experienced sudden death.

Turning toward her, Winters spoke again. "I'm really sorry to frighten you, miss. I had no choice. Someone had to stop him. If I'd known about him sooner … Can I get you some water? You're safe now, miss. No need to be afraid. It's over. Everything is going to be all right. I'll see to it personally."

The last time she was this upset, Michael had held her until she was calm. When the body was removed, she got up and walked toward the captain.

"Captain," she said, "please hold me."

"Ah … okay, miss. If that'll help." Surprised, the captain felt awkward. "Uh … I just want you to know that it's over. You don't have to be afraid anymore."

His embarrassment didn't allow him to hold her for more than a minute. By that time, Catherine had regained control of herself.

Her mind reeled at the thought that as she slept, Gauthier Robleur had somehow managed to enter her locked room and had attempted to end her life. Even more shocking, he'd died before her eyes.

"Thank you. I'm all right now, Captain. I just needed a little time." She returned to the edge of her bed and sat. The shivering was gone.

"You should put something warmer on, miss." Embarrassed at having held a pretty young woman wearing her bedclothes, the captain reached for her robe and handed it to her. He turned to the soldier's across the aisle. Murmurs about the captain holding a pretty girl had arisen from that direction. His embarrassment returned, but he was not inspired to explain the situation. He turned to her.

"If I'd known he was on the train, I would have taken him into custody. He left the dining car a minute before I did. From his description, I thought he might be the man in the colonel's report. By the time I caught up to him ... well ... you know the rest. You'd best come with me, miss. I'd feel better about it if you didn't stay here tonight. I'll move in here. You can use my compartment."

"Thank you, Captain. I'd be happy to leave this compartment."

Captain Winters handed the thin, six-inch blade with a black handle to the soldier. Catherine couldn't help seeing it. The knife, the gunshots, and the blood spoke to Catherine of the dark side of war—of the lies, the deceit, the danger, and the price one paid for failure. The events of the night had brought them all straight to the edge of her bed. She'd never forget this night.

"Captain?"

"Yes, miss?"

"Thank you for saving my life."

This time her sobs came from relief.

"You're welcome, miss. You've been very brave through all this. Colonel Conner asked me to keep an eye on you. I only wish there'd been another way. Let's go, miss. I'll have some tea sent from the dining car. Would you like that, or would you prefer something else?"

The gesture was so familiar that it put her at ease. Except for a deeper voice and Southern accent, the words could have come straight from Monroe.

"Yes, Captain Winters, I'd like that. But I should get dressed first."

"Sure, miss. I'll wait outside."

"Please, Captain. I'd appreciate it if you'd wait here. The man you killed may have accomplices. I'd rather not be left alone just now."

"I understand. I'll stand right in the door and guard the aisle, miss. No one will bother you as long as I'm here."

Spoken loud enough to be overheard, his words brought snickers from across the aisle that abruptly ended when the captain scowled.

Catherine slept tolerably well in the captain's compartment for what remained of the evening. Winters didn't sleep at all. On the chance that Robleur had not been traveling alone, he'd borrowed a stool and sat guarding her door the rest of the night.

Winters doubted that they'd ever discover the dead man's true identity or whether he was really Belgian, German, Austrian, or a paid renegade. It no longer made any difference to two people. The first was Catherine. The second was the late Mr. Gauthier Robleur. His mission had abruptly ended.

Reunited

From Ravenel to Toul, a year and nine months, John had flown for the French longer than he believed he'd survive. Not that he wasn't a good pilot. John was a better pilot than most in the squadron. He'd survived in spite of the odds. Early on, he'd reached a point where he didn't have to think about flying. He'd developed skill to the level of instinct. His airplane was an extension of his will. He could recall every detail of every combat he'd fought. The maneuvers he used in battle were designed to fit the situation that existed. His mistakes were few and never repeated.

Like Mallory had said, the limits to his skill were largely the limits of his airplane to perform the stunts he demanded of it. His skill had earned him four confirmed victories and put ten enemy fighters out of action. The twin victories over Metz didn't count, since the combat took place too far from the lines for confirmation. In truth, John had been an ace since Metz. Officially, he needed one more. John didn't think in terms of numbers. He harbored a sense of loathing at having to kill men. Unlike Rickenbacker, whose racing career instilled a need for victory, John flew to bring an end to war. It happened that his only means to that end was to shoot down enemy airplanes. That was his purpose and his duty. Shooting down them meant fewer airplanes to hunt, whether one went down or seventy, like those credited to Capitaine René Fonck.

More than once, John could have chased a crippled enemy plane and sent it down in flames. On that point, John and Rick thought differently. John sympathized with a pilot in a crippled plane, who ran from battle to the safety of his field. The reaction was natural to one who wanted to survive. Whenever a pilot went up, he courted death, whether from an enemy flier, engine failure, antiaircraft gun, collision, or just bad luck. The odds against any flier surviving more than a month were incredibly high. Death caught up to Richthofen in spite of his record number of kills and the luxury of flying with the deadliest squadron in the air. Of N. 124's seven original members, only Bill Thaw remained. The others were dead, along with eight of their replacements. John's chances for survival had matured months ago. He expected to die. The passage of time made it more realistic to expect death than anticipate survival. His calm in combat came from the knowledge that his current mission could well be his last. John's concern was prolonged war. The sooner it ended, the sooner the killing would end in the air and on the ground. Perhaps he'd live to see it end.

On the second day of the Saint-Mihiel campaign, the weather broke. Fighter patrols resumed.

"The American First Army must not be observed," said Rickenbacker. "German airmen must not to be allowed to gather intelligence to register artillery or plan a counterattack. Every enemy observer must be shot down. That's all. Good hunting."

The fliers were sent against the best German fighter squadrons.

John led a flight of four Spads whose primary mission was to intercept German observation planes headed for Saint-Mihiel. His mission included shooting down enemy balloons with incendiary bullets.

Within three miles of the front, John saw a formation of Fokkers painted in the bright colors of the Flying Circus. His most dangerous adversaries were aloft. Their new leader was Hermann Goering, the ace who'd replaced Richthofen. His fighters flew top cover for a pair of LVG C.V two-seater observation planes. John had grown accustomed to seeing the pattern. Having circled the salient from the northwest, John's squadron approached from above flying due west with the morning sun at their backs. He'd outflanked the Circus two thousand feet below and was in ideal position to attack. John signaled his three fighters to engage the Fokkers while he remained aloft. Once Goering's planes were engaged, John planned to attack the two observation planes four thousand feet below. Reed Chambers led the attack on the Fokkers, going straight at the rear of the fighter formation. The others followed Chambers on either side of Chambers's Spad.

As Chambers engaged the Fokkers, John slowly banked to the right to position his plane over the two observers. Armed and forewarned, the observers began to circle. They wouldn't continue their mission without top cover. John expected them to circle. The tactic was intended to provide mutual defense. They'd have to await top cover to resume their mission. Otherwise, they'd return to their field.

The LVGs' forward view was poor, but attacking them from the front wasn't an option. Each rear gunner could defend the other observer. The two-seater's swiveling machine gun had total command of the skies above, on either side, and behind. John increased his dive to fly under both planes. The tail of the plane above John would block its rear gunner's field of fire and eliminate half their combined firepower. Only the observer on the opposite side of the circle would have a clear shot at him. John had no choice but to take that risk. The general order was explicit. No enemy observers must be allowed over Saint-Mihiel. Far from ideal, such an attack had accounted for the deaths of some of his friends. Still, it was the only way a lone fighter could attack.

Still diving, he turned his head to look for Chambers. The fighters were completely engaged with Goering's Flying Circus.

John timed his next maneuver to come up under an observer. He reversed the Spad's dive. An LVG flew overhead just as John began firing his twin Vickers as it flew through his gun sights. The pilot immediately rolled the plane over. His rear gunner fell out, his safety belt cut in half by John's bullets. John banked to follow the plane's path. His second burst set it aflame. The German went down like a dead pheasant. The gunner's chute tangled and wouldn't open. John saw the man fall, flailing his arms wildly, lacking anything to grab onto but thin air. He immediately thought of Lufbery. Luf had died the same way.

He thought, *Jesus! That's not a good way to die!*

John kept watching until bullets ripped fabric from his left wing.

The gunner in the second LVG was pumping bullets into John's Spad. Bullets cut an inner wing strut in half, ending any chance for John to dive for safety or to make sharp maneuvers. Several came so close to his head that he heard their whiplike cracks as the bullets flashed past his ears. The flashes meant that the German was firing incendiary ammunition.

The LVG's pilot had banked the two-seater to give his gunner the best firing angle. John had expected the tactic. Taking a chance, he banked right. Halfway into his turn, he noticed the gunner frantically trying to reload his Parabellum. John's combat experience had saved his life and given him an advantage. He looked above.

He saw only two Spads. One was missing, along with at least one of the German fighters.

Looking east, he found both fighting at his altitude, half a mile below the others. One of the Fokkers had apparently tried to come down to help the observers. It was cut off by Reed. With Chambers neutralizing the Fokker, John could focus on the second LVG. It was a rare day when John had a chance to down two enemy observers. Crippled Spad or not, John didn't hesitate. He stressed the Spad to complete a slow, climbing turn to follow the fleeing LVG.

The turn brought him directly behind the enemy plane. At full throttle, the loose strut cable tore through the fabric of his upper left wing, but the Spad gained on the slower airplane. The observer was still struggling to reload. As John came within range, the gunner slapped the fuselage behind the pilot. The LVG immediately began stunting to take the two-seater out of John's gun sights, reacting like a man going home after downing too much whiskey. Even crippled, his Spad had more maneuverability than the LVG. John stayed with it, gaining with every turn of the Spad's propeller.

At fifty yards, John was in firing position. The German pilot couldn't find a combination of stunts that would shake his talented executioner from the tail of the LVG. He began to run directly for the safety of his field. As John drew near, he saw the observer hammering his fists wildly at the breech of machine gun, swearing at the useless gun and cursing its malfunction. Seconds before, he'd done his best to kill John and had very nearly succeeded. The attempt to recharge its breech was futile. The prospect of death in seconds completely unnerved him. He made a pitiful sight to John.

In amazement, John watched as the exasperated gunner grabbed the Parabellum, tore it from its swivel, and threw it over the side. John was close enough to see his eyes. With a face showing perfect fear, the gunner stood straight up and looked directly at

John. A frown of resignation turned down the corners of his mouth. Elbows bent, he raised his arms level with his chest and turned the palms of both hands upward. The gunner looked skyward, as if standing at the gates of heaven, his sins revealed to the gatekeeper. The gesture was unmistakable. He looked like a supplicant coming humbly to his last judgment before God. With no means to defend himself, his pilot, or his plane, the German was conceding death. John needed only to pull the trigger of the Vickers to confirm his destiny. John removed his hand from the firing mechanism and banked left to avoid colliding with the LVG and put the Spad on a parallel course.

As he flew alongside the LVG, its pilot turned to look. If it weren't for engine noise, they were close enough to speak. The pilot's eyes grew wide, amazed to see his enemy flying alongside. John simply smiled and waved at the startled man. He turned the Spad back toward Toul, allowing the LVG to return to its field unharmed. He didn't fire a single shot at the two men who'd done their best to kill him. Officially, John was an ace. Unofficially, he'd revisited a place hidden deep in his soul, a shadowy place of lost innocence, numbed by the war, numbed by the constant sight of death and destruction, numbed by watching men fall to their deaths in flaming machines, and numbed by the all too frequent loss of his comrades. This time, John chose life over death.

At Toul, Rickenbacker came walking toward John, his eyes downcast, his shoulders slumped, his head slightly bowed. John immediately assumed someone in the flight wasn't coming back. Rick's posture implied nothing of any good.

"John, Chaumont sent me a dispatch. It's Michael. He was in an accident a few days ago. Michael suffered a serious brain injury. I'm really sorry to have to tell you this. He died in the hospital. I found out about it after you—"

"Michael's dead?" John reacted as though he'd been punched

in the stomach. He couldn't believe his ears. Michael was a noncombatant. Disbelief forced an explanation from Rick.

"I'm sorry, John. I called to confirm the report. They said he was on the way to headquarters at Ligny-en-Barrois. He was supposed to set up aid stations before the offensive. According to the driver, they got lost. They took the wrong road out of Bar-le-Duc. Before they realized it, German artillery started shelling them from Saint-Mihiel. When they started back, the car hit a shell hole. The driver was thrown out and broke an arm. Michael was thrown headfirst against a tree. The doctor said a rib punctured his lung. The trauma to his brain is what killed him. I'm really sorry, John."

"Jesus, Rick! Ligny-en-Barrois is less than twenty-five miles from here!" The news he'd been so close to Michael without knowing shook John. Still fighting disbelief, John hoped Michael hadn't suffered. "Was he unconscious? Did he come to? Did he say anything?"

Rickenbacker paused. He knew what John wanted to hear. He'd seen men die in crashes. Those who died instantly were the lucky ones. He looked squarely at John.

"I'm sorry, John. I know you wanted to find him. The dispatch said he was unconscious most of the time. He couldn't have suffered very long."

John's head hung limply. The whole weight of the war rested on his shoulders. How on God's earth was he to tell Catherine? Michael was her favorite.

"Where is he, Rick?"

"Headquarters ordered an ambulance to take him to Châlons. There's a cemetery there where the canal splits near the Boulevard de Marne. They had a memorial ceremony yesterday. I know it doesn't help much, but someone on staff recommended him for a DSC for his work on the Marne. Probably Marshall. Pershing signed the order himself a few hours ago."

John didn't care about medals. Medals didn't bring Michael back. He had an overwhelming urge to go to the cemetery. There, he could ask Michael for a way to tell Catherine.

"I've got to get to Châlons, Rick. The major … where is he?"

"That'll have to wait, John. The major is in Ligny. He told me to pass on his deepest regrets. He instructed me to give you these sealed orders. He wants you to read them immediately."

Rickenbacker handed John a brown envelope stamped "Attention to Orders" in large red letters. John's name and rank appeared below that. Inside was a note written in the major's hand, apologizing for not being there to offer his regrets in person. The orders commanded John to proceed without delay to headquarters in Chaumont and to report to General Tasker Bliss for further instructions. The words "without delay" were underlined. It made no sense to John. Saint-Mihiel had all but been taken. The squadron would start flying defensive missions.

"Did you read this, Rick?"

"Didn't have to. The major told me what was inside."

"What's this all about, Rick? He knows about my brother. I don't understand."

"I don't know, either, John. If I did, I'd tell you. I'm not sure the major knows. He said it was important and that you should go as soon as possible. I've arranged a ride for you on the mail truck. It's due back in headquarters in a couple of hours. You've got time to clean up before it leaves. John, I didn't know your brother, but I assure you, General Pershing doesn't hand out DSCs unless they're earned. Your brother must have done some great medical work."

"If I know Michael, he did. Rick, I'll always remember him as my kid brother. I just wish I'd had a chance to see him." Numbed by the news and from flying combat patrols, John couldn't manage tears. He was tired, depressed, and totally sapped by the loss of his brother.

"John, if there's anything I can do, anything at all, I want you to let me know."

"Sure, Rick. Thanks."

John headed to his quarters. The orders didn't say how long he'd be in Chaumont or whether he should take his gear. There wasn't time to do anything but wash, shave, and get dressed. He was horrified at the thought of having to tell Catherine.

Later that evening, the mail truck reached Chaumont. General Tasker Bliss and two other officers were waiting for John in his office. John hadn't saluted an officer in a long time. The Ninety-Fourth didn't practice the custom. Bliss returned his salute and came around his desk to shake his hand.

"I was sorry to hear about your brother, Captain Morris. It may seem out of place now, but I'd like to congratulate you on becoming an ace. Under different circumstances, I'd be happier to greet someone who's fought with such a distinction under French and American flags. Your brother also served with distinction. I assure you, he will be missed. You have my profound sympathies."

"Thank you, sir."

Being an ace meant little to John. At this point, his brother, sister, and friends like Eugene, Raoul, Genêt, and Rick meant more to him than accolades or medals.

"The thanks are mine, Captain. I want to introduce you to Colonel George C. Marshall and Colonel Fox Conner. These officers were instrumental in taking the Saint-Mihiel salient. Colonel Marshall first met your brother when he arrived at headquarters. He was the officer who interviewed your brother and assigned him to an aid station."

"Yes, I did, sir," Marshall said. "I had that pleasure when the lieutenant reported. I asked him whether he'd take the assignment at the time. General Bliss, sir, with your permission, I believe someone is waiting for Captain Morris in another office."

"Yes, of course. Well, I'm glad to have met you, Captain. You come from a remarkable family."

"Thank you, sir." John spoke on his brother's behalf, not for himself. Given the choice, Michael would be standing here, not him. After salutes, Marshall and Conner accompanied John to an adjacent office.

The door boasted a sign labeled Commanding Officer, AEF. Marshall knocked firmly.

From inside, General Pershing could be heard saying, "See who that is, Sergeant."

The staff sergeant opened the door and announced Marshall, Conner, and a captain from the Ninety-Fourth Squadron.

"Let them in, please."

John was bewildered. Why was he taken to meet General Pershing?

John went in and stood at attention, and every visitor saluted the commanding general of the Allied Expeditionary Force. Pershing stood in front of his desk. He returned their salutes.

"At ease, gentlemen. I'm glad you're here, Captain. Word of your accomplishments in the service of France and your country has preceded you. It honors both countries. Before we proceed any further, someone is here whom I believe you will be interested in seeing."

Pershing nodded to the sergeant, who immediately went to the door of a dimly lit adjoining room.

"Go in, Captain, and take your time. We'll wait."

Totally baffled, John hadn't the least idea whom Pershing wanted him to meet. He hesitated a moment, looking at Pershing as though he needed confirmation.

Pershing nodded. "Go on, Captain. It's not polite to keep a lady waiting."

"A lady, sir?"

"That's what I said, Captain, a lady. And if I may say, a fine young lady indeed. Don't keep her waiting, Captain. We'll wait for you." Pershing excused himself to speak to his officers.

"Yes, sir."

When the sergeant opened the door, Catherine thought General Pershing's meeting was finished. A backlit figure appeared in the doorway. He was taller than General Pershing. In the dimly lit anteroom, John distinguished nothing of the woman's face beneath her black veil.

"Excuse me, miss, I'm not sure why I was told to meet you. Perhaps, I should introduce myself. I'm—"

"John? Is that you?"

For the second time today, John couldn't believe his ears. "Catherine!"

Catherine rushed toward him. John met her running the other way, lifting her off her feet as her father used to do. Her arms wrapped around his neck She held him tightly, as if he might otherwise disappear. Tears flowed, even John's. John closed the door to give them the privacy Pershing had planned.

"Oh, John! I'm so happy you're here." Many questions followed.

"You're a wish come true, Catherine! I never dreamed I'd see you here. I had no idea you were in France! Why are you here? When did you come? Has the general told you about Michael?"

"Yes, John. He did. I didn't think you knew, and I didn't know how to tell you. I saw Michael here, in Chaumont, shortly after I arrived. He said he'd try to find you, but you move from place to place so often. French authorities were reluctant to say anything. He really tried to find you, John. He really tried."

"If I'd only known. He was so close, Cath," John said, using Michael's pet name for her. "It would have been easy for me to see him."

"Can we go to him together?"

"Yes. I promise you." He choked on the words. "I can't help

feeling it should have been me, not him. It isn't fair. He was doing his best to help others. He wasn't in the fight."

"John, no. Never say such a thing. Nothing changes what happened. I'm so happy I've found you. That's all that matters now." Catherine began to cry.

Until now, he didn't know how much he missed her, being with her. His mental and physical strain found release. Michael was gone, but Catherine was in his arms. He couldn't help himself. His tears came as freely as hers. Catherine held on.

"I'm so glad you're here," she whispered.

John composed himself. There was so much to say, so many questions to ask. It could wait now that they were together. When Catherine's tears subsided, John remembered.

"They're waiting for us, Cath."

Before today, John had never called her Cath. In a strange way, using his brother's nickname for her gave a part of Michael renewed life. At the same time, she grew closer to John. Two years had passed since they had seen each other. They wanted time to adjust to their loss and time to be together as brother and sister.

"I'll ask the general if I can take a few days, Cath. Would you like that?"

"Yes! I'd like it very much. What happened to your face? You have scars everywhere!"

"I had a bit of trouble on a patrol. They don't frighten you, do they?"

"No, silly." She remembered the picture on her vanity table in Guilford. "You've always had a handsome face. I'm just not used to seeing scars on it." The scars didn't matter to her. John would always be her handsome, brave, big brother.

"The doctor said they gave me character. A story to tell my grandchildren. I guess I'll never be as pretty as you, Cath. I could always grow a beard."

She laughed and scolded him for making jokes about his face.

"Let's go, Cath. We shouldn't keep the general waiting."

John opened the door as Pershing was completing his comments to his officers.

"—and have never seen such a display of fortitude. Foch, Pétain, Haig, even that old tiger Clemenceau said as much afterward. Pétain sent observers to see how we'd cross the wire." Pershing turned to look at John and Catherine. "I hope we managed to surprise you, Captain, and your sister, as well."

"Yes, sir. I don't know how to thank you, sir. I didn't know she was in France."

"You've thanked us, Captain Morris. We can see that in your faces. Now, while you are both here, and with your permission, I'd like to continue with our meeting."

"Yes, sir!" John couldn't imagine what else might be in his commander's mind.

In a tone that reflected respect, Pershing faced Catherine.

"Miss Morris, obviously this is a time of mixed feelings for you. Again, I want to express my deepest sympathy to you for the untimely death of your brother, Lieutenant Commander Morris. As the commander of the American Expeditionary Force and on behalf of our allies, I present you with these awards as a sign of our deep appreciation for your brother's sacrifice. Your brother has the sincere thanks of two grateful nations."

Pershing handed her two medals and written citations. Pershing's sincerity touched her. The posthumous presentation of the Distinguished Service Cross and the Croix de Guerre brought tiny tears to her eyes. He should have been here to accept them in person. Colonel Marshall added an American flag folded into a triangle.

"I only wish I could have presented these to your brother. In his absence, Marshal Foch asked me to pass on his deepest sympathies for your loss."

"Thank you, General. I'm sure Michael would have appreciated the awards."

In a ceremonial tone, Pershing instructed, "Gentlemen, please stand at attention."

Every man in the room came to attention.

"Miss Morris, Colonel Fox Conner seems to think that you had something to do with our success in Saint-Mihiel. I happen to agree. Normally, you'd have to be in the armed services to receive this. As commander of the AEF, I'm taking the liberty to make an exception. It is my honor to award you the Distinguished Service Medal for your counterintelligence work in Belfort."

On hearing his words, John's eyes opened wide. At attention, he could not resist the strong impulse to look toward her in astonishment.

"Colonel Conner said you were instrumental in deceiving the enemy about our plans. We know they shifted several divisions toward the Belfort Gap. I can tell you that your work most definitely saved the lives of many brave men. On their behalf, as well as mine, I offer you their profound gratitude and thanks."

John stood in stunned silence as Pershing himself pinned the award on her. His speech clarified what she'd been doing in France and explained the change he'd noticed in her. She was a much more confident and mature sister than the one he'd known in Guilford.

"Miss Morris, I'd like to add my personal admiration for you and your brothers. Families like yours have sacrificed a great deal to help win a victory. Your family is exceptional in that each of you unselfishly devoted yourselves to that end. Let me assure you that in spite of regrettable losses like that of your brother, such devotion exemplifies the best we have to offer as a nation." Pershing briefly took both her hands and continued, "The war may not end today or tomorrow, but with the support, determination, and sacrifice of families like yours, there can be no doubt of its outcome."

"Thank you, General. It was the most exciting—and frightening—time of my life!"

Pershing grinned. "I hope you won't be placed in that position again. At ease, gentlemen."

Amused laughter broke the official atmosphere in the office. Catherine received a hug from Fox Conner and a handshake from Colonel George C. Marshall.

With the meeting near its end, Pershing turned to face John and made another startling announcement.

"Captain Morris, your duties in France are over. I want you to take your sister home once it is arranged. I've contacted your commander, and he is aware of my decision. He agrees completely. Colonel Marshall has your orders. I'd like you to depart within a week, two at most. Important work awaits you back home. We need a stronger air arm. America needs experienced combat fliers like yourself. The more fliers you train, the faster we'll win this war and prevent others like it."

Departure

PERSHING'S SPEECH CAUGHT JOHN OFF balance. Taking Catherine home would remove him from the fight, perhaps for the duration of the war. That prospect set off a chain of thoughts, not the least of which was the fact that he'd survive the war, a notion he'd all but given up. Since training at Pau, he'd shelved the idea he might survive the war. Now, as powerful as the thought of surviving was, a nearly equally powerful sense of disappointment arose.

Duty, the ideal he'd clung to when debating with his father, was an important part of his disposition. He'd committed to fight to the end, whatever that end meant for himself. Since the night he'd first slept in Jim McConnell's bunk at Ravenel, he'd formed a bond with his unit, a sense of obligation to the other pilots in the squadron. Joining the Ninety-Fourth had only confirmed that bond and renewed his commitment. How could he accept safety while they continued to fight? An ocean away, the trials they'd shared daily for two years would suddenly be relegated to memory. He simply could not mentally justify leaving the escadrille.

"General Pershing, sir, I can't leave the Ninety-Fourth in good conscience. I'm a flier, a fighter pilot. I feel obligated to stay with—"

"At ease, Captain Morris. No one dismisses your devotion to your fellow fliers, and no one in this office has been in the fight longer than you. Your attachment to your squadron is appreciated and admirable. What you brought to France, ahead of your country, was a resolve to win justice where you saw injustice. America waited nearly two years before we followed your example. Now that we've joined you here, the tide of the war is turning. However, your mission here is finished. I expect you to show the same dedication to duty in the States. The army needs professionals. Men like yourself must be spared to do the larger, unfinished work at home.

"We need pilots who are trained by the best—men who are familiar with the latest air combat tactics. Your expertise and experience are needed at home more than here. I'm sending you to Texas to command a new training center for fighter pilots. As of now, you are Major John Morris. Your orders give you authority to begin selecting your staff. Your most important work is just beginning, Major.

"I need an estimate of the men and equipment you'll need on the basis of turning out two hundred combat-ready fighter pilots by next spring. They must have at least thirty hours of solo flying experience. I expect a direct report on their progress at the end of each month. Colonel Marshall will be able to answer any questions concerning organization. And one more thought. Your squadron's reputation is practically legendary back home. People across America have followed the exploits of the Lafayette Escadrille and Ninety-Fourth Aero Pursuit Squadron with pride. Between yourself and Captain Rickenbacker, I can only guess which of you is the more admired."

Coming from Pershing, this was lavish praise. The back of John's neck flushed hot with embarrassment.

"I trust you will use that reputation to good effect. More importantly, you must use your knowledge of combat flying to gather your team and train pilots."

"Yes, sir." John's response was intended to forestall Pershing from heaping further embarrassment on him in the presence of his staff and Catherine. He'd have preferred combat with the Flying Circus to that.

John received congratulations on his promotion from all present. Catherine hugged him and breathed a sigh of relief. For now, the war was behind them.

"That's all for now. Good luck."

The men saluted Pershing.

"Thank you, General Pershing." Catherine didn't try to hide her joy. Pershing was more than pleased to receive a farewell hug from her.

The meeting over, Marshall took John and Catherine to his office and handed John a brown envelope containing typed instructions. He shook John's hand.

"Major, you and Catherine should take time to sort things out. If you have any questions about your new post, I'll be happy to assist you."

"Thank you, sir."

After a last salute, they left Chaumont. The first peace either Catherine or John had felt since they'd left Baltimore mingled with deep sorrow at the loss of Michael.

On arriving at the cemetery in Châlons-sur-Marne, their mood was somber. Catherine gently lowered a handful of flowers to the grave where Michael rested. John laid a wreath on the cross at the head of his brother's grave. The ribbon running through its center read "In Memory of My Brother." They didn't speak for some time.

Michael was much closer to the Marne than he'd been in the Surmelin Valley. Its waters flowed on either side of the cemetery.

"It's beautiful here. Such a peaceful spot, isn't it, John? I think Michael would have liked it. I miss him so terribly." Tears welled in her eyes. "How lucky I was to see him before he …"

"He's at peace, Cath, and in a much better place now. The Marne will always flow here, as alive as he was at his aid station. I only wish I'd known. I would have liked to have seen him again."

They delayed leaving Michael. Both realized that they might not see this place anytime soon.

The cemetery's manager approached. "I don't mean to interrupt. You are relatives?"

"Yes. My name is John. This is Catherine. Michael was our brother."

"I'm sorry for your loss. They told me about what he'd done. My son is also here, killed near the Marne in the battle when General Galliéni led the army to defend Paris in 1914. My son helped win our first victory. He and his men sent the Boche back to the Aisne. I promise you that your brother's grave will be kept as though he were my own son. He lies next to him."

Tears came to Catherine's eyes at hearing his story. John held her, both giving and receiving comfort. So many had died. So many new graves appeared in so many new cemeteries.

They went to Paris the next day, staying in the home Pershing used for his trips to the capital. Paris was gayer than it had been for weeks. John wanted badly to go to Toul, to say good-bye and take one last flight. He told Catherine, but the look in her eyes changed his mind. He called Rickenbacker to arrange for his things to be brought from Toul. Rick told him not to worry. He'd take care of everything personally. He wished John good luck in the States.

Before John put the phone down, he invited Rick to meet him in the States when he got back. Rickenbacker, now commander of the Ninety-Fourth, accepted on condition that this time he buy the meal and John foot the bill for drinks, the reverse of their last arrangement. That done, John asked Catherine to tell him everything he didn't know.

"What brought you to France? How in the world did you ever get involved with counterespionage?"

It took an hour for Catherine to explain. Afterward, she told him about Commander Fields and his proposal of marriage. The news surprised John. She hadn't written anything about it. Having seen her new confidence and the vast change it made in her, he was certain that she knew what she wanted. Wishing her happiness, he hugged his little sister. He admired and respected the woman she'd become.

Her announcement brought on as good a time as any to tell her about Michelle. On hearing the news, Catherine wanted to meet this French woman who'd stolen her brother's heart when he was alone, vulnerable, and far from the safety of home.

"Is she good to you, John?"

"She's charming, very frank, and almost as beautiful as you," he said with a wry smile. "And, if it means anything, she's written more often than you, Cath, even after your letters were delivered. I think you'd like her."

"Oh, John, I'd really like to meet her. If you truly love her, you must bring her home to America."

"Don't you think I should marry her first and then bring her to America? That would be the Victorian thing to do, don't you think?"

"Oh! You're worse than Michael! I want to meet her. We have time, don't we, John? Saint-Nazaire isn't far from Paris, is it?"

"It's well over two hundred miles, so we shouldn't waste time getting there. Our ship leaves from England in a month, and there's someone in London I also want you to meet. I'll send Michelle a cable and ask for her father's permission. I hope she'll still have me. I'm not the same man she saw the last time we were together. These scars haven't added much to my looks."

"Nonsense! Why, if she cares for you at all, they won't make a bit of difference."

"Okay, Cath. But it's only fair to tell her so she knows what to expect."

"You'll do no such thing, John Morris! Men! Sometimes I wonder if they'll ever understand women!"

"I see! You're taking her side even before you even meet her."

Pretending annoyance at his teasing, Catherine shrugged off his attempt to hug her. "You men don't know the first thing about women!"

The cable sent, they took time to walk along the quays around the Île de la Cité and toured the Cathédrale de Notre Dame on an island in the Seine. The grotesque gargoyles surrounding the building amused Catherine. They reminded her of Hugo's novel, the deaf hunchback called Quasimodo, and his forlorn love for the beautiful gypsy girl Esmeralda.

John said, "I think I see a parallel between me and those gargoyles."

Again Catherine scolded, "The scars will get better in time! That's quite enough from you about scars, John Morris! I don't want to hear another word about them."

"Yes, ma'am!"

"Good!"

The sight of the cathedral actually pleased John. Begun in 1163, it was the first he'd seen in many months that showed no damage. It had also escaped the violence of the commune in 1871. Later, he took her to a restaurant for dinner and wine. Within the day, John had an answer to his cable.

"Well? What does she say? Will she marry you?"

"Here, Cath, read it for yourself."

> Dearest John. Very excited. Will marry you and
> kiss every scar. Come now. Father will arrange
> wedding. Bring Catherine!

> Michelle

"She writes perfect English! You didn't tell me she could speak English! John Morris, what else haven't you told me about her?"

"I guess you'll have to see for yourself, Cath. I've got tickets to Saint-Nazaire."

"You bought them before the cable came! Really! Of all the arrogance! You knew all along what she'd say! Oh, men!"

Trains going south were not as delayed as those going through Paris toward the front. Catherine took an instant liking to Michelle, and the feeling was returned. For a while, John felt neglected. Monsieur du Montrey marveled at Catherine's beauty and excellent French. He said that he rarely heard it spoken as well at the university.

The wedding was informal, taking place in the church with the same name as the town. Friends of the du Montreys, passing soldiers, and curious parishioners formed the congregation. Michelle and her father were well liked and better known than John realized. She'd packed her belongings after receiving John's telegram. Her wish to go to America was fulfilled. She loved John more than French or English phrases could express. Mrs. Morris married a man who'd fought for her country. He'd given her a deep appreciation for the France her father delighted in describing for hours on end. She'd miss her father. André insisted on staying in France near his beloved Loire.

"What would I do if I couldn't walk beside the Loire? Your home is in America, Michelle. Mine will always be Saint-Nazaire."

It was a tearful farewell. Her father, as gentle and understanding as any father who might not see his daughter again, wished them happiness. As her father, he sternly reminded her to write as often as possible and to visit whenever she could.

"I promise to bring her back when I can," John said.

The channel crossing was uneventful. In Dover, they decided to take the bus to London to avoid the crowded trains. After finding a small rooming house, John called a taxi and pointed out Wren's great cathedral to them on the way to Cheapside. The Dunnes still weren't listed in the telephone guide. Catherine and the new Mrs. Morris waited outside while John went into the flat where Albert and Bertie Dunne lived. When Bertie answered the door, she was overjoyed to see John. At first, she had to look beyond his scars to recognize him. Excited as she was, she didn't lack Albert's gift for gab.

"Oh my, Albert will be su'prised ta see yah, John! I s'pose I ought to call you 'sir' now. Albert's out with the taxi just now. I expect 'im here for lunch anytime now. 'ave you eat anything? My, my, but it seems a long time since you was 'ere. 'ave yah been in London long? Was it bad over there, John? Awful, I suppose. Dear me, 'ow'd you get all those scars? If I know Albert, I can 'ardly wait ta see 'is face. Talks about cha all the time, and the night yah went to the inn. 'e should be 'ome about now. Not usually this late. Busy at the station, I expect. Will yah be in London long?"

John had to interrupt. He'd already forgotten half of her questions.

"Bertie, my wife and sister are waiting outside. I wanted to be sure you were home. We rented a small rooming house near the bus station. I'm afraid we'll only be here for a day. Our boat leaves Plymouth tomorrow evening."

"Oh, good Lord! You went and got yourself married, 'ave yah?

Well, bless my soul! That's the last thing I expected. You must bring them up, John. I'd like tah meet 'em."

Down the stairwell, a door closed, and someone came up the stairs. Bertie easily recognized his footsteps.

"That's Albert now," she said. "Shoulda been 'ere 'alf an 'our ago."

Albert began talking to her as he came through the door.

"Well, now, me old beauty. Looks like a couple of those 'igh-class whores is takin' up shop right outside our door. I s'pose the action ain't what it used to be in Soho. You there, love? Lunch ready? I'm as hungry as a bear without a tooth in 'is 'ead."

Albert was definitely home. He closed the door and saw John standing next to Bertie. Though they realized that Albert had no idea who was waiting below, they looked at him with eyes wide open. Albert's mouth opened in a perfect circle of surprise at recognizing John.

"Cor blimey! Blow me down! It's John!" Albert half shuffled, half ran to greet him, his eyes fixed on John's scarred face.

"Yes, it's me under all these scars. I'm glad to see you. You look haven't changed a bit—same mustache, same accent."

Albert grabbed John's hand and nearly wrung it off at the wrist. "Well, your mug's not like I remember! Blimey, John! Yah could knock me down with a word. Bertie, it's John! Right back 'ere in Cheapside."

"Are you daft? Did yah think I was standin' 'ere talkin' to the King of England then? And watch your mouth about them ladies below. That's John's wife and sister waitin' to come up, you old fart."

"'is wife! And 'ow's I tah know that, Mrs. Dunne? Especially as me crystal ball is at the pawnbrokers along with the rest of what we own! And before we all get to starvin', would you be so kind as to set lunch for us, me old beauty?" His words were so thick with sarcasm that you could have leaned on them as if they made a wall.

"Well, while I'm at that, Sir Albert, clean yerself up and go down and get those young ladies, if you please!" she ordered.

"Right you are, Bertie, my love."

"Mrs. Dunne, please don't go to any trouble for us. I was hoping you and Albert could come with us to Williamson's."

Pleasantly distracted by the offer, Albert answered for her.

"Now there's a man after me own 'eart. It's a grand idea, John. Bertie, save yerself some trouble. We're goin' to the tavern."

"Oh, all right, then. Tell the girls once you've cleaned 'alf of London off yer face."

For the benefit of John's wife and sister, Albert gave the ladies the same tour on the walk to Williamson's as he'd given John that December two years earlier. John listened, once again marveling at the pride that Albert had for London. When Albert spoke, the houses on the avenues came alive. At times, Michelle asked Catherine to explain what Albert meant by certain phrases, never having heard such a strange accent.

The following morning, Albert and John took the ladies to Westminster Abbey, where Albert gave them an education for life. He was in his glory, showing them every nook and name on the walls and floors of the famous abbey. For Catherine and Michelle, it was a morning of memories, mostly memories of the Dunnes.

"I'm really grateful to you, Albert."

"Blimey, John. I'm not often embarrassed by a Yank, though I suppose George the Third was, if you catch my meaning."

The time to leave London came, and the farewell to Albert and Bertie was filled with promises to write. John said they'd try to come again when they returned to visit Michelle's father. Before going, John told Albert that he was going to Texas. This news prompted some serious advice from Albert.

"Mind now, John. I 'eard Texas was at peace, but yah ought to carry a little somethin' just in case the Indians change their minds."

The comment brought smiles from John and Catherine.

Misconceptions of the American West lingered throughout Europe. In France, John met French soldiers and civilians inclined to believe that America's frontier was still filled with hostile natives, train robbers, cattle thieves, and six-gun smoke on unpaved streets.

Michelle wasn't any different. Excited to sail to America, her questions her reflected impression that the West was still wild.

"Are there Indians in Texas, Jean?"

"I'm sure there are, but I couldn't name any tribes."

"Do they still fight with the wagons?"

John took her hand, chuckling at the thought. "No, they don't do that anymore. Those days are gone. I want to visit a ranch in Waco that belongs to the father of a friend I knew when I was training in Pau. He said it was a quiet place."

"Who was your friend? You didn't tell me about him."

"One of the pilot trainees ... a good man. We called him Outlaw."

Michelle saw a hint of concern cross his face but misread its meaning. She'd always wondered about the stories she'd heard as a child. After a moment, she said, "I have read about outlaws like Jesse James."

John laughed. In defense of her new sister-in-law, Catherine scolded him.

"John! Stop! She doesn't know! You shouldn't laugh about what she read as a child."

"Actually, I'm laughing because I was remembering Outlaw, Cath. He was quite the character. You'd have liked him once you got to know him. I meant no offense to Michelle. I'm a very lucky man to have found her."

"You certainly are, John Morris, and don't you forget it!"

"I won't, Catherine. I've learned a lot since I joined the escadrille."

He wasn't thinking of Michelle when he spoke. Since learning he'd survive the war, John had time to think. He realized that Europeans held no monopoly on misconceptions. In 1914, Americans believed that Europe should solve its own problems. They were wrong, and they knew less about Asia. The safety of two oceans gave America reason to stay out of foreign entanglements. Its isolationism forfeited its influence over the start of the war in Europe. Trade with the Allies had forced it into the war. John believed future isolation was impossible. America had a stake in European events, and the airplane was bound to make the world even smaller.

As they passed the torch held by the copper-clad statue in New York's bay, they were reminded that they were entering a free land. The energy symbolized in its flame was unappreciated in European capitals until the doughboys arrived at the battlefields.

Inside, John was still at war. He had to think about those things. The death and destruction the war brought and the effects of its cost would come from analysts for years. He'd seen things most Americans hadn't seen. How could he explain it to anyone who hadn't seen it for themselves? He'd seen men at their best and worst. He was both proud and troubled. The most troubling was what he'd discovered about himself. He'd become capable of suppressing emotion and morality. Under normal conditions, he'd have never taken a life. The war made him choose life and death.

John had yet to engage in his inner war. Life had become cheap. War made men targets for bullets, children were made fatherless, churches were targets for artillery, towns were piles of shattered brick and stone, wells became burial pits, clouds were places for ambush, women were objects of rape. The war had nearly killed his generation. Everything he'd loved had either died or been destroyed. Yes, he had Michelle and Catherine. But John's mind would be at war long after peace was signed. He made it his mission to see to it that such a war never came again.

Weeks later, the guns on the western front went silent. The slaughter of a generation officially ended at the eleventh hour on the eleventh day of the eleventh month of the year 1918, and a new phrase was born—"the eleventh hour." It would come to mean the last minute, not when something ended but when something took place. Something did take place after the war. They called it the Treaty of Versailles.

Peace Terms

After four years of war and the relentless efforts of each side to inflict as much death and destruction the world had ever witnessed, weariness demanded that the guns finally go silent and end the slaughter. With Foch's permission, a German deputation was allowed to pass through the western front on November 7, 1918. Matthias Erzberger's route was planned by Foch himself. Saint-Quentin lay along its meandering path, a wasteland that Hindenburg left in retreat. Foch wanted the German deputation to see it. Along the way, sentries delayed the German deputies, examining papers, reexamining them, all within the sound of French guns.

Near the end of the road tour, they were put on a special train, its destination unknown to them. At seven in the morning, they arrived at a small railroad siding in a secluded wood somewhere in northwestern France. Erzberger met Foch in the French commander's personal coach. Foch's expression was stiff but civil.

Once they were seated, Foch opened the talks by asking a simple, sharply pointed question. His guests could either impale themselves on it or immediately be put on the defensive. In either case, Foch had the advantage.

"What is it that you want from me?"

"Marshal Foch, we came to ask for a cease fire and to discuss the Allies ... that is, your proposals for an end to the war."

It was the response Foch expected. His four-word reply destroyed the German overture and implicitly placed the complete responsibility for four years of war and its future course squarely in his enemy's lap.

"We have no proposals."

Erzberger was noticeably shaken. "Surely, sir, you must have some wish for peace!"

Foch wanted no debate. The reply had come with an economy that was foreign to the battlefields. Foch made his and their position perfectly clear.

"Your kaiser sent his armies to invade France. If he wishes to save himself and his armies from further destruction, he must sue for peace. The terms of peace are not debatable."

As far as Foch was concerned, the German army was beaten, and the war could end as easily here as in Berlin when the Allies marched down Unter den Linden. Foch held the high hand, and Erzberger was well aware of it. Foch had not come to them. They had come to Foch. The situation in Germany was well known to both men. If the war continued, the kaiser would hear terms of surrender dictated to him in Berlin.

Germany's mountainous military losses were irreplaceable. Their economy was near total collapse. Their navy was in the midst of mutiny. Hunger and civil riot raged throughout the streets of their cities. The Hohenzollerns were in total ruin. The war Germany brought to France would either end here and now, or it would end in Berlin. Why else would Erzberger have come? Erzberger knew the need for truth had come.

"Marshal Foch, it is the wish of my government to end the war. We are prepared to agree to a mutual cease-fire while we discuss the terms for an armistice."

"There will be no cease-fire!" Foch's memory of his son's death in battle was still fresh. He nodded to his assistant. "Proceed, General Weygand."

General Maxime Weygand read the terms for peace like an assistant bank manager reviewing a petitioner's request for a loan. They amounted to terms for surrender. Germany would withdraw to the frontiers of August 1914; they would return Alsace and Lorraine and repatriate prisoners. The bitter loss of Alsace-Lorraine in 1871 was still fresh in the minds of Frenchmen. These Erzberger expected, but the cost to Germany was higher.

"Germany must evacuate the Rhineland in thirty-one days as a buffer zone to deter any future plans it may have for war with France. Moreover, the military and naval forces of Germany must be dismantled. The kaiser must give up his crown. The East African colony and Black Sea ports must be evacuated. France demands full war reparations."

It was a price tag that that would keep Germany impotent and indigent for decades. The terms were harsh, but Germany had not accepted earlier calls for peace.

Protest was pointless. The arrival of the Americans assured total victory. Either they agreed, or the war would continue to its logical conclusion in the enemy's capital. The choice was theirs. Foch rejected pleas for a cease-fire while the terms were sent to Berlin for decision.

"The kaiser has seventy-two hours to reply. This meeting is ended."

His terms made clear, the deputation was dismissed.

Unable to win concessions, the German deputies awaited reply in Rethondes. With Ludendorff absent, Hindenburg informed the kaiser.

"Your Majesty, I can no longer tell you to depend on the army."

Hindenburg bore the kaiser's anger. Later that day, they met again.

Hindenburg said, "I cannot offer a guarantee for Your Majesty's personal safety. I advise Your Majesty to abdicate and proceed directly to Holland."

Once again, the kaiser's anger flared. Wilhelm responded, "Then you no longer have a warlord!"

With that, the Prussian monarchy ended. Wilhelm's flight to Holland came without the pomp and parade of his accession to the throne. His passage to Holland was not immediately announced. Foch's terms were accepted.

At the fifth hour of November 11, 1918, Germany signed the armistice, and word was sent to every commander. The war would end at the eleventh hour. By agreement, the killing would continue for six hours at the expense of well over a thousand Allied lives. When the hour came, every artillery battery wanted to go on record as firing the last shell. At one minute before eleven in the morning, one last grand crescendo of artillery shells blew more holes in French soil. Then, almost unbelievably, it ended. The war was over.

A long-forgotten silence fell on the battlefields of northern France, a strange silence, a silence unheard since the echoes of a young Serb's revolver had died after an Austrian archduke's car had took a wrong turn on a street in Sarajevo. Each side had grown used to the sounds of war. Silence was no longer the sole realm of the dead. It was foreign and literally disarmed them.

Armistice brought an enormous release from fear. The realization that the war was over meant that the killing was over. Cheers sprang from French and German trenches. Some sat quietly; some cried. Enemies ventured cautiously into No-Man's-Land, their rifles left behind. Some swapped helmets. Some offered cigarettes. Some danced.

On an average day, the war meant that twenty thousand men had either died or were made casualties. Had their loss mattered? The cannons and machine guns were quiet. The war was over. They had survived. The death of fear brought men together who'd recently tried their best to kill each other. The first peaceful minutes made war a thing of the past, an event that faded into purgatory. Peace forced a conscious effort to relegate the war to history. The end of war brought a need to leave the hated trenches without rifles at the ready, without bayonets pointed, without running into the teeth of death. For the first time, they could advance toward their enemy's lines without fear raging in their stomachs, without confusion, without screams of pain, without the sight of comrades falling, without visions of dead bodies. They were no longer men at war. They were simply men.

War's end brought pride to America. That pride was put on parade in New York on February 17, 1919. John held Michelle's hand next to Commander and Catherine Fields. They watched as James Jefferson marched with an unsure gait next to his father in a parade that had no color lines. New York cheered the men who'd fought Germany from France. Decorated as a regiment, the 369th Infantry was proud of their victory in the Argonne Forest. They'd helped to clear a corridor through German lines in the costliest single battle America fought, the Battle of Meuse-Argonne.

Waving a tiny flag, Catherine stood next to John, cheering as James blew his cornet walking on two legs up Fifth Avenue. Next to him, his beaming father loudly beat his drum, followed closely by Elijah Tanner Martin in the grandest band ever, led by Jim Europe.

"Look, John! I don't think I've ever seen Monroe so happy."

"He's in his glory, isn't he, Cath?"

"Jean, James is well, is he not?"

The formation narrowed as they entered Harlem, where the regiment had first formed to go to war. Friends and wives met them with flowers to welcome them home. There wasn't a dry eye when Hayward and Little preceded the band into Harlem. They were home.

Catherine and John were all that remained of the Morris family. Their sorrow took temporary leave watching the parade. John managed to suppress the anger that often consumed him after the war. John hoped to be rid of it with Michelle and their children to come. In fact, children became the topic when they went back to Kew Gardens after the parade.

Catherine's thoughts dwelled on children after her marriage. "John, do you think we should decide the names we'll give to our children when they come?"

"Why not? How about Michael for your first son?"

"Really? How many boys do you think I'm going to have? I like Michael. But, what will you call your first boy?"

"I've asked Michelle. She prefers Samuel or André."

Catherine sighed. Michelle's wish to remember her father was kind. But another possibility arose.

"What if I have a second son? Would you mind if I named him James? Monroe would like that."

"It's a great idea. What if it's a daughter?"

"I'll call her Elizabeth, of course!"

Names couldn't bring back their former life in Guilford, but they seemed right. New life always brought new hope.

"So much has happened, John. I'm glad it's over. If only Michael could have been here."

"He must have known the war was almost over, Cath. He was

closer to it than I was. He had to be aware after what happened on the Marne."

"He'd want us to remember, to get on with our lives, wouldn't he, John?"

"Yes. He was like Father. We'll visit him, Cath. France isn't as far away as it used to be. Besides, Michelle wants to see her father."

"It sounds wonderful. Shall we make it a promise?"

"Yes! We'll all go together. That's a promise!"

Epilogue

The war made promises too. James would recall plucking the flesh of his lieutenant from his tunic after a barrage on the Marne. Major Eddington would remember the skull of a soldier, first a trough and then a home for a rat in the sodden muck of a field in Flanders. John would never forget a man falling to his death with three miles of air between him and eternity. There are no winners in war, only two kinds of losers—big losers and bigger losers. The Great War also promised a Second World War.

The men who met in Versailles gave shape to that promise. As they wrote the epilogue of the war, none of them realized that their treaty was to become the prologue of the next war. Signed and sealed, the next war would be considered a sequel to the Great War. The curtain of the first had closed to permit the rebuilding of sets and time to gather both old and new actors. It gave time for the rise of new producers, new directors, and new weapons before its tickets were sold—many one-way tickets for more young men. The only question was when the curtain would rise and the Second World War would make its debut. Twenty-one years later, in September of 1939, the world again became embroiled in a total war—a war that surpassed the death and destruction of the First World War. They'd learned nothing from the first and nothing about how to make peace.

The millions of young men who'd gleefully gone to war in 1914 believed they'd fought the war to end all war. The Second World War would take its name from the first and return the favor. Men had not foreseen the length and breadth of the First World War. Their offspring would not foresee the length or breadth of the second. The world had little time to recover from the affects of the First World War. Nature itself needed more time to cleanse the battlefields. Many of the same characters would participate in the Second World War. There were differences, but the plot was familiar. And as the curtain reopened, the world would again witness the heights to which men could soar and the even greater depths to which men could sink.

Recommended Readings

(A few of these books may not be common to public libraries.)

Eddie Rickenbacker's autobiography, *Rickenbacker*, Prentice-Hall, 1967, relates his trip to Europe on the ship St. Louis and his experiences as a pilot in the US 94th squadron, the famed "Hat in the Ring." The pilots of the Lafayette Escadrille and their missions are described in books written by its members. Edwin C. Parsons's, *I Flew With the Lafayette Escadrille*, E.C. Seale & Company, 1937; Captain Georges Thenault's, *The Story of the Lafayette Escadrille*, The Battery Press, reprinted 1990; James Norman Hall's, *High Adventure*, Houghton Mifflin Company, The Riverside Press, 1918 (with photos); Charles Nordhoff and James Norman Hall's, *Falcons of France*, Little, Brown & Company, 1929.

Historical works like Edward Jablonski's, *Warriors with Wings*, The Bobbs-Merrill Company, Inc., 1966, includes rare photos; Arch

Whitehouse's, *Legion of the Lafayette*, Doubleday & Company, Inc., 1962, and Dennis Gordon's, *The Lafayette Flying Corps*, Schiffer Military History, are collected short biographies with photos of the flyers in the Lafayette Escadrille and Lafayette Flying Corp [two separate entities]. Finally, Herbert Molloy Mason, Jr.'s nonfiction, *The Lafayette Escadrille*, Random House, 1964, is a well-researched history of the Lafayette Escadrille, includes maps, and a list of the flyers and their fates in the appendix.

On the ground war, essays collected by Herbert J. Bass, *America's Entry into World War I*, Holt, Rinehart, and Winston, 1964, explains the accepted theories of America's late entry. Frank H. Simond's five-volume work, *History of the World War*, Doubleday Page & Company, 1918, is readable from start to finish in the style of the time. Gouraud's full message to the 4th Army appears in Volume Five. *A Doughboy with the Fighting Sixty-Ninth*, by Albert M. Ettinger and A. Churchill Ettinger, White Mane Publishing Company. Inc., 1992, offers an inside view of that unit and contains many photos. The graphic nature of battle in the British trenches comes from journalist Sir Philip Gibbs's prophetic book, *Now It Can Be Told*, Harper and Brothers Publishers, 1920. From an American, who became a British "Tommie," comes the humorous experience of Arthur Guy Emprey in his book, *Over the Top*, G.P. Putnam's Sons, The Knickerbocker Press, 1917, a biography that includes a comic dictionary of British trench jargon. A detailed study of life and death in the trenches is found in John Ellis's book, *Eye Deep in Hell*, Johns Hopkins University Press, undated, ISBN 0-8018-3947-5. Arthur W. Little's book, *From Harlem to the Rhine*, Covici-Freide, 1936, gives the history of New York's 15th Regiment [the 369th French regiment] from the view of its proud commander.

General Pershing's talk with his staff in the chapter *Senard* is invented, but expresses his known sentiments as written in his report to the Secretary of War, *Final Report of Gen. J. Pershing*, Government Printing Office, Washington, D.C., 1920. The discussions between Foch and Pershing are fictionalized, but reflect their sentiments and conversations. Pershing's own account appears in his two-volume work, *My Experiences in the World War*, Fredrick A. Stokes Company, 1931. Lawrence Stalling's account comes in his book, *The Doughboys*, Harper & Row, 1963. Published years later, and written in very different styles, these last two works have useful maps. Barbara W. Tuchman's book, *The Guns of August*, Macmillan Publishing Company, 1962, details the events that led to war. The Pulitzer Prize winning author's work goes well beyond its elegant style.

Dozens of purely historical works provided the means to create an accurate chronology in order to set the characters in real time and in real places.

CPSIA information can be obtained
at www.ICGtesting.com
Printed in the USA
BVHW031305240619
551819BV00001B/1/P

9 781491 743836